FROM
Venice
With Love

With Love
COLLECTION

February 2017

February 2017

February 2017

March 2017

March 2017

March 2017

FROM *Venice* *With Love*

TRISH MOREY **ALISON ROBERTS** **KAT CANTRELL**

First Published in Great Britain 2017
By Mills & Boon, an imprint of HarperCollins*Publishers*
1 London Bridge Street, London, SE1 9GF

FROM VENICE WITH LOVE © 2017 Harlequin Books S.A.

Secrets of Castillo del Arco © 2012 Trish Morey
From Venice with Love © 2013 Alison Roberts
Pregnant by Morning © 2014 Katrina Williams

ISBN: 978-0-263-92788-7

09-0217

Our policy is to use papers that are natural, renewable and recyclable products and made from wood grown in sustainable forests. The logging and manufacturing processes conform to the legal environmental regulations of the country of origin.

Printed and bound in Spain
by CPI, Barcelona

SECRETS
OF CASTILLO
DEL ARCO

TRISH MOREY

With grateful thanks to Ellen, Charlie and Claire
for being my captive carpool brainstormers.
Thank you so much for your interest and
your input and energy and most of all,
thank you for Venice. You guys rock!

And with thanks, as ever, to my fabulous
Maytoners, for Coogee Beach and fish and chips,
for making me laugh and cry and commiserate
and celebrate, but with thanks, most of all,
for once again making magic happen in
the shape of words.

For it must be a kind of magic.

Thank you!

Trish
Xxx

Trish Morey always fancied herself a writer—so why she became a chartered accountant is anyone's guess! But once she'd found her true calling there was no turning back. Mother of four budding heroines and wife to one true-life hero, Trish lives in an idyllic region of South Australia. Is it any wonder she believes in happy-ever-afters?

Find her at www.trishmorey.com or https://www.facebook.com/trish.morey

PROLOGUE

Paris

'PROMISE ME something, Raoul. Grant a dying man one last wish.'

The old man's voice was thready and thin, little more than a whistle on his breath and no contest for the battery of machines beeping their presence around the bed. Raoul leaned closer. 'You mustn't talk that way, Umberto.' Raoul placed his hand over the old man's, trying not to damage the papery skin or nudge the needle projecting from the back of his claw-like hand; trying to pretend it was nowhere near as bad as it was. 'You are as strong as an ox,' he lied, wishing it were true. 'The doctor said—'

'The doctor is a fool!' the old man interjected, dissolving into a fit of coughing that left him wheezing in its wake. 'I am not afraid of death. I know my time has come.'

Wiry fingers clumsily overturned those of his visitor's, squeezing down as if to emphasise the urgency of his words, even though his once-legendary strength was gone, his fingers grown weak. 'But I fear what might

happen once I am gone. Which is why I summoned you. You must promise me now, Raoul, before it is too late…'

The old man sagged against the pillows, his eyes closed in an ashen, sunken face, his sudden outburst taking its toll. For the first time Raoul was struck with the realisation that there would be no coming back: this time his oldest friend, his mentor—and the closest thing to family he had known for more than a decade—was dying. He had to force himself to stay and not flee from the room and the heavy knot tightening in his gut.

'You know I would do anything for you, Umberto,' he uttered in a voice that felt like gravel in his throat. 'You have my word. Ask, and it shall be.'

An eternity passed, an eternity filled with beeping machines that were the only sign Raoul had that his old friend had not already passed, until with a sigh his eyes fluttered open, watery and dim, his voice tinged with affection. 'Look after Gabriella for me. When I die, she will be vulnerable. I will not rest unless she is safe.'

He touched his free hand to the old man's shoulder to reassure him, his fingers encountering little more than bone. 'Then rest easy, old friend. Nothing will happen to her. I would be honoured to act as her guardian.'

The old man surprised him, snorting a protest instead of uttering the thanks he'd half-anticipated. Raoul was halfway to celebrating this spark of life, a glimpse of the Umberto that once was, until the words his old friend had said in response registered in his mind—impossible words, words that made the blood roar in his ears, sending thoughts of celebration tumbling and smashing

like debris caught up in the first destructive wave of a tsunami.

He stood, unable to sit while the roar of the wave churned through him, and turned away from the bed, raking a damp hand through his hair and tugging at his tie, looking ceiling-ward for the air-conditioning vents. God, but it was hot in here.

'Raoul, did you hear me?' The thread of Umberto's frail words came on a thin wire that dug its way into him, slowing his retreat.

'I heard you,' he said—*every last word*—but that didn't stop Umberto from repeating them now, driving that sharp wire deeper and deeper into his psyche where it twisted and grew poisoned barbs.

'You must marry her, Raoul! Promise me you will marry Gabriella.'

Madness! He dragged in air tainted with the smell of impending death, disinfectant and the chemical sprays designed to disguise them all yet failing miserably, and threw his head back, hating what was happening— hating even more what he was hearing. Wasn't it bad enough that his old friend was dying? It had to be some kind of madness, he decided, for his friend to propose such insanity. 'You know that is not possible. Besides,' he added, remembering the last time he'd seen the girl, 'Even if I was crazy enough to marry again, surely Gabriella is too young?'

'A woman now.' Umberto blinked away tears, his voice breaking with emotion. 'Twenty-four years of age.'

Raoul was shocked by the invisible slide of time; cursed the years he had lost in the mire of another age.

Had it really been that long? Then again, maybe this made it better, easier. 'Then surely she is old enough to choose her own husband?'

'And if she chooses Consuelo Garbas?'

'Manuel's brother?' Raoul lifted disbelieving hands to his temples, driving fingertips deep into the veins that pounded like drums. God, but could this nightmare get any worse?

The name Garbas was seared on his soul, the letters burned deep, so deep that his bones ached at its mention. It was a name he'd hoped he'd heard for the last time a long, bleak time ago.

Yet he should have known that ridding himself of this curse would never be that easy. The Garbas family was like a black hole, sucking life from the world around, devouring anyone and anything in its path. He turned back, moved closer to the bed, needing to know despite himself. 'What does he want with Gabriella?'

'He's been sniffing around her like a hyena waiting for a carcass, waiting for her to turn twenty-five when she can claim her inheritance.' The old man paused, catching his breath, although the rise and fall of the covers over his chest was barely discernible. 'He knows I would never permit her to marry him. So now he waits for me to die before he makes his move.'

Raoul nodded. 'Hyena' was right. It was the way his kind operated: scavengers; scum, the lot of them. Only their massive wealth gave them entree into high society, lending them a veneer of respectability so brittle it was a wonder it didn't shatter every time they drew breath.

And now one of them was after Gabriella? 'She doesn't know?'

Umberto scoffed. 'He would hardly tell her the truth. She knows only that his brother died in tragic circumstances. She thinks that gives them something in common.' The old man sighed and gave a hint of a wistful smile as he shook his head. 'I have tried to warn her but Gabriella sees only the good in everyone—even the likes of him. And all the time he plays her like a fish on a line, knowing he has the advantage of time. So, you see, I have no one to turn to but you. You must marry her, Raoul,' he said, lifting his head shakily from the pillow in a supreme effort that saw the cords in his neck stand out tight, his watery eyes turn glassy in their intensity. '*You* must keep her safe. You must!'

He collapsed back into the pillows to catch his breath, the rapid beep of machines filling the void, while Raoul sat down by his side and bowed his head, his thoughts in turmoil, conflicted beyond measure.

Damned if he would let a Garbas worm his way into Umberto's granddaughter's fortune. Damned if he would ever let that happen after what he had suffered. But Raoul was the last person who could keep her safe.

Besides, did Umberto really think it would be such a simple matter to get a twenty four year old woman—any woman, for that matter—to agree to marry him? Why should she give him a second glance when he could give her nothing in return? She would be some kind of fool if she did.

He took his friend's hand again, half-wondering, half-knowing that this would be the last time they met.

'Umberto, old friend—*my friend*—I love you with my life, but this makes no sense. There must be a better way to keep Gabriella safe and I will find it. But I would be no kind of husband for your granddaughter.'

'I'm not asking you to love her!' he blustered from the bed, the machines beside him going into overdrive. 'Just marry her. Keep her safe!' The door burst open, a nurse rushing through, pushing the visitor aside as she checked her patient.

'Visit's over,' she snapped out without looking over her shoulder. 'You're upsetting my patient.'

Raoul raised his face to the ceiling in supplication and frustration. When he looked back at the bed where the nurse fussed, checked and adjusted drips and machines, his old friend looked so forlorn and desperate and beyond tired, a shadow of a man who had once been great. It struck Raoul that his last moments, his last days, should not be wasted in worry such as this, even if it meant promising the impossible so that he might at least die in peace. Umberto deserved that at least.

'I'll marry her, old friend, if that is what you ask,' he said, ignoring the warning scowl he earned in reward from the nurse, grinding the words out between his teeth as the wire in his gut pulled inexorably tighter and trying desperately not to think of the cost to them both. 'I'll marry her.'

CHAPTER ONE

Three weeks later

WINTER had come early, the late-September day dressed in drab colours as if the planet itself was mourning the death of her grandfather. But the inclement weather found only empathy with Gabriella D'Arenberg, the damp air and misty rain matching her mood as she stood beside her grandfather's flower-strewn grave in the Cimetiere de Passy. Then the last of the mourners whispered condolences and pressed cold lips briefly to her cheeks before drifting away along the path.

She would leave shortly too, once Consuelo had returned from the call he had excused himself to take, and they would join everyone at the hotel where the caterers were no doubt already serving canapés and cognac. But for now Gabriella was happy to be left alone in quiet reflection in the cold, dank stillness of the graveyard. Here, under the shadow of the Eiffel Tower, there was nothing to intrude, the sounds of the city barely penetrating the stone walls.

Until a dark shadow made her gasp and look around.

He appeared out of the fog, tall, broad and dark as

night as he moved stealthily between the funeral sculptures, the winged angels and fat cherubs suspended ghost-like in the swirling mist as he passed. A shiver of recognition—or was it of relief?—washed through her and bizarrely, for the first time that day, she felt warm.

Raoul.

She had seen him at the service; it had been impossible to miss his dark presence in the back of the tiny crowded chapel. Her heart had lifted at the prospect of seeing him again after so many years, only to exit the chapel to a bubble of disappointment when she had found him nowhere amongst the mourners gathered outside.

Raoul, who with his intense black eyes and passionate mouth had been her every adolescent fantasy—dark fantasies she'd had no right to imagine. Wicked fantasies that brought a blush to her cheeks just thinking about them. And, when she'd got news that he'd married, she'd cried for two days solid. She'd cried for him a year later when she'd learned of his wife's death. Thank God he had no idea about any of it or she could never face him now. Thank God she was over all that.

The crunch of boots on gravel grew louder, his long leather coat swirling about his legs, his hair pulled back into a ponytail that served to accentuate the strong lines and angles of his chiselled features. His eyes, if anything, were even more intense than she remembered under that dark slash of brow. Tortured, even. And something about that intensity frightened her a little, just as if his purposeful stride held a portent of danger, sending a tremor skittering down her spine.

The mist, she thought in explanation, as she contin-

ued to log his approach with her eyes. The cold, swirl-
ing air...

The air shifted and parted before him and then he was
there, standing before her, a mountain of blackness in a
mist-shrouded world, so tall that she had to tilt her head
back to look up at him and his unflinching expression.
He didn't smile. She didn't expect him to, not really, not
this day.

But this was Raoul, an old family friend, so she dis-
missed her feelings of foreboding and danger and ven-
tured a nervous smile of greeting, slipping her hands
instinctively into his as easily as she had once done, rel-
ishing their instant warmth, thinking, *you came*. 'Raoul,
it's so good to see you.'

For a moment he seemed to tense, and she wondered
if she'd overstepped the mark by presuming familiarity.
Then his hands squeezed hers and the tightness around
his mouth relaxed just enough to give an answering
smile that still spoke of sadness and loss. 'Gabriella,'
he said in a way that seemed to cherish every syllable
as he uttered it.

Then he leaned down to kiss first one cheek, and then
the other, slow, lingering kisses. She shuddered under the
brush of his lips against her flesh, his warm breath curl-
ing into hers and peeling back the years. She breathed
him in, taken by the way he smelt so familiar, of clean
skin and warm leather and the same woody notes of his
signature scent that she recalled—yet there was so much
more besides, as if what she'd remembered had been but
a shadow of his essence.

'I am so sorry for your loss.' He drew back then, let-

ting her hands drop, and she tried desperately not to be
disappointed by his absence, shoving her hands in her
coat pockets, not just to keep them warm but more to
stop them reaching out for him. Those teenage fantasies
might have been behind her, but Raoul was here now,
real, broad and achingly close. Inside her pockets, her
hands curled into fists.

'I didn't know you were coming,' she managed a lit-
tle shakily, surprised he could still affect her so deeply
and so fundamentally, even after so many years. 'Or you
could have stayed at the house. Where are you staying?
You should have let me know.'

He rattled off the name of a hotel that barely regis-
tered in the force of the impact of seeing him again. But
then, she was hardly herself right now. Memories, es-
pecially memories of anything and anyone connected
to her grandfather, seemed all too willing to bubble to
the surface. Raoul had been close to her grandfather for
longer than she had, their two families intertwined as
long as she could remember, at least until the tragedy
that had wiped out both sets of parents. 'And of course,'
she said, acknowledging that truth, 'It's your loss too.'

'Umberto was a good man,' he said with a nod, his
deep voice rich with emotion. 'I will miss him more than
I can say.' Then he blinked and something skated across
his eyes, something so sharp and painful she could al-
most feel its sting, so fleeting it was gone before she
could make sense of it, even if he hadn't turned his head
to look down at the grave.

Remembering, she assumed, as she studied his pro-
file and catalogued the changes time had wrought. He

had always been on the outer edge of good-looking, his dark, strong features organised in a way that was compelling rather than handsome in any conventional sense, the shadows in his features hinting at unknown dangers and untold secrets.

How many nights had she lain awake imagining all those dangers, all those secrets, wishing she might one day know them all?

Age had lent him even more mystery. The angles of his jaw looked sharper. The secrets hinted at in the shadows seemed darker, his eyes more haunted. True, there were lines around his eyes, but he was simply *more*, she decided, more than he had been before. More edgy. More mysterious.

More Raoul.

And with a start she realised that, while she'd been lost in her musings, he had changed his focus and was now studying her.

Dark-as-midnight eyes scanned her face, a hint of a frown creasing his brow, and she wondered if something was wrong before he nodded, gave her another of those slight smiles and stepped away a little to look at her. 'Whatever happened to the Gabriella I used to know? The skinny girl with plaits who always had her head in a book.'

She hid her embarrassment under a laugh, secretly hoping his comments meant that he approved of how she looked now, for it seemed important somehow that he did. She had long since come to terms with the knowledge that she'd never be classically beautiful—her eyes were too large and wide, and the chin that she'd hidden

under a hand for much of her early teenage years was too pointy. But it was *her* face and over the years she'd learned to accept it, if it had taken finishing school to give her the skills to emphasise her eyes and learn to like how she looked. 'She grew up, Raoul. That skinny girl was a long, long time ago.'

'It was,' he agreed, and then he paused, as if remembering another time, other bleak days filled with funerals... 'How have you been?'

She shrugged. 'Good. And sometimes not so good.' She glanced at the open grave, felt the anguish of loss bite hard and bite deep. 'But, even so, better now for seeing you.' She paused, wondering how much she could say without revealing too much of herself, and then decided simply to be honest. 'I'm so glad you're here.'

'And me.' His dark eyes looked past her. 'But you should not be alone now.'

'Oh, I'm not. Not really. Consuelo—a friend—is here. He left...' She looked around, pushing a loose tendril of hair from her face as she scanned the cemetery. 'He left to take an urgent phone call.' *That seemed to be taking for ever.* 'Probably for one of his foundations, I expect. He heads a charity for children with cancer and leukaemia. He's always on the phone chasing contributions.'

She was babbling, she knew, making excuses for him as she glanced at her watch before scanning the grounds again, wondering how he could let one of his donors keep him so long, today of all days. 'We're heading to the hotel shortly for the wake. Everyone's already there.'

She looked back up at him, suddenly fearful that this man was about to step out of her life as quickly as he

had stepped back into it, leaving her with no idea when she might ever see him again. The thought of going another ten-plus years was suddenly too awful to contemplate. 'You will come, won't you? I saw you in the chapel but you'd disappeared by the time I got outside, and I thought I'd missed you. There's so much I want to talk to you about.'

He lifted a hand and pushed that wayward coil of her hair from her cheek with just the pads of his fingers, the lightest touch that sent a rush of heat pulsing through her. 'Of course I will come. It will be my pleasure.'

Breath stalled in her lungs; his fingers lingered as he coiled the strands behind her ear, as he looked down at her with those dark, dark eyes...

'Gabby!'

She blinked, registering her name, but registering even more that Raoul had still not removed his hand. His fingers curved around her neck, gently stroking her skin, warm and evocative, even as she angled her head towards Consuelo's approach. The touch of an old friend, she told herself, reaching out to someone over a shared loss; it was nothing more than that. It would be rude, an over reaction, to brush his hand away.

'Are you coming?' Consuelo asked, still metres away and frowning as his eyes shifted from one to the other, taking in the tableau. 'We're going to be late.'

'Gabriella was waiting for you, as it happens,' Raoul said, and she looked up at him, surprised. For, even if he had correctly assumed this was Consuelo, that would hardly explain the note of barely contained animosity in his words.

Consuelo didn't seem to notice. He seemed far more interested in staring at Raoul's hand where it lingered at her throat, as if just the heat from his glare would make it disappear. For the first time she wondered if maybe it had been there too long. She put her hand to his and tugged it down, but wasn't about to let him go completely, sandwiching it between her own instead. She noticed he made no move to withdraw from her completely.

'Am I missing something?' she asked, looking from one to the other, for the first time realising the similarities in the two men—and the differences. Both shared Spanish colouring, with dark eyes and hair, but that was where the similarities began and ended. Raoul was taller, broader, more imposing. He made Consuelo look almost *small*. 'Do you two know each other?'

'Consuelo and I are old friends,' Raoul uttered slowly, in a measured tone that suggested they were anything but. 'Aren't we, Consuelo?' The other man's eyes skittered with something approximating fear before he turned to Gabriella, tugging on his tie.

'Phillipa said the priest wanted to say a few words,' he said, ignoring the other man as much as it was physically able. 'He's waiting for you to arrive to begin. Now.'

'Phillipa called you?' Was that the phone call that had kept him so long? That was odd. Her friend had never before called Consuelo; Gabriella wasn't convinced Phillipa even liked him. Unless Phillipa had figured— correctly, as it turned out—that her phone would be off and that Consuelo, with his twenty-four-seven phone addiction, would be a better bet. She nodded. At least that

made some kind of sense. 'Then we should go. Raoul, can we offer you a lift?'

Consuelo stepped closer alongside her, tugging at her arm. 'Look, the car's waiting. We should get going.'

Raoul smiled. 'Thank you for your kind offer, Gabriella, but I wish to have a few words with your grandfather before I make my own way.' He lifted his hand, capturing one of hers as he raised it to his mouth, pressing his warm lips to her skin, his dark eyes glancing up at her as dark tendrils of his hair fell free from his ponytail to dance around the sharp angles and shadowed recesses of his face. 'Until we meet again, Bella,' he said, using his old pet name for her, an endearment she hadn't heard in over a decade.

But he had remembered.

And then those same eyes turned to meet the other man's and somehow turned ice-cold in the interim. 'Garbas,' he said with a nod, so simply that it took Gabriella only a second to realise he'd dismissed the other man out of hand. Consuelo felt it too, for he took her hand and tugged her away.

Raoul watched them disappear along the misty path, unable to suppress a growl when Garbas looped a proprietorial arm around Gabriella's shoulders and pulled her in close.

For his benefit, he had no doubt. Umberto had been right about the hyena sniffing around, watching and waiting for his chance to strike—not that he would see a penny of Gabriella's fortune if Raoul had anything to do with it. Not now the dogs were closing in.

It hadn't taken much. He'd known there would be dirt and plenty of it if he just dug deep enough. Now he just had to sit back and wait. It wouldn't be long and then Gabriella would be safe from his clutches.

Gabriella.

Bella.

Forgotten for years, lost under the weight of time, yet still the endearment had come to him automatically, as if all he had to do was see her before it tripped from his tongue. Yet she looked so different now from the last time they had met. When had twelve years ever passed so profitably? For him, it had been a period of loss, betrayal, death and ultimately of his own self-imposed exile. For her, it seemed those years had worked some kind of magic, transforming her from a gangly child into a very beautiful woman.

They might just as well have been living on different planets.

Huddled alongside the grave, her coat lashed tightly around her slim waist, her glossy chestnut hair coiled behind her head, she had been almost unrecognisable from the child he remembered, yet he should have seen it coming. Her mother had been beautiful after all, half-English-rose, half-Italian-royalty, her father the *crème de la crème* of French aristocracy. Her heart-shaped face somehow captured the best of all of them: her mother's cat-like eyes and smooth-as-silk complexion, her father's passionate mouth. Beautiful. Fragile.

Much too good for the likes of him.

What had Umberto been thinking? Dealing with the likes of Consuelo was one thing, but why would he want

to saddle his own granddaughter with a broken creature like him? Why make him promise to marry her?

"You don't have to love her!" Umberto had said.

Just as well. What would a woman like her want with his love, even if he were able to give it? And why would she waste hers on him? Why would a woman like her ever want to marry him?

And why should she have to? Consuelo would soon be history, untouchable, locked away where he could not reach her—and not even someone who saw the good in everyone would want to defend him when she discovered the truth. Raoul could just as simply deal with any other Consuelos if it came to that. He could weed out the hyenas and the jackals, the parasites who came to prey on a rich, beautiful woman.

He could take care of them all.

Except then he remembered the touch of her skin, the smooth column of her throat and the trip of her pulse under his fingertips. He remembered the press of her cheek against his palm, remembered that moment when she had looked up at him and he had imagined the impossible, had wanted the impossible. For the first time in a long time he had felt his body stirring with want.

And that knowledge shamed him.

He hadn't meant his fingers to linger. He had wanted just to establish a contact between them, as if that might help eradicate the years that lay between them. But one touch had not been enough, and when a stray strand of hair had blown free from the knot behind her head he had been unable to resist tucking it away, using the excuse of Garbas coming upon them to leave it there.

It had been worth it just to see the look of unbridled hostility in his eyes. It had been worth even more because she had felt so damned good under his fingers.

He squeezed his eyes shut on a groan. What was he thinking? She was his oldest friend's granddaughter! The last time he had seen her she had been twelve, and it didn't matter how old she was now; she was still more than a decade younger than him. And he had been charged with taking care of her, not with taking advantage of her. He was supposed to keep her safe.

By mauling her at her grandfather's grave?

He shook his head. 'I'm sorry, Umberto, but what were you thinking?' he muttered, as he stood by the grave of his friend with just the tangle of his conflicted thoughts and the mist for company. 'Why would you make me promise such a thing when no good can come of it?'

The soft, damp air swirled around him, whispering no answers, offering no solutions, and leaving him with just one truth. He had promised his dying friend it would be so.

So he would make it happen.

CHAPTER TWO

'WHAT is he doing here?' Consuelo demanded as he strode along the path like a man with the demons of hell after him. 'Why did he have to come?'

Gabriella skipped a step to keep up with him. 'Raoul is an old family friend. Of course he would be here.'

'But the way he was touching you—like he owned you. Like he meant something to you. You let him touch you!'

'We grew up together, Consuelo. Our two families were practically inseparable, at least until I was twelve years of age. The last time I saw him was at our parents' funerals. Of course there is some feeling between us. He is like a brother to me.'

He looked across at her suddenly, his eyes wild and frantic, and she wondered what else must be troubling him for him to overreact in this way. 'And that's all he is to you?'

'But of course,' she said, wanting to soothe, but mostly because there was nothing else she could say, even if she might so foolishly have once dreamed of more.

He wrapped his arm around her shoulders and tugged

her close in to his body. She needed to be hugged but she wondered why this contact didn't stir her blood or warm her as Raoul's touch had done. Perhaps because she saw more of him, or because he was more familiar to her, more comfortable to be around. She shouldn't encourage him—she knew he wanted more out of their relationship than she could commit to right now—but today she was glad to have someone to hold on to, even if his touch didn't stir her like another's…

She shuddered now with the memory of it, of how just the gentle touch of Raoul's fingertips had set her blood fizzing. How was that possible—a man she hadn't met other than in her dreams for so many years? Or had she just wished and hoped for it so much, she'd believed it had happened?

But then he'd always had that impact on her. He'd always seemed larger than life, and she'd always been drawn to his dark mystery. Why should it be any different now, simply because a dozen years had passed?

'How do you know Raoul?' she asked, curious as he hastened her towards the waiting car. 'Is he one of the foundation's benefactors?'

He laughed, a short, derisive laugh. 'Him? No, he would not give to a charity such as ours, not even to save the lives of sick children.'

'Why do you say that? Have you ever asked him?'

'I do not bother with his sort. His kind have no heart.'

'No, Consuelo,' she protested, remembering back, thinking that Raoul had had the biggest heart of anyone she knew. Nothing had been too much trouble for him back then, nothing too much effort for his family

and hers. And when the police had called that fateful evening with the shocking news it had been Raoul who had cradled her, letting her cry her eyes out, offering her the remnants of his own shattered heart. 'That cannot be right.'

'Then you do not know him very well, after all. Come,' he said, opening her car door so she could precede him into the vehicle. 'Forget Raoul; there are more important things to think about right now.' He tapped the waiting driver on the shoulder to let him know they were ready. 'Like arranging for your things to be moved from the house into my apartment. Given you're on leave, it would be the perfect time.'

She blinked, momentarily stunned. Where had that come from? 'What are you talking about?'

But he was engrossed in the traffic, scanning it, almost as if he was looking for someone. Raoul? Surely he was a long way behind. And then he turned back to her, smiling, and she wondered if she'd imagined his nervousness. 'Come on, darling. Now that your grandfather's gone, there's no reason why we should live apart any longer.'

'We haven't talked about this.'

He took her hand in one of his, patted it with the other. 'Come, Gabby, you know as well as I do that half the reason you haven't moved in already is because your grandfather needed you. Now there is no reason for us to be apart. Now it is time you were looked after the way you should be. The way I want to look after you.'

She shook her head. 'Consuelo...'

'Of course, I can always move in with you, but I

thought you might prefer a fresh start somewhere else, somewhere without the memories.'

'I like where I live,' she said, stiffening and wondering what she had said or done to make him think she was ready to move in with him. 'And my grandfather is barely cold in his grave. I would actually prefer not to have to deal with this today.'

He sighed and lifted her hand to his lips, although his eyes lacked any warmth to go with it. 'I'm sorry, Gabby. I'm rushing you. Of course we can talk later.'

Much later, she thought, clutching her coat at her neck and wondering what it was that was throwing Consuelo so off-kilter today; he was so very anxious as he resumed his busy scanning of the traffic.

They were almost at the hotel when Consuelo's phone buzzed again. He pulled it from his pocket and held it to his ear, and Gabriella looked across, wondering if it was Phillipa again wanting to know how far away they were. But even as she watched the colour drained from Consuelo's face.

'Mierda!' he said, before he snapped it off and shoved it away, tapping the driver on the shoulder. 'Stop here. Let me out here.'

'Consuelo, what's wrong?' she asked as the driver cut across two lanes of traffic, to the squeal of tyres and the blare of horns, to double park on the side of the road. 'Who was that?'

But he was already climbing out. 'A problem at the office. I have to go.' And then he slammed the door and disappeared into the crowd.

* * *

The priest's words were moving, the condolences she received from old friends and associates heartfelt, and Gabriella felt one kind of peace descend on her soul. Her grandfather had been much loved by all who had known him, had touched so many lives, and it was clear that it wasn't just her who would be left with an Umberto-sized hole in her heart.

But now the wake was winding down and she felt suddenly deflated with it. She'd turned her phone on to silent, hoping that she might get some news from Consuelo, some kind of explanation, but there had been no messages explaining his sudden disappearance or when he might join her. She was beginning to think he wouldn't make it at all.

And maybe she could have lived with that if Raoul had bothered to turn up like he'd promised. She'd hoped he'd soon follow them from the cemetery. From the very first minute she'd stepped into the hotel's plush reception-room, she'd been anticipating his arrival, scanning the room for a hint of his broad, dark-clad shoulders or a glimpse of his blue-black hair. She longed for the dark solidity of his presence. She longed for the comfort she'd found in it at the cemetery, a comfort she yearned for now.

He'd promised he'd come. She ached with wanting him to come. So where was he?

Phillipa appeared at her side and put a hand on her shoulder. 'How are you bearing up?'

'Do men always let you down?' she mused as she stared blankly into a cold cup of coffee in her hands that she battled to remember picking up. First Umberto, the

grandfather who had taken her in as a grieving twelve-year-old and had been both mother and father to her, was gone. Then Consuelo, who couldn't even stop thinking about his foundation for just one day, disappeared to who knew where and for how long? And now Raoul, who she'd lost before she'd even found again.

'Hey, don't worry,' said Phillipa. 'You know how he is,' she continued, clearly only seeing one side to Gabriella's concerns. Her friend squeezed her hand as she prised the neglected cup from her fingers. 'The foundation is everything to him. He's got caught up in something, that's all. And, for the record, men don't always let you down. Not all of them, at any rate.'

'I'm sorry,' she said, remembering Phillipa's gorgeous husband. 'I'm just feeling maudlin. You have a keeper of a man. He is a wonder to bring you all the way from London just for me and with such a young baby.'

She kissed Gabriella's cheek. 'Nothing is too much trouble for you, but you're right; Damien is a keeper, but he will need rescuing from our baby soon. Will you be all right if I leave?'

'I'll be fine. You've been so wonderful today. Oh, and I meant to say before, thanks for calling while we were at the cemetery. I lost track of time completely out there.'

Her friend looked blank.

'You phoned Consuelo,' Gabriella prompted. 'To tell him the priest was waiting for me to begin his talk.'

Phillipa frowned and shook her head. 'I never called. I don't even have his number.' It was Gabriella's turn to blink. Why had Consuelo made out that she had? Unless

he'd been so desperate to get her away from Raoul that he'd resorted to lies to do it. What had happened between the two men that nobody was letting on about?

Phillipa put a hand on her elbow. 'Gabriella, are you okay?'

Suddenly it was too hard to think. She put a hand on her brow. 'I'm sorry. I've got a rotten headache. I must have misunderstood.' Her friend smiled and squeezed her arm.

'Let me get you some painkillers and some water. It might take the edge off it.'

Gabriella sighed, letting herself sag, hidden for a moment behind a marble pillar, trying desperately to relax. Her head hurt. Her feet ached. And her heart felt like a giant void. If only she could take a pill for that. Today she'd said goodbye to her grandfather, the man who had taken on the role of both her parents and more when they had been ripped from her life. Such a good man. Such a brilliant man. Why did the world—why did she—have to live without him just yet?

She looked around the room, looking at the few remaining guests talking over their coffee and cognac, wondering if anyone would notice if she simply disappeared. But she was kidding herself. Of course she couldn't just slip away. She would have to stay until the grim and bitter end.

Then the air in the room seemed to still and intensify until it shimmered with expectation. The hairs at the back of her neck stood up as she felt the scorching gaze of dark eyes drinking her in. Phillipa joined her, blinking as she held out a glass of sparkling water—not that

she was looking at Gabriella. 'Oh, wow, forget keeper husbands for a moment. Who on earth is that?'

Gabriella didn't have to turn around to know who it was. She could feel his identity in her rapidly liquefying bones. She could feel it in her heated flesh and empty lungs.

He had come.

And then he was beside them, so broad, tall and dangerous-looking that his presence should darken the world, except that it only served to brighten hers.

'Raoul Del Arco,' he said, bowing to her friend. 'At your service.' Although it was the fingers pressed to the small of her back that had Gabriella's full attention, the press of them against her flesh sending an electrical current surging along her spine, needles of sensation that radiated out to take anchor in the suddenly sensitive tissue of her breasts and dark places inside, deep down in her belly.

'I thought you weren't coming,' she said a little breathlessly when she'd managed to unglue her tongue from where it had been stuck to the roof of her mouth. And then, because she realised it sounded like it contained a note of desperation and even accusation, she forced herself to smile. 'But thank you for coming now. And let me introduce Phillipa Edwards. We went to the same boarding school in England.'

Raoul nodded, taking her hand. 'It is a pleasure.'

'Raoul was like a big brother to me growing up,' she continued. *And my personal hero.*

'Umberto was a very important influence in my life and Gabriella has always been very special to me,' he

said as his arm moved upwards, his long-fingered hand cupping her shoulder, pulling her close against his heated body, a gesture that seemed a world away from brotherly, at least the heated way her body seemed to be interpreting it. 'Unfortunately we lost touch for several years, so to meet again under such circumstances makes for a bittersweet reunion.' He looked down at her, his dark eyes intense, mesmerising. 'I see now I will have to ensure I do not allow such a lapse to occur again.'

Clearly she should have eaten, because she felt dizzy at his words, so light-headed that she could have fallen into his eyes right then and there if Phillipa had not excused herself, saying she needed to get back to her baby. Gabriella hugged her friend and then she was alone with Raoul.

He dropped his arm to face her; absurdly she missed his touch and the warm solidity of his body pressed against hers. Then he tilted his dark head and smiled in a way that transformed his features from darkly threatening to something warm and dangerous that could melt cement as easily as it could buckle her knees. 'I am sorry to have kept you waiting, Bella. You said you wanted to talk and I felt that might prove easier after everyone had gone. I thought, I hoped, you might allow me to take you to dinner.'

Bella.

There was that name again.

'I was just going to go home.'

'Ah, but of course.' He looked around the room, the remaining stragglers exchanging stories and talking over

old times. 'It has been a very long day for you. Then maybe I can take you home?'

'No, not home,' she decided suddenly. At home there would be no treasured grandfather waiting for her, ever again. Why had she ever thought 'home' would offer some kind of sanctuary?

Besides, with Raoul beside her she didn't feel so enervated, so drained. Instead, it seemed like every nerve ending in her body was suddenly awake and acutely aware of the man before her.

And acutely aware of a sudden hunger. It felt like she hadn't eaten for ever. 'Thank you, Raoul. If the offer still stands, dinner would be lovely.'

He stayed by her side while the wake wound up, lending her his strength when mourners departed and succumbed to a final burst of tears as they kissed her goodbye, and then he took her to a tiny 1890's bistro on the Left Bank that greeted them with the scent of roasted garlic and tomatoes, with its *belle epoque* decor, quaint etched-glass and globe lamps. It was not somewhere she'd been expecting to be taken and definitely somewhere she was sure Consuelo would not know existed. There were no billionaires here that she could see, no players, politicians or film stars. Simply ordinary people enjoying a night out.

Well, ordinary apart from Raoul. There was nothing ordinary about his broad shoulders and strong black hair that glowed blue in the subtle lighting. He shrank the tiny room with his sheer presence, blotting out the other diners until they might just as well have been cardboard cut-outs. It felt good to be able to sit opposite and have

no reason not to look at him and drink in his strong features—those dark eyes with their depths only hinted at under that dark slash of brow; those sculpted cheekbones, strong blade of nose and those lips, their passionate lines as detailed as if chiselled by a sculptor's hand.

It felt good to be here with him.

'Twice today I have found you alone,' he said after they had ordered their meals. 'Could Garbas not stay until the end of the wake?'

She fiddled with the napkin in her lap. Consuelo hadn't made it at all, not that Raoul needed to know that, not when he clearly harboured enough resentment towards the man already. And not when there had been no word and she still had no idea herself what was going on. 'He was called away. Something important, I guess.'

'More important than you?'

She flushed and waited while the waiter poured them both a glass of Beaujolais, ruby red in the light cast by the lamp in the centre of the table. Consuelo always had good reasons when he was delayed or had to suddenly change their plans—it happened so often that she was used to it. To let her down today of all days... But he would have good reason, she was sure.

Although, what reason would he have for assuming they would now move in together?

She picked up her glass on a sigh, admiring the colour of the wine. Maybe he'd just felt neglected, with her attention going firstly to her grandfather and then to Phillipa when she'd needed her recently. And maybe he hadn't been uppermost in her thoughts these last few weeks and wanted to change that. But, still, when had

going to a few parties and dinners together been a sign
of imminent cohabitation?

Then she saw Raoul waiting for her and decided to
worry about the missing Consuelo and his distorted per-
ception of their relationship later. She gave an ironic
smile. 'Clearly much more important. Anyway, I didn't
come to dinner to talk about him.'

'Touché.' Across the table Raoul smiled and lifted his
glass to hers in a toast. 'To us, Gabriella. To old friends
and new beginnings.'

His words stirred her soul deep. 'To us,' she said, tak-
ing a sip, feeling the sensual slide of fine wine down her
throat. She watched him watching her over the rim of
her glass, liking the way he watched her, wondering if
he liked what he saw.

And she knew she was in danger of reading too much
into this. She was feeling things and hearing things that
couldn't possibly be there or mean what she thought.
And for all his talk of new beginnings and expressions
of regret that it had been so long, he would most likely
disappear from her life tonight and not even Umberto
would be there to bring him back to her.

After all, this was Raoul, and her teenaged fantasies
had been just that—fantasies. She put her glass down
before the alcohol might convince her otherwise. 'You
visited Umberto the week before he died?'

Across the table Raoul stilled. 'Umberto told you
that?'

She shook her head and the lights in her hair danced
under the lamps. She'd worn it up for the funeral, a se-
vere knot at the back of her head, but time and the damp

had worked tendrils loose, so now the ends softly framed her face. 'No, his nurse. He died before—before I made it home from London. I was too late to see him.'

'I'm sorry,' he said, praying that his visit had done nothing to hasten his old friend's death and prevent his granddaughter one last opportunity to see him.

'I think he knew he was dying and he didn't want me there.' She looked at the ceiling and pressed her lips together in a thin white line. 'He sent me away, you know.'

'I didn't know.'

'Phillipa was almost due to give birth. Her husband was overseas and booked to get back—there should have been plenty of time—when a coup closed all the airports. He was stuck in a war zone and she was frantic with worry; little wonder the baby came early. And I didn't want to leave Umberto, but he told me he was fine and that I must go to help my friend. He promised me he would be fine...'

He took her hand, squeezed it in his own. 'He was looking out for you. He was trying to spare you.'

'By denying me the opportunity to share his final days, his final moments?' She hauled in a breath and shook her head. 'Why don't I feel blessed in that case? Instead, I feel cheated. I didn't even get a proper chance to say goodbye.'

'Bella,' he said, his hand stroking her cheek, his thumb wiping the moisture welling from her eyes, 'He didn't want you to see him like that.'

'But why wouldn't he want to say goodbye to me?'

'Because maybe he wanted you to remember him as he was before, strong and happy, not confined to a bed

with a battery of machines beeping out his existence while you waited for them to fall silent one by one. He loved you too much to subject you to that.'

She sniffed and rested her cheek against his hand, staring blindly at the table as if considering his words. She looked lost, a little girl in a woman's face, a little girl who had suffered too much already in her short life; a beautiful face that was no hardship to stare at, no hardship to caress. Even with leaking eyes and tear-streaked cheeks, even with that trembling bottom lip, she was indeed a beauty. Even without her fortune in waiting, she would be a catch.

What a waste.

For she deserved only the best. She deserved happiness and love and a good man who could give her both.

She deserved so much more than a man who would marry her simply to fulfil the terms of a promise.

And that wretched knot he seemed to endlessly carry with him grew in his gut, twisting, tangling and pulling tight. Why was he even considering going through with this? Garbas would be no threat now. Garbas could not hurt her. So he should just take her home, say goodnight and walk away. He should let her go. If he had any sense at all, he would just let her go. Umberto would never know.

Except he had promised.

And *he* would know.

Besides, perversely perhaps, a part of him was beginning to think it would not be such an impossible feat to get her to agree to marry him. Indeed, the longer he was with her, the more certain he was that he could achieve

the unthinkable. She had worshipped him as a child. She certainly didn't hate him now, not from the way she seemed to lean into his touch, not from the way he found her glancing at him when she thought he wasn't looking. And, whatever she'd heard of his past, it didn't seem to make her wary of him in any way. *Foolish, foolish woman.*

'So what did he say?'

He looked up to find her eyes on him, sad eyes wanting answers.

'You talked to Umberto,' she prompted. 'What did he say?'

He hesitated, his hand dropping, his fingers toying with the stem of his wine glass, knowing what her reaction would be if he told her what Umberto really wanted from him.

'Surely I'm entitled to know something of his last words? Can't you tell me anything?'

'*Si.*' He nodded. 'Of course you are entitled. Because mostly, Bella, he talked of you.'

'Me.' She blinked and swallowed and he followed the movement down the long, smooth column of her throat until it disappeared into her chest, a slow, sensual slide. He had to drag his eyes north again when she said, 'What did he say about me?'

'That he loved you,' he said, embellishing the truth, because he knew she needed to hear it and because he knew it to be true. 'More than anything or anyone in the world. He talked about how special you are and how much you mean to him. He talked about how afraid he

was for you when he was gone, how he would miss seeing you married with children one day.'

She dragged in air and bit down on her plump bottom lip with her teeth in the way he remembered her always doing whenever she'd been upset years ago. He remembered her trying not to cry out loud at her parents' funeral and biting down so hard on her lip those teeth had drawn blood, blood she'd later smeared on his white shirt when he'd hugged her and held her close. How her twelve-year-old's tears had reduced him to tears too, even though he'd promised himself to be strong that day.

God, but she'd been through so much. He could well understand Umberto wanting to protect her and ensure nothing bad ever happened to her again. He wanted that too. And, the longer he was with her, the more he wanted it. But he still knew in his crusted heart that he was the last person who could make it so.

'He told me that you see the good in everyone, that you do not judge, that you have a good heart.'

Across the table, she sniffed. 'Thank you. It would have been nice to have heard these things first hand, but it is good to hear them at all, so thank you.'

'Sometimes it is not possible to say these things face to face. Your grandfather was old-school. Did he ever tell you he loved you when he was alive?'

'No, but I still knew.'

'Yes, you knew. Some things, Bella—some things do not need to be said for us to know them to be true,' he said, feeling only slightly guilty for the things he'd told her, the things he'd embellished and the things he'd omitted when he saw how happy she was to hear them.

And she smiled, tears once again welling in her eyes. 'Thank you, Raoul,' she said as she clasped his hand in hers, only letting go as their meals were served. 'Thank you so much.'

CHAPTER THREE

'WHAT will you do now?' he asked while they ate. 'Will you stay in Paris?'

She tilted her head as she toyed with a mushroom, contemplating his question and letting herself appreciate for the first time just how much she was enjoying tonight. She hadn't expected to enjoy anything today, and there was still an Umberto-sized hole in her chest. But she felt, if not entirely happy, then almost *good*, she decided, although she was in no doubt that the company was a major factor in that. Just being with Raoul seemed to make her feel good, to feel warm.

'I have my job at the American Library here in Paris. They've given me leave, as long as I need, although I think I really should get back to work. I've been off more than a month already.'

'You don't look like any librarian I've ever seen,' he offered. 'In fact, if librarians had looked like you when I was at school, I might have spent more time studying in the library.'

She smiled and tilted her head. 'Why thank you, kind sir, but I think perhaps that is the wine talking.'

'No,' he countered. 'That is definitely the man talking.'

She felt his words in the quake that rumbled its way down her spine and lodged deep in her belly; she had to suck in air to cool and mitigate its far-flung effects. 'I'm the special-collections manager,' she said, squeezing her legs together under the table to quell the buzzing between her thighs. 'Maybe the library gods give us a bit more leeway in that department.'

And to her relief he laughed, a rich, deep sound that resonated through her bones. 'Come to Venice with me.'

Her breath caught—or maybe it was her heart—and it was her turn to laugh, but this time nervously. 'Excuse me?'

'I have business in Venice. Come with me, Bella.'

She shook her head, once again blindsided by the events of the day. She was torn to think he was leaving already after such a short time, tempted to do something wildly un-Gabriella-like and take off with him. But she didn't work that way. 'I can't just take off to Venice.'

'Why not?'

'I have my job.'

'You're on leave.'

'But... But...' She was thinking of all the reasons going to Venice with Raoul would be so wonderful: the chance to renew their acquaintance, the opportunity to feel his warming presence; logic momentarily deserted her.

'What do you have to stay for? A change would do you good.'

When he put it like that, it *had* been a long time

since she'd had any kind of holiday. Once she went back to work it would be months before she could ask for more time off, and the thought of going to Venice with Raoul... 'No.' She shook her head, much more emphatically this time, half to convince herself. 'That's silly. What were we talking about again?'

He shrugged, as if it didn't matter one way or the other. 'So, think about it. No rush. Meanwhile, we were talking about you. Where did you go to school? I seem to remember Umberto mentioning boarding school once or twice when I visited him.'

She nodded, feeling warmed by the thought of Umberto talking to Raoul about his granddaughter and what she was doing—and Raoul actually remembering—while in the back of her mind she kept hearing his words, *Come with me, Bella.*

She took a sip of water, wondering if it was the wine making her feel reckless enough to want to say yes. Then she marshalled her scattered thoughts enough to answer his question properly.

'From the day I was born, my mother had me booked into the same ladies college in the Cotswolds she'd attended as a girl. I'd always known I was going there and, while I didn't want to leave Umberto, it felt good being there and nearer her parents, too, while they were alive. And I'd see Mum's name on winners' boards and amongst lists of past prefects and it made me feel good— walking those same corridors, sitting in those same classrooms that she had. Like I was closer to her, if that makes any sense.'

Suddenly she wasn't sure what made sense and

what didn't. She gave a nervous laugh, tilted her head. 'Did you actually mean it about coming to Venice?' Immediately she dismissed it. 'But, no, sorry, it's a crazy idea. I'm probably not making any sense.'

'You make perfect sense,' he said, raising his glass to her. 'And it's not such a crazy idea.'

Oh, but it was. If she went to Venice she might get used to the warm, wonderful way he made her feel—as if she had one hundred per cent of his attention all the time, as if she were the only person, the only woman, in the world.

And that would be crazy.

'Anyway,' she pressed on, determined to get back to her story and not dwell on things that could not be, 'That's where I met Phillipa.'

'Your friend I met today?'

She nodded, remembering the first day they'd met, the two girls who'd teamed up in desperation because they'd known nobody else in the entire school and yet had stayed friends ever since. 'She was my very best friend from day one, even through the couple of years when her family shifted to New York. She came back to study librarianship at uni as well, and we ended up living together during terms. We'd each go our separate ways in the holidays, her to New York, me to Paris, or we'd take turns at visiting each other's homes.' She smiled. 'Phillipa's the most brilliant friend. Better than a sister—not that I've ever had one.'

She stopped, and looked at him, leaning back and smiling patiently at her. 'Oh God, I'm talking too much, aren't I?'

'No, I could listen to you all night. I wish I had been there more for you, Bella.' Maybe if he had, he wouldn't have ended up so lost himself... 'I should have done more.'

She shrugged. 'Come on, Raoul, how could you? The last thing you needed was to be bothered with a girl barely in her teens. And I was fine. I actually liked boarding school. It was hard at first, but in a way it took my mind off things. Besides, what could you have done? You were busy with your own life.'

Busy? That was one way to put it. And, realistically, what could he have done? He'd spent the two years after his parents' death either drunk or aiming for it, playing every casino he could find, throwing money at every game and every horse it was possible to lose on and finding himself a new family into the deal. A family that loved someone who could splash money around and not care, a family who had adopted him for one of their own, if only to suck him dry.

And then, emerging out of the bleakness of that time, he'd found Katia—or she had found him. Playboy of the year, bachelor of the year; he'd been awarded so many of those meaningless titles he couldn't remember them all. But she had wanted him above all others and they had been so absorbed in their own special world that nothing else had mattered. Or so he had thought. Not until much later when the foundations of his world had once again been torn apart...

He shook his head, wondering at the insanity that had driven his actions then, knowing he should know better now. For it had to be a form of insanity to be contem-

plating what he was doing, to be undertaking what he was doing.

Even now he'd primed Gabriella perfectly; she was still thinking about Venice even though he'd said nothing to encourage her after that first exchange. Even now she was still thinking it through, working out the angles, making it possible in her own mind, making it her own decision.

Even now it could still happen—and he could get her to Venice and clear of Paris before the news of Consuelo's inevitable arrest broke. For Consuelo would be arrested, nothing was surer.

But right now, looking into Gabriella's eyes flickering brandy-gold in the lamplight, he wasn't so sure of anything else. The way she looked at him...

She wasn't the girl she had once been. She was a woman now, and his body was reacting the way a man's body did to a woman he desired.

He shook his head, trying to dispel those images. 'You were no doubt better off without me.' *As you would be now.*

She reached over, took his hands in hers. 'I'm sorry. How about we make a deal? How about we don't think about the past? Maybe it's time we let it go. You yourself toasted to a new beginning, so can't we just leave it at that? Can we let the past go and start again?'

If only it were that easy!

His past *was* him. It was his past that had made him, shaped him and moulded him, even broken him along the way. It had made him who he was now.

How could he let that go without losing himself, without losing who he was now?

He didn't know how.

He wouldn't know where to begin.

And, promise or no promise, suddenly he couldn't do this—not to himself and definitely not to her. It was suddenly too hot, the air like poison as the walls of the bistro closed in on him. He knew he had to get outside into the fresh air, into a world where he could disappear and be alone and where she would be safe from him.

'Are you finished?' he asked, already standing, his voice like gravel as he threw some notes onto the table.

She blinked up at him in surprise, grabbing her coat as he moved like a dark cloud past her out of the restaurant and into the night.

It was raining, the lamps along the Seine throwing jagged zigzags of colour sliding along the wet pavement and across the dark water. 'Raoul,' she said, as she skipped to keep up with his long stride. 'What's wrong? What did I say?'

'It is nothing you have said, nothing you have done.'

'Then, what?'

'It is me, Gabriella.' It stung like a slap to her face that he had dropped the use of Bella, dropped the endearment. 'You are better off without me.'

'No, Raoul, how can you say that?'

'Because I know! You were right to decide not to come with me.'

He hailed a taxi and bundled her and she thought he would follow until he rattled off her address and made

to close the door. She threw out her hand against the door to stop him. 'What are you doing?'

'Sending you home. Good bye, Gabriella.'

She shoved open the door and stood up to him, face to face, the door—and a world, it seemed—between them. 'No. Not until I know when I will see you again.'

'You do not want to see me again.'

'Don't tell me what I want!' There was a spark in her eyes he hadn't seen before, a hint of rebellion about that sharp chin he hadn't seen since she was a child. Not that it would do her any good.

The driver uttered a few impatient words and she turned and let go with a torrent of French of her own before she turned back. 'I don't want to wait another twelve years to see you again, and I damn well won't.'

'Who can say how long it will be?'

'So, what time do you leave? We could still meet for lunch if it's late enough.'

'No.'

'Then maybe breakfast at your hotel?'

'That is not possible. I leave mid-morning.'

'Can't you change it?'

'I told you, I have business to attend to.'

'And it cannot wait?'

'No.'

Infuriating! He was like a mountain made out of a single piece of solid granite, She could pound her fists against his chest except she knew he would not feel a thing. 'Then maybe I was too hasty before. Maybe I could come with you after all, even just for a day or

two. Like you say, the library will not expect me back immediately.'

'I'm sorry, Gabriella, but I was too hasty with my invitation. I should have realised it would not work.'

'But you asked me. Why would you do that? Why would you ask and then change your mind?'

'Because it is pointless! Because I cannot do this—please do not try to make me.'

'For God's sake, Raoul, you blast into my life after a twelve-year absence and then you disappear before we've had a chance to get to know each other again. Can't you at least offer me something?'

'But I am, Bella—I am offering you your freedom. Treasure it.'

And he turned and strode off into the wet, dark Paris night.

She watched him go, wishing she could run after him, knowing it would be a mistake. But what had he meant about offering her her freedom? Why should she treasure it?

Why couldn't he at least have explained what he meant?

He dreamed of Katia that night, Katia emerging from the mist with all her grace and long, lithe limbs, her dancer's eyes and beckoning smile. He dreamed of parties floating on a champagne cloud; he dreamed of laughter, dancing and sex that went long into the night and the following day, and then doing it all again the next. Until the mist turned dark and putrid and a mocking

smile became a call for help, became a scream, and he tried to make his feet move, tried to run…

He woke to a pounding heart, covered in sweat and tangled in sheets. It took seconds to realise the pounding was coming from the door and not only from his chest. Thank God! He swung his legs over the side of the bed and sat up, snatching up his watch and throwing it back when he saw the time and realised it had taken him so long to get to sleep last night that he'd slept later than he'd intended. It was room service, no doubt, with his breakfast order, although why they had to make such a God-awful noise…

He called out that he was coming and lashed a towel around his hips, pulling open the door in the same movement. But it was Gabriella who fell into his arms, tear-streaked and brandishing a newspaper in one hand, and it took him a moment to remember, to work out how she'd found him. 'Raoul, I'm sorry,' she sobbed, clinging to him. 'I'm so sorry. I know you'll be angry with me, but I didn't know who else to turn to.'

He put a tentative hand to her head, trying not to think too much about the push of her breasts again his chest or the fact his early-morning body had reversed its decision to relax. Hating himself that it had. 'What is it, Gabriella?' he asked gruffly, shifting slightly and still feeling a building sizzle of satisfaction in his veins, already half-knowing what the news must be.

'It's all over the papers,' she sniffed, thrusting it into his hand. 'It's Consuelo. He's been accused of using the foundation as a front for money laundering. He's been arrested for fraud.'

Already? he thought as his eyes flicked over the article, taking in the pertinent details. So it was done and she was safe. Surely Umberto would not quibble about the exact letter of his promise not being carried out? He'd done her a favour, after all, and if all went to plan Garbas would be locked up for a very long time and Gabriella could find and marry someone decent. 'But what brings you here? What do you think I can do?'

'We have to help him. It can't be true. We have to—'

'We?'

'Surely you would help me?'

'But if it is true, what they accuse him of?'

She blinked watery eyes up at him and exhilaration almost gave way to regret for causing her more tears after she had shed what seemed like an ocean of them. 'What?'

'If the police are right? That he has been using the foundation as a front?'

She buried her head against his chest again, as if to block out the truth. 'But that would make him some kind of criminal.'

'Then maybe, just maybe, you should brace yourself for that eventuality.'

She stilled in his arms. 'You think there is a possibility?'

He shrugged, unable to prevent himself from stroking her back through her coat, trying to show indifference when all he wanted to do was tell her that he knew it to be true and that she had had a lucky escape. Could she not tell from the gravity of the reports that this was no frame-up? Then battling to care about Garbas and

whether he was guilty or innocent when she was in his arms this way, and so very beautiful, so very desirable...

With a groan, he hauled his libido and his thoughts back to where they should be.

'The police must have evidence. They do not go around arresting people on such charges lightly, Bella.'

The use of her pet name sliced through her tears and through the dense fog that had occupied her mind ever since he had abandoned her last night, leaving her sleepless and unable to cope with this morning's revelations.

And suddenly she was aware of so many other things—of the spring of chest hair under her fingers; of the broad width of naked chest that lay heated under her cheek and pressed against her breasts; of the rough towel that was the only barrier separating them.

'You called me Bella,' she said, lifting her head to look up at him. 'I thought you hated me.'

He stroked her hair back from her face. 'I could never hate you.'

And she smiled. 'Nor me you. I think we are destined to be friends for ever, Raoul.' Even though, with his warm, firm flesh under her hands, she wished it could be more.

He kissed the top of her head. 'I believe so. I'm sorry I was so—abrupt last night, Bella. There are things you do not understand.'

'I would be happy to try, if only you would let me.'

He let her go and turned away, so suddenly that she was left to find her balance in a world that had somehow subtly shifted while she was in his arms. 'I should

get dressed,' he said, opening his wardrobe. 'So, what do you intend to do?'

It took her a moment to work out what he meant. 'I have to do something. Maybe I should go to the police station—tell them there must be another explanation. Offer to be a character witness.'

Halfway pulling out a shirt from a wardrobe, he stopped and looked at her. 'Do you always believe the best of people, Bella? Always? No matter what?'

It was her turn to shrug. 'But how can it be true? The foundation does such wonderful work. I have seen the children he has helped—tiny children with no hope until his foundation funds their treatment; tiny children who have lost so much and yet are still able to smile because of what his foundation has done for them—offering them hope for some kind of future. What will happen to them?'

He growled as he shrugged the shirt on. Was she so naive that she couldn't see that Consuelo's purpose was to hide behind those very children he pretended to care about in order to cover his filthy tracks? 'They will not suffer because of this.'

She shook her head. 'I don't know. I keep thinking someone must have made a mistake. Maybe it's someone working for him behind the scenes who might have done this. And I can't help feeling there must be something I can do to help.'

His fingers stabbed the last shirt-button home, his blood running cold in his veins while he watched her over his shoulder. 'Do you love him, Bella—this man who abandoned you yesterday on a day you needed

friends to stand by you? Is that why you are so desperate to help him?'

'No.' She made a sound like a whimper. 'No, but does it have to be about love? He's a friend, and he's going to need all the friends he can to get through this.'

'And yesterday, when you needed a friend? Where was he then, if not already running, if what the paper suggests is true? Why else would his offices be raided? Why else would he have been arrested at the airport like that article says if he was not trying to flee? Unless he had plans to travel that you knew about?'

'No.' She squeezed her eyes shut. 'We were planning on having a quiet dinner together.'

'Then how much help do you think you can be, without proving him to be a liar with your evidence?'

She collapsed on the un-made bed, her face in her hands. 'I'm sorry. I don't know! I just don't know what to do.'

She looked so vulnerable and broken, so desperate and despair-ridden, that he could not help but feel guilty, even when Garbas was scum and had it coming to him. There was little triumph here. In kicking Garbas, he'd kicked her too when she was already down, even if it was to save her.

But there was no way now he would walk away and leave her here in Paris, not like this. All she knew was death and loss here, and a friend she was determined to defend. She was just as likely to go to the police and ask to speak to him. If she asked him if he had done it and Garbas said he had not, of course she would believe

him. She would never be free of him, not really, not un-
less…

God, what a mess.

'Bella,' he said, sitting alongside her, pulling her into
his arms. 'I will tell you what you must do. You must
pack your bags and come with me to Venice and you
will forget all about what is happening here.'

She sniffed again against his chest, a fresh torrent of
tears hot against his fresh shirt. 'But you don't want me
there,' she sobbed. 'You said you didn't.'

'I'm asking you now.'

'So why now and not last night? You didn't want me
to come last night. You sent me home.'

He sighed, stroking her hair, looking across the room
at nothing in particular. 'Last night I was reminded of
things I would rather forget. Not because of you, Bella,
but Umberto's death reached me in places I did not want
to go. And I was angry. Unthinking. Careless of your
feelings. But I cannot leave you here like this in Paris,
all alone, with Umberto gone and your friend in jail.'

She shook her head. 'But…'

He took her chin in his hand and lifted it so he could
see her eyes. 'You have leave. Why not make the most of
it? How long has it been since you had a real holiday?'

Too long, if the lost look in her eyes was any indi-
cation. 'You said it has been years since you were in
Venice,' he said, knowing she was swayed. 'I have an
apartment on a canal, big enough that I could do my
work and you could sightsee to your heart's content.
And we could sip wine in the evening on the balcony
and watch the gondolas slip by. What do you say?'

Her eyes swirled with the possibilities. He saw them; he saw her hesitation and felt her temptation as she tasted the opportunity before her. And still she wavered. 'I don't know.'

'Of course you do,' he said. 'And then in a few weeks, when all this has all settled down and you are feeling stronger, come back and see what you can do for your friend then. Maybe it will have all blown over. But things will be clearer then, I know.'

She looked up at him, and he could see she was torn. 'You really think so?'

'I know so.'

Her teeth found her lip—swollen and bruised from yesterday's stresses he realised—and he put a thumb to her lip if only to stop her injuring herself further. 'You've hurt yourself. Don't do that.' And even as he brushed her lips apart with his finger she looked up at him with those wide cat's eye. Even though he knew it was folly, even though he knew it could lead nowhere good, he could not resist. So he dipped his mouth to hers, tentatively, whisperingly soft, no more than a brush of skin against skin.

Yet she shuddered against him like the world had quaked beneath her feet.

My doing, he thought with a touch of satisfaction as he tasted her lips and felt the foundations of his own soul shift and stir and bring him reluctantly to awareness— where he had no intention of going.

He returned the finger to her lips, pushing himself away, reminding himself why he was doing this. He would have to kiss her, he told himself, if this was to

work. It meant nothing. And then, once she was safe, he could let her go. She would be free to find someone worthy of her, someone who could offer her a future filled with life and love.

She looked up at him, all blinking eyes and breathlessness, her lips parted as if she could not draw in enough air any other way, as if waiting for him to kiss her again.

Later, he thought, knowing he shouldn't rush her, knowing he should take his time. Because he had no choice, even though it was the wrong choice. He couldn't leave her here.

Because, like it or not, Umberto had been right all the time.

There was no other way.

CHAPTER FOUR

VENICE enchanted her. From the moment she first caught sight of their destination as their plane came into land at Marco Polo airport, Gabriella was struck by the soft beauty of this ageing city perched upon the sea. From the air it had looked like a fantasy land, seemingly floating atop the waters of the lagoon, the tell-tale S of the grand canal slicing through its many islands.

From the *vaporetto* as they approached the city, it appeared even more magical. She sighed with pleasure, soaking up the soft sun on her bare arms, the breeze dancing through her hair. It felt like for ever since she'd felt the sun's kiss on her skin or the whispering breeze in her hair and she tossed her head back, letting her hair flick and dance on the warm air.

There was something exotic and timeless about approaching the city by water. She could almost imagine herself as a mediaeval princess being ferried across the sea to meet her new husband, a wealthy Venetian merchant, mesmerised by the sight of such beautifully decorated buildings jostling shoulder to shoulder for space. Some were topped with intricate domes, others with towers pointing upwards as if in the search for

space, while the water lapped at their feet. There were palaces, churches and rows of gondolas tied to candy-striped posts bobbing on the water. It was all utterly unreal. Utterly magical.

'Happy?' Raoul asked alongside her, his blue-black hair pulled into a short ponytail, his eyes covered with sun-glasses that only added to his dark appeal. Her eyes drank him in. Already he looked different, as if he'd lost some of the tension that had lined his features just yesterday. His shirt softly draped in the breeze, sculpting against his broad chest, while the unbuttoned collar revealed a tantalising vee of olive skin at his neck with a sprinkling of dark hair.

A sizzling heat zipped its way up Gabriella's spine and momentarily struck her dumb. If the mediaeval princess was lucky enough to have someone like this man waiting for her, she would be one very lucky woman indeed.

But, no—this man was more likely the pirate who came to retrieve his bride from the clutches of the wealthy merchant.

He tilted his head and smiled. 'You certainly look happy.'

Happy didn't come close. She was arriving here in Venice, in a magical city with a man who took her breath away every time she looked at him. How had she ever imagined there was anything sinister about him when she had felt that sliver of apprehension yesterday in the cemetery? For his was a dark beauty that erred on the side of danger but erred deliciously, so that every glance was like a guilty pleasure to be sinfully enjoyed.

Would the fair princess stay with the rich Venetian merchant? she wondered. Or would she let herself be taken by the pirate?

No contest.

Exhilarated beyond measure, feeling suddenly more alive than she had in months, she laughed into the wind, letting the sound get taken away over the water. 'I love it. I'd forgotten how beautiful Venice is. This is just like seeing it for the first time.'

'How long has it been?'

'Years. I think I was only ten or eleven and on a school trip. I don't remember much beyond feeding the pigeons in St Mark's Square.' She shook her head, smiling as she remembered the chaos she and her class mates had caused. 'Twenty squealing girls. Those poor pigeons.'

He looked at her. 'I remember now. You told us that first night we were in the mountains while we sat around the fireplace. Everyone was laughing. I had forgotten...'

It was no wonder he had forgotten, she thought, quietly reflective for a moment. That time in the mountains had been their last holiday together. She could remember little of those first few days, either. All that stuck in her mind was the helicopter ride over the glaciers she'd been so looking forward to, and the night of illness that had put paid to any chances of her going. It was Raoul who had generously offered to stay back and look after her so their parents could go together and not miss out. Gabriella had spent the day dozing and sipping lemonade, listening to Raoul read her story after story. And they had thought nothing of it when the day had begun

to darken and the night closed in. Not until the police had come calling...

'You're biting your lip again, Bella,' he said, wrapping an arm around her shoulders. 'Don't worry. We are here together now and I promise to save you from any pigeons with long-term memories.'

She laughed and turned towards him, turning away from the buildings, the water and the ladylike beauty of the city to his intensely masculine face. She was grateful that he had turned the mood around, grateful just to be here with him in this beautiful city. 'Thank you so much for allowing me to come,' she said, and reached up on tiptoes, wrapping her arms around his neck and kissing his cheek. She sighed as she relished the warm, clean scent of man, the brush of his blue-black whiskers against her lips and the feel of her body pressed length-to-length with his.

He took her arms, easing them away from his neck. She wondered if once again she had overstepped some unseen line, but he surprised her by turning her around in front of him and linking his hands at her waist where they sat, snug and disturbingly comfortable.

'We are nearly there, Bella. Look,' he said as the water taxi turned off into a smaller canal and then into another set, like a canyon amidst the tall buildings. Flowers spilled from flowerpots under arched windows; quaint bridges appeared from a wall and forded the canal, disappearing into the buildings on the other side like secret tunnels.

With Raoul's warm body at her back, his arms around her waist, she never wanted this journey to end. She was

acutely aware of the constriction of his arms every time she drew breath; she was achingly aware of the proximity of them to her breasts. And then there were his hands, crossed and perched so low across her belly; she knew if he just stretched out the fingers of one hand he could touch her *there*...

It was so deliciously close it was almost impossible to breathe.

All too soon they arrived at the water door of a large *palazzo*. With a lightness that belied his size, Raoul released her and jumped to the private landing, offering his hand to help her. She looked up at the exterior of the building, drinking in the detail of walls the colour of sunset, soft blue accents around the windows and archways on the lower floor. The next boasted high-arched windows, with even a balcony complete with arched doors and marble columns. Strange; when Raoul had mentioned having an apartment in Venice, this gothic masterpiece was not what she had envisioned.

'Welcome, Raoul,' a voice said, and she looked around as an ornate arched grille swung open, revealing a man younger than Raoul by some years. 'We've been expecting you.'

'Thank you, Marco,' he said, passing him their luggage. 'This is Gabriella D'Arenberg who will be my guest for a while. Gabriella, Marco and Natania comprise my staff. I'm sure Natania will soon be along.' As he spoke, Gabriella saw a woman skip down the stairs, her layered mini skirt fluttering around her thighs. A wide smile directed at Raoul lit up her face as she appeared, her expression turning more wary when she took

in their visitor. With one vertical sweep of her beautiful eyes, she gave Gabriella an inexplicable stab of jealousy. Natania was lush, gypsy-beautiful and she got to live with Raoul on a permanent basis. How on earth could he resist anything so gorgeous?

'Ah, here is Natania. Anything you need, simply ask.'

'It is a pleasure to meet you, Gabriella,' the younger man said, smiling. Gabriella could see that, while he shared Raoul's olive skin and Mediterranean colouring, that was where the similarity ended. His long, dark lashes and lush lips softened his face; even the hint of mischief in his eyes gave him a boyish charm.

'I should have warned you, we don't stand on ceremony here,' Raoul explained. 'Unless you prefer a title— miss? *Mademoiselle?*'

She shook her head. 'No, not at all. Thank you, Marco, it's lovely to meet you too.'

Natania edged closer; big hoops pierced her ears. 'It will be lovely to have another woman around for a change,' the newcomer said, holding out her slim hand, gold bangles jangling at her wrists. She moved like a colt, loose-limbed and lithe, her scooped tank top and skirt fitting smoothly, accentuating her perfect figure, the perfect complement to her wild, gypsy eyes. 'I get so bored being surrounded with just men.'

Marco jerked his head up at this, a wry grin on his lips, something heated skating over his eyes as their eyes met. Gabriella reined in that unfamiliar streak of jealousy. So Marco and Natania were a couple? That was comforting news. As was the knowledge the *palazzo* didn't see a passing parade of women.

Unjustifiable, perhaps, because what Raoul did or did not do was no real concern of hers; it wasn't as if she had any kind of stake in him. But, still, it was there and the knowledge warmed her in places still humming from his touch.

'Thank you, Natania,' she said, meaning it. 'I know I'm going to enjoy it here.'

Raoul led the way to the *piano nobile*, the noble floor, where his suite sat high above the water's edge, with views over the canal and no fear of flooding. Downstairs were the minor and service rooms, he pointed out as they climbed, while Marco and Natania shared a smaller suite of rooms on the floor above.

'You need all this space just for you?' she asked as he led her to his suite of rooms.

'Maybe not, but I won it in a card game many years ago. I was not about to quibble with the size.'

'And you kept it for an investment?'

'No. I was merely lucky enough not to lose it on the next game. Or the one after that.'

She laughed, because she could not imagine gambling with a property so clearly valuable. 'You are kidding? Surely you would not risk making the same mistake someone else had?'

'Why not? It was no risk for me because it meant nothing to me. Maybe that's why I was lucky enough to keep it. Anyway,' he said without bothering to explain as he pushed open the door to the apartment, 'Come inside.'

It wasn't a living room or even a lobby the suite opened on to, it was a library, lining four walls of the

long, narrow room, bookshelves stacked high, even over doorways to the impossibly high ceilings. Gabriella did a double take, blinking with disbelief as she took in the titles, some of them recognisable treasures.

'You have a library?' she said, suddenly spinning around, a smile lighting up her face, illuminating her features with a child-like delight that twisted his gut.

So much enthusiasm.

So much life.

Such a waste.

And then she stopped spinning and stood there, almost incandescent with wonderment as she inhaled deeply, as if she could breathe in the collective wisdom contained in a room filled with old books. 'It's wonderful.'

He could not bear it. First her excitement at the *vaporetto* as they'd approached the water-borne city, an excitement that had made it impossible not to want to wrap her in his arms and feel that excitement first hand.

And now here. But this time he resisted the urge to collect her into his arms and feel first-hand the excitement in the shape of her feminine curves.

Did she always see the joy in everything?

Did she not realise it couldn't last?

'This way,' he said gruffly, almost rigid with control as he pulled open a set of double doors, unable or unwilling to stay in the room a moment longer with her. 'The living room.'

She'd done something wrong. One moment, Raoul had been warm and welcoming—even, she thought, remembering the warmth of his touch pressing against her

back and the iron-like feel of his arms around her waist, more like a lover than a friend. His touch had been filled with both tenderness and desire.

Had she been the only one to feel that desire?

But now, it seemed as she watched him both physically and mentally retreat from her, there was nothing warm about him. His back was ramrod straight, the air about him frosty. Yet all she'd done was express her delight at the unexpected discovery of his library.

Had she been too easily impressed? Too gauche? Raoul was more than a decade older than her. She must seem so young and unsophisticated compared to the women he was probably used to, even if they weren't permitted here. But there would have to be women...

With a heavy heart, she followed him through the doors and into a long, richly decorated room with two long blood-red velvet sofas lining the richly frescoed walls. Four arched doors opposite led to the balcony she had seen from the sea-door landing, she assumed. But it was the chandelier that hung from the decorated ceiling that was the *pièce de résistance*. It was so exquisite that she stopped following Raoul for a moment to simply absorb its beauty. From its base swept long white plumes tipped with red, all swaying and curving, like the necks of peacocks dancing and craning their heads this way and that. The artist had captured the motion so well, it could almost have been alive.

'This is the dining room,' she heard him say. And then he must have turned, looking for her. 'It's Murano glass—an original.'

'It's exquisite,' she said, cautious, conscious of not

gushing over every last thing in case she further aggravated him.

'Have you been there? To the island, I mean, to see the glass factories?'

'Yes, my class did a tour, but I don't remember seeing anything this beautiful then.' Probably because they'd all been too fascinated with the tiny animals, the dolphins, fish and the *millefiore*—the tiny coloured flowers and hearts set in the glass—to take note of any of the more spectacular work.

'I will take you again, in that case.'

'You will?' Then she remembered not to look so excited and schooled her face into something she hoped looked far more sophisticated and calm. 'Thank you. If it's not too much trouble, that would be lovely.'

Something scudded across his eyes, and just as quickly disappeared. 'I will organise it.' Once again, he pointed to the room off one side of the living room. 'The kitchen is behind the dining room. Natania cooks most nights. And this,' he said, crossing to the other side of the living room and opening another door, 'is your room.'

She followed him into another long room, as large as the living room they had just left, with more large sofas and an amazing red Persian rug splashing colour and depth into the furnishings. But it was the king-sized bed to which her eyes were drawn. It was set into an arched alcove at the end of the room, columns at its entrance, the walls decorated with a mediaeval mural featuring nymphs and satyrs along with gods and goddesses engaged in various acts of love. It was an orgy of colour,

passion and sex—the perfect lover's retreat. And he expected her to sleep there? Surrounded by that?

'Surely this is the master suite?' she said, trying not to blush and knowing she was failing miserably. She was no prude, and the art was sublime, but the images were not exactly easy to look at, not if the last thing you needed to think about was sex.

'You are my guest. And this is the most comfortable room.'

Comfortable, maybe. Confronting, *definitely*.

'There is a bathroom through here,' he said, his arm reaching for a door handle past the buttocks of a god engaged in an activity that was clearly giving him and the recipient great pleasure.

'You're blushing,' he said. 'Are you shocked by what you see?'

It wasn't that. It wasn't the sight of the images that shocked her, exactly. It was that she didn't want such thoughts put in her head when she was with Raoul. She didn't need them. It was like her every night-time dream had been captured by a mediaeval artist five-hundred years ago and had been splattered across these bedroom walls. *Raoul's bedroom walls.*

'I wasn't expecting such *unique* decor, it's true. But it's a beautiful room. In fact...' she said, fleeing for the safety of the bathroom, before realising there was no sanctuary in a place where she could just as easily imagine Raoul naked and soaping himself in the wide marble shower. She squeezed her eyes shut, trying to blot out those images too—but how did you blot out the image of a perfect male specimen, naked under the cascading

water, droplets beading on the ends of his hair, rivulets sluicing down his long, hard body?

She swallowed hard and slapped on a too-bright smile as she turned. 'It's a fabulous apartment. How old is it?' As an attempt to find something safer to talk about, even if maybe it was groan-worthy, it was the best she could come up with. The fact she hadn't used the word 'naked' was something to be proud of.

'At least seven hundred years,' he said as he showed her through the rest of the apartment: the second bathroom, a small room given over to an office and a still-generous but much more modest and unassuming second bedroom. With no lovers' alcove, she noted wryly, and with which she would have been perfectly happy. 'Originally it was built on a Byzantine design, and then redesigned during the fourteenth century to what you see today.'

'It's magnificent, Raoul,' she said, no stranger to luxury herself. But there was something special about this place. It spoke of a time of both massive wealth and an unprecedented interest in the arts and all things beautiful. The *palazzo* was a temple to the beautiful, the fine, the rich and sensual.

And Raoul was like a beautiful, tortured dark angel in its midst.

'I must leave you now,' he said when they had finished the tour and he once again stood stiffly before her in the library. 'I have something I must see to. Please make yourself at home.' And then all too suddenly he was gone, leaving the air swirling in his wake.

She wandered through the apartment alone, stopping

to admire a painting or an exquisite detail on one of the many frescoes, admiring the chef's kitchen with a zillion gleaming utensils hanging from the hooks.

She stopped by the *quadrifora*, the four beautiful doors that led to the balcony, and on impulse opened them and stepped outside. A breeze tugged at her hair, and on it the scent of cooking from a *trattoria* she could see along the canal, its tables and chairs spilling out onto a terrace alongside the water. She stood there and listened to a gondolier serenade his passengers and just breathed in the scents and sounds of a city built upon the sea while her tangled thoughts lay elsewhere.

What was it that troubled Raoul? she wondered. That coloured his moods from light to dark in an instant? What was it that drove him to such dark, explosive depths, that turned his eyes unreadable and closed him off to everyone?

She stood there, long after the gondolier's song had faded along the canal, thinking about the riddle that was Raoul. Finally, finding no answers amongst the stuccoed buildings, the overflowing flowerpots or the slow, eternal slap of water against building, she sighed and thought about unpacking instead so she could go and explore.

She found Natania in her bedroom with the job already half done. 'Oh, I don't expect you to do that.'

'I don't mind. There is not enough to do otherwise, and anyway—' she lifted a cashmere sweater and rubbed it against her cheek '—you have such beautiful clothes and you wear them so well. Do you know my Marco said you looked like a flower when you arrived? Dewy and fragile and just waiting to be picked.'

Gabriella stilled as she retrieved her toilet bag from the case, heading for the bathroom. 'Marco said that?'

Natania nodded gravely, slipping tissue paper between the folds of the sweater before reverently placing it in a drawer. 'Please don't be offended. It was meant as a compliment. Only he was worried that to put you in this bedroom...' She waved a hand '...well, it might make you unsettled.'

Gabriella was still trying to work out how to answer when the other woman unzipped a compartment in her suitcase, unfolded a dress and laid it on the bed, smoothing the fabric with her hands, almost worshipping the formal gown. 'So beautiful,' she said, slipping a cover over the dress before hanging it in the closet. 'Maybe we could go shopping together while you are here?'

'I'd love to.'

The other woman's eyes lit up. 'You would? *Bene.* Anyway, I told Marco he was wrong. A woman as beautiful as you, you would know men. You would be no unpicked flower who would become unsettled by a little nudity. Am I right?'

Gabriella looked around the alcove and wondered at the other woman's definition of 'a little nudity', but she wasn't about to debate that now. For, while it was nobody's business but her own, she got the impression this was no time to act coy. She was no shy, retiring flower after all, even if she lacked the raw sensuality of this gypsy princess. 'I'm no virgin, if that's what you mean.' *Even if she could count the number of times she'd had sex on the fingers of one hand.*

The other woman's eyes opened wide, her lush mouth

in a broad self-congratulatory smile as she planted her hands on her hips and nodded. 'You see? I knew that. A woman senses these things.' She gestured to the walls around them. 'Then you will understand this art. You will appreciate it for its true beauty.' She glanced at her watch and then back at the suitcase. 'And now I must start dinner, but...'

'It's okay,' Gabriella said. 'There's not much to do. I'll finish the unpacking.'

'*Grazie!* And I promise you tonight I will make a feast fit for a king—and his queen, for that matter.' She gave an abrupt nod, as if she'd just made up her mind about something. 'Yes, it is good to see Raoul with a woman at last.'

'Natania, please don't think... It's not like that. We're old friends, that's all.'

'*Si.* Maybe for now.' And with a toss of her beautiful head she spun on her heel and headed for the kitchen, the bangles on her hand jangling in time to the sway of her hips.

What was that supposed to mean? Was Natania a fortune teller as well as a cook? But, with her spine still tingling from the gypsy's unsettling prediction, there was no way Gabriella was going to ask.

Not when she half-wished it could be true.

Raoul stormed across the square behind the *palazzo*, sending pigeons scattering while he cursed the black tide inside him that threatened to rise up, bitter and turgid, from his gut like the thick, black sludge that stuck to the piles below the water. A black tide that would not let

him out of its clutches, that clogged his veins and would not let him think or act like a normal man.

He had never wanted this. He was in no position to keep anyone safe, not when he lurched from one dark mood to the next—not when he had been unable to save his own wife.

But he hated the way Gabriella had flinched back there in the library, as if he had physically lashed out and struck her—all because he was incapable of dealing with someone who saw light when he saw dark, who saw hope where there was none.

And afterwards she had withdrawn into herself, quelling her natural spirit until she had become a stilted and stunted facsimile of who she really was, and he hated himself for doing that to her even more.

If he could not repress that side of himself, he would surely frighten her away and she would never agree to marry him.

And he had promised to.

Damn himself to hell and back for it, but he had promised. What happened when you broke a promise to the dead? Did they rise up and come after you? Did they toss and turn in their graves and haunt your dreams and turn your days to nights?

He didn't want to find out. He already had enough ghosts to last a lifetime.

So he would have to woo her, court her and let her zest for life wash over him. And then afterwards, when Garbas was safely locked away behind bars and could not touch her, he would let her go.

CHAPTER FIVE

MAYBE it was Natania's cooking and the superb platter of *frittura*, the fried fish and calamari she had prepared, or maybe it was the rich *risotto al nero di seppa* made with squid ink, which Gabriella found surprisingly delicate, that served to soothe Raoul's dark mood. Or maybe it was just that his appointment had gone well. But, whatever the reason, Raoul was back to his charming best when he returned to the apartment. When he suggested an evening walking-tour of Venice after dinner, she could not resist the chance to explore the city.

The air was heavier tonight, full of humidity as a cooler change worked through, but for now it was still warm. Raoul reacquainted her with the big tourist sites, with the highly ornate Basilica di San Marco and the grand Palazzo Ducale in St Mark's Square where once long ago she'd fed and raced after pigeons with her friends. He pointed out the domed bell-tower of San Giorgio Maggiore standing on its own island across the dark slapping waters. He took her to the Rialto Bridge, the stone wonder spanning the broad Grand Canal, its central portico lit up so it looked like a grand lady dressed up for a night out. Then he showed her places

that were off the main trails, wending his way through the darkening city, showing her architectural treasures and little-known pictures carved into stone walls and known only to those who knew Venice beyond the tourist routes.

He could do this, he decided as he led her to a tiny trattoria overlooking the lagoon for coffee. He could force back that black tide inside him and be civil—pleasant, even. He could be interested and attentive. And he could do this not just because he had to but because he honestly wanted to know more about her, more about those lost years when he had missed out on knowing her.

'What made you decide to become a librarian?' he asked, watching the ends of her hair play on the soft breeze as she sat down. She'd tied her hair back in a loose knot behind her head before they'd come out, but tendrils had worked their way loose and now danced around her face. He envied them their playfulness. His fingertips itched to brush them away, to linger on her soft skin…

Their coffee arrived; she thanked the waiter and looked back at him, her eyes bright and clear, smoothing the hair from her brow and tucking it behind her ears. 'I don't think there was ever a time I didn't want to do something to do with books. I actually think my profession chose me.'

He realised he liked listening to her too. He liked the sound of her accent, the blend of half-French, half-English, the best of both, Cognac over cream.

'Tell me what you love about it,' he urged.

'It's just working with books, all of them, every one

of them an entire world between the covers. Every new one is a discovery and until you dip into them you just never know what's inside: new worlds; new discoveries; new characters who leap off the page. It's all there, just waiting for you to open the cover and turn the page.'

She was so bright, so passionate, and even while he felt the darkness rise, even as his gut churned and rebelled, still it was impossible not to feel that light shine out from her and warm him in places where light had not touched for so long.

'The books in my library,' he bit out, coming up with an idea that might hold her, something to keep her interest while she stayed. 'I don't even know what's there.'

He watched her brow pucker as she sensed the almost-crime. 'Maybe while I'm here—if you didn't mind, that is—maybe I could look at them and catalogue them for you.'

'You would do that for me?'

'I would love to.'

She was so excited, he believed she would.

'What about you?' she asked as he finished his coffee, so suddenly that he was taken by surprise.

'What about me?'

'What have you been doing all these years?'

Standing still.

Trying to forget.

'Nothing half as interesting as you.'

She tilted her head. 'I was sorry to hear that your wife died. You were married such a short time.'

The black tide grew closer. 'What did you hear?'

'Only that there was some kind of tragic accident.

But it's such a long time ago now. Did you never think of remarrying?'

Never.

He pushed his chair back. 'Why don't we walk?'

A mist had grown while they'd sat in the café, rolling in over the sea, devouring everything in its path. Gabriella forgot about her question and thought there was something so utterly fascinating and serene about watching an entire world slowly vanish, a fantasy world disappearing into the fog as if it had never been real, as if it had never existed.

They found a bridge looking out over the water where the deepening mist rolled in over the lagoon, obliterating and absorbing everything, even sounds, so that it was as though Venice had been buried under a dank, white cloud. Every now and then a light would appear, or the dull rumble of an engine would herald the ghostly shape of a vessel making its way back to shore. She shivered. 'Are you cold?' he asked, putting his arm around her shoulders.

'It's spooky,' she said, looking up at him. 'Don't you feel it?'

He looked out into the mist-covered lagoon and she wondered what he was looking for when all anyone could see was white. 'The ghosts come out,' he said, 'When there is a night like this.'

'Oh, Raoul, please,' she said, trying to laugh while she fought down the prickles rising at the back of her neck and the shivers running down her spine. 'I'm not a child you can frighten so easily.'

'No, it is true. There are many, many ghosts in Venice. And many, many stories.'

And, because she had told him she was no longer a child and could not be frightened so easily, she felt she had no choice but to boldly ask, 'Like what? Tell me one of your ghost stories, then.'

Still looking out in the mist, a look so intense it was almost enough to make her regret her rash challenge, he began, his voice low and heavy with foreboding. 'Once there was a wealthy merchant who had the world at his feet. He had riches beyond measure—he was good-looking, some even said—and he had a beautiful wife, famous and talented. And he thought that he had it all. He thought that he was happy.'

She held her breath as the fog swirled silently around them, knowing this could not end well.

'And then one night, a night filled with the pleasures of the flesh as so much of his life had become, he introduced his wife to two brothers, supposedly two friends of his. But the two brothers conspired against him. They promised the merchant's wife the world and spirited her away.'

'She went willingly?'

He shrugged. 'Who can say? The man was a fool, you see, who saw nothing before him but his perfect life, and nothing afterwards but a blind rage. And when he found her one storm-ridden night, lying with one of the brothers, it almost destroyed him.'

'What happened?'

'They died that night, both the woman and her lover.'

'The merchant killed them?'

'He might as well have. Because she haunted him every night afterwards until he thought he was going mad with the darkness. And even now, on nights such as these, you can hear her voice on the mournful breeze calling for him, searching for him, waiting for him to pass by so she can suck him into the watery depths.'

Through the gloom of the fog the soft wind moaned and a light flickered faintly once, twice, before it disappeared back into the swirling fog. Gabriella grabbed hold of Raoul's arm, chilled beyond measure. 'It's late,' she said, trying not to tremble as she clung to him. 'And it's been a long day. Let's go home.'

They walked back hand in hand, the soft lamps along their route and Raoul's solid presence banishing thoughts of ghosts, legends and what must have been just wild imaginings, turning her thoughts away from the ghostly and much more towards the physical and the real. Her hand fitted well in his, she mused; his long fingers were warm and strong. She squeezed her hand and he squeezed back, looking down at her. 'I want you to be happy, Bella. Are you glad you came to Venice?'

She smiled, thinking she would be happy to be with Raoul anywhere when he was like this—charming, warm and the perfect host. But to be here with him in Venice, against the backdrop of mediaeval *palazzos*, with the rumble of the *vaporettos* and the snatches of love songs from passing gondoliers, she couldn't think of a better place to be. 'It's magical, Raoul. Thank you for insisting I come.'

He stopped and pulled her to him, his free hand curving around her neck and sending delicious shivers cours-

ing through her as leaned down, his eyes on her mouth. She gasped as their lips met, breathing in the taste of him, dark, rich and potent, much like the man himself. His mouth weaved some kind of magic on hers. So tender and evocative was his kiss that she wanted to fall into it and go with it wherever it might lead so that, when he lifted his head, she almost mewled a protest.

'What was that for?' she asked, suddenly breathless and dizzy, hoping for all kinds of things that were probably as unlikely as building an entire city on water—yet here it was.

'Because,' he said, his dark eyes swirling with heated intent, 'There was no way earthly way I could not.'

She lay awake a long time that night in the big king-sized bed surrounded by the endless orgy, a celebration of the act of love in all its iterations, still reeling from Raoul's kiss, still tingling at the memory of his touch and the sensual brush of his lips against her own.

Buzzing at the erotic images on the walls around her.

On the wall before her a nymph kissed her lover, his hand at her plump breast. She could almost imagine that hand on hers, tweaking her nipple, coaxing it to hardness. With a groan she turned over, willing herself to think of something less sensual, less arousing—only to be welcomed by a wild-eyed woman, her head thrown back in ecstasy as her lover pressed close behind her. She turned on her stomach, buried her face in the pillow and tried to ignore the ache in her breasts and the pulsing insistence between her thighs.

Such a big bed.

Such a lonely bed.

Such a waste.

And when she did fall asleep it was to restless dreams of potent, well-built gods, wicked satyrs—and a dark and dangerous man who kissed like one of those gods, who probably made love like one of those gods and who was sleeping a mere room away...

Raoul was out when she rose the next day, so she pulled on jeans and sneakers and a singlet top that could afford to get dusty and threw herself into the task of cataloguing the library while he was away. Marco found her a step ladder so she could reach all but the highest shelves and promised he would help her when she got to those. Even on the lower shelves, the breadth of the collection dazzled her. Mostly they were books printed in Italian, as she had expected, but a quick scan revealed titles on geography, the sciences, history and the arts, with some dusty tomes at least a century old; a veritable treasure trove.

She flipped through one volume, a history of the *palazzos* of Venice by the looks of it, its spine creaking with age and stiffness. But the illustrations were still wonderful, leaping from the page with life, the buildings along the Grand Canal instantly recognisable even now. Her heart raced with the possibilities of her task—maybe there were volumes here that had never been documented before. Why not?

But with only her schoolgirl Italian to help her she would need help. One of her colleagues from the library would be able to help her, she was sure. She needed to

call her boss anyway. She would call later today, when she had more idea of the size of the task ahead.

Then with a pang she remembered she needed to find out what was happening with Consuelo. She had barely spared him a thought ever since she'd arrived, yet there must be news by now. Even if he could not answer her messages, someone must know what was happening to him. Raoul had intimated there was nothing she could do, but there had to be something she could do to help. She was a friend, after all, and he would do the same for her; she was sure of it.

She was just about to descend the ladder when she saw it—the slim volume wedged tightly between two others. Even with her imperfect Italian she could make out the title: *Ghostly Tales of Venice*.

Thinking it must have been the source of Raoul's story, she pulled it out, curious, leafing through the pages and searching for his story of the wealthy merchant who was haunted by his lost love. She flipped the pages, just able to decipher a few words here and there. One was a story of children lost in the mist who had disappeared for ever, their gondola found floating listlessly the next day. Another was of a murdered soul who haunted the bridge where he was brutally killed, and yet another told of a woman lost at sea whose unearthly casket could be seen floating on the lagoon on mist-shrouded nights.

Maybe Raoul had been right, she thought as she flipped through the book, her blood running cold with even just a snatched word here and there and a pencil-sketch illustration. Maybe there really were ghosts in

Venice's mist-shrouded waterways. She had felt something last night; she was sure of it.

But she reached the last page of the slim volume and closed the book without finding what she had been looking for. There was no mention of Raoul's wealthy merchant, nothing that came close to the story he had told her, of the wife lost with her lover who had haunted her merchant husband ever since.

And like the cold slice of steel through flesh an idea came to her and she wondered...

Had it been a legend?

Or had Raoul been telling his very own ghost story?

The lost wife, the tragic death, the darkness he seemed to carry around with him as if the past still had hold of him, weighing him down, refusing to let him go. Was Raoul that haunted merchant?

She clutched the small book to her chest and shivered as she remembered the cool detachment with which he had related the tale, as if it had had nothing to do with him. But Raoul too had lost his wife in tragic circumstances. And he had cut Gabriella off earlier when she had expressed her sympathy, changing the subject. Had the story been his way of explaining something he found too difficult to talk about?

Her heart went out to him. Hadn't they both suffered enough when they had lost their parents? Yet Raoul had suffered another blow by losing his wife not long after.

She started down the ladder, the book still clutched in her hand. It was so unfair.

It would be enough to drive any man to despair.

She resolved that she would not cause him more pain.

As he had come to her rescue with Umberto's death, rescuing her from her sudden loneliness, so she too would do everything she could to ease his suffering so that he would never rue the day he had invited her here.

She was almost at the last step when the door swung open behind her. One-handed, she turned and lost her footing, and would have fallen, but he was there to steady her, his hand like a steel clamp around her wrist, the other at her waist, easing her gently down to the floor. 'Bella, what are you doing?'

She looked up at him, breathless and grateful, intending to find him a sympathetic smile, to let him know she understood about his pain and his loss. But just the very sight of him warmed her soul so much—his dark features, the angles, planes and dark recesses that combined to stir her senses—that her smile became so much more besides. 'Raoul,' she said as he bent down to kiss her cheeks, leaving her almost breathless as his evocative scent filled her lungs. 'I thought I would get started on your library. To earn my keep.'

'I have a better way,' he suggested. 'It is a beautiful day outside. Come and share it with me.'

'But the library?'

'Has waited this long. It will still be there tomorrow. Come, Bella—you *do* want to see something of Venice while you are here?'

'Of course. I'll just go and get changed.'

'Please don't,' he said, his voice tight. 'You look good in anything you wear—but in those jeans, Bella…' And his words put a sizzle all the way to her bones. Then he tilted his head and looked almost genuinely contrite.

'I probably should not say such things.'

'It's okay,' she said, licking suddenly dry lips—the dust from the books, she assumed. 'I don't mind. I... I'll just grab my jacket.'

He had her. From the moment he had kissed her on that Venice path last night, he had sensed that she was his. Ridiculously easily, as it happened. He could not imagine why any woman, let alone one as beautiful and filled with life as Gabriella, would be drawn to someone as dark and as accursed as him. But for whatever reason—maybe that trait in her that had her believing the best in everyone—she seemed all too ready to forgive him his faults, if he could only repress that dark part of him and act civilised every now and then.

So he donned the air of a civilised man, not one plagued by dark deeds and darker moods. In the ensuing days, he showed her the best of Venice. He walked her to the Castello area in the evening, lingering in the Giardini—the gardens created only two short centuries ago after Napoleon's invasion—then spent time in the Via Garibaldi, where they sipped bitter spritz with fat green olives amongst the locals taking time out. He took her to the museums and galleries, both the well-known and obscure, and he treated her to the best and least well-known of Venice's restaurants on the outlying islands, while treating her to the most exclusive of Venice's boutiques nearby.

He listened to her talk, seemingly endlessly, about the books she'd discovered in his library where she explored every day. And he let her joy of discovery wash over him, knowing he must if she was to trust him.

He had been the perfect host. And tonight would be no exception, he decided as he slipped on his jacket. Tomorrow he would take her to the glass-making factories and shops of Murano, but tonight would provide one more piece for the fairy-tale picture she was building up of Venice. And, if tonight's excursion went as well as expected, they would be shopping tomorrow for more than just glass.

He swallowed back on the now-familiar pang of guilt, that what he was doing might be wrong or unfair, or was somehow taking advantage of her. Because it wasn't as if he didn't like her. It wasn't as if he had to pretend to be attracted to her; it wasn't as if he had to lie about those things. They were old friends, he told himself, and it wasn't as though he planned to hurt her. He was protecting her, just as her grandfather had requested.

And Umberto had been right—there would be nothing worse for her than if she fell into the clutches of someone like Garbas.

If marrying her was what it took to prevent that, he would do it.

Gabriella's body hummed with anticipation as she waited. Raoul had promised her something special tonight, a secret he had refused to reveal, even when she had teased him and begged him to let her in on the secret.

He was different, she decided as she looked down from the balcony at the never-dull vista that greeted her. Could one ever get sick of the sight and sounds of Venice? It was a world unto itself—a place of incredible

beauty on the one hand, of secrets and hidden depths on the other.

Just like Raoul himself.

For even lately in these last few days, even when he had played the host role to perfection, there had been times—glimpses, really—when she would turn her head and look at him, catch him unawares and see *something* lurking in the depths. Something troubled, menacing and sometimes even sinister that made her want to reach out with her hands, smooth his brow, untangle his thoughts—and then he would look up, see her watching him and smile, chasing the shadows away.

Venice suited him, she thought, sighing into the soft breeze and, just like Venice, he was unique. One of a kind. Impossible not to fall in love with.

She stilled at the railing, her heart skipping a beat and then resuming just that slight bit quicker. She couldn't love him, could she? Not really?

Sure, she had always loved him; he had been almost family.

Except that wasn't what she was thinking now.

When she had been no more than a child, she had worshipped him as a child worshipped someone she adored like a hero, someone she could look up to.

As an adolescent, her fantasies had been based more on fairy tales and rampant teenage hormones, of a fantasy Raoul that was larger than life that she could only dream about, the product of her own wild imagination.

And now?

Now she was a woman. Surely she did not imagine

that tingle every time they touched? Surely she did not imagine the magic of their kiss?

Those things were no fantasy.

Those things were real.

But love? Could she really be falling in love with Raoul? They had been together just a few short days, after all.

She must be crazy even to think it.

She must be.

And yet the magic of the last few days had not simply been all about Venice. Venice delighted her, it was true. But it wasn't Venice that had her blood pounding or her heartbeat quickening right now, it was the thought of spending the evening with Raoul. Of losing herself in his bottomless gaze and feeling the heat from his body feed into hers, warming her in an endless, sensual glow.

It was more than just Venice.

It was Raoul, and she was falling in love with him.

He found her waiting for him in the living room, standing on the balcony overlooking the canal, her expression pensive. She was more beautiful than ever in a soft pastel-print dress with a cinched waist and full skirt that made the most of her tan skin, chestnut hair and the near-sinful proportions of her figure, the feminine curve from breast through waist to hip.

When had he gone from merely noticing that she had grown up to thinking she had grown into a very desirable woman? When had just a glance at her turned from benevolent approval of the changes time had brought about to something deeper and more fundamental, something

that stirred his blood and sent it simmering? Right now, it seemed like he had wanted her for ever.

She turned when she heard him approach, her smile wide, welcoming and totally innocent—and that pang of guilt made itself known again, twisting this time, mercilessly so. He wished there was something about her he did not like, something he could find fault with aside from her unswerving faith in her human companions.

Except that it was that very fault—the trait that made her see the best in the likes of that scum Garbas—that was also making his job so very, very easy.

'Are you ready, Bella?' he said, taking her hands in his. 'For tonight's adventure?'

Her eyes held so many stars he could not count; her eager smile was infectious and he laughed in spite of his own misgivings and his own endless doubts. 'Then let's go.'

Tonight the air was warm and blessed with only the lightest of breezes, the architecture of Venice turning honey gold under the westering sun.

'This evening,' he said as he handed her into the gondola waiting at the sea door, 'We continue our exploration of Venice from the water.'

Together they sat back on the plushly cushioned reclining seat as the gondolier let the vessel drift away, setting it moving along the canal with long, languid sweeps through the water.

They ventured into the Grand Canal, past St Mark's Square, still heaving with tourists and its cloud of pigeons, past all of the sights that Raoul had shown her on foot. Only this way showed Venice as it was always

meant to be seen—from the sea, where the water offered an unbeatable perspective of the wonders that rose all around them.

He had judged his timing well. Gabriella sat entranced, reclining in the curve of his arm, as comfortably wound against him as a cat, and he sensed that if he asked her this day to fly to the moon she would say yes.

Right on cue, the rich tenor voice of their gondolier rang out in the balmy evening air.

'Raoul,' she said, her eyes so bright and brilliant they threatened to rival the moon's pearlescent glow. 'Did you plan this?'

He drew her closer to him and smoothed a loose tendril of her hair with his hand. 'Are you happy, Bella?'

'I don't think I have ever been happier.' And she settled deeper, curving her delicious body against him, making him burn. Tonight, he thought, she was his. All he had to do was ask the question.

The gondola slipped along the canals, gently slicing through the water, taking the route Raoul had instructed the gondolier to take, getting closer and closer to that moment—and to the task he had promised himself he would undertake tonight.

Except, the further the boat ventured, the heavier and darker his gut felt. How was he supposed to keep her safe? What if he couldn't? What if he failed again? For she was beautiful, too beautiful for him. Too beautiful to be shackled to a man with a dark past and no future, even if he told himself it need only be for a few months, just until he knew she was free from Garbas. Too beauti-

ful to be shackled to a man who could not keep anyone safe, not even his own wife.

'It's a beautiful night,' she said, nestling closer to him. 'At least we will be safe from your ghosts tonight.'

He stilled, for there were always ghosts. She had been gone ten years and still she would not let him go.

She would never let him go.

He felt Gabriella shift against him, protesting his sudden stiffness. 'Raoul, is something wrong?'

'I'm sorry, Bella,' he said, trying to force himself to relax. Tonight was no time to remember, to think of ghosts, horrors and mistakes that belonged in the past. Tonight there was a job to be done. 'Look,' he continued, pointing ahead, wanting to change the subject for his own sake as much as to distract her. 'The Bridge of Sighs.'

Before them the white limestone bridge arched gracefully over the Rio di Palazzo, connecting the old prison to the interrogation rooms in the Doge's Palace. 'I read about that,' she said. 'And how Lord Byron gave it that name for the prisoners who would sigh as they took their last view of the city from the windows of the bridge before being taken away to meet their fate.'

He nodded, feeling an uncomfortable tightness constrict his chest. 'That is indeed one story of the bridge,' he managed, his heart beating faster, his blood pumping louder in his ears as the moment he had been planning drew nearer. 'There is another—much more romantic, as it happens. They say that if lovers kiss at sunset under the Bridge of Sighs they will find blissful happiness with each other for the rest of their lives.'

The boat glided along the canal, its companions the gentle slap and whisper of water and the gondolier's evocative serenade. He looked down at her where he cradled her in his arms, her face close to his, the slanting rays of sunlight warming her brandy-coloured eyes, eyes filled to the brim with expectation as she waited for his kiss.

This was it.

It was time.

CHAPTER SIX

RAOUL looked down into her eyes. Neither the darkness of his past nor the ghosts that plagued him were enough to stop him now.

And, even though he knew it was insane, that he was the last person to deserve her, he wanted her—wanted all of her, at least for tonight. For the promise he had made, he told himself. Only so she might believe it to be true.

The setting sun turned the air molten around them, shimmering with a thousand wishes, a thousand hopes. The first of his wants, he knew was in his control. His lips brushed hers as he sensed the shadow of the bridge move over them while his lips tasted, explored, tested.

Her mouth melded to his willingly as she gave herself up to his kiss, her sweet, sweet lips parting in invitation, an invitation he had no power but to accept as he felt the heat in his body build as her body curled into him, her hot mouth dragging him in.

And it was his turn to go willingly, losing himself in her liquid depths, plundering her mouth, wanting to reach deeper, harder. Needing more.

Their kiss started at the Bridge of Sighs, but it did

not end there. It did not end anywhere close to there. For the first time in her life, she felt truly alive, every part of her tingling with hot awareness, as if a switch had been thrown and her body was humming with electricity looking for somewhere to go. Looking for release of a charge that would burn her up if she couldn't let go.

Until all too soon they were back at the *palazzo*.

'We are home,' Raoul whispered against her sensitive lips, tracing the pad of one finger down her cheek. 'It is time to go.'

'Already?' she asked, too comfortable to move, and he chuckled softly, a satisfying, rumbling sound that said he wasn't done with her yet either.

'It does not have to be the end…'

She blinked up at him, sensing the invitation in his words, giving her the choice when there was really no choice at all. 'Make love with me, Raoul.'

This time he didn't chuckle. Instead he growled and scooped her up into his arms, not letting the sudden sway of the vessel throw him from his stride as he lifted her bodily from the gondola and through the sea door, his lips once more meshed with hers as he negotiated the route up the stairs and into the apartment.

He found her room, lit in the soft night glow of the city, hesitating momentarily before laying her almost reverently on the wide bed. For the first time she didn't see the endless orgy going on around her, didn't envy them, because Raoul was here with her and soon she would be his.

He growled again as he joined her, collecting her into his arms as he pulled her into his kiss.

She was drowning, she decided. She had been drowning all night, finding it impossible to draw air, finding it impossible to breathe or to think or to anything but drown under a torrent of sensation.

And drowning had never felt so good.

His hot mouth was at her throat, his hands moulding her to him, length to delicious length, joining them at breast and thigh and making her gasp when she felt him against her belly, hard, insistent and wanting.

What little air there had been was consumed in a raging heat that started and ended between her thighs.

Her hands tangled in his hair, urgent and busy, sliding the tie from its length. Her fingers luxuriated in its silky weight as he dipped his head and took her breast in his mouth. Even fully clothed she felt his hot breath sear her skin, felt his teeth graze one sensitive nipple until she cried out with the pleasure of sensation and the frustration of the barrier of clothing.

He was already ahead of her, his long fingers working at the buttons of her blouse, peeling it away, dispensing too with her skirt and sliding it down her legs, unwrapping her, opening her up to his gaze. She waited, afraid and tremulous, unable to breathe while he lifted his head, wanting him to like what he saw, needing both his approval and his desire.

In a face built of shadows and darkness, his eyes gleamed in the soft slanting light as his hands traced their way back up her legs, resting flat-palmed on her belly, his fingertips tracing the line of her lace bra. 'Bella,' he said. His voice was so low and filled with gravel that it seemed she felt his words through the touch

of his fingers rather than heard him speak. 'You are so perfect.' He dragged in air, his dark eyes looking suddenly tortured, confused. 'But I... Bella, I do not deserve...'

'I want you,' she said, empowered by the raw admiration she had seen in his eyes, the raw power before whatever doubts had crept into his mind, about whatever sense of wrong he was committing. This was not wrong and it never could be. She raised herself onto one elbow, unclipping her bra with her free hand, coaxing the strap down her arm, letting the scrap of lace fall from her breasts. 'I want you to make love to me, Raoul. I want to feel you deep inside me.'

He groaned then, a sound that seemed rent from his very soul. It was so very dark and anguished that for a moment she was afraid he might leave her—but then he looked at her, his chest heaving, and his eyes told her he was going nowhere. His fingers worked at his shirt, reefing it off, and she could not resist putting her hand to his skin, drinking in the complexities of his skinscape—the sculpted flesh, the wiry brush of hair, the nuggety nub of a nipple.

He hissed in air when she flicked that nub with the nail of her thumb, already shrugging down his trousers, kicking off his shoes, brushing off his underwear with the sweep of one hand that exposed all of him to her gaze.

She gasped at his size, her body sizzling at the raw, masculine potency, and she saw his eyes glint at her reaction before he tumbled her back on the bed.

'You're beautiful,' she said, awed by the power and

beauty of his body under her hands as he rained kisses on her skin, her throat, her belly, her breasts, making her cry out as he rolled his tongue around one sensitive nipple, drawing it into his hot, liquid mouth.

All the time the need inside her coiled tighter and more insistent, so that when his hand scooped down her side and brushed her last scrap of clothing she thought she might explode.

'Raoul!' she cried. He shushed her with his kiss, tangling his tongue with hers, pulling her deeper as his fingers slipped under the lace and through her neat curls, parting her with just the tip of one incendiary finger. Never had she felt like this, breathless, overwhelmed and on the cusp of something so magnificent, so momentous. Never had she felt so out of control.

'I need you,' she said—yet Raoul showed no mercy, drawing her nipple into his mouth, sliding his fingers deeper into her hot, slick darkness, his thumb circling that exquisitely sensitive nub, where it seemed all her nerve endings coalesced, one finger pushing inside her, almost sending her over the edge.

Her hands flailed on the bed, searching for something—anything. She found him, rock-hard, hot and already beading with moisture, and it was his turn to groan as he pulsed and bucked in her hand.

'Bella,' he said, grinding the word out between his teeth as though she was hurting him.

'I want you,' she repeated, writhing under him, knowing that if he didn't make love to her right now she would surely burn up in these desperate, all-consuming flames. 'Please, I need you!'

This time he showed blessed mercy, whisking off her remaining garment with an efficiency she might have congratulated in other, less urgent circumstances but right now any delay was too long, any time a waste, when all she wanted in the entire world was to be joined with this man.

Then he was back and she mewled with pleasure and surprise to realise one of them had been aware enough to think of protection as she pulled him into her kiss. He eased her legs apart, his clever fingers returning to once again caress, tease and drive her wild with need until she could not bear it a moment longer.

She tilted her hips in invitation, thrashing her head from side to side, driven crazy with longing, need and something like insanity. Just when she could not stand it any more, he was there at her entrance, and everything in her body seemed to concentrate and focus down on that one, tenuous, madness-inducing contact; that one hitched moment in time where the whole world—the satyrs, sirens, gods and goddesses—all waited with bated breath.

And then he entered her, filling her with one long thrust that drove her head back into the pillows and the breath from her lungs as her body stretched to accommodate his fullness.

Nothing, nothing in the world—not the first sun of spring on her skin, the fresh whisper of breeze through her hair after a long summer day or even seeing Raoul appear through the swirling mists that day—had ever felt so good.

Until he shifted inside her and the best got better.

Her eyes found focus, found his dark eyes watching her as he slowly withdrew and waited on the brink only to fill her even deeper, so that she gasped. But she kept her eyes on his, even as the storm inside her built with every slow withdrawal, with every sliding thrust; even as the rhythm between their bodies built, even as the pace became frantic and their breath with it, even as sensation coiled, intensified, built and built.

Built until there was no place higher to build, no place yet to go. With one final, urgent thrust, one cry of triumph, he made the stars and moon collide and sent their tiny sparkling shards raining down all around her, spelling out the words she already knew to be true.

I love you, Raoul.

It wasn't supposed to be like this. He collapsed alongside her, dragging in air as if his life depended on it, wondering what the hell had just happened. Make love to her, he had thought. Seduce her. That was what he had planned.

So why did he feel like he was the one who had been seduced? Why did he feel like he had been the one handed a precious gift?

She had told him that she wanted him.

She had told him that she wanted to feel him deep inside.

She had wrapped those hot fingers around him and brought him to the very edge of his control.

And, in the sex-fogged recesses of his mind, he knew only one thing: that, for both their sakes, this marriage could not come soon enough.

* * *

The call came the next morning. He should have slept, and slept late, given the night of love-making they had had, but Raoul had slipped out of her bed early, unable to rest under the lover's alcove. He had been feeling claustrophobic, hemmed in by the audience, mocked by the smiling satyrs and pitied by their lovers, as if they knew the truth.

So when the call had come he had been there to take it—to hear the news that Garbas, courtesy of the finest criminal lawyers in Europe, had been granted bail against all odds. Worse still, word from the street was that one of the first places he had visited on his release was Gabriella's home, looking for her. No doubt needing access to her wealth to fund his defence.

So he had been right to bring her to Venice with him, he acknowledged as he terminated the call. Now he just needed to finish the job he had set himself.

With Garbas on the loose, he would have to do something sooner rather than later—otherwise he would soon track Gabriella down, discover she was in Venice and try to play the friendship card. He could not let that happen.

He glanced at his watch and then back towards the bedroom where Gabriella still lay sleeping and probably would for hours. Half of him yearned to rejoin her in bed, to be there when she woke up, make love to her warm, willing body and blot everything out—the deathbed promise, the past, Garbas. Blot it all out with the glories of her body and the passion of their love-making.

But he could not afford to think that way. Making love

to her was a means to an end, nothing more. He could not afford to let it be more.

So he would leave for Paris now, talk to his contacts and find out what had gone wrong with the police case. And meanwhile Natania could take Gabriella on the promised trip to Murano.

She might be disappointed he would not be taking her, but he would make up for it tonight.

'I don't know whether to stay in Venice or go home.'

On the other end of the call, Gabriella heard Phillipa's soft expression of concern. 'Do you really have a choice?'

That was exactly Gabriella's problem—she didn't know. She'd woken deliciously warm cocooned in the bed clothes, wondering if last night's love-making had been a dream, being told by the protest and creak of unfamilar muscles that it was not. She'd woken with a smile on her face and with joy in her heart.

And if Raoul had been there to hold her close and make love to her again there would have been no question in her mind. There was no place she would rather be.

But she had woken up after the most wondrous night of her life *alone*.

And Natania's explanation that Raoul had apologised but had promised to be back in time for dinner went no way to diminishing this overwhelming sense of abandonment.

Hadn't last night meant anything to him? All night his body had told her he loved her. All night she'd waited for him to say the words, expecting him to say the words

she had found herself so close to saying every time she looked at him.

Yet this morning he had gone without a word.

'I don't know,' she said, shaking her head, trying to clear her muddied thoughts. 'I guess I really should go home and sort out the estate some time, and then I have to do something about returning to work. And Consuelo finally texted this morning and wants to catch up…' Then she thought about leaving Raoul, the man who had blown her world apart. 'But…'

'But what? Is it Raoul?'

'He makes me feel so good, Phillipa. He makes me feel so alive.'

'Ah.' There was a pause. 'Do you love him?'

Gabriella breathed out in a rush, 'I think so.'

'And does Raoul feel the same way about you?'

That was where Gabriella came unstuck. What did a man feel for you, if he could make love to you all night and then disappear with the morning without so much as a sweet kiss to remember him by—a man who told you nothing of how he felt?

Unless he was deliberately trying to give her the message that their love-making didn't mean anything. But that made no sense when she thought of how he had almost worshipped her body. Surely he could not be that callous?

'I don't know, Phillipa. It's driving me crazy, but I just don't know.'

'Then it's easy, Gabriella. Everything has happened so quickly, it's no wonder you're confused. So, go home. Sort out the estate, go back to work and catch up with

Consuelo if you must. But just take some time to clear
your head. And, if he's the one for you, if he truly loves
you, you will know.'

'How will I know?'

'Because he won't be able to live without you.'

When Phillipa put it like that, it all made such sense.
She was too close to him here, in this fantasy *palazzo*
in one of the most romantic cities in the world, it was
no wonder she couldn't think straight.

She would tell him tonight at dinner.

The decision made, her flight home booked for the
next day, Gabriella spent the afternoon with Natania.
They wandered the fascinating shops and factories of
Murano, shop after shop filled with the beautiful, the
most stunning and even the most whimsical expressions
of the glass-makers' art in colours of brilliant blues and
reds, some laced with gold.

Cabinet after cabinet was filled with intricate bottles,
glasses and ornaments, while chandeliers, hung from
every ceiling ranging from the traditional to the ultra-
modern.

The two women prowled the shops, stopping here and
there to admire something beautiful, Gabriella found
herself enjoying the day out much more than she had
expected, maybe because she'd made her decision and it
felt like she was taking back control of her life; maybe
because Natania was such good company. One of her
cousins worked on the island and her knowledge of the
various glass-making techniques and styles was better
than any guided tour.

Gabriella took the opportunity to buy an intricate per-

fume-bottle for Phillipa. And, while Natania was busy talking to her cousin, purchased a necklace that simply begged to be around Natania's neck—a glass heart, a brilliant red with splashes of gold, wild and sensual like the woman herself. It would be her thank-you gift.

She was just paying for her purchases when Natania said farewell to her cousin and they moved onto the next store—the last one, she had promised herself, before they caught the water taxi home so she could pack.

'Why must you leave so soon?' asked Natania beside her.

'I can hardly stay here for ever. I have a job I have to get back to in Paris some time. And a house waiting that is being neglected in my absence. Plus, there are the friends I want to visit.'

Natania nodded to her long list of reasons and asked, 'So, do you love him?'

Gabriella simply blinked. Natania was the second person to ask that question today. Was it so obvious? She sighed, conceding the point, knowing there was no point beating around the bush with her. 'I think I have always loved him, Natania—as a friend. But lately, that love has changed…'

The other woman nodded, as if satisfied. 'He is not an easy man to love. He has a dark past that colours his world.' Almost immediately she moved away to investigate another table of ornaments. Gabriella followed, intrigued. 'How long exactly have you worked for Raoul?'

She shrugged, setting the gold hoops in her ears bouncing while her eyes searched the past. 'Ten years, maybe eleven. I am not so good with numbers.'

'Did you ever meet his wife?'

She threw a glance over her shoulder. 'That was not a good time for him.'

'So you met her?'

'No. But I saw what it did to him. I saw what it cost. It was an ugly time.'

Gabriella wanted to ask why, and what else she wasn't telling her, except then she found it—what she had been looking for all the time she had been on Murano and hadn't even realised.

A gift for Raoul.

It was sitting amidst a sea of pretty ornaments, so many, too many to choose from, but this one was different. This one spoke to her. A paperweight. And at its base it swirled with darkness, clouds of purple to black, like the dark, dank sea. As it rose, the colours shifted and turned, still complex and rich in density but with the promise of light captured in the darkness. At the very top it was the clearest, sparkling crystal while at its heart sat a brilliant splash of red.

It was Raoul, she realised as she picked it up and held it in her hand. It was Raoul and all his complexities, all his moods. And his heart, locked away somewhere deep inside it all, the heart he had shown her these last few days—the heart he had all but given her last night.

Maybe she would leave and he would not follow her, be able to live without her—but she could leave him with this, and maybe one day he would understand.

CHAPTER SEVEN

GABRIELLA found him in his office, already back from Paris on their return. 'Raoul?' He turned at her voice. 'Am I interrupting? Is this a bad time?'

'No, of course not,' he said, closing down his laptop. 'Come in.' He rose to meet her, kissing her cheeks, warming her senses with his signature scent, bringing back last night's memories in a rush that had her cheeks flushing and her body preparing all over again for their coupling. 'You are a sight for sore eyes, Bella. I'm sorry I could not have been with you today.'

'It doesn't matter,' she said, only a half lie. While it had mattered at the time, now it merely increased her resolve that what she was doing was right. Time and distance were what she needed, despite what her body kept trying to tell her. 'How did your business go?'

He waved his hand as if dismissing it. 'A nuisance, nothing more, but unfortunately it had to be dealt with today.' He took her hand. 'I hated to leave you like I did but I was loath to wake you, knowing how little sleep you got. Can you forgive me?'

She tried to ignore the flush of heat that flowed into her arm at his touch but there was no ignoring the heat

that infused her face. They both knew he was the reason she'd had so little sleep. 'I found you a present,' she said, wanting to change the subject before she thought about what he could do to her to earn her forgiveness. 'While we were in Murano.'

He stilled, sensing something was not quite right. She was nervous and distant, as though she'd erected a wall between them in the hours since he'd left her sleeping. He cursed the impulse that had seen him take off for Paris rather than handle what was happening here. But then, something had changed last night, something that he had not planned, and he had needed the space to deal with it.

'You do not need to buy me gifts,' he said. *You would not want to, if you only knew...*

'It's nothing. Here,' she said, holding out the package to him.

He regarded it solemnly before taking the surprisingly heavy gift, strangely touched by this unexpected gesture.

'Open it,' she urged. Once again he caught a glimpse of that enthusiasm she had, that bright spark of life he'd once found so challenging, a quality he now associated with her and that he looked for—because it would mean his dark heart had not extinguished that spark, despite his early moodiness. 'Unless,' she added, a little sadly, he thought, 'You would rather open it later?'

'No,' he said with a shake of his head, not wanting her to be sad now, knowing that there was enough disappointment and sadness ahead of her. Cursing himself,

because with Garbas free he could see no way around it. 'I want to see what you have found me.'

So he slipped off the ribbon and peeled open the tissue paper until he held the cool, glass weight of her gift in the palm of his hand.

'It's a paperweight,' she said unnecessarily. 'I thought you could use it in your office. It reminded me of you.'

He lifted it to the light, examining the mix of dark and light, the skilful melding and weaving of the different levels of colour with a core of intense red at its centre. With an electric charge up his spine, he saw what she so wanted to see.

She was wrong, of course.

'Do you always see the good in people, Bella?' he said, looking at her. *Even when they are not good? Even when they want something from you that you should not have to give?*

She looked confused. 'I just wanted to give you a gift, Raoul. I'm sorry if you don't like it; I just wanted to get you something to remember me by.'

And suddenly every hair on the back of his neck stood up. 'Why would I need something to remember you by? You're not going somewhere?'

'I have to go, Raoul. I've had the best time—really I have—but I'm in your way here; I know. And besides, I have a job to go back to. I can't stay here for ever, after all.'

He had blown it. There was a tightness in his throat, but it was no match for the ball tearing its way through his gut. She had been eating out of the palm of his hand

and he had blown it by leaving her alone because he had had to go to Paris.

No, that wasn't true; he could have handled his business from here, over the phone, could have given his contacts new leads to follow up in their investigations. It was because he had been afraid of getting too close— and now it had cost him. 'When are you planning on leaving?'

'Tomorrow. I've booked my ticket. Marco said he'd take me to the airport.'

So soon!

'Are you mad at me, Bella, for abandoning you today? I knew I should not have left you that way...'

'No, Raoul. It is more than that. This has been a lovely escape, truly, but I need to get back to my life. It is not like we won't see each other again, surely?'

'Of course,' he said, knowing there was no way he could let her return to Paris. Not yet. Garbas would need funds and plenty of them if he was to mount any kind of serious legal defence against the criminal charges already laid against him. He would have his dogs watching. He would know the moment she returned home. And then he would make up some excuse for her about why the charges had been laid in the first place, and ask if she could lend the money from her inheritance to fund his defence.

It wasn't going to happen.

Which meant he could not let her go.

'I'm sorry you feel you must leave,' he said cautiously, careful not to overplay his hand. 'But if that is what you believe you must do...'

'I must go, Raoul,' she said, though her eyes were tinged with sadness, as if she was half-disappointed that he did not argue the point. He took heart from the observation, realising that maybe all was not lost after all. 'My stay in Venice has been wonderful, but I have to return to the real world at some stage.'

'In that case,' he said, knowing that he only had one more shot at this, 'We must not waste a moment of tonight.'

Raoul had suggested formal for the dress code, so she decided on the golden gown Natania had admired that first day that now seemed so long ago. They took a *vaporetto* to Lido, to the five-star Excelsior hotel, a palace of a hotel, no stranger to royalty, film stars and other celebrities. Gabriella tried not to think about how devastating Raoul looked in his black dinner suit but in the end she had to. It was either that or think about how easily Raoul had taken the news she was leaving tomorrow. Maybe he had been expecting it. Maybe even hoping for it.

She wasn't disappointed, she told herself, it was simply validation that she was doing the right thing.

Even if the thought of leaving him hurt like hell.

What had she expected, though? That Raoul would beg her to stay? No, that was pure fantasy. One night in a man's bed didn't mean for ever. Phillipa was right, she needed distance. They both did. She was doing the right thing...

They dined in the restaurant upstairs. Sparkling champagne and the finest wines provided the lubrica-

tion, a pianist playing Vivaldi the musical score, and Venice provided the spectacular view—a view that only got better as the sun set behind the city, transforming it into a city of gold. Gabriella forgot about being disappointed because, even though she was going home tomorrow, there could be no better view in the world and no one better to share it with.

After their meal the pianist started playing dance music and Raoul put down his wine glass. 'Dance with me, Bella,' he said, and there was no way she could say no. Why should she? Besides, she was flying home tomorrow; she and Raoul both knew it. There was no reason she should not enjoy tonight.

So she let him take her in his arms and let him masterfully, superbly, spin her around the dance floor until her blood was dizzy. In his arms, she felt his strength and his darkness, and it was hard to separate either, just as it was impossible to separate reality from fantasy. Because this was how she wanted to remember him, a swirling, evocative explosion of feeling.

So they danced, and afterwards she couldn't remember if there had been anyone else on the dance floor with them, absorbed so totally in the man she was dancing with, and it didn't matter because she was with him. He held her close, so close that she could barely breathe, so close that there was no distance between them, no barrier to the growing heat, the building tension as they whirled, entwined, around the dance floor.

Would he take her to bed and make love to her again tonight? She wanted nothing more to end this night, other than a promise to meet again soon. And mean-

while every sensation, every powerful, evocative feeling, was stored away in Gabriella's memory so that until that time she could pull them out and examine them all over again, one by precious one, in the nights when she would inevitably be alone.

Meanwhile, she lost all sense of time. She only knew that the sun had long departed and the moon had risen and she feared the night must come to an end. But he saved her from the end just yet and suggested a walk along the beach before they went home.

She slipped her jewelled sandals off before venturing onto the sand and he offered her his hand so she might carry her sandals and the skirt of her gown without losing balance. She slipped her hand into his. She saw his heated smile and felt his warm grip and let both seep deep into her bones. So what that she was leaving tomorrow? She was going to enjoy every moment of this last night with him.

Just one last night...

The beach was long and almost empty, the season late; what day trippers there had been had long since departed. The beach was theirs, a long strip of sand glowing under the light of the full moon, the air balmy and still, the dark waters laced with silver.

'Did I tell you,' he said after they'd walked hand in hand in companionable silence for some way, 'How beautiful you look tonight?'

Her breath hitched, her heart fluttered in her chest like a winged beast. 'No,' she said. 'I don't believe you did.'

'Then I am remiss. So let me tell you now.' He stopped

walking then and turned to her. 'Tonight you are more beautiful than I have ever seen you. More beautiful than the sun setting over the most beautiful city in the world, more beautiful than the pearl of a moon hanging heavy in the sky.'

There was so much power in his words, so much depth and feeling, that her heart almost burst from her chest to embrace him. But at the same time she knew she dared not believe him. 'Thank you, Raoul, but I wish you wouldn't say such things.'

'Why shouldn't I tell you what I think?'

'Because I am leaving tomorrow, and you will only make it harder—for me, at least.'

'Then don't leave.'

She laughed a little uncertainly and turned, starting to walk back the other way. 'We've been through this. I have to go. I can't stay here for ever.'

'And what about what happened last night? Didn't that mean anything to you?'

'Hey, I wasn't the one who left this morning without saying goodbye.'

'I knew you were angry with me.'

'No. I'm not angry.' She thought about the talk she'd had with Phillipa earlier today, the sense her friend had made, even though the thought of leaving and missing out on more nights like she'd spent last night... But, no, space and distance were what she needed now. Head space. Physical distance. 'Last night was amazing. But everything has happened so quickly, I need some time to work it all out. To work out what I want.'

He took her hand and squeezed it. 'I understand.'

They walked a little way to the sound of the sea lapping at the shore, music and laughter wafting on the breeze from a party somewhere up the coast, and she thought that was the end of the matter until he said, 'Can I let you in on a secret?'

She turned to him. 'Of course.'

He stopped her and took her hand to his mouth, pressing his lips against her palm, sending a sizzle all the way to her toes. 'A long time ago, I made a promise to myself. Last night, in your bed, I was tempted to break it.'

She shook her head, confused, laughing just a little to try to ease the tension. 'I'm not sure I understand.'

'You see, I do not break promises easily. And wanting to break a promise made me hurt you, I think, by leaving this morning without a word.'

'You had business, you said.'

'I did. But I did not have to leave you to do it. I was afraid of what might happen if I stayed.'

'Raoul,' she said, her heart tripping, 'What are you saying?'

'A long time ago I vowed never to marry again. I promised myself that I would never take another wife. But last night, in your bed, I came close to breaking that vow—so close that it scared me.'

Every cell in her body froze; her lungs squeezed tight, so tight she could barely get out the words. 'I don't think I understand.'

'I panicked this morning. I behaved stupidly and left you, and I hurt you and made you angry when that was the last thing I wanted to do. What I really wanted to

do was ask you, Bella, if you would do me the honour of becoming my wife.'

'Raoul…'

'I know I don't deserve it, Bella. I know I am the last person you would want to marry, and the least deserving, but would you consider my proposal anyway? Would you marry me?'

'You're serious. You're actually serious.'

'I have never been more serious in my life.'

She looked up at him, his eyes so intent that for a second she was tempted—oh, so tempted—to fall into those dark depths and believe him.

But, no! She shook her head and started walking down the beach away from him, her heart thumping like a drum, making so much noise it was no surprise she couldn't think straight. 'Raoul, that's just crazy.'

'Don't you think I know that?' she heard him call. 'Don't you see why I couldn't face you this morning?'

No. She couldn't think. And she couldn't see that. She couldn't see anything, not with the sudden tears streaming down her face as she stumbled along the sand.

She wasn't even sure what she was running from. Didn't she want Raoul to want her? Except that it almost seemed too much, too soon. Too perfect. Too imperfect. Oh God, what should she believe?

'Bella!' he yelled, catching her arm, pulling her to him.

'You didn't want me here,' she remembered as she slammed into his hard chest. 'You never wanted me to come to Venice in the first place, and yet now you tell me you want to marry me?' She punched him on the arm,

on the shoulder, would have punched him on his chin if his wrist hadn't snagged hers and dragged it down where her fist could do no damage. 'So what are you trying to prove by asking me to marry you?'

'What are *you* trying to prove? I've told you I want to marry you. Why do you fight that? After the night we shared, why can't you believe that?'

She shook her head. 'That was one night! We need more time. It's too soon.'

'I thought it was too soon. How could I think of breaking a promise I had made for life after such a short time with you? Don't you think I have tortured myself all day for leaving you like I did? For leaving you thinking I didn't care?

'But let me make it plain—this is not about one night. Because I wanted you the moment I first set eyes on you. I wanted you then, Bella. I want you now. And I am willing to break every vow I have ever made in my life to have you, if you will only have me.'

'But wouldn't it be more sensible to wait?'

'Why wait, when we feel this way? Why live apart when we are made to be together? Because if I am not mistaken you feel it too, don't you? You feel this magic between us. Do you really believe this is going to go away? Why should we wait when we are so good together?'

There was something exciting about his words, something urgent and powerful that tugged on that part of her that wanted to believe him. Wanted to believe his words were true—maybe because they so closely mirrored her own feelings.

She didn't really want to leave. Logic told her she should, but her heart would always stay here with Raoul, no matter how far she moved, no matter where she lived.

But *still* he hadn't said the words that she so wanted to hear. 'You tell me how much I mean to you, and yet you haven't told me that you love me.'

'Haven't I?' He took her in his arms and kissed her then, so deep and deliciously that it felt like his kiss had touched her very soul and sworn his love. 'But then, if I didn't love you, why else would I want to marry you?'

He kissed her again and she knew she had not imagined it the first time—that there was no way he could not love her, not when his kiss touched her so deeply, not when she knew in her heart he was the man for her.

It might be crazy, rash and all kinds of madness, but it was a madness they clearly both shared—and what point was logic and waiting when what you wanted was clearly right?

'You are really sure about this?' she asked one final time to be sure of what he was asking. 'You really are serious about wanting to marry me?'

'I have never been more serious in my life.'

And the zipper of heat that flushed out from her spine confirmed that she had no choice, no choice at all...

'Then I will marry you, Raoul. Please, yes, I will marry you.'

'I so wish Umberto could be here,' she mused as Phillipa handed her the bouquet, a glorious rose concoction in soft apricot, peach and cream colours from which long ribbons fluttered. It was two minutes before the wed-

ding ceremony was due to get underway and they were expecting a knock at the door at any moment to let them know it was time. Meanwhile she had time to think about Umberto and a moment they had both missed out on.

'He would be so proud of you,' Phillipa said.

Gabriella could only agree. Umberto would have had no objections to her marrying Raoul. He would have approved wholeheartedly, no doubt, which was some consolation, given he was not here to give her away. She just wished he could be here to see how she looked today.

The beaded gown clung to her body like a second skin and the hours she'd put in today at the spa and hair salon had been well worth it. Her skin was smooth, her nails perfectly manicured and her hair had been pulled up into a classic style, sleek and polished, with a few tendrils coiling around her face, a face that today even she conceded came close to beautiful. That was probably more due to the fact she couldn't stop smiling rather than her perfectly applied make-up, but whatever it was it was working.

Today she felt like a princess from some long-ago fairy tale about to marry her fairy-tale prince. And the only thing that could have made her feel better was her grandfather being here to see her get married.

'Strange, really, how it was Umberto's death that brought Raoul and me together. Do you think he'll be here somewhere today watching over us?'

'I know he will. And he will be as happy for you as the rest of us are.'

She smiled as she looked down at the bouquet. 'You

know, I really thought you might try to talk me out of marrying Raoul, but you've been fantastic. Thank you.'

'Why on earth do you say such things?'

'Because you told me to wait and to take my time, and now I've gone and done neither. I thought you'd be lining up to tell me I'm about to make the mistake of my life.'

Her friend laughed. 'Okay, so I thought you were being rash and I was worried about you. But I've seen you with Raoul, and do you really think I would interfere in anything, or in your dealings with anyone, who had obviously made you so happy? It is clear Raoul loves you with all his heart.'

Gabriella wrapped her arm around her friend and squeezed her tight, for she had needed to hear that. 'Thank you so much for that. Because it is crazy, how fast this has all happened. But I love him so much. I love him with all my heart. I want to spend the rest of my life with him.'

She turned away then, pretending to be interested in the sparkle of the diamond-encrusted pearl earrings in her lobes, wondering where the hell the knock on the door she was waiting for to tell her it was time to start the ceremony was, knowing she should take courage from her friend's words.

It is clear Raoul loves you with all his heart.

Was it clear? She wanted it to be true. Because still he had not said the words to her. And then she thought again of the words he had said to her, letting them lend her strength…

Some things do not need to be said for us to know them to be true.

And she knew he would say it. He was just waiting for the right moment. *Like tonight.*

A sizzle of raw heat slid down her spine and sparked a fire deep in her belly. Tonight they would consummate their marriage in that place where it had first happened, under the lover's alcove.

She could hardly wait.

She heard a knock on her door and felt a hand on her arm, seeing Phillipa in the reflection in the mirror. 'It's time,' her friend said.

The chapel was lit with burnished golden light, the sun already descending over Venice and gilding the assembled guests. There weren't a lot, not that Gabriella noticed anything once she saw Raoul standing at the front waiting for her, his hair blue-black under the light, slicked back into his signature ponytail, his dark suit showing his height and the breadth of his shoulders to perfection.

And, although she believed in Raoul with all her heart, although she knew that he loved her, still she looked for some kind of sign—something to confirm that she was not acting crazy, agreeing to marry a man so quickly. Something to confirm he was the man she wanted, who wanted her.

She watched him say something to Marco standing alongside him, when the music heralding her entrance started. Marco glanced up and stopped him with just a tap to his shoulder and a nod, and Raoul stilled and turned around.

Their eyes meet across the small chapel and she felt the impact of his like a blast of heat. *Raoul*, her soul seemed to whisper, relief infusing every part of her as their gazes tangled and meshed, knowing nobody could look at her that way unless he truly loved her. Unless he was her soul mate. Nobody else could make her feel so alive, so desired.

Phillipa turned to her and beamed. 'Oh my God,' she said. 'Did you see the way he looked at you? This guy is seriously in love.' And then she threw her smile and turned, setting off slowly down the aisle.

'I now pronounce you man and wife. You may kiss the bride.'

It was done.

Raoul felt the rush of success lift the weight of a promise made to a dying man clean from his shoulders in a tidal surge. But then he made the mistake of looking down at his new bride, who was watching him through that veil with those damned cat-like eyes, anticipating his kiss, full of expectant hopes, dreams and wishes; the tide crashed right back over him.

'I love you,' she mouthed and he wanted to run right then and there from the chapel. Guilt crashed over him. Hadn't he done enough? He'd married her, hadn't he?

He'd never wanted her love.

But people were waiting; the priest was waiting, and she was waiting. She looked more like a goddess than any woman had a right to, every diamond hanging from her ear, every bead on her dress, even the moisture in

her eyes, catching the light so that she sparkled before him like a glass of fine champagne waiting to be sipped.

So he forced himself to smile. Forced himself to look at her like a man who had realised his ultimate dream and had not just fulfilled a promise to a dying friend. He lifted the veil that separated them and dipped his head, curling a hand around her slim neck and trying not to think about how good she felt under his hand, how taut her skin was, how smooth. Then they kissed and he tried not to think about how good she tasted—sweet, ripe and willing. While the 'willing' was difficult enough to forget, it was her whispered, "I love you," that tortured him the most.

Because she wouldn't love him when this was over.

She would never speak to him again.

She would hate him for ever.

Anticipation bubbled in her veins as Raoul handed her into the *vaporetto* and then tucked her in beside him. The wedding and reception had been everything she'd ever dreamed of and more, every little girl's fantasy come true. And now she was anticipating a wedding night that was her big-girl fantasy come true, the night she'd been dreaming of ever since he had proposed those few long weeks ago.

It was late, the moon already wearying of the night, and she didn't mind at first that he had little to say. They'd spent a night talking, laughing and being congratulated, barely having time to speak to each other. So it was good to have the time to sit in the curve of his arm and contemplate the coming pleasures.

With every passing minute she felt anticipation coil and grow inside her. Tonight they would once again join the parade of nymphs, satyrs, gods and goddesses engaged in the act of love. The thought brought a secret smile to her face. She snuggled in closer to her new husband, breathing in his signature scent, relishing it, knowing that from tonight it was just one more pleasure at her disposal.

'I love your scent,' she murmured, nestling closer, thinking about returning to the *palazzo* and spending their wedding night in each other's arms in the lover's alcove. 'I don't think I'll ever get enough of it.'

Something about the way his body stiffened and shifted against her made her look up. She noticed the lights around them looked wrong; they seemed to be heading away from Venice instead of towards it.

'Where are we going?' she asked, curiosity getting the better of her.

'The airport.'

'Raoul,' she said, half-disappointed they were not going straight home to the apartment, half-delighted that he had gone to some trouble to make this night special. 'You actually planned a honeymoon and you didn't tell me? Where are we going?'

'Spain.'

'Tonight?' she said with a tinge of regret. 'But it's already so late, and I was hoping…'

'It's not far,' he said abruptly, apparently more interested in looking out to sea in the direction they were going than looking at her, and letting whatever she was hoping slide right on by. 'You can sleep on the plane.'

She swallowed down the bubble of disappointment. It was thoughtful that he'd wanted to surprise her, really it was, but she didn't want to sleep on a plane. Not tonight. Not when she'd been hoping that soon she would be once again lying with her new husband in her big, wide bed—*their* big, wide bed—amongst the nymphs and satyrs, joining them once again in their endless celebrations of the flesh, only this time as a married couple.

But, while it was sweet he'd wanted to find somewhere more special for their first married night together, something seemed wrong.

'Is everything okay?'

'Of course'

'Are you sure? Something seems to be bothering you.'

'It's nothing,' he said.

And then she remembered. 'Didn't your family have a place somewhere in Spain once?' she asked, remembering a snippet from her past. His head snapped around towards her, but before she could read anything in his eyes his mobile phone rang.

He pulled it from his pocket and checked the caller ID before holding the phone up to his ear and turning away. 'Excuse me, I must take this call...'

Gabriella jerked awake as the car came to a halt. She'd slept fitfully, first on the charter jet and then in the back of the car that had been waiting for them at the airport when they had landed.

'We're here,' Raoul said beside her. She stretched and blinked, wondering where the resort was when she could see nothing through the gloom and swirling mist

except a glimpse of grey stone walls that were just as quickly swallowed up again.

She yawned, bone weary, wondering what time it was as a light snapped on somewhere, turning the outside world a glaring white as her door was pulled open. 'Marco,' she said, shivering as he helped her alight to the misty outside world, a world that carried the scent of salt and sea and the sound of surf crashing somewhere nearby. 'How did you get here so quickly?'

He nodded. 'Natania and I left straight after the ceremony to get things ready. Welcome, Signora del Arco.' Through her weariness shot a burst of pleasure. She was a married woman now and the idea was still so novel it sent a thrill coursing through her. A married woman, as of tonight—soon to be married in every sense of the word. She shivered again, this time less due to the cold and more to the anticipation of what was still to come.

'Did you hear that, Raoul?' she said, looking around for him, but he mustn't have heard or was thinking about something else—because he was scowling, his features tight as he rounded the car from the other side.

'Get the luggage, Marco,' he snapped, before turning perfunctorily to her. 'It's cold out here. Let's go inside.'

Something was definitely on his mind, she gathered. He'd been abrupt ever since they'd left the wedding. Or maybe he was just as tired as she. Still, she wished for the warmth of his arm around her or even the warm gesture of walking hand in hand. She realised he had barely touched her since the *vaporetto* trip across the water. 'What is this place?' she asked, still wearing her heels and cautiously following him up a short flight of

ancient stone steps worn low by the footprints of a hundred generations. 'Where exactly are we?'

'Galicia,' he said. 'On the Atlantic coast of Spain.'

Around them the mist swirled, danced and kissed her bare skin with cold, damp lips, while above them rose high stone walls that looked grim and austere and that disappeared into the fog. The surf continued to crash unseen somewhere below.

A door opened before them, massive and heavy with enormous iron fittings. Natania was there to welcome them into the massive entrance hall, looking rumpled and sexy, but sullen with it, as though their arrival had inconveniently interrupted the other couple and she'd had to hastily pull her clothes back on.

'Do you want something to eat?' she asked unconvincingly, looking from one to the other. Gabriella waited, hoping Raoul would say they were going straight to bed.

'You show Gabriella to her room,' he surprised her by saying instead. 'I'll be in the study. Unless,' he said, turning to her, 'You're hungry?'

She was too shocked for a moment to respond and she wasn't sure what bothered her more: the talk of *her* room instead of *ours*, or the fact he was not coming with her. 'Not at all, but...'

'Then Natania will show you upstairs. You must be tired.' He kissed her on the cheek, a platonic kiss, a benevolent kiss. A kiss that went nowhere near to being the kind of kiss she was looking for this night of all nights. 'I will see you in the morning. Sleep well.'

'This way,' Natania said, bangles jangling on her

wrists as she headed for a curving staircase, a sound that jangled on Gabriella's already shot nerves. But there was no way she was going to follow the woman when her new husband was already going in the other direction.

'Raoul!' she said, her heels clicking on the flagstone floor. She caught up with him halfway across the floor, took his arm and attempted a smile and a laugh, as if there had been some kind of mistake. There *had* to have been some kind of mistake. 'It's our wedding night, Raoul. Surely you're not going to spend it in the study working all night?'

Something in his expression softened. He touched a hand to her hair. 'I'm sorry, Bella.' It was the first time, she realised, he had used his pet name for her today. 'But it is very late and there is something I must attend to. And I thought you would appreciate a rest after our long day.'

'Can't it wait?'

'No.'

'Then I will wait for you, Raoul. You have to sleep some time.'

He just looked at her, and his dark eyes looked so empty it chilled her all the way to her bones. 'As you wish.'

She pushed up on her toes and kissed him on the lips, brazenly letting her breasts press against his chest, lingering there so could be in no way unclear as to whether she would rather sleep or make love, no matter how long his work took or what time he came in. 'I wish.'

Natania was waiting for her on the stairs, her dark gypsy eyes missing nothing of the exchange.

'He'll come up when he's finished,' Gabriella said with a brightness she had to plaster on to make stick. 'If you just show me the way.'

Natania said nothing, merely performed a slow blink of her wide eyes and turned to lead the way up the long staircase, her bangles again sounding too bright and discordant for the grim setting and Gabriella's equally grim mood.

A long gallery met them lined with heavy drapes, heavier furniture and paintings of windswept cliffs and boiling seas. A castle featured in one, severe and solid, complete with battlements and turrets, clinging to the edge of the cliff like it was part of it. This castle? she wondered. It could be, judging from the interior, dark and brooding, like a slumbering giant waiting for the light. Not exactly the honeymoon resort she'd been anticipating. Then again, she thought with a pang of hurt, so far this was nothing like a honeymoon.

'What is this place?' she asked, catching Natania up outside a door.

'Castillo Del Arco,' she said, leading her into the big high-ceilinged room. 'It is, Raoul's *other* place.'

'It's very—grand,' she said, wondering how she could subtly ask where her husband's room was.

'I hate it,' the other woman said. 'It is a bad place.'

Gabriella wandered into the vast room. So this was to be *her* room. Clearly it was not Raoul's. It was too soft, with its patterned wallpaper and rich, red velvet curtains; a fireplace lit with gold flames ran along one

wall, a four-poster bed standing proudly against its opposite, an ornately carved blanket box at its foot. There was a door alongside the bed, and she opened it, curious to see if it led into Raoul's room —*hoping*— and immediately was disappointed when she found only an en suite.

Natania's words finally wormed their way into her consciousness. She spun around, reminded of Phillipa's warning in the frisson of fear that ran down her spine. 'Bad? In what way?'

But Natania wasn't listening. Marco had arrived with the luggage someone else had clearly packed for her and he was leaning down, kissing her.

Gabriella disappeared into the bathroom, feeling simultaneously shocked, breathless and guilty that she had witnessed the intimacy, even though logic told her she had done nothing wrong. *I'm just tired*, she told herself; *strung out*. She took a couple of deep breaths while she ran cold water over her wrists, willing the colour in her face to subside.

But there was no way she could will away her own desires, or the buzz of need that bloomed, insistent and pulsing, deep in her belly and tight in her breasts. For it should be Raoul with *his* mouth on *hers*; Raoul in her bedroom.

Damn.

Marco had left when she returned; Natania was busy unpacking her luggage. 'There's no point doing that,' she told her. 'We'll only have to repack it all when I shift rooms tomorrow.' *Because there was no way she intended to let herself be shunted off into her own room*

another night. 'Right now I just want to crawl into bed.' Natania's eyes flared with a wild flame that told her that was exactly what Natania intended herself—except she would not be spending the night alone in hers.

'If you are sure...'

Gabriella just nodded, the beginning of a headache tugging at her temples. 'You go.' *At least one of us might as well have a good night.* She was just leaving when Gabriella remembered. 'Natania, what did you mean when you said this was a bad place?'

The other woman gave her a look of such abject pity that she was almost crushed under the weight of it. 'I am sorry, I should not have spoken of such things. Good night.' And with that she was gone.

What things?

She prowled the room, wanting to shriek at the closed door, at the walls, the bed and the rich, dark drapes. She wanted to shriek with the insanity of it all. This was her wedding night. *Her wedding night!* And yet here she was, tucked away in a lonely room in a castle on some godforsaken stretch of coastline shrouded in mist.

And where the hell was her husband?

She threw off her sandals and flung them across the room, where they smacked into the wall and it was still nowhere near satisfying enough.

What the hell did he think he was doing?

Nobody worked on their wedding night. Nobody!

Thunder boomed in the distance, a low, rumbling growl that went on and on and echoed her own rumbling discontent. A flash of lightning painted the room with the curtains' vivid red.

Damn it! Natania would know where he was. She should just have asked her. Barefoot, she rushed to the door and pulled it open to the darkened hallway. She could see nothing and nobody, until another clap of thunder that seemed to shake the very walls was followed by a light so bright it transformed night into day.

And there, at the end of the long passageway, she saw a shadowy figure—*Natania?*—disappearing into a room.

She called out to her but the sound was lost in the sudden crash of rain on the windows and the doors as the castle descended once again into blackness, only a thin, ghostly glow through a window at the end of the passageway providing any illumination.

She wanted to follow the woman, but right now she was probably already in the arms, if not the bed, of Marco. Did she really need to interrupt them in the act of love-making? Did she really need to remind herself of what she herself would have been doing—*should have been doing*—if only her husband had not decided to abandon her on their wedding night?

What would they think of her? The lonely bride, still in her wedding gown, searching desperately for her husband.

She had seen the pity in Natania's eyes. Did she really need to see more?

The rain pelted down on the roof and walls until the pounding itself sounded like thunder. She shivered. It was freezing out here in the dark passageway; her head was thumping and she was tired beyond measure. Bone weary. Across the room the fire crackled in the hearth;

the bed looked cosy and inviting. And down the end of the passage the thin, grey light was just a shade lighter. It was later than she thought. It would be dawn soon.

No wonder she was so tired. She would lie down for a while to get warm. And maybe Raoul would come to her when he had finished his work like she had asked him to. She would wait up for him.

And tomorrow—*today*—things would make more sense. They had to.

He stood at the rain-streaked windows, looking out into the bleak nothingness of the storm, wishing bleak nothingness for his mind to erase all thoughts of the woman lying upstairs waiting for him.

Right now she would be confused and angry. He could deal with those things, he expected them. It was the hurt he could not deal with; the hurt he knew she must be feeling.

But she was tired, she would sleep. And soon she would understand that this was the way it had to be.

'It is done, Umberto,' he said, gazing unseeingly into the night through the rain-streaked windows. 'And I hope you are satisfied.'

CHAPTER EIGHT

HE HADN'T come.

It was after midday when she awakened to the sound of Natania bringing in a tray, and the sickening, hollow feeling that Raoul had not come to her bed.

Natania swished open the long curtains with a flourish to reveal a bright blue sky and turned to watch her through hooded eyes. 'Raoul asked me to check on you.'

'That was very considerate of him,' Gabriella said snippily, her disappointment turning to anger, thinking it might have been just a tad nicer if Raoul had come to check on her himself. 'And how is my husband today?'

The woman gave a lazy shrug. 'I have learned not to ask such questions.'

'Because you don't like the answers?'

'Because sometimes it is better not to know.'

Gabriella didn't agree. She had a few questions she intended to ask, and she wanted to know the answers. She padded to the window while Natania poured the coffee, and her gaze was met by a scene of staggering beauty. The castle was built on some kind of rocky headland with a small sandy cove off to one side. Below them the sea foamed white onto the rocks at the foot of

the cliff, a sea lit with sparkling diamonds and so dazzlingly blue, it rivalled the brilliant sky for supremacy. Everything looked bright and calm and perfect.

So different from last night with the fog and the storm; maybe she had been overly tired and feeling melodramatic with it. Already she felt better, brighter, just for feeling the warmth of the day through the glass. She would feel much better again when she had talked to Raoul.

Armed with Natania's directions to the library, and feeling refreshed after breakfast and a bath, she wandered the passageways of the labyrinthine castle. Even in daylight it was a gloomy place, filled with dark timber furniture, beams and heavy wall-hangings, all seemingly impenetrable to the outside sunshine. She shivered in her sundress and light cardigan—a choice inspired by the sunny view from her window rather than the ambient temperature—and wondered if it ever warmed up inside.

There was hush all around her, no other signs of life, and only the tick of a grandfather clock at the top of the stairs intruded on the silence, jarring her nerves as she wended her way slowly down the long staircase. She treaded lightly, careful not to make any noise herself, feeling like she must comply, and only hesitated when she neared the bottom step, knowing the sound of her low heels on the flagstones would echo in this vast space. So unnaturally quiet it was almost as if the castle, that sleeping giant from last night, was awake and waiting, holding its breath, and she didn't want to be the one to make it spring into action...

Suddenly there was the creak of a door, a bang. And so lost was she in her quiet world that she jumped and gasped.

'Gabriella! There you are, at last,' Raoul said, smiling as he strode towards her. 'I thought you were going to sleep all day.'

He took both her hands and kissed her cheeks, and she drank in his scent, letting it feed into her soul, letting it comfort her. And here, two steps up, so she could look him in the eyes, she told him, 'I waited for you.'

He tilted his head, a lock of his black hair falling free from his ponytail and curling around his eyes, his expression truly contrite. 'I'm sorry, Bella.' He used his pet name for her again at last, giving her a glimpse of the man she thought she had married. 'I finished way too late. I didn't want to disturb you.'

And in the rational light of day her concerns of last night seemed overblown, exaggerated.

'Come on,' he said, taking her hand. 'How about I give you a tour so you can find your way around? And then I suggest lunch down in the cove where the wind will not bother us. Natania has promised to make us a picnic basket.'

It all sounded so wonderful—Raoul sounded so wonderful—that Gabriella just laughed, feeling the weight of last night's worries float away.

The castle was even larger than she had anticipated, stretching from one length of the headland to the other. One side of the central staircase was given over to a massive feasting room, big-beamed and with a central fireplace on which it would be possible to roast an entire

ox. The library where Raoul had his office set up was an incongruous blend of technology atop antique desks and cabinets, its walls stacked so high with books that he had to practically drag Gabriella out of it, in order to show her the rest of the house, with promises she could visit and explore whenever she wanted.

Upstairs he showed her room after room; there must be a dozen bedrooms and just as many bathrooms, so many with their furniture covered in dust covers. She had to concede she had been given the prettiest of them all, which was still no consolation. *Which one is yours?* she itched to ask; *where do you sleep?* But she wanted him to surprise her and show her and invite her inside and make her his wife...

'And this one is Natania's room?' she said, wanting to speed up the tour in her quest to find his when they reached the end of the hallway.

'No. Natania sleeps downstairs. There's an annexe above the garage she and Marco share.'

'But I saw her last night during the storm. I called out to her but she didn't hear me.'

Every hair on the back of his neck stood up. She reached for the handle before he could stop her. 'It's locked,' she said, turning to him. 'Do you have the key?'

'It's nothing but a store room,' he said coarsely, tugging her away. 'Nobody uses it. Come, let's go. Lunch will be ready.'

He excused himself at the bottom of the stairs, showed her how to find the kitchen and told her he'd meet her there in a few moments, before striding towards the library.

She found the kitchen where he'd indicated, Natania packing their lunch into the basket, Marco by her side helping. They were a team, the two of them, almost inseparable; she stopped dead, feeling like an intruder again. *Feeling jealous.* Not of Natania, exactly, for she wasn't interested in Marco. But she wanted to feel Raoul close by her side, wanted to enjoy such simple intimacies with him.

'So you found him?' Natania said, noticing her, brushing her hands together and setting her gypsy bangles jangling before she reached for a bowl of salad topped with fat red tomatoes.

'Thank you, yes; he's just gone to get something.'

'You will like the cove,' she said. 'It is very private. Very intimate. You can swim naked and nobody will see you.'

If Gabriella blushed any more she was likely to end up in the salad instead of eating it. 'Good to know. Maybe when it's warmer.'

'You would be surprised. It is very protected from the wind. And some men cannot resist a taste of bare flesh.' She shrugged her bare shoulder, smiling at Marco, whose eyes were glinting with heated agreement. For all their shared secrets, Gabriella got the distinct impression the other woman was giving her advice.

Would she take it? Maybe she wouldn't need to. Maybe Raoul had been planning sinful seduction for this afternoon the whole time; maybe that was why he'd decided on the picnic. 'I'll keep that in mind,' she said as Raoul joined them.

'What will you keep in mind?'

'That the mist and storms blow in quickly,' Natania said, looking levelly at Gabriella. 'To watch out for them.' Gabriella felt almost like she had found an unexpected ally.

'The weather is perfect. There will be no storms today.' He picked up the basket. 'Let's go.'

Natania pressed a blanket into her hands. 'Take this. It is not good to get sand in your food.'

The sultry images that advice put into her head had her halfway to blushing again, but then she suddenly remembered. 'Oh, Natania, Raoul says that door at the end of the corridor is locked, but you must have a key—I thought I saw you go in there last night.'

The atmosphere in the room chilled to ice as the two exchanged glances, Marco standing stiffly alongside; she wondered what it was she'd said wrong.

'I was not there last night.'

'But I saw you, after you came to my room. Well, I *thought* I saw you, when the lightning struck. I called your name, but you mustn't have heard me over the sound of the storm.'

'No. I went straight downstairs after leaving your room. You could not have seen me.'

'Oh.'

'Forget it,' said Raoul, his voice thick and gruff. 'It was obviously just the drapes moving in the wind and making shadows, that's all. Let's go.'

It was not possible, he told himself as he led her along the path towards the stone steps leading down to the beach. It was impossible, he knew, but still he had needed to

check. There had been nothing in the room to say anyone had been there, let alone her. There was no way it could be possible. Katia was his ghost, his nightmare.

Although not his only nightmare now.

For now he had another one, and this one was of his own creation.

He'd headed off her questions when he'd met her at the bottom of the stairs. He'd been expecting a fight, or at least some kind of remonstration about her having been expected to sleep alone. It had to come at some time. It would come. Nothing was surer.

And all he was doing now by taking her to lunch and treating her as she deserved to be treated was delaying the inevitable, hoping to draw out this time with her as long as possible. She had to believe this marriage was real, at least until Garbas was put away for good.

But there was a far more selfish reason for wanting to be with her—because it was impossible to abandon her completely, even though he knew that, the way he burned for her, it would be a safer course of action to do so. Maybe this way would draw the pain out longer, cause them both unnecessary torture, but there had to be some benefit for doing what he was doing for Umberto, some pay off other than knowing she was safe from the likes of Garbas.

He wanted her near. He knew he was playing with fire, but he wanted that pay off. He wanted more of those moments with her to remember and to hold with him for ever long after she'd discovered what he was really like or why he had really married her and was long gone. For she would leave him, that was for sure.

And that knowledge alone was enough to clamp his gut.

'I thought your family used to live in Barcelona.' They were halfway down the path to the beach before she spoke—maybe because he'd taken off like the devil himself. 'I'm sure we visited you all there one year.'

He turned, wondering how much she remembered. 'We did.'

'You don't live there now?'

'No.'

'You sold it?'

He wished. As it was, he could barely remember that night long ago when he had been so furious with the world and the hand it had dealt him, so unprepared for dealing with his own inadequacies. 'I lost it in a card game.'

'Oh.'

'You win some, you lose some.' The phrase came nowhere near to describing the pain he'd felt on losing the property at the time. He'd thought himself indestructible. Invincible. That had made him the worst kind of fool. Even now his failure, his sheer recklessness, appalled him. The knowledge of those wasted years was like a millstone around his neck, weighing him down. He had learned to rationalise his loss since then, see it for what it was, a moment in time when he'd made both some bad decisions and some good. But it didn't make him feel any better about it.

'Like your apartment in Venice?'

He shrugged, wishing himself a past that was one whole lot more glorious. 'Exactly like Venice.'

'And this place? Another card game? Another win?'

He looked back over his shoulder, up at the castle that imposed itself on the clifftop almost as if it were part of it. He realised the truth, maybe for the first time in his life, and only because of what he was doing to her—he hated this place.

Was that why he had brought her here? Not from some noble desire to keep her safe, but so he might taint thoughts of her with this toxic castle and its toxic memories? So it might make it easier when she left?

Or because it was easier for him to remember why he was wrong for her? Because a man who did not hold out a hand to a woman in desperate need...

She deserved better.

She was like a breath of fresh air in a stale room. She was a candle glowing in a dark cave.

And it crushed him like a weight on his chest that, for all he had given her, he might be the one to extinguish that light.

'Another win,' he conceded, although it hardly seemed a win now when it was the last place he wanted to be with Gabriella. She should be somewhere far more deserving of her company right now. Somewhere light, beautiful and free from the darkness of the past. And she should be with someone far more worthy.

But she was with him now, and there was a picnic waiting, the curve of sand in the cove lying inviting below. If he could not give her happiness, he could at least give her a taste of what she deserved.

He turned, holding out his hand to her as they negotiated the first of the uneven stone steps down to the

beach, and she smiled her thanks, her hand warm and surprisingly strong in his. Surprisingly addictive. He wished it could be more than just her hand he held, and for a moment he just looked at her.

The soft breeze tugged at her fringe over those smiling, brandy-coloured eyes, toyed with the skirt of her white sundress, kicking up the hem around her long, tan legs. For a moment he almost forgot himself and thought about taking her into his arms and crushing her to him, wanting to possess her in every sense of the word.

'Raoul,' she whispered. He saw her mouth form the word and for the first time he noticed how good his name looked on her lips.

And he turned away, setting off down the stairs, knowing he could not afford to notice such details, knowing there was no point to it. But he would accept her smiles and laughter. He would take them and store them away in a special place in his mind so that, once she was gone, he could take them out, dust them off and remember how precious it had been to have her if only for such a short time…

The beach was as protected as Natania had promised, the cove acting like a sun trap, the air still and surprisingly warm. Gabriella kicked off her sandals and wiggled her toes in the sand. Delicious.

Just like Raoul's gaze had been moments before. She was still half-breathless with its impact, still dizzy with the anticipation and the desire.

He wanted her. And that knowledge made her body bloom in readiness. Was that why he had brought her

here, to seduce her on the sandy shore today, before they joined as a married couple tonight?

The cove was larger than you could tell from the castle, full of secret grottoes hidden behind giant boulders so they were utterly private. She glanced up at the castle where it sat heavy and imposing on the cliff, recognising it from the painting in the hall near her room. She mentally counted rooms, working out which one was her bedroom, checking out the angles from where the kitchen must be, frowning when she noticed the turret.

'What's that room?' she asked. 'The one with the turret?'

He shook his head without bothering to look that way. 'Nothing. A store room.'

'It must be somewhere over that locked door. Are there stairs inside?'

'Perhaps. It is not something I bother to think about. Do you want to eat?'

She squeezed her eyes against the light and put a hand up to shade her brow, trying to make out details. 'The view from there must be wonderful.'

'How about the view from here?' he suggested, and she turned back to him to see. He had found a place bathed in the warmth of the sun and yet totally private from any inquisitive eyes at the castle. Not that she imagined Natania and Marco would be bothered to watch them when the pair were clearly more involved in each other. They laid the blanket down upon the virgin sand and set the picnic basket in the middle.

'I hope you're hungry,' he said. 'Natania has prepared an entire feast.'

He pulled out a plate of chicken, a dish of plump, green olives stuffed with feta, another plate of cheese, some crusty bread and the rustic salad. Everything looked and smelt delicious; she was more than hungry, but food was not her greatest need at this time.

She accepted a glass of the local village wine, though, ruby-red and spun with gold in the afternoon sun. And she lay sideways on the blanket, one arm propping up her head, the other hand nursing the wine glass. She didn't have large breasts but she knew the angle would spill them together and accentuate their curves. She was determined to seduce him, if he didn't seduce her first. 'How long have Marco and Natania worked for you?'

'Ten years,' he said, selecting one of the fat olives. 'Maybe longer. Maybe shorter. Why do you ask?'

'They seem very close.'

'They have been together much longer than they have been with me.'

'They clearly love each other very much.'

He did not look at her, she noticed. He did not take the opportunity to say he loved her, as she hoped he might. Instead he looked out to sea. 'Perhaps. It is not my business.'

'You mean you haven't seen them together? They're very affectionate. Very—*close*.'

'They do their work. That is all I ask.'

'He is very good-looking, of course.'

He looked at her now, she noted with satisfaction as she sipped on her wine. He had taken no time at all to swing his head around to her. 'Who is?'

'Marco, of course. I can see what Natania sees in him.'

He picked up a small pebble from the sand and flung it at the sea where it landed with a plop. 'You find Marco attractive?'

She shrugged. 'Maybe I like what he does for Natania. I like the way he is so fascinated in her, so drawn to her. She seems happy enough.'

He didn't answer, just turned his gaze out to sea again. She propped her glass in the sand, slipped off her cardigan and flicked her hair off her neck. 'That's better. It's warm here. Natania said it was warm enough in the cove to swim naked.'

'I wouldn't know.'

'Maybe we should give it a try.'

'The water will be freezing.'

'I can think of a way we can warm up afterwards.' She sat up and popped the first two buttons on her dress. 'I'm game if you are.'

His arm snaked out, his wrist ensnaring hers like a manacle before she could attempt the third. His eyes were dark and storm-tossed. 'Don't do this, Gabriella.'

'Don't do what?'

'What you're doing.'

But she refused to give in that easily. She knew he wanted her; he just had to see it. 'I thought you liked to see me naked?' she said innocently enough, her words couched as an invitation, designed to inflame him.

'Anyone might see you.'

She shook her head, unwound his fingers from her wrist and took them to her mouth, kissing each one in turn, sucking them, rolling her tongue around each fingertip, a blatant promise. 'Not here,' she said, taking his

hand lower, curling his fingers around the third button, popping another so her bodice parted and exposed a wide wedge of her breasts that she held the palm of his hand against. 'We're completely and utterly alone. The only one who will see me is you.'

For a moment she had him, his dark eyes molten, his fingers moving over her skin, exploring, brushing a nipple so that she mewed with pleasure, arching her back to press further into his hand.

'Raoul,' she whispered. 'Make love to me.'

He spun away so suddenly she was left reeling with his absence. 'I have to go,' he said, his chest rising and falling like a bellow. 'Take your time. I will send Marco later on to fetch the basket.'

And then he was gone. When she recovered enough to look around, she saw his long legs eating up the stone steps three at a time until he reached the top. She watched him stride towards the castle, and she collapsed on the sand, lacking even the energy to rebutton her bodice, feeling as stung and sick as if he'd physically slapped her.

What was happening to her? She was barely married twenty-four hours and her husband was rejecting her, refusing to make love to her when he had already shown how good they could be together.

So what the hell was his problem?

CHAPTER NINE

BY THE time she returned to the castle, Raoul was gone. 'To the village,' Natania told her, looking sullen again.

'Did he say when he would be back?'

She shook her head and passed her a cup of hot, sweet tea; Gabriella gave up. Natania could not help. How could anybody help when she did not know what the problem was herself?

So she sat in the library to await his return. Maybe Phillipa had been right, after all. Maybe she had rushed into this marriage without talking through the details of each other's expectations. Maybe she should have waited. But it was not too late; they had only been married one day. She flatly refused to believe it was too late. He loved her, she was sure. Otherwise why would he have married her?

So she would wait, and when he returned they would talk.

She busied herself with studying the books in his collection, trying desperately to be interested and get absorbed when she found a rare or first edition, but her heart wasn't in it. Her ears were permanently pricked, waiting for any sound that might signal Raoul's return.

Natania eventually came and brought her a bowl of chunky soup filled with vegetables, crusty bread and local butter; it smelled wonderful but Gabriella could not stomach it and sent it back barely touched.

And, as day slipped into evening, Gabriella knew he intended not to return while she was awake, so she pressed Natania to take her to Raoul's room. 'Are you sure?' the woman asked.

'I have to,' she said. Natania nodded and showed her to his room, not on the first floor as she had expected, but a modest room tucked away behind the kitchen, barely better than servants' quarters.

'He sleeps here?'

Natania nodded. 'Ever since we have worked for him. He will not sleep on the floor above.' She fetched Gabriella a robe and laid it on the bed. 'I am sorry. Even I did not think he could be this cruel or I would have not have let you marry him.'

'I love him,' she said, feeling weak, stupid and totally shell-shocked. 'Nothing could have stopped me marrying him.'

The gypsy woman nodded, her eyes sad. 'I know.'

He watched her sleep, her chestnut hair splayed across his pillow. He physically ached to join her, but he knew he could not. Not if he was ever to let her go.

And he must let her go. She was too precious, too beautiful. She deserved far more than he could ever give her. She deserved better. She deserved a man who might save her if she ever fell...

And yet here she was in his bed, curled up like a kit-

ten, and here he was, rock hard with wanting her. He could take her right now. He could climb into bed, kiss her into wakefulness, caress her sweet curves and bury himself deep in her sweet depths.

He ground his teeth in frustration and growled low in his throat, forcing his feet to stay right where they were.

Why didn't she give up? How many times did he have to reject her before she hated him enough to leave him alone?

He had never taken her for such a fighter.

And he had never taken himself for such a fool. He knew he was capable of being a fool; God, he'd more than proved that eleven years ago, marrying a woman at the end of her career who had wanted the safety blanket of a marriage, while refusing to be satisfied with being out of the limelight, still lusting after the adoration of everyone. The adoration of just one man had not been enough.

He thought he'd learned his lesson then.

But no. He had been a fool to agree to this. He had known it would come unstuck. He had known it could not work. There were other ways to get revenge against a family he hated with his soul without holding someone so precious and innocent hostage in the process.

It was so wrong to hold her hostage.

But he could not afford let her go yet. If he did, she would flee straight into the arms of Garbas and this would all have been for nothing; Umberto's plans would backfire in spectacular fashion. He had not come this far to let a Garbas win now. So he needed to keep her here just a little while longer, just until Garbas was put away

for good, and then he would let her go. There had to be someone decent out there for her—someone worthy of her love.

And in the meantime there would be no more picnics on the beach. No more occasions where they could be alone together, even if it meant no more smiles, no more laughter to add to his bank of memories. And, given what he was doing, the last thing he deserved were smiles and laughter.

'I'm sorry, Bella,' he whispered, aching for her, aching for what he had lost before he had ever known the full extent of her love. 'So very sorry.' And he left her sleeping and walked away.

'We need to talk.' It was after lunch and he'd been avoiding her all day, taking his meals alone and forcing her to do likewise, but finally she had managed to track him down to the library.

'Bella,' he said, rising to his feet to greet her with a kiss to her cheeks. 'How lovely to see you. Did you sleep well?'

'Forget it, Raoul. I'm not in the mood.' She didn't want empty platitudes. All morning a storm had been building outside, thick, dark clouds building on the horizon, sweeping in from the sea until they formed a heavy dark bank. All morning a storm had been building inside her, dark and brooding and increasing in intensity.

'Is something wrong?'

'You know it is. I want to know what's going on.'

'I'm afraid you have me at a disadvantage.'

'I don't think so. I think I'm the one at a disadvan-

tage. I gave up on waiting for you to come to my bed, given that was apparently too onerous a task the night we were married, so I slept in your bed last night, hoping you would join me some time through the night.'

'Bella, I am so sorry. I was held up…'

'Doing what? I want to make love with my husband. What is wrong with that?'

'You don't know what you're saying.'

'I do! I just don't understand what you're saying or why you're saying it. I'm your wife, Raoul, and I am going mad here wondering what is wrong with me that you are so interested in doing something else—anything else! But there is nothing wrong with me, so it must be with you. You hide yourself away from me every night; I won't let you do that again. Because I love you, and I want to make love to you. I want you in my bed. I want to be in yours. Why won't you make love to me, now that we are married, when you found no such barrier before? Or is there something painfully wrong with me you haven't told me about?'

'There is nothing wrong with you.'

'Then what the hell is wrong with you? We are married, Raoul. You took me for your wife. What is it you intend to do with me that you bring me to this godforsaken end of the earth and as good as hang me out to dry? What's with that? This is supposed to be our honeymoon.'

He stiffened. 'I did not realise you were so inconvenienced by being here.'

'Inconvenienced? How ungrateful of me to imply such a thing, when clearly I'm having the time of my life! And

when I try to seduce you—my own husband—you reject me. You turn me down. How do you think that makes me feel?'

'Gabriella…'

'Do you know how humiliating it is for everyone to know that your own husband will not make love to you?'

'Nobody knows.'

'Except for Natania and Marco. Or is that why you brought me here? To save me the humiliation and indignity of the entire world knowing? Should I thank you instead for your kind consideration?'

'Gabriella, it's not like that.'

'Isn't it? You know, I used to think you had bricked up your heart behind walls so high and thick that they could never be breached. But I thought there was hope for you when we spent those days in Venice. I thought there was hope when you asked me to marry you. But I was wrong.

'Because you don't have a heart at all. You're empty inside. You're not a man, you're a shell. An empty, hollow shell of a man. Devoid of emotion. Devoid of feeling. And I wish to God I'd never met you.'

His jaw was set tight, the cords in his neck pulled taut, and when the words came they sounded like they were ground out. 'You have no idea what I feel.'

'No, I don't. Because you won't tell me. You won't share the slightest thing with me. Me, the woman who is supposed to be your wife! And yet you give me nothing. When I tell you that I love you, I get nothing in return. I don't even know if you love me. I thought you did. I believed you when once you told me that you do

not have to hear the words to be true, but now I need to hear those words. Can you say them? Do you love me, Raoul?'

'Bella…'

'Don't *Bella* me! Don't pretend I mean something to you when clearly I mean nothing. Do you love me? It's a simple enough question. Yes or no, Raoul; what's it to be?'

He spun around, his hand raking through his hair. 'Why are you doing this?'

'Because I need to know. I need to hear those words. I need you to prove that they are true.'

His hand slammed down hard on his desk. 'Do you think I wanted this?'

'What are you talking about? You're the one who asked me to marry you. Who insisted on not waiting? Who told me that I was the one who made him want to break his vow never to marry again? You're the one who asked *me* to marry *you*!'

He shook his head wildly from side to side, like a stallion readying for a fight. 'Do you think I wanted a wife who needed a man to love her and cherish her? Do you think I *needed* another wife?'

Thunder rolled overhead, a long, booming sound that filled the silence in the room and turned it toxic.

'But you asked me…' She heard a sob, recognised it as her own and knew she had to escape, knew she had to get as far away as she possibly could from him. She turned and fled out of the room and across the stone entrance-hall, her shoes slapping on the stones.

'Gabriella!' she heard, but she didn't stop. Couldn't

stop. She had to get away, as far away as she could. She tore through the kitchen, looking for escape, finding it in the doors leading to the terrace and the path to the cove, thinking she could hide there, amongst the boulders on the beach, and find the time to work out what she should do.

She would have to leave. She would have to run away, her tail between her legs. Humiliated. Defeated. Phillipa would take her in—Philippa, who had warned her to take her time.

Two short days ago she had been so happy. So wondrously happy. So sure that he loved her.

Do you think I needed another wife?

Hadn't he wanted to marry her? Then why had he asked her? What had she been thinking? Tears streamed down her face, blurring her vision. The bank of dark clouds blotted out the sun, the loose edges like thick, black fingers rolling dark dough across the sky; they rumbled and grumbled with discontent. But still she ran on, faster, towards the stone steps that led down to the beach.

Behind her, she heard him call her name again and ran faster, her grief pushing her on. She flung herself down the time-worn steps to the beach, her feet barely touching the stones, before launching herself onto the sand. The skirt of her dress flew around her; she kicked her flat shoes from her feet at the first opportunity to give her purchase on the sand.

'Gabriella!'

Above her the sky darkened, the waves crashed against the cliff. She heard his voice on the wind that

whipped through her hair, filled with salt and moisture from the sea, but she didn't look back. She dared not. There was no point. What was the point of looking back at a man you loved—a man you *thought* you loved—who seemed incapable of loving you but had married you nonetheless?

She could not bear to see him.

Why had he done this to her?

Why?

Her feet pushed on, fighting the loose, soft sand, searching for somewhere to hide, somewhere she could be safe in her misery and despair.

But the sand had been eaten up on the incoming tide and there was nowhere to run. The tide lapped at her feet and she turned back only to collide with a rock that should not have been there. Except this rock was warm, had a thumping heart and had arms that clamped tightly around her.

Raoul.

She looked up at him, panting, desperate and afraid. She saw her storm reflected in his eyes, wild, insane and wanting, as above them the storm broke in a thunderclap that shook the ground and sent the vibrations spiralling through her. They fell on each other like that storm, hungry, wild and insatiable.

Their mouths meshed, their tongues dancing, duelling, her cheek scraping hard against his blue-black beard as she pulled his clothes free with busy, seeking hands, needing to touch him, to feel him; needing to feel his hot flesh against her own.

Rain pelted down upon them, fat droplets that tugged

on their hair, their clothes and stuck the fabric to them, but his hands were hot and liberating; the wet fabric was no barrier to those seeking hands. He groaned in her mouth and spun her away, finding their own private grotto, where he pressed her hard against the stone, and pressed himself hard against her, making her gasp with his size and his need while her own need spiralled out of control. Her hands explored him, fingernails raking his back, relishing the firm, hard flesh, the muscled tone; her fingers traced the lines of his ribs, the nub of his nipples, the thick column of his erection.

He made a sound like a hungry beast, half-growl, half-roar, and she felt her dress tear apart, felt the rain on her hot skin and his hotter hands at her breasts. Felt her bones dissolve as he dropped his hot mouth to one breast, sucking her nipple in tight until she thought she would explode with the agony and the ecstacy, while his large hands travelled her body, heading south, taking away her last remaining scrap of cover.

She battled with his waistband and, still locked together with her at the mouth, he pushed her hands aside and did the job himself; she felt him hard and hot and bucking against her belly.

She felt herself lifted, pressed hard against the smooth stone, her body pulsing as her legs encircled him, throbbing with need, anticipating completion.

Thunder boomed again and lightning rent the sky. She caught sight of his face, wretched, desperate and tortured, and she pulled his face to hers and kissed him so deeply, she knew he must feel her very soul.

She was lost to the storm going on around her, the

storm going on inside, the fury building with the need until he lowered her slowly down.

She felt his hardness in a nudging press, her muscles working to pull him in; her body ached for completion. And yet he held her there, suspended, for what seemed like for ever as his tongue drove into her mouth, demanding every part of her for his own. Until he let her fall as he pressed inside, her mind blew apart in a raging storm of stars.

Nothing could ever be better than this.

The fleeting thought came to her in that one moment of clarity when the world and everything in it was suspended and there existed just this one, intense moment.

Then he moved inside her and her world threatened to come apart. He was so large she felt that she could not let him go without feeling the suck of his organ on her womb, without feeling the need to have him back inside.

She was already on the brink. He thrust again and she gasped with the spiralling sensations shuddering around him, and with the next he cried out and buried himself so deep inside her she wondered if he could ever find his way out.

Her orgasm came in a rolling wave, like the dark clouds had done this day, building and intensifying until there was no way to go but be lost in the thunderclap of her release as she felt him lose himself inside her.

He carried her to the castle wrapped in the shredded remnants of her dress and his damp shirt; he carried her to his bathroom where they soaped each other in

the steamy shower, exploring each other's bodies, taking the time they had not had before.

And then he laid her reverently on his bed and acquainted his mouth with every part of her, tasting her, suckling her until she once again cried out, begging for release.

Afterwards he held her close. 'I love you,' she said, and he stilled and kissed her cheek.

'Go to sleep,' he said, holding her close, his voice a husky promise.

She snuggled closer. For she knew in her heart that he loved her, even though he still could not bring himself to say the words for whatever reason he must love her.

She knew it.

Until she woke in the morning to find him gone.

There was a letter on his pillow, barely a note, just two short lines:

I'm sorry.
Please forgive me.

And the bottom dropped out of her world.

CHAPTER TEN

HE HAD gone. Some time this morning before light, according to Natania who had heard the car, he had left her.

Why?

'I thought he loved me,' she said, sitting in Natania's kitchen, sipping sweet tea.

'I told you this was a bad place. You should leave.'

Nothing had ever sounded so tempting. But where to go? Back to Paris, and the big empty house? Or Venice, where she would not be welcome if Raoul was there? 'I don't know where to go.'

'You have a friend in London. Marco can take you to the airport.'

She bit her lip, thinking through the options. Wondering how Phillipa's husband would take the news of her separation so soon after dragging his wife and young baby to Venice for the wedding. 'I don't know. I have to call her, see if it's okay.'

'Call her, then. Or email. There is a computer in the library.'

'You're right. I'll book a ticket while I'm at it. Thank you, Natania. I'm sorry that we could not have met in better circumstances.'

The gypsy woman shook her head, setting the hoops at her ears dancing. 'It is not your fault. I thought you were the one.' She sent her gaze in a wide arc. 'But it is this place. It is what it does to Raoul. It is what it reminds him of. It is a bad place.'

It was a toxic place as far as Gabriella was concerned. It got worse when she realised the computer was password-protected and she couldn't even access her email account, let alone book a flight.

'Damn you, Raoul,' she snarled as she stared at the blinking cursor. On a hunch, she typed 'Raoul'. No luck.

'Raoul Del Arco' met with the same 'invalid password' response.

Out of frustration she typed in 'bastard', half-expecting that one would work—but then, she rationalised when it didn't, anyone could have guessed that; it was hardly secure.

She scanned the desk, looking for somewhere he might have jotted down the password, but the desk was irritatingly paper free. She pulled open a drawer, searching through the papers for something, anything, on which he might have written it down. But she could find nothing and slammed it shut.

The drawer on the other side got similar treatment. This one was almost empty though; mostly stationery supplies. A few pens. A stapler. A key.

That drawer got slammed shut too.

Damn!

Unless, she thought a moment later, there was a filing cabinet somewhere. She opened the drawer again, picked up the key, which was heavy, despite its small

size, and ornately carved. Maybe it was not like any filing-cabinet key she had ever seen before, but then this was Raoul and his filing cabinet was no doubt antique.

She prowled the library, testing any piece of furniture with a lock, but most were already unlocked and the key did not fit. She studied it in the palm of her hand. Why keep a key that fitted no lock?

Then she remembered the door at the end of the passageway.

The locked door. And she wondered...

What had he done? Raoul drove aimlessly through village after village of simple white stone buildings and small fields set amidst the rocky hills, knowing only that he needed to get away—except there was no getting away from his own black thoughts.

For he had done the unthinkable. He had done what he had promised himself he would not do. He was supposed to keep her safe; he was supposed to protect her.

Instead he had given in to his basest self. He had taken advantage of her sweet body, and he had not been able to stop at just once.

And it didn't matter that she had provoked him, that she had goaded him with her taunts and her words. Nothing mattered except that he was in the wrong, whichever way he looked at it. He had been in the wrong from the very beginning.

He had set out to marry her, to do anything it took to keep her and Garbas apart, and he had done that. But in the process he had lost Gabriella.

You don't have to love her.

The old man's words came back to him. He'd taken the words at face value. They had seemed cold but they had made sense. And he had intended to keep himself apart. He would not love her; he could not afford to, not if he was to set her free.

He hadn't meant to love her.

He pulled the car to a halt near a *horreo*, a corn shed that looked like a miniature stone cathedral, his palms sweating on the wheel.

He hadn't meant to love her.

But he did.

He looked at the *horreo*, reminded of the stone castle where he had brought her and then abandoned her. What would she be thinking? How would she be feeling? After giving her the cold shoulder since their wedding, they had shared a night of exquisite pleasure—he had lost count of how many times they had made love—and then he had cold-heartedly walked away.

His hands were sweaty on the steering wheel.

Their love-making had been so frantic and desperate that he had not even thought to use protection.

Even now she could be carrying his child.

What had he done?

He had run from the truth. He had not even been able to bring himself to tell her he loved her. Surely she deserved at least that?

But then, she deserved so much more. She deserved an explanation. She deserved his apology. After which she probably would not want his love.

But he had to tell her.

He put the car into gear and turned it around on the

narrow road, only then noticing the dark bank of cloud that extended along the coast. And with a sizzle of apprehension he was reminded of another time, another day long ago, when the cloud gathered heavy over the castle and he had been rushing to get back.

Only to have his world crash and burn when he had.

He wasn't superstitious; he didn't believe in Natania's gypsy folklore that she would spout whenever she got the chance. But, still, there was a bad feeling in the pit of his stomach and he put his foot down.

She slipped the key into the lock where it fitted like a hand in a glove and held her breath, turning it with a solid click. She looked around, wondering if anyone had heard her. But Natania was busy in the kitchen and Marco was with her. Besides, the way the wind outside was building, nobody would possibly hear.

She turned the knob, easing it around, her heart hammering in her chest as she pushed open the door. It was dark, soft, grey light filtering in through a grimy window, dust motes playing in the shifting air. She found a switch and flicked it to and fro but nothing happened. And then she could see enough in the dim light to make out a dresser, an oil lamp on top, a stack of boxes in one corner and a circular staircase rising up on the other side of the room.

Everything was musty. The dust tickled her nose and she thought about leaving. Some kind of store room, he had said, and she could believe him. Clearly she had imagined it when she had thought she had seen someone entering.

But why would Raoul keep it locked and why would he secrete the key in his desk downstairs?

Something banged upstairs and she jumped. Then it banged again. A shutter come loose in the wind, she guessed.

The staircase beckoned. Maybe the answers were upstairs, in the turret room itself. She found matches by the lamp, lifted the glass and held a match to the wick, hissing and spluttering, filling the glass and the room with soft white light. Then, holding it carefully, she started to climb the creaky stairs.

Outside the wind started to howl, a sound that conspired with the banging to make a home in the back of her neck, prickling as if someone unseen had run their finger along her skin.

She shivered. *Next she'd be seeing ghosts.* Warily, tentatively, she peered through the hole at the top of the stairs, the doorway to the turret room. It was dark but for the shutter slamming repeatedly against the wall letting in a thready glow of grey light. She stepped up into the room, holding out the lamp as she circled, stunned beyond measure.

It was someone's idea of a fantasy bedroom, something from *The Arabian Nights* or similar. The bed was low and covered in rich red silks and brightly coloured cushions with gold trim and tassels, dusty now, but still a glorious splash of colour. The walls were hung with jewel-coloured silk wall-hangings and covered in portraits: a ballerina, stunningly beautiful, photographed in costume in every ballet imaginable, *Swan Lake, Giselle, Romeo and Juliet.*

And there on the dresser was a close-up of her laughing into the camera, beautiful, glamorous and so full of life. Gabriella put down the lamp and picked up the picture in her hands.

To Raoul, she had written in large, elegant letters. *All my love, Katia.*

Katia. *Raoul's first wife.*

A chill went down her spine. This was Katia's room, kept as it must have been when she was alive. Kept locked and preserved, like some kind of shrine.

Was that why he hadn't wanted another wife? Was that why they had come here, to be close to his first wife. Because he was still in love with Katia?

Pain lanced her heart. She'd thought she had sensed something holding him in reserve. It had not been there when he had made love to her; he had loved her then.

Or so she had thought.

Raoul drove the last few kilometres with a growing sense of dread. It wasn't the approaching storm, but the fear that Gabriella had already left. What had she to stay for, after all? He had left her. There was nothing for her here.

But as he neared the castle something else caught his attention and froze his blood solid. There was a light on that shouldn't be there, a flickering light in the turret room—*just as there had been that day all those years ago.*

And suddenly he wasn't afraid that she had already left.

He was afraid that she had stayed…

* * *

The wind howled around the windows, cold fingers searching for a way in, the shutter banging endlessly, threatening to shatter what was left of her already bruised and battered nerves. She put the picture down and crossed to the window, testing the latch. It was stuck, probably grown shut through years of disuse.

Down below she could hear the surf smashing against the cliff, sending spray raining skywards. The window budged, little by little. If she just pushed a little harder, it would come unstuck.

He took the stairs three at a time, bellowing for Marco and Natania, wishing Gabriella would stick her head out of a door and demand to know what was wrong, fearing all the time that she would not—that he was already too late.

He reached the landing and turned right, standing panting and gutted when he saw it—the door to the turret room open, the flickering light from the lamp dancing down the stairs.

'Gabriella!' he shouted, leaping onto the stairs. 'Gabriella, where are you?'

She pushed against the glass with all her weight just as the clap of thunder burst from the skies, but it was the feeling that someone had just called her name that had her looking over her shoulder at the same moment the window finally gave. She didn't have time to see if there was anyone there; the wind clamped icy fingers around the open window and flung it open, dragging her from her feet. She screamed, clinging to the catch, her legs battling for purchase on the window sill while the surf boiled and spewed on the rocks below.

'*Nooo!*' he roared, feeling the past come crashing back, dark and horrific.

This could not be happening again!

He flew across the room, red spots before his eyes, the colour of blood in the white sea foam. He caught hold of her leg and then her waist. 'Let go!' he yelled at her. Her fingers were still wound deathly tight around the window clasp.

Finally she seemed to realise he had her and let go. He spun her inside, into his arms and against his frantically beating heart, stroking her hair with one hand, keeping the other wound tightly around her while the wind swirled and screamed into the room. 'What the hell were you doing?'

'The shutter was banging.'

'No,' he said, relief giving way to anger. 'What the hell were you doing in here?'

She pushed him away, ran her hands through her hair as if she was fine, but she was trembling and as white as a ghost, her chest rising and falling quickly as she tried to catch her breath. 'I was looking for a password for your computer so I could book a flight out of here. I found a key instead.'

'And you thought you'd go exploring?' Behind them the shutter and the window both slammed, rain slanting inside, feeling like icy needles against their skin. He growled and yanked the shutter closed before securing the window.

'You told me it was a store room.'

'It is.'

The storm let loose outside, the thunder overhead,

lightning piercing the gloom and letting loose a fresh burst of rain against the shutters. 'You didn't tell me what it stored. You didn't tell me you kept it as a shrine to the woman you love.'

'Is that what you think?'

'What else could it be? No wonder you said you never wanted another wife. You already had one—all her photographs, all her mementos, locked away safe and sound for whenever you wanted to spend a moment or two with her. I never believed you slept downstairs near the kitchen. This is where you spent the first two nights of our marriage, isn't it? Tucked away with the memories of a dead woman!'

And he cursed himself for thinking he could lock away his past behind a closed door and keep it there for ever. 'You have no idea how wrong you are.'

'Am I? You brought me here because you couldn't bear to be apart from her. You married me, but once we were here you had no use for me. Because there was no room for me in our marriage, not when you had her.'

'No!'

'Because you are still in love with her!'

'No! That's where you are wrong. If this room was kept as a shrine, it was as a shrine to my own stupidity— a reminder of how naive a man can be when he believes in love.

'I stopped loving Katia a long time ago when I discovered my love was worth nothing. When she used this room to betray me!'

She looked around uncertainly. 'Katia...?'

'She brought her lovers here. Her little secret room,

her *love nest*, complete with an escape route in case someone came looking. In case I called for her.'

She shook her head, holding her arms around her waist, her hair stuck down around her face. 'I didn't see any escape—'

'There is a railing outside the window—or there was—and footholds in the rock. Easy enough when the weather was fine, perilous when it was not. But she didn't seem to care. It was a game she played, you see, a risky, dangerous game—trying to outsmart me, and succeeding. Until that storm-ridden night.'

She swallowed, remembering the surging sea, angry and frothing below the castle like a wild animal snapping and snarling to be fed, and felt a chill run down her spine. She could not imagine trying to be out there with just a railing and footholds between her and the violent sea. 'Katia died here, didn't she? She and her lover fell to their deaths.'

'Now do you understand why I keep that door locked?'

He turned away, closing his eyes to blot out those images, his hands fisting in his hair. But he could still picture the scene just as clearly as if it had happened yesterday—Manuel, already disappearing from view as Raoul had run up the last few stairs into the room, roaring and almost frothing at the mouth in his fury and rage; Katia urging Manuel to hurry, as she herself had taken one look at Raoul, her eyes bright with the thrill of the game, her hair whipping around her face and her laughter still ringing out in his mind.

He had been so angry and filled with rage, rage that

filled the black empty hole from where his heart had been ripped; he had been paralysed with shock. His feet had been stuck to the floor while his world, his dreams and his love had disintegrated around him.

For she had betrayed him.

She had laughed at him.

And, even when he had heard the grating, tearing sound of metal from rock, even when he had heard Manuel's cry as he had fallen from the broken railing— even when he had heard Katia's desperate cry as she had realised the game was no longer fun—he had stood there a moment too long, transfixed, broken and shattered, wondering what the hell had gone wrong.

A moment of inaction he would pay for for his entire life.

He reeled away from the window. What use was a pathetic lock? He should have bricked up the door to this poisoned room and its sordid memories years ago.

He felt her hand on his shoulder. 'Raoul...'

'Don't,' he said. 'You would not want to touch me if you knew.'

'If I knew what?'

'The truth. I came back to tell you. I could not leave you like I had, not without you knowing everything.'

Spiders crawled up her back; the light from the lamp flickered ominously. 'What do you mean?'

'I mean the truth about why I married you.'

CHAPTER ELEVEN

THE air in the turret room was too thin to breathe, the raging storm outside a soundtrack for what was going on in her head. Here, in this room, her future lay in the balance. He had come back. He had left her this morning but he had come back, as she had wanted him to, as she had prayed. Except now she wasn't sure she wanted to hear what he had to say.

'So why did you marry me?'

'Gabriella—Bella—I have so much for which to seek your forgiveness.'

'No, forget about forgiveness. Tell me why you married me. Clearly it was not, as I imagined in my pathetic little brain, because you loved me.'

'I… It shames me to say that it was not.'

She squeezed her eyes shut and sagged into a chair, uncaring about the dust that welled up in a cloud. Right now she had more important things on her mind, like the heart that lay trampled and bleeding all over the floor. 'Then tell me why.'

'I made a promise. To a man I loved and respected above all others. A man who had been like a father to me. Even though I knew it was wrong, even though I

knew I could not be the husband you needed, I made that promise to him.'

She looked up at him, chilled to the bone, knowing there could be only one man who would have made him promise such a thing. 'My grandfather made you promise to marry me?'

'He was dying, Bella. He was worried about you.'

She remembered the visit he'd made before Umberto's death, the conversation he'd skirted around when she'd asked him for the details. But it was too impossible to believe, too horrendous; hysteria built inside her like magma ready to erupt at any moment. 'You promised to marry me because my grandfather asked you to?'

'He wanted to be sure you would be safe when he was gone.'

She put the heels of her hand to her forehead, the drumming in her temples growing louder, the pressure growing heavy and insistent behind her brow. It was insane. Did he actually realise what he was saying?

Suddenly she couldn't sit. She sprang to her feet, pacing the floor. 'And you agreed to this? You said, *anything you ask, Umberto; of course I will marry her?*'

'I tried to tell him—'

'You told him you would marry me—so you lured me into a loveless marriage only to dump me in a godforsaken castle in Spain where your dead wife rides shotgun—'

'*No!* I told him it wouldn't work. I told him I would make no kind of husband. I told him you would hardly be safe with me—a man who had not been able to save his own wife. How could you be safe with me?'

'And yet you still said yes. You took me to Venice and you set out to seduce me. You made love to me! I thought you loved me, Raoul. When you held me in your arms and you made love to me, I thought you *loved* me! But you lied, every one of those times you kissed me. Every one of those times we lay in bed together, every one of them was a lie!'

He took a step closer and held out one hand to her. 'No, Bella.'

She turned away. She never wanted to touch him again. 'And all the time you couldn't wait to be rid of me. You couldn't wait to drop the pretence and dump me.'

'It wasn't like that.'

She spun back around. 'You deceived me!'

'What choice did I have? Marry you, or say no to Umberto and watch Garbas get his greedy hooks in you?'

She stilled, her breathing hard and frantic in her chest, her mind seizing on the one thing that finally pulled the pieces together. 'This is all about Consuelo? Grandfather was so worried about my friendship with him that he would get his henchman to marry me? Why couldn't he have just warned me if he was so worried?'

'Would you have listened—you, who always sees the best in everyone? You, who could not believe he was a criminal even when he was charged with fraud by the police? Try to see it from Umberto's point of view: Garbas knew you would inherit as soon as you turned twenty-five. Umberto wanted to ensure you would be safe from his greed.'

She shook her head. 'Even if what you say is true,

what danger is Consuelo to me now that he's been charged?' And even as she said the words a creeping suspicion filtered into her psyche, no more than a floating piece of black silk on the wind at first, it took shape and form and became three-dimensional and ugly.

'You were responsible for that, weren't you. It was no surprise to you that day of the funeral—no surprise that Consuelo had disappeared. Because you already knew. You were the one who tipped off the authorities. You— you wanted to be sure he could not touch me. You got Consuelo arrested.'

'He's a criminal, Bella. It's no more than he deserves.'

She blinked, appalled at his implied confession, horrified by the sheer magnitude of his machinations—all to ensure she would marry him. 'You don't even try to deny it. You always hated Consuelo. Always!'

'And why wouldn't I hate him? He was the one who called me asking for money one too many times and, when I refused and told him he was a fool, he gloated that I was the fool and that his brother was having an affair with my wife! He gloated that I was the last to know, that everyone—*everyone*—knew and were laughing about me behind my back.'

A bolt of lightning squeezed through the shutters; a blast of thunder rent the skies and rumbled long into the distance.

'Consuelo's brother died here...' she said.

'Manuel was having an affair with my wife. He was supposed to be a friend. They were *both* supposed to be my friends.'

'And you were so worried I would marry someone

who did the dirty on you that you put me through all this. How considerate of you.'

'He's a scumbag, Bella. You deserve better.'

'*He's* a scumbag?' She looked up at him, wondering how she could ever have imagined that she loved him—someone who manipulated people, facts and the truth to gain his own ends. 'So what the hell does that make you?'

She saw him flinch. She was glad that she could cause him half the pain he had caused her. 'The joke's on you, of course,' she continued. 'For I had no intention of marrying Consuelo. Yes, I liked him—but as a friend, that was all. Maybe you might have given me some credit for making my own decisions.'

'You think he would have left you alone, knowing you were coming into your inheritance? Don't kid yourself. It was the money he was interested in.'

'Maybe you're right. It would not be the first time I had fallen prey to a man who wanted nothing more but to use me and abuse me for his own purposes.'

'Bella, listen to me…'

'Why should I, when all you have ever told me is lies?'

'No. Hear me out. Yes, what I did was wrong, but I was bound by a promise I had made to a dying man. I would marry you, I had decided, but I was going to let you go—once I knew you were safe. I wanted you to find someone worthy of you, who loved you for who you were and not how much money you had.'

'How very noble of you. And meanwhile you lock me up in some cold, barren castle in Spain and pretend you

are not interested in me. Or were you pretending when we did make love?'

'That was never a pretence.'

She nodded but she could not bring herself to look at him. 'Maybe. But your love was. That's where I have an issue. Our marriage is a sham, Raoul, a complete and utter sham. I want a divorce as soon as it can be arranged.'

'Bella—Gabriella—please, give me a chance to explain. I left today because I was disgusted with myself. I had promised myself I would protect you. I would keep you safe, and when it was safe I would let you go where you could find the love of a good man—a worthy man. I would not stop you.

'Except I did not realise I was already falling in love with you. I thought that, if I didn't say it, it wouldn't matter, that it wouldn't count. But last night, when we made love in the storm, and afterwards in my bed, I could not deny what had already happened to me in Venice. And today, instead of fleeing, I had to turn around to tell you. I love you, Gabriella. I had to come back and ask for your forgiveness and to tell you I love you with my life.'

She laughed. Insanely. Manically. Whether it was a delayed reaction to the shock of almost falling from the window onto the rocks below, or a reaction to the callous way he had treated her, she didn't know. But the sound was cathartic, strengthening her, increasing her resolve. 'And now, when everything else has come unstuck, you serve up with the one thing you know I have

been waiting for. The one thing I have been begging for you to say all along.'

'Bella, it's not like that.'

'Isn't it? Isn't this the last card you have to play, the final roll of the die? Your last feeble attempt to keep me prisoner in a loveless marriage? But it won't work, Raoul. Not now. Because I don't believe you. And, even if I did, it doesn't matter any more because I don't want your love. Not if this is the way you show it.'

'Gabriella…'

'No,' she said, standing strong now with a new resolve. She'd been a fool but she had survived, and she would keep on surviving all by herself. 'I don't want to know. Just arrange that divorce, Raoul. I want to be free of you and I want it now.'

CHAPTER TWELVE

Marco told him she was there, waiting for him at the sea door—with the signed papers, no doubt, though why she hadn't sent them via her lawyer he had no idea. Maybe she thought she had left something here.

He was on his way down to her when he spotted it, the paperweight sitting on his desk, the paperweight she had bought for him that day in Murano. He lifted it up to the light, watched the way its dark layers spun and floated around the blood-red core, the darkness lightening as the layers rose until they faded into the clear glass. He shook his head.

Even Gabriella, who had always seen the good in people, would not make the mistake of selecting such a thing for him again.

He remembered the way she had presented it to him, intending it to be a parting gift, except he had not been able to let her go. Not then.

Except he had not realised why.

What a fool he had been.

He sighed, replacing it on his desk. It was all he had of her now, and even that was more than he deserved.

She was waiting in the gondola, looking more beauti-

ful than he had ever seen her, a soft pastel dress showing off her long, tan legs, her hair braided around her face, falling free around her bare shoulders. Just looking at her was enough to slice his broken heart anew.

'Gabriella,' he said, relishing the taste of her name on his lips. 'Would you not come inside?'

She smiled a little, or maybe she just pressed her lips together, and shook her head. 'I thought we might meet on neutral ground. Or, in this case, neutral territory at least.' This time she did smile and he noticed for the first time the strain lines around her eyes, the tightness in her features, as though she was battling to keep herself in control. 'Will you join me?'

She could have asked him to fly to the moon with her and he would have said yes. As he climbed aboard, he noticed the folio tucked by her side. 'You brought the papers?'

'I brought them.'

And something inside him died, something unreasonable—because it was unreasonable to hope that she had changed her mind after all he had put her through, even if he wished it could be so. He had spent two months in his own personal hell, wishing he had done things differently, wishing he had never agreed to Umberto's deathbed wishes, wishing he had been man enough to follow his gut and refuse.

But he had not refused, and now she had come with the papers that would be the death warrant to their marriage.

'How did you know to find me here?' he asked as the

gondolier gently negotiated the vessel into the wider canals, and she smiled again, easier this time.

'Lucky guess. I figured that not even you would want to stay in that mausoleum of a castle a moment longer than you had to.'

Even he had to smile at that. 'It is good to see you, Bella.'

She blinked up at him. 'And you.'

'You could have posted the papers.'

'I know, but there were still some things I didn't understand. I have spent two months trying to hate you. Two months trying to forget. But there are still some things that will not let me go.' She shook her head. 'I could not ask those things by mail.'

'What things?'

'Like the ghost story you told me that foggy night we were here in Venice—the story of the merchant who lost his wife to two brothers. That was no legend. That was your story, wasn't it?'

'It was mine.'

She breathed out. 'You made it sound like the merchant had killed them both. But it wasn't like that, was it?'

'It might as well have been.'

The gondola slipped along the canals, turning this way and that, the movement of the boat strangely soothing despite the subject matter.

'So tell me.'

And it was his turn to pause. 'I should have seen it coming. She was a ballet dancer, as you know, famous the world over. But she was at the end of her career, and

she craved the adulation of the audience. I should have known she would never be happy with just one man when she was used to the adulation of a crowd. Everyone but me, it seemed, knew about her secret room. I think in the end she hated me because I didn't know, that I was foolish enough to believe that she actually loved me.

'And, when I found out it was true, I was in such a rage, it was no wonder that even in the midst of a storm they fled from me. I could not have saved Manuel—the railing was old and rusty and pulled away from the stone—but Katia…'

He squeezed his eyes shut. 'She cried out and I was so angry, so tortured, that for a moment I could not move. And when I did it was too late.'

He felt her hand slide between his and he opened his eyes in surprise. She smiled sadly. 'How do you know you would have reached her in time?'

He shook his head. 'That is my curse. I will never know.'

She gazed up at him. 'That's why you feared you could not keep me safe, isn't it? You feared you could not keep anyone safe.'

'How could I keep anyone safe? I could never trust myself again.'

'But you did save me, Raoul. Don't you remember? When the wind caught that window and pulled me from my feet, you were there to stop me falling. You saved me, Raoul.'

He shook his head. 'I surprised you. I made you turn. If I hadn't come…'

'I could have fallen. But you saved me.' She nodded

then, taking a deep breath. 'I think I understand now, at least some of it.'

'What do you mean?'

'I mean I've been spending a lot of time thinking these last two months. Remembering. Pulling those weeks apart and trying to work out what happened. And I keep coming back to you trying to walk away. That night in Paris when you put me in a taxi and strode into the rain—you were walking away from Umberto's promise then, weren't you?'

'I didn't want to hurt you. If there was another way to keep you safe, I would do it. But you would not let me.'

'Because I came to your hotel in the morning.'

'You wanted my help to defend Garbas and when I refused you were going to do it all by yourself. I had to get you out of Paris.'

'And so you brought me here to Venice, to seduce me, to convince me to marry you.'

'Bella, I'm not proud of what I did.'

'Maybe it's not so bad, what you did. Or maybe why you did it.'

He turned towards her, trying to find a meaning to her cryptic comment. But she was looking ahead, avoiding his gaze, staring at the buildings now turning softly golden with the lowering sun. 'They called me, you know, several times—Consuelo's lawyers.'

'What did they want?'

'Money. I turned twenty-five last week. Consuelo thought I might like to donate to his defence fund.'

'What did you tell them?'

'That I had better things to do with my money. You were right; he would have sucked me dry.'

She looked at him then. 'I went to the hospital where Consuelo's foundation was based. I went to talk to the director to see what I could do about providing for a new foundation to support those children undergoing chemotherapy, those left in the cold without funding after the collapse of the foundation. He told me that someone had already taken care of it. That someone had already covered what they had lost in the foundation and more.'

She hesitated and looked up him with tears in her eyes. 'That was you, Raoul. You funded the programme, so no child's treatment would be interrupted. So those children's lives might be saved.'

He saw the setting sun in her eyes, saw the golden light dance in her tears. 'I felt responsible.'

Moisture tracked down her cheeks. 'And for two months I have been trying to find a reason to hate you, to believe you had no heart—but everywhere I look, everything I remember, makes the pieces fall another way. And then, with learning of one generous act of kindness, I knew I was wrong. How could I hate a man who did such a thing?'

He smiled, her words a balm to his soul. 'I am glad you don't hate me, Bella. I have lived in hell these past months thinking that.'

She sniffed. 'And so I was wondering...'

He lifted her chin with one hand and rubbed the tears from her cheeks with the thumb of the other; his touch made her catch her breath. 'Tell me,' he said, his voice a

husky, deep whisper that carried an urgency that rippled through her bones.

'You once said that you loved me. I threw it back in your face. I thought you were lying. But did you mean it? Was it true, Raoul?'

'That I love you?' He exhaled in a rush. 'Oh, Bella, I know I have betrayed your trust. I know I hurt you so much. And God knows I didn't want to fall in love with you. I didn't think it was possible. But every time we made love, every time I looked at you, I couldn't help but fall in love with you that bit more.

'And it scared me, Bella. I knew you would leave me one day, and I knew it would kill me—so I tried to push you away, but it didn't work.

'Because I do love you, Bella, and I always will. And, if there is ever a way to make up for the way I have treated you, so help me I will track it down, I will pin it to the ground and I will spend my entire life making it up to you.'

'Oh, Raoul.' She put a hand to his cheek, felt the familiar brush of his blue-black beard against her palm, never wanting to have to remember what that felt like again. 'I love you so much, Raoul.'

His mouth found hers and they kissed as the gondola slipped silently beneath the Bridge of Sighs.

'About those papers...' she whispered when finally they had come up for air.

'What about them?'

'Do you think it would hurt if we didn't fill them in? If we gave our marriage another go? With just you and me this time. Nobody else. And no ghosts from the past.'

He smiled at her and her heart flipped over. 'Definitely no ghosts from the past. Just you and me, starting again.' He picked up her hand and kissed it. 'You have made me the happiest man in the world, Bella. You have given me something I thought I would never have, something I thought I had forfeited any right to for ever: you have given me your love. And I will treat it like the treasure it is.'

He dipped his head and kissed her again, so sweet and rich with feeling this time that her head spun and the blood fizzed her veins until she was dizzy on bubbles and the hot taste of him in her mouth.

And that night, in the big bed in the lover's alcove, they solemnly repeated their marriage vows, with the sirens, satyrs, gods and goddesses as their witnesses, smiling this time. Knowing this time it was for real.

* * * * *

FROM VENICE
WITH LOVE

ALISON ROBERTS

Alison Roberts lives in Christchurch, New Zealand, and has written over sixty Mills & Boon Medical Romances. As a qualified paramedic she has personal experience of the drama and emotion to be found in the world of medical professionals, and loves to weave stories with this rich background— especially when they can have a happy ending. When Alison is not writing, you'll find her indulging her passion for dancing or spending time with her friends (including Molly the dog) and her daughter Becky, who has grown up to become a brilliant artist. She also loves to travel, hates housework, and considers it a triumph when the flowers outnumber the weeds in her garden.

CHAPTER ONE

THE SOUND OF more than one person shouting got steadily louder as Nico Moretti turned into the narrow Venetian alleyway that would get him to his destination a little faster.

He tried to ignore the sound. He was in a hurry and it wasn't as if the sound of shouting was anything unusual for a large Italian city but he could feel his frown deepening. It was a disturbing echo of what was already occupying too much of his head.

The noise was loud enough to have people stopping in the street now. Turning their heads and asking each other what they thought it might be about. The slowing pace and knots of people forming made it harder to move forward and Nico heard a growl of frustration escape his own throat.

He could tell them what it was about if he had either the time or the inclination. It was about people who wanted different things. People who were passionate about what they believed in. People who weren't prepared to even try and understand each other and left broken lives in their wakes. But he didn't have the inclination. Not when he felt so out of place in this city of

his birth and with the sound of his childhood language surrounding him and reinforcing that exclusion. And he certainly didn't have the time. Not when the real reason for his return to Venice was due to start in less than thirty minutes.

At least he had the advantage of his height. And plenty of practice in cutting through obstructions to get to the heart of an emergency. All he needed to do was take on the mantle of an expert consultant en route to an urgent call in an emergency department or at an accident scene.

'*Scusi.*' The word was a command, not a request, and, as always, it had the desired effect. A path appeared through the gathering crowd. Those closest to him actually stopped talking to stare at him but that only made the sound of whatever was happening ahead clearer.

Whatever it was about, it wasn't simply a misunderstanding or disagreement. There was a language barrier as well. He could hear English being spoken by a forceful, female voice.

'Stand back. Don't move him yet. Call an ambulance. *Ambulanza.*'

More shouting. In Italian. Had someone called an ambulance? Where was it? Why wasn't it here yet? They were right beside the Grand Canal, for heaven's sake. Practically a highway in Venice. Where were the police? Where was a doctor when you needed one?'

'*Sì.*' The English woman had understood something in the furore. '*Dottoressa.* I'm a doctor. Let me get close. I have to find out if he's breathing.'

'He's not,' someone close to Nico muttered. 'He's

dead. He has to be, falling off the roof like that. He must have broken his sorry neck. Who does that English woman think she is? An angel who can work some kind of miracle?'

'It's almost Christmas,' a black-clad Italian grandmother said sagely. 'A good time for a miracle to happen.'

'*Scusi.*' Nico schooled himself not to show any personal frustration as he recognised the inevitability of what he had to do. He raised his voice and spoke in Italian. 'I'm a doctor. Let me through. What's going on?'

Charlotte Highton heard the commanding male voice that overrode the almost hysterical barrage of Italian around her. She could also hear the faint sound of a siren. Please, God, she breathed. Let that be an ambulance.

Getting caught up in an accident scene had been the last thing she'd needed after getting lost in the back alleys of Venice, trying to take a shortcut to her destination near St Mark's Square, but what could she have done? She'd seen the man fall from the scaffolding. More than that. She'd been caught by the way he had been doubled over and clutching at his chest seconds before he'd fallen. There was no chance of him surviving any injuries the fall might have caused if he'd already been in cardiac arrest before it had happened.

But they wouldn't let her near and precious seconds were being lost. One of the man's workmates was probably the first-aid officer for the building company and he'd decided that the fall had caused a spinal injury. He

was holding the victim's head still and shouting at any-body who so much as bumped the unconscious body.

Now he was shouting in response to a query from the newcomer, who Charlotte couldn't see because other people were also trying to tell him the story and some were gesticulating madly—pointing to the roof of the house and circling their arms in the air to represent the fall. For a crazy moment Charlotte almost smiled.

Here she was in this beautiful, ancient city with the water of a canal lapping almost at her feet. Surrounded by the sounds of a language she loved but had never had the time to learn. Caught by the passionate involvement of people who were, for the most part, probably com-plete strangers to the unfortunate man who had fallen. This would never happen in England. It was *so* Italian.

Then a single, curt word from the newcomer and everybody fell silent. And shifted enough to make an opening. The man who stepped in to fill the gap was as Italian as everything else. Tall and dark. Strong featured and exuding a masculinity that was supremely confi-dent. Such a stereotype that, for another crazy moment, Charlotte was sure she'd met him before.

Or maybe she just recognised that kind of confi-dence. It didn't come from any awareness of his effect on women. This kind of quiet power came from being in a situation where he knew exactly what needed to be done.

'You're a doctor?'

'Yes.'

'And you speak English?'

'Yes. I'm a specialist in emergency neurology.' He

was bending over the unconscious man now. 'Did you see the fall? Has he been moved at all?'

'Yes, I saw the fall.' Charlotte was right behind the man and she was reaching for the victim's neck. The newcomer caught her wrist in a grip that was as powerful as everything else about this man. His confidence. His voice. The eyes that were locked on hers right now.

'What do you think you're doing?'

'I *saw* him fall.' Charlotte spoke the way she would to anyone who was preventing her doing her job. Or some unfortunate junior doctor who was getting the basics dangerously wrong. 'I saw him *before* he fell. He clearly had severe chest pain. He didn't trip. He *collapsed*. I need to see whether he's got a pulse.'

For a stunned heartbeat the dark eyes continued to hold hers. Charlotte could see how swift his comprehension was. She actually felt the moment when he stepped back from confronting her action and they became a team. He let go of her wrist.

Rapid instructions in Italian followed. The Italian specialist took over holding the man's head and guided a log roll that had the patient on his back with his airway opened in an admirably short space of time. The nearby siren was getting louder but it wasn't yet close enough. Charlotte was crouched with her cheek against the patient's mouth, one hand on his neck with her fingers searching for a pulse and the other resting gently on his diaphragm seeking the movement that would indicate breathing.

'Nothing,' she snapped. She wasn't exactly dressed for performing CPR. She had to hoist up her slim-fitting skirt so that she could kneel on the rough cobblestones

of the alleyway. Her equally neat-fitting blouse beneath the skirt's matching blazer hadn't been designed for vigorous movement either. Charlotte felt a seam ripping within the first seconds of pushing her body weight down hard enough to depress the chest of the large man.

Her unexpected medical colleague was still communicating in Italian to those around him. Explaining what was going on perhaps. And then he was showing the person who'd been guarding his patient so effectively from Charlotte how to support the man's cervical spine but do a jaw thrust at the same time.

As she stayed in position, with her body weight directly over her straight arms, Charlotte could look sideways. She saw the way he demonstrated the required position, with his large hands splayed, the palms pushing against the angle of the man's jaw and his thumbs resting on his cheeks. She knew the pressure required to keep that kind of hold and yet he made it look like he was being gentle with the critically ill patient.

And then he let the first-aider take over the hold and shifted so that he was kneeling right beside Charlotte. The shafts of pain from the movement of her knees on the cobblestones seemed to fade as his body lined up so close beside hers their arms were touching.

That eye contact was extraordinary. Reassuring and encouraging at the same time. The almost invisible movement of his head told Charlotte that he was in sync with what she was doing. That he was ready for her to pause so that he could deliver a breath. With an equally subtle nod, Charlotte began counting aloud. She had no idea how many compressions she'd done already but it was standard international protocol to deliver two

breaths for every thirty compressions and a lead-in was given so that minimum pumping time was lost.

'Twenty-eight, twenty-nine…thirty.' Charlotte raised her hands and sat back on her heels as her CPR partner bent down, pinching the man's nose and covering his mouth with his own. She watched the man's chest rise and fall. Twice. And then she was back in position and the compressions continued smoothly.

Wow. Not only could this guy get air into someone without disturbing the protected position of a C spine, he was prepared to do mouth-to-mouth resuscitation on a stranger. A risk very few medical people would be prepared to take these days. And compressions were deemed the more important component of CPR now. If an ambulance was on its way and the compressions were effective, you had a window of ten minutes or so before the lack of extra oxygen would cause irreversible brain damage.

Charlotte was impressed. She was also sweating despite the deep chill of Venice in December, and her knees felt as if someone had attacked them with a baseball bat. She'd never been more grateful to hear the sound of a siren so close. Looking up, as she paused to let another two breaths be delivered, she was astonished to see that it was a jet boat, arriving on the canal, complete with flashing beacons and a uniformed paramedic, with a defibrillator in his hand, waiting to jump ashore.

She knew better than to stop what she was doing and wait for these emergency medics to take over the scene. Automatically, she rocked forward, her hands back in position on the centre of the man's chest with one flat and the other locked around the wrist to give her extra

strength as she pushed down and began the count that would remain silent until the warning of breaths needed.

One...two...three...

Nico could hear the shouts of the paramedics arriving and securing the ambulance. Thank goodness! The discomfort of kneeling on cold, hard cobbles to perform CPR was truly unbearable.

Not that the English woman was showing any signs of discomfort. Nico had been watching her, waiting for the signal to deliver another couple of breaths but also because she was so...so *in control*. So very British.

She had that English peaches and cream type of complexion and the kind of reserve that always felt so foreign to Nico, but he had spent so many years away from Italy it was very familiar. So familiar, in fact, that he could imagine he'd met this woman before. He'd certainly met the type.

Virtually the exact opposite of the type of women he preferred.

It was perhaps unfortunate that he'd inherited his father's taste in women. He liked them small and dark, curvy and vivacious. With an appetite for life and fun that could negate any tendency to take life too seriously out of working hours. But as long as he didn't make his father's mistake of marrying a woman like this, he wouldn't end up abandoned and broken-hearted when someone on another continent offered something more exciting. Like when his father's beloved Irish wife had simply taken their only child and made off for greener pastures.

Nico shook off the thought. Normally, snippets of

family history would never distract him from a situation like this but his mind had been full of it until the moment he'd intervened in this rescue scene. Even now, he was aware of the small object in his pocket that the solicitor had insisted he take with him. It should be small enough to dismiss out of hand but unfortunately it carried a significance that could never be dismissed.

He had to push it firmly to one side right now, however. After a second glance to reassure himself that the paramedics were coming in the right direction, Nico took another look at the woman who hadn't missed a beat in performing the chest compressions.

Strands of her blonde hair had worked themselves loose thanks to her current physical exertion but the rest of it was still tightly bound into an intricate kind of knot that removed the feminine allure of long tresses. She had grey eyes that could have looked attractively smoky but she was so focused on the clinical aspects of this situation that they were devoid of an identifiable emotion.

Even now, as the paramedics set up the defibrillator and prepared to take over the management of this patient, he couldn't detect any sign of relief or distress, perhaps, that she'd been caught up in this traumatic event. She was watching what the paramedics were doing with hawk-like intensity. She might not speak Italian but Nico had the distinct impression that she wouldn't hesitate to correct these medics if she felt things were not being done to an expected standard.

He filled them in as they attached the patches to the man's chest. He provided the cervical spine support as preparations were made to secure the airway and

the first shock was delivered, but then a second crew arrived, along with the police, and Nico found himself stepping back and merely watching, along with the crowd of people the police couldn't manage to disperse.

The English doctor was in the same position. Nico saw her tucking the hem of her blouse back into the tight waistband of her skirt. He noticed the holes in her tights and the red, grazed skin of her knees. He could feel the ache in his own joints and it gave him an oddly powerful feeling of connection with this stranger. He tried to catch her eye and smile but she was looking at her watch and frowning, as though she was running late for something.

And then she looked over her shoulder and her frown deepened. Whatever she was looking for was obscured by the crowd of people who were watching in fascination as the resuscitation scene reached fever pitch.

The man's airway was secured and a paramedic was delivering oxygen via a bag mask unit. An IV line was in place and drugs had been administered. And then the shout was given to stand clear and another shock was delivered.

There was a collective gasp from the onlookers as the man's body jerked in response to the shock and then silence fell as everybody held their breath. Only those closest could see the blip on the screen of the life pack and then another and another as the rhythm picked up. One of the paramedics felt the neck of the patient and grinned at his colleague.

'We have a pulse.'

A cheer went up from the crowd and the atmosphere only became more excited as the emergency services

prepared to transport the man to hospital as quickly as possible. People were moving away in response to the shouted instructions of the police officer and Nico saw the English woman disappearing behind others.

He couldn't let her vanish. Somebody had to thank her for her contribution to saving the man's life.

'Scusi.' Again, Nico pushed his way through the human obstruction. He was going against the flow towards the canal and where they were trying to manoeuvre the stretcher that now carried the still-unconscious man into the ambulance, but that was also the direction in which the woman was going. She was still looking for something, her head bent as she peered around people, and suddenly Nico spotted what she was after. A black laptop case, propped against the wooden piling the ambulance launch had been tied up to.

He could get to it first. She'd have to stop and talk to him then and he could thank her. Get her address, maybe, and then follow up on the patient and let her know the outcome. With a determined effort Nico stepped in front of a man and reached for the case. He had it in his hand when someone bumped into him from behind with such force that his hand simply opened. The case fell, bounced on the cobbles and fell again, in a graceful arc, to land in the canal. For a second or two it floated on the surface. And then it sank.

Charlotte watched the laptop case disappear under the murky water of the canal, its disappearance hastened by the wash of the ambulance as it took off with its beacons flashing and siren sounding.

If she took her shoes and jacket off...

Good grief…was she actually considering diving in to try and retrieve it before it sank too far?

The downward glance towards her shoes had hammered home the reality of what was happening. Straightening and dusting off her skirt after she'd got to her feet hadn't cured the creases and streaks of grime. Her tights were shredded and one knee was grazed enough for a trickle of blood to be obvious.

Her armour had been dented.

But worse than that—far, far worse than that—her shield had been ripped away from her and destroyed.

'Oh…my…God…' Charlotte had about a heartbeat before she knew the fear would try and kick in.

The man was turning towards her, clearly appalled at what had just happened.

She couldn't let him see her fear. Couldn't let anybody see it because if they did it would become real. It would take over and she would be sucked back into that place where she was utterly powerless. Where she became nobody.

It wasn't going to happen. Charlotte fought back, gathering fury as if it could repair the amour. Replace the shield.

'You *idiot*,' she snapped. 'Have you *any* idea what you've just done?'

The dark eyes widened, startled by her ferocity.

'I'm so sorry,' he said. But the apology in his eyes was being replaced by something more like astonishment. Anger, even, at being attacked for something that had clearly been an accident.

Charlotte knew that. She'd seen the person behind being pushed and stumbling, only prevented from fall-

ing by the safety barrier this man's back had provided. It didn't help, though, knowing that the action had not been deliberate. How could it, when the effect was the same?

'That laptop has my presentation on it,' Charlotte snapped. 'The presentation I'm supposed to be delivering to an international symposium in...' She jerked her gaze to her wrist. 'In exactly *ten* minutes.'

His face was changing again, along with the expression in his eyes. He was putting pieces of a puzzle together with the same kind of swiftness that had been obvious when they had become a team, working in sync to try and save the life of the unfortunate man who'd fallen from the scaffolding in the wake of his cardiac arrest.

They weren't a team now. They were on different sides of a battle and Charlotte felt as if she was fighting for her life. He couldn't possibly understand how important this was to her but he obviously knew more than she would have expected.

'Not by any chance the symposium on critical interventions in the emergency department? Being held at the Bonvecchiata hotel?'

'Yes. I'm Dr Charlotte Highton. Due to open the symposium in...' Charlotte had to swallow hard '...*eight* minutes.'

'*You're* Charlotte Highton?'

'Yes.' Charlotte glared at the stranger, who was looking at her as if he'd seen a ghost. As if he couldn't believe she was who she'd said she was.

He gave his head a sharp shake. And then he held out his hand. 'Dr Nicholas Moretti,' he told her. 'Nico.

We've met before. Twice, in fact. At St Margaret's Hospital in London. And that night at The Cosmopolitan Club. It was a few years ago now...' His voice trailed off. He was frowning and still staring as if he could barely recognise her. As if he couldn't make sense of what he was seeing.

Well...no surprises there. He was talking about a lifetime ago. She'd been a different person then.

A person she couldn't afford to be reminded of because it would only make this situation even worse. How incredibly unfortunate was this? To not only lose the protection she depended on but to meet someone who had known her back then? Before...

Before her life had turned so sharply it had virtually doubled back on itself to take the path she was now on.

For just a moment Charlotte could remember what it had been like at that crossroad.

She could feel the fear.

She didn't remember meeting him. Oh...she'd felt the beat of familiarity when she'd seen him. She probably *would* remember him if she allowed her mind to go back to that time. To when she'd been the rising star of a prestigious London hospital and her academic brilliance had been enough to erase the shadows of a painfully shy youth. To when she'd had the world at her feet and she had been courted by albeit distant royalty and wined and dined at places like The Cosmopolitan Club.

A time that it hadn't even occurred to her that she might be reminded of today.

Not only reminded of but stripped of any protection she would normally have to ward it off. How long had it been since she'd felt this vulnerable?

To Charlotte's *absolute* horror, she could actually feel the prickle of tears at the back of her eyes. Tears that could unleash weakness that might undo her completely. She blinked. Hard. She dragged her gaze away from yet another expression she could read in this man's eyes. He had such an open face. He was probably a very nice person but she didn't need anyone to be *concerned* about her.

She could look after herself. And succeed. She'd learned that long ago.

A police officer had come to stand beside them. This man who had an Italian name that matched his looks but who, curiously, spoke perfect English with an Irish accent, translated his query.

'He wants to know if you need assistance of any kind.'

A snort of something akin to laughter escaped Charlotte. She alone was the only person who could provide the kind of assistance she needed right now. Unless by some miracle a police diving team could be available within seconds and an even more impressive miracle would reveal a laptop that could survive total submersion.

But a rapid conversation in Italian led to the police officer nodding and indicating, with a wave of his arm, that Charlotte should follow him.

Nick was also following. 'He's going to take us to the symposium venue,' he said briskly. 'In the police launch. It will only take a few minutes.'

Charlotte looked down at her ruined clothes. She couldn't appear anywhere looking like this.

'We will explain what's happened.' His hand was on

her arm, guiding her through the crowd that was only now dispersing properly. 'Please let me help if I can. I feel responsible for this unfortunate turn of events and I will do anything I can to put things right. Perhaps they can rearrange the order of the presentations. And do you have a back-up of your material?'

Having a man step in and try and solve this problem was the last thing Charlotte needed.

'Of course I do. It's on a flash drive.'

'Which is where?'

Charlotte focused as the police officer offered her a hand to step into the speed boat. She ignored the hand, climbed aboard unaided and then turned back.

She had to speak through gritted teeth. 'It's in the side pocket of the laptop case that you *threw* into the canal.'

It was a totally unjustified accusation in the wake of an obvious accident. It was also an undeserved slap in the face given that he was trying so hard to help.

But Charlotte didn't care. She couldn't afford to.

'Please don't concern yourself any further.' She turned away and nodded to the pilot of the boat, who revved the engine. Waved at him imperiously enough to indicate that speed was of the essence and it was time to leave. 'This is my problem and I will deal with it.'

Nico watched the police launch speed away down the canal.

He could walk to the venue in only a few minutes longer than the boat trip would take. He hadn't actually told her that he was booked to attend the sympo-

sium himself so he couldn't really take offence that he hadn't been invited to share the ride.

Besides…he needed a few minutes to try and get his head around this extraordinary development.

She might not remember him but he remembered Charlotte Highton very well indeed. He'd been looking forward to seeing what that dynamic young doctor was like further down the track of her brilliant career.

Not that she'd been his type when he'd met her all those years ago but he'd been able to appreciate her attributes. The soft femininity that had been such a delightful contrast to the skill and intelligence she'd radiated as a young clinician. The sparkle of a woman who'd had the world and most of its men at her feet.

Now she was a female clinician who exuded power and control. There wasn't even the slightest hint of softness.

Or emotion, other than anger.

Except…just for a moment there, when he'd told her that he'd met her before, Nico could swear he had seen real fear in her eyes. A vulnerability that had been so out of place with the external appearance of this woman that he'd thought he'd been imagining things.

What he certainly wasn't imagining was the stark contrast between the woman he remembered admiring in the past and the one he'd just encountered.

What the hell had happened to Charlotte Highton?

And what was she trying to hide?

CHAPTER TWO

'CHARLOTTE...THERE YOU ARE! Thank goodness...I've been seriously worried about what might have happened to you.' The tall, grey-haired man was hurrying towards her. As he got closer, however, his step faltered and his eyes widened. 'Oh, my goodness. What *has* happened to you?'

The hotel Bonvecchiata had a water landing for gondolas and motorboats so Charlotte had entered the foyer moments after leaping out of the police launch. She knew she looked a fright but there'd been no chance to duck into a restroom and at least tidy her hair and sponge some of the mud from her clothing. Richard Campbell, the co-ordinator of this select symposium and the man who'd invited her to open it, must have been pacing the foyer as he'd waited anxiously for her to arrive.

'Long story, Richard. I'm very sorry, but I got caught up in an emergency. A man went into cardiac arrest and fell off some scaffolding right in front of me. I had to keep up the CPR until the ambulance got there.'

Charlotte was speaking quickly but her mind was working even faster. There were about fifty people

who'd been invited to attend this symposium. Where were they? Sitting in the conference room already, drumming their fingers on the tabletops and muttering about the substandard organisation of this gathering?

Richard was an old friend. Charlotte felt terrible about letting him down like this by being late and he didn't even know the worst of it yet. How was she going to tell him that she'd lost her presentation material?

He'd noticed her gaze sweep the foyer.

'They're serving coffee and cake in the restaurant for everybody. As soon as I knew you were running late I put back the start time for half an hour. There's a couple of attendees that aren't here yet as well.'

'Oh…' Charlotte nodded. She had been given a small breathing space. Now she had to decide if there was any way in the world she could rescue the situation. 'Richard…about my opening address…'

The older man smiled. 'Catchy title. "Miracles or Mutilation?" It's caught everybody's attention already, I have to say. But, Charlotte…' Richard was frowning now, looking down at her shredded tights and grazed knees. 'Are you going to be able to deliver it?'

Richard Campbell's reputation was on the line here. There were people from all over the world who'd chosen to come to this satellite symposium—a breakaway group from the much larger conference that had finished in Rome yesterday—plus others who had chosen to come to this forum without attending the main conference. They were all leaders in the field of emergency medicine. Exceptionally busy people who would not be happy to have their precious time wasted.

Charlotte's presentation had been researched meticu-

lously. The medical illustrations department of her university hospital had spent hours preparing the graphics that represented the facts and figures, the trends and the controversies about cost-effectiveness. It didn't matter how phenomenal her memory was, there was no way she could do justice to her presentation.

If she could get hold of someone at St Margaret's they could find the presentation on her desk computer and email it to her, but that would take too much time. They only had a matter of hours to fit in the other presentations and discussions before the symposium dinner this evening. And someone needed to open the day's programme.

How would it look it she backed out? Even with the best excuse in the world it would still dent her reputation as a young leader in this field, and Charlotte *needed* that reputation. It was who she was. The professional Charlotte Highton was strong enough to hide the *real* Charlotte. The inadequate, shameful one who wasn't a real woman at all.

She was caught between a rock and a hard place here. If she explained that there was no way she could do this, she would tarnish her reputation with the taint of failure and that chink in her armour might never be mended. It might grow, in fact, and eventually split open and the whole world would know what she was hiding.

They might look at her the way Nico Moretti had. As if they knew she was a fraud.

Charlotte could feel her heart thumping rapidly and there was a sinking sensation in her stomach that threatened to spiral into nausea.

'I've got a small problem,' she confessed to Rich-

ard. 'I've lost my presentation. My laptop ended up in the canal.'

'Oh…Lord…' Richard shaded his eyes with his hand. 'Can you manage without it?'

Charlotte opened her mouth to tell him how unlikely that was, but before she could force the words out she was distracted by the sound of her name being called from somewhere near the reception desk.

'*Charlotte Jane Highton…*'

The voice was as familiar to her as her own but Charlotte didn't want to believe that there was yet another problem she had to deal with. She kept her gaze on Richard, who gave her a rueful smile.

'Sorry. I hadn't got around to telling you. Your grandmother's here.'

Charlotte shook her head sharply. 'No. She's not supposed to arrive until tonight. After the symposium. We're travelling back to London together tomorrow.'

But the voice was much closer now. It couldn't be ignored.

'Charlotte Jane… What on *earth* have you done to yourself, child? You look like you've been run over by a gondola.'

Charlotte closed her eyes. She might be thirty-one years old but her grandmother could make her feel like a child again in a heartbeat. Flame-haired and larger than life, Lady Geraldine Highton was never one to stand on ceremony.

'Gran…what are you doing here?'

'I'm supposed to be here. I booked a room for us tonight.'

'Yes, but you were flying in this evening.'

'I changed my flight and arrived first thing this morning. I decided I wanted to hear you speak and this lovely man has told me I can sit in with all the translators and hear you on some headphones.'

Richard was nodding now and his smile was intended to reassure Charlotte that this problem, at least, had been dealt with. Clearly, he had been charmed by Lady Geraldine. Or intimidated. Either way, she had made arrangements that she now deemed satisfactory.

'But, Gran, you hate hearing anything about medical procedures. You've never wanted to hear me talk about my work.'

'Today's different.'

Something *was* different. With the kind of skill Charlotte found invaluable in her dealings with people in traumatic situations, she could sense that there was something important her grandmother was keeping to herself.

'I might not like hearing it,' Lady Geraldine continued, 'and I might not understand it, but it won't stop me wanting the chance to be proud of my granddaughter. Who knows? It might be the only chance I ever get.'

Yes. There was a shadow there in her grandmother's eyes. Eyes that usually sparkled with the determination to squeeze the best that life had to offer out of every opportunity. What was going on?

Charlotte knew she was staring. She also knew that her grandmother could read her like a book.

'We'll talk later,' Lady Geraldine said crisply. 'What we have to do now is get you tidied up. Thankfully, I have spare hosiery in my bag. And a hairbrush. Come on, Charlotte. Where's the nearest bathroom? There's

no time to waste. You don't want to keep all these important people waiting, do you?'

'But...'

There was a plea on Richard's face now. 'You don't have to give the presentation you prepared,' he said quietly. 'I have every confidence that you can think of something to say that would be an appropriate way to open this symposium. Could you do that, Charlotte? Please?'

The space between that rock and hard place suddenly got so small that it squeezed the breath out of Charlotte's lungs. She couldn't think. Maybe because she had no choice.

'I'll do my best.'

So it was that Charlotte found herself looking almost presentable again fifteen minutes later, standing in front of a room full of people who sat at a huge, U-shaped table. Some wore headphones to receive the translation service. Most had laptops or tablets on the table in front of them, along with pads of paper, pens, pitchers of iced water and even bowls of mints.

Charlotte had nothing other than a microphone clipped to the lapel of her jacket. From the way her heart was pounding and how exposed she felt, she could have been standing here stark naked.

She tried to smile at the group but failed. She did, however, manage to introduce herself and apologise for the delay in starting.

'I'm sure you've all heard by now of the reason why I was delayed and you, more than most, will understand that emergencies happen.'

Oh, help. Charlotte could hear the sound of her own voice, magnified by the loudspeaker system. Where was the calm, professional tone she always used in public?

What would her grandmother think of this? The niggling worry that there was something wrong that her grandmother wasn't telling her couldn't be allowed to surface until this was all over but it was impossible not to have a flash of shame that the pride her only living relative had taken in her achievements was going to be dented.

'Ah…' Charlotte stared at the group, totally at a loss for what she could say next. Please, God, let the ground open and swallow me up, she thought.

The ground didn't open but the door of the conference room did, to admit a latecomer. Everybody's head turned at the interruption but Charlotte's gaze had got there first and now it was stuck.

The worst moment of her life had just taken a dive to a new low.

How on earth could Nicholas Moretti have the nerve to show up here, knowing he'd ruined her preparation for this talk? He'd already revealed his disbelief that she was who she said she was. Did he now want to see if she was going to make a fool of herself and confirm that disbelief?

He was about to get what he came for, then, wasn't he?

Nico gave a very European hand gesture, apologising for his interruption as he took the empty space at the table. His body language conveyed complete confidence that he had the right to be here, though. That he was, in fact, eager to take part in the proceedings. And then his

gaze locked with Charlotte's and that weird spinning sensation in her gut seemed to catch fire.

Anger?

Quite possibly.

Charlotte Highton wasn't about to let the actions of a man even threaten to destroy her.

Not again.

She took a deep breath, jerking her gaze away from Nico and vowing not to let it return to that section of the table until she was finished. In a way, he'd done her a favour. His entrance had covered her stumble and now she was fired up. Whether it was from anger or desperation was immaterial.

'Some of you might be asking whether I should have let myself become involved in that emergency situation, especially when the result has deprived you of the audiovisual accompaniment you were supposed to have this morning.'

A ripple of sympathy went through the gathering.

'It's a fair question,' Charlotte continued. 'How far should any of us go in getting involved? How far should we go as emergency medicine specialists? Out in the field or in our own departments?'

Her words were clear and her tone as professional as ever now. Everybody was listening. Looking at her. She could feel one gaze in particular so strongly that she knew exactly who it was coming from. Good. Let him watch and listen. Let him see who Charlotte Highton was now.

'We can do so many things that can be done in an operating theatre in our emergency departments or out

in the field. Burr-holes, tracheotomies, amputations, thoracotamies, Caesareans.' Charlotte paused for effect. 'Extreme measures in desperate circumstances. How many are justified? Does the weight of evidence suggest we're performing miracles? Or guilty of performing mutilations?'

Another pause. This was the moment that would make or break this talk.

'I had a presentation that was full of statistics about these kinds of extreme procedures and graphics to show you the controversial relationship between patient outcomes and cost-effectiveness. Obviously it's not possible to do those facts and figures justice from memory, so instead...' The solution to this problem came to her in a flash of inspiration. 'I'm going to present a case history.'

Nico sat back in his chair.

He could feel the surprise of the people around him. What was this? They were all intelligent people who were hungry for new knowledge. They wanted to be presented with the results of cutting-edge research that they could use to improve what they did for a career. But they were going to be told a *story*?

'The man I'll call Bernie was forty-three years old,' Charlotte was saying. 'He went to the corner shop very late one night, because his pregnant wife had a craving for chocolate ripple ice cream. The timing was unfortunate. The shop was held up and Bernie got stabbed. A small knife with a short blade was buried to its hilt in his chest, deflected by the sixth rib, maybe five or six inches to the left from the midline.'

Nico could sense the interest picking up around him. The injury had been dangerously close to the man's heart.

'The ambulance crew knew not to remove an impaled object. Bernie's still conscious when they arrive but his blood pressure's dropping. Fortunately, this corner shop is only about two minutes' drive from St Margaret's hospital. They put a doughnut dressing around the knife to stabilise it, give Bernie some oxygen and load and go. They establish IV access en route.'

The way Charlotte had changed to the present tense drew them all into the urgency of this case. Clever. Or were they all drawn in, as he was, by the sound of her voice? Soft, but as clear as a bell. As under control as her hair was again, all scraped back into that complicated knot thing.

Nico had preferred it the way he'd seen it after that resuscitation scene, with enough loose wisps to suggest that the whole knot could be released if you buried your fingers in it, wiggled them and then dragged them gently through the length of the hair. How long was it when it was loose? he wondered. And then he sharply dismissed the errant speculation and concentrated again on what she was saying.

'By the time Bernie comes through our doors, he's lost consciousness. His BP's unrecordable. His cardiac rhythm goes from SVT to VF to asystole within thirty seconds of my team getting him hooked up to the monitors.'

Nico was really listening now. So this was a case that Charlotte herself had managed? He could imagine her there, in the emergency department of St Marga-

ret's. Wearing scrubs, probably, with a white coat over them. No…she'd been expecting a major trauma. She'd have a plastic apron on. And gloves. And a head covering that probably had a plastic face shield to protect her from blood spatter. She would have been in charge. In control. Her voice might have been louder than it was right now but just as clear.

'We know our protocols inside out but how do we start CPR? This man's got a knife in his chest that's probably punctured his left ventricle. He's bleeding out. We can pull the knife out and push fluids but there's a hole in his heart so that would be futile.'

Nico was holding his breath without realising it. Everybody here knew that the only option was to do one of the most invasive procedures that could ever be done out of an operating theatre. Cracking open this man's chest and getting to the heart of the problem, so to speak.

'He's dead already unless we do something major and do it fast.' Charlotte's tone told them she agreed with the conclusion they'd all reached. 'A thoracotomy is the only option but I know as well as everybody else in the team what the odds are for a successful result. Virtually nil. But, hey…we have to try, don't we? This man is about to become a father. Right now, his pregnant wife is probably wondering why it's taking him so long to get back with her ice cream.'

Charlotte seemed to straighten her back. 'I'm the one who has to make the call and, as far as I'm concerned, it's a no-brainer. We take out the knife and I do a clamshell thoracotomy. There's a gaping hole in the left ventricle and I suture it shut while we deal with more blood in a thorax than I've ever seen before.'

Nico closed his eyes for a heartbeat. He could picture it. A nightmare scene. The tissue of the myocardium would have been slippery. The visual field would have been impossible to keep clear with all that blood so you'd have to work almost blind.

'We start pushing fluids and begin CPR. I'm riding that stretcher to Theatre with my hand inside Bernie's chest, doing internal compressions and praying that my rough suturing is going to hold.'

Oh, Nico could imagine that scene too. Charlotte would have had to have been astride the man's legs, with one hand on the side rail to steady herself. Amongst the bank of monitoring and ventilation equipment that would have been in place. Speeding along with her team running to get them to Theatre as fast as possible.

It felt like he was standing in one of the wide corridors of St Margaret's right now, watching the dramatic spectacle rush past him. Opening his eyes again, he knew that he was looking at Charlotte with growing admiration. This was some woman.

'The cardiac surgical team is waiting for us. They do a much better job than me in repairing the damage. They replace the blood volume and get Bernie's heart started again. By this time his wife is at the hospital. Bernie's taken to the intensive care unit. He's still alive but what none of us know is whether we've done the right thing in saving him. Will he wake up? And, if he does, how much brain damage has been caused by the lack of oxygen? His wife is distraught and, just to add to the tension, she goes into labour three weeks before her due date.'

A soft groan came from her audience. This might be

nothing like what they'd expected as an opening talk but they were all invested in the story now. They had to know the outcome.

'I've told you this story because it does, unlike so many, many others, have a happy ending. Bernie did have a degree of neurological compromise. His cognition and speech were affected and he had a unilateral weakness on his right side.'

It was the first time Nico had seen Charlotte smile. He felt his own lips curve in an unconscious response.

'But his weak arm didn't stop him being able to cradle his newborn daughter a couple of days later. His difficulty in finding words didn't dim the way he could communicate his joy to his wife.'

Dammit. Was that a *lump* Nico could feel in his throat? He swallowed it away. His own career was full of success stories like this, wasn't it?

'The bottom line,' Charlotte continued quietly, 'is that our job is about the people who come under our care. Bernie was a miracle. But if he hadn't made it, that resus scene in my ED could have been denounced as unnecessary mutilation. We couldn't know how it would go before we started but is it just a coin toss?'

Charlotte was looking around the room. Nico was waiting for her gaze to cross his. He was oddly disappointed when it didn't.

'No.' She answered her own question. 'That's what our chosen specialty is all about. Working towards being the best we can be in our field of expertise. Knowing when there's a choice that pulling out the big guns is going to make the difference between life and death.'

Nico saw Charlotte take a deep breath. She was

wrapping up now and the unusual introduction had clearly been a huge success. Everybody was leaning forward, totally engrossed and eager to participate in the programme that was about to start.

He felt the same way so how on earth could he be distracted by the way that deep breath pushed Charlotte's breasts against the material of the plain blouse she wore under that tailored jacket? The way a hint of cleavage struggled to appear over the top button. Good grief. She was so buttoned up with that hairstyle and the fitted clothes she wore, it was almost as if she was trying not to look remotely feminine.

Maybe she was batting for the other team. Nico tucked the thought away with satisfaction. That would explain a lot. Maybe she had been trying to deny her true preference when he'd seen her out with that man in The Cosmopolitan Club all those years ago. And even if she was now comfortable with who she was, in her position Charlotte probably wouldn't want to come out of the closet and travel in the company of her girl-friend. Or wife, perhaps. It was none of his business and it didn't bother him.

So why did that curious feeling of disappointment in not making eye contact with her a second ago suddenly deepen several notches?

'The papers you are going to be privileged to hear today are from invited speakers who are leading their particular fields. I'm looking forward to hearing the discussions that will follow the presentations. Again, I must apologise for my unorthodox keynote speech but, on behalf of Dr Richard Campbell, our chairman for today, and the others involved in organising this satel-

lite session, let me welcome you to our symposium on critical interventions.'

Nico joined the round of applause. His neighbour leaned sideways to say something about how moving the story had been and how good it was to be reminded of the human aspects of their science. But Nico merely murmured agreement. He couldn't take his eyes off Charlotte. As if she felt his intense gaze, she looked up from her position at the front of the room.

So there, her gaze seemed to say. *I did it—even if you did do your best to stop me.*

After the awkward start to the day things were running smoothly. Richard was delighted. He smiled at Charlotte as they were preparing to follow the others out of the conference room for the lunch break.

'Do you know, I think your introduction has allowed for some very interesting questions to be raised that people might not have considered appropriate otherwise. You've given this whole forum an informality that has brought people closer together. It was a stroke of brilliance.'

'Thanks.' Charlotte rubbed the back of her neck, trying to ease the tension that still hadn't gone away completely. 'It could have taken things in the opposite direction. I was lucky.'

'I think everyone was impressed.'

Had Nicholas Moretti been impressed? And why did it matter so much that he had been?

'I'm sure they'll want to tell you that themselves, over lunch.'

Charlotte wasn't at all sure she wanted that to hap-

pen. She might be used to talking to colleagues while balancing a plate of food and eating but the idea of doing that in Nico's company seemed disturbingly...intimate?

Whatever. She had the perfect excuse.

'I'm going to skip lunch, if you don't mind, Richard. I'll grab a sandwich or something but I really need to check on my grandmother and make sure she's being taken care of. And that she has something to do for the afternoon. Goodness knows what kind of mischief she could get up to otherwise.'

Richard was grinning now. 'She's quite something, your grandmother. How old is she?'

'Eighty-two. Going on about sixteen, I think. I often feel as if I'm in the company of a wayward teenager.' Charlotte's smile was fond. 'And then, at other times, she comes out with the kind of wisdom and advice that only someone who's experienced life to the full could have. She's amazing.'

Richard patted her arm. 'Go and catch up. I'll give your excuses to anyone who asks.'

'Thanks.' Charlotte hurried out to the reception area, away from the dining room, and asked whether her grandmother had left a message for her.

'No. But she's had lunch delivered to your room. Would you like your key now?'

The room was massive and decorated in Venetian style with sumptuous drapes, bed coverings and deep armchairs all in tones of silver and soft bronze. There was a Persian rug on the floor beneath the chandelier hanging from an astonishingly high ceiling. A small table with spindly legs supported a silver tray that had

plates of delicate-looking sandwiches and cakes, a pot of tea and cups.

The first thing that struck Charlotte was that the tray hadn't been touched.

Almost at the same time she noted how tidy the room was. Where were the clothes strewn about that always happened when Geraldine was choosing her next outfit? The open guidebooks as she chose her next adventure?

And why on earth was her grandmother lying on a bed in the middle of the day? Lady Geraldine Highton might be eighty-two but she didn't *do* naps. 'Life's too short,' she always said. 'And it's getting shorter for me by the day. Why waste it by sleeping? I can sleep when I'm dead.'

'Gran…' Charlotte moved towards the bed. 'What's wrong?'

'Oh…' Geraldine clearly hadn't been expecting a visitor. She sat up swiftly, looking…embarrassed. No, make that *guilty*. 'Charlie…I didn't think I'd see you until this evening.' The odd expression vanished, to be replaced by a beaming smile. 'That was a wonderful talk you gave, darling. I can't tell you how proud I was. And I understood every word. Well, almost every word. The next speaker was terribly dull in comparison. I went for a walk and watched the gondolas for a while. I might go for a ride in one after lunch. It's been years…'

Charlotte sank down onto the edge of the second bed, facing her grandmother. Something here was off-key. Terribly off-key.

'Gran…' She reached out and took hold of a soft hand decorated with several diamond rings. 'What's going on?'

'Whatever do you mean? Nothing's going on, Charlotte. Come and have lunch with me.' Lady Geraldine got to her feet but then her face changed. She couldn't hide a grimace of pain and her hand went to her stomach.

'You're not well,' Charlotte gasped. 'That's why you haven't touched your lunch. Why didn't you *tell* me?'

'I'm fine. There's nothing wrong with me.'

'Lie down,' Charlotte ordered. 'I want to have a look at you.'

For a long, long moment Geraldine looked undecided. But then she quietly lay down and answered the barrage of questions. Yes, she had abdominal pain. No, it wasn't the first time. Yes, she'd been to see a doctor about it. She'd had a scan. She was booked to have a biopsy between Christmas and New Year.

A *biopsy?*

With absolute dread giving her a chill that almost made her shiver visibly, Charlotte quietly asked if she could feel her grandmother's tummy and when she did, the hard edges of the mass she could feel confirmed her worst fear.

'Did…did your doctor tell you what he thought it was after the scan?'

'Oh, yes…' Lady Geraldine took hold of Charlotte's hand with both of hers. 'He's sure it's some form of bowel cancer.' Her voice wobbled. 'I didn't want you to find out, darling. Not yet.'

Charlotte's voice was thick with tears. 'Why not? You should have told me. I should have been there with you when you had your appointments.'

'We've been planning this trip for so long. Going on

the Orient Express has been on my bucket list for far
too long.' Unbelievably, Geraldine was smiling mis-
chievously. 'And what better time to fulfil a bucket list
item than when you've been told the end probably isn't
that far off?'

'Gran... We can't spend thirty hours on a train. We
have to fly back to London tonight. I'll talk to people.
We'll find a way to bring that procedure forward so we
can start treatment earlier.'

'No way, Jose.' The way Lady Geraldine's eyes nar-
rowed was a warning that she was not about to be con-
tradicted. 'I've taken some painkillers. I'll be as right
as rain after a little rest. You're not going to spoil this
for me, Charlotte. Are you?'

It wasn't really a question. And the look coming from
those faded blue eyes wasn't disapproving. It was full of
absolute love. The kind of love Charlotte had received
from this remarkable woman ever since she'd been or-
phaned as a small, terrified child.

This was why her grandmother had wanted to hear
her speak today. Why she'd wanted to tell her how proud
she was of her. Well, that cut both ways, didn't it?

'Let's enjoy this time together,' Lady Geraldine
added softly. 'Before we know anything for sure. Let's
pretend you didn't find me like this. The way I wanted
it to be. Go back to your conference, darling. I need a
little rest and then I'm going to choose my outfit for
the dinner tonight.'

Those words stayed with Charlotte during the after-
noon's symposium proceedings and it was the hardest
thing she'd ever done, to keep up her professional image.

The papers being presented were fascinating and the discussions lively, and Charlotte had learned long ago to firmly shut the door between her professional and personal lives, but today it was impossible.

Today had started badly. She thought she'd made the best of a bad situation and survived but now it felt as if the world had tilted far too sharply on its axis. What did her brilliant career matter if she was about to lose the person she loved most? The only person she truly loved, come to that.

The conference attendees were invited to a cocktail session before a break to get ready for the dinner but Charlotte quietly slipped away from the group. She had to pull herself together. Had to find the strength to deal with what was undoubtedly coming. Did she really want to deprive her grandmother of the long-awaited pleasure of the train trip tomorrow and whisk her back to London and into hospital? Did she have that right?

The balcony leading off the now deserted dining room offered a private space with the bonus of an idyllic canal view where more than one ornate gondola could be seen floating past.

One of the gondolas held a pair of young lovers who were locked in a passionate embrace, oblivious to their surroundings for the moment. Maybe they were practising. Wasn't there a bridge here in Venice and if you kissed while going beneath it, it meant that your love would last for ever?

If her grandmother was here on this balcony with her, she'd be poking Charlotte with a bony finger right about now. Clicking her tongue.

That should be you in that gondola, Charlotte Jane,

she'd be saying. *Kissing some gorgeous young man whose baby you can't wait to have. You don't know what you're missing, child, and it's the most important thing in life.*

But Charlotte knew all too well what she'd be missing far too soon and hearing her grandmother's voice so clearly in her mind was the final straw.

Tears rolled down her cheeks. Hot, burning tears that felt like acid. No surprise there. They were pretty concentrated given that she hadn't shed a tear for six years now. They were such a sign of weakness. Feminine weakness.

She knew there was no point in trying to stop them.

Thank God nobody could see her.

The room Nico had been given at the hotel Bonvecchiata was luxurious. He eyed the huge bed, pulled at his tie to loosen it, and looked forward to putting his feet up for a while before heading off to the symposium dinner.

What a day!

Shedding his jacket, Nico walked to the tall windows of his room and looked through the ornate iron grille to find he had the bonus of a canal view. A gondola floated past with a young couple locked in each other's arms.

Nico smiled. Nice. His gaze drifted lazily and then it caught.

His smile faded.

There was a balcony on the floor beneath his. Charlotte Highton was standing there, her shoulders bowed as if she carried the weight of the entire world on them.

And she was *crying*?

Dio, but this woman was so full of contradictions.

For a moment Nico stared in fascination. He would never have believed that she was capable of showing such a depth of emotion. But why was she so upset?

Did it have anything to do with being unable to present what she'd intended to present this morning?

Because of the trouble he'd unwittingly caused for her?

For another, long moment Nico kept staring, unsure of how to unravel the conflicting emotions being stirred in his own gut. Why did he feel such a strong urge to try and help this prickly, complicated woman? It was more than having contributed to a bad start to her day. More, even, than being curious about how someone's personality could have changed so much in just a few short years.

Being aware that there was some indefinable extra motivation should be enough of a warning to stop him getting involved any further, but did he want to listen to that warning?

He turned away. Stared at the huge, inviting bed for a moment. And then, with a soft growl, he turned on his heel and headed for the door.

CHAPTER THREE

OH...NO.

As if she could cope with her day getting even worse!

Of all the people to discover her at her lowest point in so many years, it had to be Nico Moretti.

Charlotte did her utmost to stem the tide of her tears. She turned her back on Nico and leant on the balustrade of the balcony, gripping the roughened concrete so hard she could feel tendrils of pain in her fingers that flickered into her arms. She fixed her gaze on the canal beneath and blinked again and again, trying to clear the wetness that didn't want to stop. Why couldn't it go back where it had come from, instead of continuing to roll down her face in these humiliating tears?

He didn't say anything. He just came to stand beside her. He, too, seemed to be gazing at the view and he spread his hands on the balustrade as if the only reason he was there was to admire their surroundings.

Charlotte's panic ebbed a little as he just stood there, a silent presence.

She'd never had company during the most unhappy periods in her life. Her first instinct, even as a young child so bereft at the loss of her parents, had been to

hide. To cry alone. And feel alone. To accept that life was a terribly lonely business and you just had to deal with that.

There *was* comfort to be found in simply being close to another person. To feel the presence of another living, breathing human.

The fact that Nico wasn't saying anything made it easy to accept his presence. She didn't have to try and find excuses or explain anything, and to have someone there who was clearly prepared to accept the state she was in made it feel as if it was okay not to be coping. As if she had support.

Strong support. Bit by bit, Charlotte found her thoughts creeping out from the dark knot in her head. She was aware of how big Nico was. Well over six feet in height and broad with it. His hands against the ancient concrete looked huge and powerful but his fingers were long and artistic looking. Clever hands, no doubt capable of performing the careful, intricate movements that were needed when you were dealing with something as precious as brain tissue.

Charlotte blinked again and, amazingly, her vision wasn't blurred any more. Without raising her head from its bowed position, she could study his neatly trimmed nails and olive-brown skin and the smattering of dark hair on the backs of his hands that disappeared under the turned-back cuffs of his white shirt.

Her head turned, as if her gaze was being pulled up by an external force. Up his arms, across his chest, where a loosened tie hung like a necklace and the top buttons of his shirt were undone. It was impossible not to flick her gaze up to his face now, but it was safe. He

was still staring down at the canal so Charlotte let her gaze linger for a moment on the strong profile. Unfairly luxurious eyelashes that brushed his cheeks when he blinked. A nose that made no apology for the space it took and deep creases on each side that ran down to meet a mouth that looked as if it smiled often and easily.

A jaw that looked like it hadn't seen a razor in a fair few hours. And a firmness to it that suggested tension. Was he gritting his teeth? Was he standing there not knowing what to say? Wishing he was somewhere else?

'I'm sorry.' The words came out as a whisper. 'I've had… It's been…' she had to take a tiny gulp of air '…a weird kind of day.'

'I understand.' Nico moved finally, but only his head. He angled it a little towards Charlotte. And then he smiled at her.

And…dear Lord…*what* a smile. Slow and so full of warmth. The most genuine smile she had ever seen. And it was for *her*. She had to catch her breath again.

'And I have a horrible feeling I might have contributed to your day not being the one you hoped for,' Nico continued. 'I really must apologise again.'

His voice was as warm as that smile. The Irish lilt was unmistakeable but, if he had been in Ireland, they would hear something else. An Italian inflection that made it unique. An astonishing accent colouring a depth that was as masculine as his size and aura of power.

How many women had fallen in love with that voice already?

Not that she was about to join the ranks. Charlotte cleared her throat.

'No…really. Losing my laptop was nothing com-

pared to…' Oh, help. Had she really been about to break one of her most ironclad rules and share personal information with a professional colleague?

'Compared to what, *cara*?'

It was the endearment that did her in. An endearment in a foreign language that somehow made it inoffensive and genuinely caring.

'My…grandmother is here. She's not well and…and it's possible she might not have…' Charlotte's intake of breath was a small sob. 'Might not have much time left.'

'Ohhh…' The sound was a drawn-out note of understanding. Empathy.

This man was a stranger even if they *had* met before. She would probably never see him again after today. So it didn't really count as sharing personal information, did it? Nobody would be giving her meaningful glances at work or gossiping about her in the cafeteria at St Margaret's. As if it would help with the anonymity, Charlotte fixed her gaze on the canal again. She could be simply talking aloud to herself.

'She's the most important person in the world to me,' she said softly. 'My parents both got killed in a horrible accident when I was eight years old. I was in the accident too and came out as a terrified shell of a child who wouldn't even speak to anyone for months. Gran never cared how tough it got, she was always so patient and so loving. So proud of any achievements I managed.'

'She would have had a lot to be proud of.'

Charlotte's breath came out in a huff of incredulity as she twisted sharply to glare at Nico. He was so used to giving women compliments, wasn't he? Meaningless

compliments that demeaned what she was trying to tell
him about her wonderful grandmother.

'What makes you think you know anything about
me?' The words came out tight and accusing. And then
Charlotte shook her head and swallowed fresh tears.
'You know *nothing*.'

There was a flash in his eyes but, while he might be
startled by the verbal attack, he didn't look away.

'I know that a few years ago I met a woman who
would have made anybody who loved her immensely
proud,' he said calmly. 'But you're correct…I know
nothing about you on a personal level.'

His gaze still held hers and there was something else
in his eyes now. Respect? Curiosity?

'So tell me,' he invited. And then he smiled again.
'I'm listening.'

She was about to walk away.

Nico could sense the internal struggle but, dammit,
he *wanted* to hear more. He knew perfectly well he
was taking advantage of finding Charlotte in a state
that made her vulnerable but he wasn't about to use
the situation to his own advantage. Quite the opposite!
His only motivation for coming out to this balcony and
interrupting an obviously private moment had been to
offer assistance.

He owed her that, surely?

Even though she had dismissed any contribution he'd
made to her having such a bad day, he knew he hadn't
helped it get off to a good start. And it was frustrat-
ing not to be able to think of a way to make up for that.
Nico Moretti was an expert in making other people's

lives better, even in the most dire of circumstances. He firmly believed that you could find at least a little patch of joy anywhere if you didn't take life too seriously.

Maybe that was why he knew he had the reputation of being a playboy. But play was the key, wasn't it? Like when he took the time to actually play with one of his smaller patients or do something silly enough to make them smile. And…good grief…he'd never encountered a woman who couldn't accept a compliment, even if it had been an automatic and possibly less than genuine response.

Nico had a strong sense that anything Charlotte told him would be completely honest, no matter how badly it reflected on herself. In his experience, this was an unusual trait, particularly for a woman on first acquaintance.

What really surprised him, however, was how much he wanted to hear more about her. His curiosity about Charlotte Highton was increasing rapidly. He remembered the brilliant young doctor. He'd seen the icy-cool clinician in action. He'd seen a speaker not only cope with facing an international audience having been deprived of her resources but engage them to the point where she'd had them in the palm of her hand.

And now he'd seen a glimpse of a loving granddaughter. Beneath all the layers he could detect there was an orphan who'd been a desperately unhappy child. A woman who currently looked alone. And lonely.

Just who was the real Charlotte?

He tried to send a silent message with his smile. And his eyes.

Talk to me. Please. You never know, I might be able to help. I'm good at helping.

It wasn't working, though. It was as though he was trying to hold a wild creature in his hands and it was struggling to be free. An injured wild creature that wanted to crawl away and lick its wounds somewhere it felt safe.

He needed something more to keep her here. He needed to tap into something that would give them a bond, however tenuous.

'I've met many people at many conferences over the years,' he told her. 'They are often accompanied by their husbands or wives. Or their lovers. Sometimes by their children. You are the very first I've met who is accompanied by a grandparent. That's…intriguing. Special.'

He watched Charlotte take a ragged breath. He heard her sniff and had to hide a smile because it sounded so… unprofessional. Childlike, even. It wasn't as if he'd never witnessed a grown woman crying, of course. They usually did, when he told them things were over, but this was different. The tears had nothing to do with him and they touched a spot in his heart usually reserved for those younger patients or their families. Something poignant.

'Gran *is* special,' Charlotte said, her words a whisper. Then she cleared her throat. 'But she doesn't usually accompany me. In fact, I'm not allowed to talk about anything remotely gruesome or medical when I'm around her. She says that you can always find something uplifting to talk about if you try hard enough.'

'A woman after my own heart,' Nico smiled. 'A

finder of joy who can make people around her feel better.'

He let out a quiet breath as he sensed Charlotte relaxing. He knew she was almost smiling herself because he was watching so carefully and he could see the softening of her lips. The imperceptible curling at their corners.

'She always has something to look forward to. A new adventure planned. That's why she's here. As soon as she knew I was going to be speaking in Venice she looked up the timetable for the Orient Express going from Venice back to London and when the dates were perfect she said it was meant to be and I couldn't say no because it was well up the bucket list.'

'The bucket list?'

'You know...' Charlotte really smiled this time, as she looked up and caught his gaze. 'The list of things you really, really want to do before you kick the bucket?'

'Kick the...? Oh...' Just occasionally, the fact that English was a second language tripped him up. '*Sì...*' The Italian word slipped out unconsciously as he contemplated the euphemism for dying. 'I understand.'

Her eyes were grey. A dark, stormy sort of grey at the moment. He always expected blonde women to have blue eyes so the colour struck him as different. As unusual as this woman was herself, perhaps?

'But it's a crazy idea. How can we take a slow train trip across Europe when she's so sick? We should fly back to London tonight. I could have her in a hospital by tomorrow, getting the kind of investigations she needs to plan treatment.'

'Is that what she wants? Your grandmother?' It was

a relief to be given a problem to solve at last and Nico was more than ready to focus on it, but he needed more information. 'What is her name?'

'Geraldine. Her friends call her Jendi.'

'And what are the symptoms of her illness?'

'I don't really know. She's kept this from me. I wouldn't have known about it at all yet except I found her resting and could see she had abdominal pain. And...I could feel a mass...'

'She has medication for the pain?'

'Yes. She seems fine now. She totally refused to consider cancelling the train trip and getting a flight to London. She told me to go away so she could have a bath in peace and get ready for the dinner tonight. She wants to dress up.'

'If there are no obvious signs that it would be detrimental to her condition, then maybe that's exactly what she *should* do.'

Charlotte's jaw dropped. 'And the train trip? You think that's a good idea, too?'

'Another day or two will not make any difference to the course of her illness,' Nico said. 'And look at it from her point of view. What would be better? To be lying in a hospital bed waiting for possibly a painful procedure or being able to forget about what lies ahead for a brief time and enjoying a wonderful experience in the company of someone you love?'

'But...' Charlotte caught her bottom lip between her teeth and tugged on it. It was another childish gesture that caught Nico in that soft spot in his heart. But then she let go with her teeth and soothed her lip with her

tongue and suddenly it was quite another, very unexpected spot that Nico could feel waking up. 'How could *I* forget enough to help her enjoy it?'

'Because you have that kind of strength.' This time the compliment was completely sincere. Nico already knew enough about Charlotte to be convinced of it. 'You can choose the part of you that you want other people to see and the rest you can keep hidden.'

Something very odd flickered across Charlotte's face. The kind of expression that suggested…guilt? As though she'd been caught out trying to hide something huge and important?

No. The expression was gone as fast as it had appeared. And now Charlotte was turning away. Nico wasn't ready to let her go. Not just yet.

'I think you should make the most of any time you can have together. Be proud that you can help her achieve this bucket-list thing. Maybe you can find out what the other things on her list are too and tick another one off soon.'

A rueful laugh escaped Charlotte. 'Oh, I know what's on the top of that list and it's not something that's ever going to be ticked off.'

'Oh?' Nico tilted his head encouragingly. 'They say that nothing is impossible.'

'*This* is.' Charlotte was looking up at the sky now. Assessing the clouds to see if the forecasted snow might arrive or was she seeking divine inspiration? She flicked Nico the briefest glance. 'Gran's greatest wish is to see me get married. Settled down and ready to present her with her first great-grandchild.'

'Ohhh...' Nico nodded slowly. 'That could be tricky.'

'Impossible.' The word was final.

'Hmm.' He had solved the problem of the train trip. Surely there was a way of at least getting around this one? 'Would there be any harm in letting her *think* it might be possible?'

'Gran's not stupid. She knows perfectly well that I'm not in a relationship. I haven't been for years. I'm hardly likely to get away with pretending I've met "Mr Right" within the next few months, am I?' She took a step away from him, raising her hand to smooth her already perfect hairstyle. 'And I really can't believe I'm having such an astonishingly ridiculous conversation.'

Nico had been distracted for a split second, wondering again what Charlotte's hair would look like if it wasn't so tightly coiled and clipped into place. He wanted to pull out some of those pins. To force her to loosen up a little.

'Because it's not so ridiculous,' he said. 'What if you attended this dinner tonight with...with your new boyfriend? How happy would that make your grandmother?'

This time it was real laughter that escaped. A delicious, totally unexpected chuckle of real mirth. 'Is there a "hire a boyfriend" agency in Venice that you know about?'

'There's no need to hire anybody.' Nico's grin stretched his mouth. 'It's the least I could do to make up for this morning's unfortunate happenstance.'

It was perfect. Here it was on a plate. The opportunity to not only make up for contributing to any dis-

tress caused by this morning's incident but to do it in a manner that would be *fun*.

Except that Charlotte was looking at him as if he was totally crazy.

This was surreal.

Just having a personal conversation with a professional acquaintance would have been weird enough but this incredibly good-looking stranger seemed to be offering to pretend to be her *boyfriend* for an evening.

Imagine that!

Unfortunately, Charlotte *could* imagine it. She could imagine herself introducing him to her grandmother as a…as a *friend*…and Nico turning on his most charming smile and Gran putting two and two together and letting wishful thinking make the impossible a reality.

Oh…God…how happy would she be?

The distraction of a train trip to take her mind off what was coming was nothing compared to the joy she would have if she thought Charlotte had finally found 'the one'.

It was crazy. Wasn't it?

'That's crazy,' she said aloud, hoping the spoken words would confirm it.

'It's only for an evening.' Nico shrugged as if it was no big deal. 'We could tell her we've met before, which is perfectly true. We could say that there's something about Venice being such a romantic city and we've realised we can't fight the attraction any longer. It was meant to be.'

Oh…my… If the look he was giving her right now

was any indication of the performance he could put on for her grandmother, she would be totally convinced.

For a skipped heartbeat kind of moment, Charlotte almost believed it herself. She could feel it right down to her bones. How could anyone be so good at looking as if they had just fallen madly in love with someone? It was doing very strange things to something deep inside her. A process that had to be stopped immediately.

He's acting, she reminded herself. And he's only this good at it because he's clearly had a lot of practice.

'You may be an expert in pretending,' she snapped, 'but it's not something I could carry off. I wouldn't even want to try.'

He was still giving her *that* look.

'I watched you this morning,' he said softly. 'I think you can carry off anything that's important enough to you.'

There was a glint of mischief in those dark eyes. Good heavens, he was actually *enjoying* this, wasn't he? He *wanted* to do it?

'You might be surprised at how easy it is,' he continued. 'You might enjoy it.'

Charlotte snorted. 'I don't think so.'

'And wouldn't you even want to try? For your grandmother's sake?'

'No. It would be completely dishonest.'

'Completely?' Nico injected a hurt tone into the word. 'Could you not summon even a tiny bit of attraction to me to work with?'

He tilted his head, moving it closer to her own, his gaze dropping from her eyes to her lips.

And, heaven help her, but Charlotte could actually

feel a curl of desire unfolding deep in her belly. It escaped from that place that was locked away. A place she could never enter because, if she did, she would have to remember... Have to face up to what was so wrong with her...

'No.' The word came out like the slamming of a door. It was time to get away from there.

Away from this man who was making her think about ridiculous things.

Feel things she had no desire to feel.

'At least think about it.' His words followed her as she almost ran to get off the balcony. 'I'll see you at dinner.'

CHAPTER FOUR

'OH, MY...'

'What's wrong, Gran? Are you all right?' The lighting wasn't so great in this dinner venue. A restaurant within easy walking distance of the conference venue, this ancient stone vault of a room had been transformed into a winter wonderland in honour of the season.

White church candles with multiple wicks, in a nest of holly leaves and poinsettia flowers, made a centrepiece for each of the small tables set for four. Sheets of fairy lights in icicle form hung from the high ceiling and, on one roughened stone wall, a slide show of Christmassy scenes was softly fading in and out as the scenes changed.

It was a beautiful setting for a dinner but the flickering light levels made it impossible to see things as clearly as Charlotte would have liked. She was convinced her grandmother had suddenly gone pale.

'Stop fussing, Charlotte, for goodness' sake.' Lady Geraldine gave her a surprisingly sharp poke with her finger. 'If you weren't half-blind, you would have noticed what I just noticed.' Her smile was almost gleeful as she lowered her voice. 'Eye candy...'

'*Gran*. Wherever did you learn an expression like that?'

'I blame television,' Lady Geraldine sighed. But she was still smiling. Still watching a point well beyond Charlotte's shoulder. The entranceway, most likely, because Charlotte had deliberately chosen a table as far away from the door as possible. A nice, dark corner. With a bit of luck, Nico Moretti would be late and either he wouldn't be able to spot her or the two unoccupied settings at their table would have been taken by another conference attendee and his or her partner.

But no. With a sinking heart Charlotte realised that to have grabbed her grandmother's keen interest, this 'eye candy' would have to be spectacularly good looking. And judging by the way her elderly relative was practically fanning herself with her hand now, he was coming in their direction. Slowly, she turned her head.

Oh, my...was an understatement. Dr Moretti was wearing a beautifully fitting dinner suit, which always made men look good, but so were most of the other male guests here. Maybe the soft lighting had something to do with the way he stood out. Or more likely, it was the man's sheer presence as he wound his way through the tables, pausing to smile at people he knew or share a few words in greeting.

He seemed to have a spotlight on him, in any case, and Charlotte knew her gaze was as transfixed as her grandmother's. As focused as every other woman in this room.

If Nico was scanning the room, looking for her as he kept moving, he certainly gave no indication of it. Anyone watching would assume he knew exactly what

table he was expected at. Charlotte could feel her grand-
mother's interest sharpen into astonishment as he fi-
nally made a beeline for their corner, his face lighting
up in a smile of sheer joy.

'Carlotta. *Cara*…' With his gaze locked on hers,
Nico reached out and cupped one side of her face with
his hand. It was an exquisitely tender touch. Over-
whelmingly so. Charlotte had no hope of collecting
her thoughts, let alone expressing them. His gaze sug-
gested that if she didn't want him to play this game she
only had to say the word, but how could she when she
couldn't even draw a breath?

And she saw the moment the question in his gaze
turned to delight.

Game on.

With a smoothness that suggested Nico was far too
good at acting, he turned his charm onto the unsus-
pecting Lady Geraldine. He gently picked up the hand
with its diamond rings flashing in the candlelight. He
pressed his lips to it.

'And you have to be Carlotta's *nonna*. I've heard so
much about you. This is…*such* a pleasure.'

And then Nico took hold of one of the two spare
chairs and moved it so that it was as close to Charlotte's
as possible. He sat down and adjusted the silverware
and then nodded at a nearby waiter, who instantly came
to fill his champagne glass.

Lady Geraldine was watching this little show with
rapt attention and she seemed as lost for words as Char-
lotte. Until Nico raised his glass, tilted his head in a
silent toast to the women, took a long sip and then…
smiled.

'Um…Charlotte?'

'Yes, Gran?'

'Is there something you haven't told me?'

This was her chance to pull the plug on this crazy plan that Nico seemed perfectly happy to put into action. To pretend—in public—that they were a couple in love.

Trouble was, even for the short time it had been happening, it was casting a spell that was unbelievably powerful.

They said that falling in love was magical. Maybe even pretending to be tapped into some of that incomprehensible power.

Whatever. Charlotte could feel the waves of envy coming from the other women in this space. She could see the gleam of joyous disbelief in her grandmother's eyes. Worst of all, she could almost feel what it *would* be like having someone like Nico head over heels in love with her.

And, God help her, she wanted more.

Just for an hour or two.

Just enough to give her a bubble of whatever this magic was so that she could remember it when times were bleak.

And there *were* going to be bleak times ahead.

Could there possibly be a greater gift she could give her beloved grandmother than to let her die with the peace of believing that the child she had raised was happy at last? That she would be loved and cared for in her absence?

It was a very strange feeling, this…giving in. Living in the moment without trying to weigh up any consequences or complications. It was incredibly liberating.

Fun—like Nico had suggested it could be? Something was certainly lifting the corners of Charlotte's mouth.

'Gran…this is…Nico.' Her words sounded hesitant. Breathless. The way they would if someone was about to reveal something secret. Something personal and precious.

'Nico Moretti,' he expanded. He laid his hand over Charlotte's on the crisp, white linen tablecloth as he smiled at Lady Geraldine. 'I am Charlotte's…' He hesitated, clearly at a loss for the right word to describe his relationship to her, and she held her breath. Could he really pull this off?

Nico turned his head and she could swear his sigh was one of pure happiness. 'I am whatever Carlotta will give me the honour of being,' he murmured.

'Charlotte?' The gentle word belied the 'please explain' undertone.

'It's been s-sudden,' Charlotte stammered. 'I was going to tell you today, Gran, but…'

'But then you started worrying about me.' Lady Geraldine clicked her tongue. 'For heaven's sake, child. This is *far* more important. I want to know everything.'

Oh, help… Charlotte tried to buy some thinking time by picking up her champagne glass. The Italian prosecco being served was astonishingly light. Delicious. She took another long sip.

'We actually met years ago,' Nico said into the expectant silence. 'At St Margaret's in London. It was my bad luck that Carlotta was unavailable at that time.'

Uh-oh… It took Lady Geraldine less than a split second to work out exactly what time Nico was refer-

ring to and that earned Charlotte a glance she would rather have avoided.

Gran knew there had been far more to the break-up of that relationship—the only one she'd ever known Charlotte to have—than she'd ever been privy to. It was the only aspect of Charlotte's life she'd ever been shut out of and it was a cloud that had hung over them ever since. Something that was never mentioned but always there.

Charlotte drank the last of her wine and barely noticed the waiter refilling her glass as she listened to Nico continuing to talk.

Why hadn't she thought that this pretence could open that particular can of worms?

And it was too late to stop it now. She was already in too deep.

About to drown?

He knew he'd said the wrong thing.

Nobody could have missed that electric glance that Lady Geraldine had speared her granddaughter with when he'd said that she had been otherwise attached when he'd first met her.

What the hell was that about?

Never mind. He knew he could redeem himself. He'd been quite confident of pulling this off from the moment he'd walked into this exclusive restaurant and spotted the table he needed to aim for.

The table where the two most beautiful women in the room were sitting.

Maybe Charlotte often wore an elegant silver dress to such a formal occasion but Nico had a strong sense

that it was not usual practice for her to leave her hair loose like that—a tumble of soft waves that gleamed an ash blonde in the candlelight. Had she be thinking of him when she'd brushed it out and chosen not to wind it back into its prison of pins?

And the grandmother! Nico had expected an English dowager of some kind. Tall and forbiddingly aloof. He had smiled the moment he'd set eyes on the old lady sitting beside Charlotte. Even from a distance he had caught the flash of her bejewelled hands and even a small tiara nestled in fiery red hair. He could sense her interest in the people around her and an ability to see beneath the surface of social niceties. This was going to be a much more entertaining evening than he could have hoped for.

'I can't tell you how often I've thought about her since then,' he told Lady Geraldine with palpable honesty. 'And then fate brings us together in the most romantic city in the world.' He shrugged, his smile suggesting he hadn't made much of an effort to stand firm against the winds of fate.

Was he overdoing things? Judging by the mistiness in Lady Geraldine's eyes, she was swallowing this very happily, but from the corner of his eye he could see that Charlotte was simply sitting there, staring at him, her lips slightly parted and her expression dazed.

He still had his hand covering hers, so he picked it up. Such a soft hand. Such elegant, long fingers and neat nails that were not disguised by any unnatural colours. He touched his lips to her hand and then leaned forward as though drawn irresistibly to kiss her lips next. They looked soft, too, and when Charlotte uncon-

sciously dampened them with the tip of her tongue, Nico realised that he actually *did* want to kiss her.

Dio… That wasn't meant to happen. He closed his eyes for a heartbeat to take control of the unexpected shaft of desire but then he let his breath out in a soft sigh. Did it matter? Charlotte wouldn't need to know it was anything other than good acting and it would certainly make his performance more believable. He opened his eyes and focused on the owner of the hand he still had imprisoned in his.

'It was meant to be,' he said softly. 'I'm lucky enough to have been given a second chance and even luckier that this beautiful woman seems to feel the same way.' He added a few words in Italian, knowing how limited Charlotte's grasp on the language was, and hoping that it would add to the impression of sincerity.

It had more of an effect than he had anticipated. Lady Geraldine sniffed delicately and picked up her linen serviette to dab at the corner of her eye.

'*Bella*,' she said, her Italian accent flawless. '*Carlotta è una ragazza fortunate.*'

Beneath his fingers, Charlotte's hand stiffened with tension. 'What?'

'She said you are a lucky girl,' Nico murmured. 'That the story of how we met is beautiful.'

'At last…' Lady Geraldine smiled mistily at her granddaughter. 'Oh, darling. I can't begin to tell you how happy this makes me. This…this is the best night of my *life*.'

Charlotte's lips trembled but she managed to smile. In the instant before she turned to look at her grand-

mother Nico caught the flash of emotion in her eyes that told him how huge this gift of happiness was.

And she couldn't have given her grandmother this if it hadn't been for him. It made him proud.

It made him want to give *more*.

The interruption of the first course of their dinner arriving was a welcome distraction that gave Charlotte time to try and collect herself. Not that she had the slightest appetite and she couldn't help her gaze straying sideways to look at Nico at noticeably frequent intervals as she wondered how he could be so incredibly good at this pretence, but that was just the sort of behaviour a woman who'd just fallen head over heels in love would display, wasn't it?

No wonder Gran believed it all. Charlotte had been sucked in herself. She'd totally forgotten the fear of the conversation touching on that no-go period in her life. And the way she'd felt when he'd picked up her hand and kissed it… No. What had been utterly shocking had been the way she'd felt when he'd leaned closer and looked as though he was about to kiss her on the lips.

The hum of conversation around them and the elegant strains of the Christmas carols being played by a quartet in the restaurant foyer had faded into nothing more than background static. The flickering light of the candles seemed to mirror the tiny flames licking her skin. Heating her blood and pooling somewhere deep in her belly.

A moment's madness, fuelled by what she could swear was an equal level of attraction in Nico's eyes. But they were dark eyes and the light was low. She

couldn't possibly have seen his pupils expand and she must have imagined the electric charge that came through her fingers where his skin was still in contact.

The shock of hearing her grandmother respond to Nico in Italian had been enough to break the extraordinary spell being cast, which was just as well. Nico was enjoying himself quite enough. How appalling would it be if he knew he was having a genuine effect on her?

Lady Geraldine wasn't eating much either, and that was enough to send Charlotte's thoughts in a darker direction. Her grandmother might be in her eighties but she had always been a woman of amazing energy who lived life to the full. Nobody would deny her the maximum extent of whatever modern medicine could do to prolong that colourful life, but you had to balance additional time earned by what the quality of that life would be. Major surgery and chemotherapy would be a miserable time and it was possible that the end would not justify the means.

Something like despair gathered in a cloud over Charlotte as she toyed with her entrée. Thank goodness Nico and her grandmother were so engaged in conversation. Nobody would thank her for destroying the joyous atmosphere that had been created at this particular table.

'So your mother is still living in Ireland?'

'Yes. With husband number four.'

'Good gracious! What was wrong with the first three?'

'My mother has trouble resisting offers that seem to give her a better opportunity to experience the best that life can give. She is a free spirit, Lady Geraldine, who

is not bothered by what others think. A bit like your-self, I'm guessing?'

Gran actually laughed with delight. If she'd had a fan in her hand, Charlotte thought, she might have smacked Nico's hand with it. Instead, the old lady gave him an almost shy smile.

'You can call me Jendi, dear,' she told him. 'As my friends do.'

'I'm honoured…Jendi.'

'And your father? Is he still living, too?'

'No.' Charlotte saw the way Nico laid down his fork as though he had caught the lack of appetite around him. 'He died some years ago now.'

'Oh…' The sound was one of sympathy. 'Too young. Was it an accident?'

'A broken heart.' Nico's voice was expressionless. He was stating a fact.

Charlotte couldn't help her eyebrows rising at such a non-medical notion from a man with his training. She didn't say anything but maybe her breath had escaped with a disparaging sound because Nico flicked a glance in her direction. His words, however, were directed at Lady Geraldine. His new *friend*.

'They called it a heart attack, of course,' he said. 'But his heart broke when my mother left him and on every visit I made back here, I could see his slow decline.'

'That's terrible,' Lady Geraldine declared. She was frowning now. 'But at least it hasn't put you off mar-riage, Nico.'

'M-marriage?'

The word was so shocked that Charlotte knew the game might be up. Had it not occurred to him that it

was a natural direction for someone's thoughts to go in when faced by two people who were 'meant to be together' and had made the connection at last?

'Early days, Gran,' she said in a stage whisper across the table. 'Don't frighten the poor man.'

'Frightened? Me?' To give him credit, Nico recovered fast. He actually winked at Lady Geraldine. 'We men like to pick our own time, that's all. The element of surprise, you understand?'

'Oh, of course.' Lady Geraldine beamed at him. 'I promise I'll be surprised.'

She wouldn't be the only one. Nico was only supposed to be posing as her new boyfriend, that's all. Something that would make Gran happy because it offered hope for her not having a lonely future. This was getting out of hand. He was sharing family secrets as though he was already a prospective grandson-in-law.

How on earth was she going to explain what had happened here tonight if, by some miracle, her grandmother's treatment was effective and she lived for years after this?

The interruption of formal speeches in praise of the symposium and its organisers filled in the time between courses and prevented any further bonding between her gran and Nico, but it didn't lessen the increasing tension Charlotte was experiencing. It only got worse as people began to mingle between the tables and Richard Campbell came to say hello.

'Did you enjoy listening to Charlotte this morning, Lady Geraldine?'

'Oh, I did. So much. Thank you for arranging things,

Dr Campbell. I am the happiest woman in the world tonight.'

'So I see.' It was impossible not to respond to the glow her grandmother was exuding. No one would believe that she could be facing confirmation of a terminal disease within days. And the misty look she was giving the young couple at her table was just as easy to read. Richard's jaw sagged visibly as he followed her gaze.

'Charlotte? You and…?'

'Nico Moretti,' Nico said, extending his hand.

A new challenge, then. Could he pull off this pretence with the people who worked with Charlotte?

'Delighted to meet you, Richard. Although I think we met some years ago. At St Margaret's?'

'That was where he first met Charlotte,' Lady Geraldine put in.

'Mmm.' Richard was giving Charlotte a strange look and Nico's heart sank. He remembered that impression he'd had when he'd been listening to her speak this morning. That her playing down her femininity might reveal a sexual preference that didn't include men. Maybe her closest colleagues were aware of something that was kept strictly private. Something she didn't want her grandmother to know, either.

Was that what had been hidden beneath that absolute conviction that she would never be fulfilling her grandmother's dearest wish of settling down and having babies? Suspicion on Jendi's part might also explain that charged glance directed at her granddaughter, which he'd inadvertently provoked.

Charlotte certainly seemed bothered by something.

As soon as possible after Richard moved on to another table, she excused herself, muttering about needing a bathroom. He saw her ask a waiter for directions and then head out a door that led to a long balcony. Presumably the bathrooms opened off the balcony to one side of the restaurant.

Which meant that Nico could also excuse himself and head in that direction. He could catch Charlotte before she came back into the dining room and just check that he wasn't causing even more trouble for her, although exactly how to broach the subject of her sexuality in a sensitive manner was entirely beyond him at the moment.

The balcony ran right along the canal side of the restaurant. It was quiet out here with the added darkness that came from the still water of the canal. Nico didn't need to use the facilities so he paced back and forth, waiting what seemed an interminably long time for Charlotte to reappear. What was she doing in there? Twisting her hair back into some impossibly tight 'hairdo'? He hoped not.

A gondola drifted past below with just a single light making the ornate brass ornament on the prow of the boat gleam. A couple sat, wrapped in blankets against the cold and silent as they gazed in wonder at the magic of touring this city at night with only the ripple of the boat to disturb the serenity.

The tap of high heels on stone disturbed the moment for Nico. He turned and Charlotte's step faltered.

'What are you doing out here?'

'Waiting for you.'

The only light now that the gondola had passed

came from the fairy lights of the restaurant and a small Christmas tree that was being used to reveal where the door to the bathrooms was. Silver light that made Charlotte's dress shine and cast a spotlight on the way the fabric clung to her body and revealed noticeable curves. It also caught matching strands in her hair. It would look golden in the sunshine, Nico thought. Chameleon hair. He could imagine her eyes could create that illusion too. Maybe they would take on a blue hue under a summer sky. Or when she was happy?

Right now they were a stormy, slate grey.

'Why?'

She sounded nervous and added to that impression by pushing her fingers through her hair. The gesture ruffled the loose waves. It was a supremely feminine movement. Confusing, given what Nico was there intending to find out. The reminder made him shake off his focus on how unexpectedly attractive Charlotte was looking. He cleared his throat.

'I...um... It seems to be going well. Your *nonna* is happy.'

'Mmm.' He could see Charlotte swallow. A ripple that ran the length of her elegant neck. 'Too happy, maybe.'

'Is there such a thing? Especially at a time like this?'

Charlotte sighed. 'She *is* happy. I don't think I've ever seen her look so...so contented.'

'There you go, then. It's been a good thing to do. A reprieve from thinking about less happy things. One that you may be able to use for some time.'

Charlotte looked away, watching the tail end of the gondola as it turned a corner. 'But I didn't think things

through. I thought other people would just think you were sharing our table for dinner.' Her voice rose and the words sped up a little, revealing how unsettled she was. 'I didn't expect to start a rumour that will follow me back to St Margaret's. I have no idea what I'm going to do about that.'

'You don't have to do anything.' Nico paused, trying to select his words carefully. 'Unless it's going to cause personal distress?'

She frowned at him. 'What kind of personal distress?'

'Well…you might have someone in your life that wouldn't be happy to know about this…this illusion you're creating.'

'I don't…' She was trying to process his meaning. Then she made an impatient sound. 'I told you I wasn't in a relationship.'

'Not with *Mr* Right,' he murmured.

There was a moment's dead silence and then Charlotte's eyes widened. 'Oh, my God…you think I'm a—' An incredulous huff broke her words. 'Are you *serious*?' And then she turned away but not before Nico had seen a fierce sparkle in her eyes.

Oh…*Dio*… He'd really put his foot in it now, hadn't he? Was she about to start crying again?

No matter. He had come prepared. He reached for the neatly pressed handkerchief he'd pushed into his jacket pocket just before he'd left his room. He pulled it out and, as he did so, something glinted in the light and bounced on the stones with an audible *ping*.

Charlotte turned her head. 'What was that?'

'Nothing important.' Nico knew what it was. It had

been weighing his pocket down earlier today. But then he'd forgotten all about it after he'd arrived at the symposium. After he'd been swept along by listening to the story Charlotte had told them. Weirdly, it hadn't occurred to him to think about it again all day. Or remember to take it out of his pocket.

His grandmother's ring. The one his father had given his mother. The one she'd left behind when she'd broken the marriage and Nico's true family. Maybe it was better if it got left behind at the bottom of a Venetian canal. Drowned and lost. Like his belief in true love and marriage and happy families for ever had been lost so many years ago.

But no. This ring was the only thing his father had left him as his inheritance. The only link he could touch that went back to his early childhood. It was important. Nico ignored Charlotte and his gaze raked the rough stones as he searched for what he'd dropped. It must have come out of his pocket at speed, propelled by being caught in the folds of the handkerchief. Had it already bounced irretrievably into the waters of the canal?

Like Charlotte's laptop?

No. There it was, precariously balanced right beside a stone balustrade on the very edge of the balcony. He would have to be careful not to nudge it over the edge, he realised as he stooped. Trying to slow his movement, Nico dropped to one knee and reached for the ring.

'What on *earth* are you doing?' Nico could see the ripple of the long, silver dress as Charlotte stepped closer. He sighed and held the object up to show her.

'It's my grandmother's ring,' he said heavily. 'It's a long story…'

He wasn't going to get a chance to tell her any of it, however. A startling shriek cut through the night air.

'Charlotte! Nico! Oh, my goodness…' Lady Geraldine had come out through the restaurant doors and was standing there, her hands clasped in front of her as though in prayer. 'Is this…? Are you…? Oh…how *romantic*. A proposal. In Venice, of all places…'

It took a long moment for the full horror to sink in but, yes…here he was, on one knee. Kneeling in front of a beautiful woman with a backdrop of a Venetian canal, holding up what was obviously an engagement ring in his hand.

He bought a fraction of time by getting to his feet somewhat awkwardly. He caught the panicked look in Charlotte's eyes. They were going to have to confess now, weren't they? Ruin the happiest night of this sick old lady's life.

No. He could fix this.

With the ghost of a wink to let Charlotte know he had things in hand, Nico grabbed her hand and shoved the ring onto her finger. It was a tight fit but he gave it an extra push to get it over her knuckle. Was it pain that made Charlotte gasp? Maybe it was the shock of how fast he'd moved or this unexpected twist in the show they were putting on. That didn't matter either. Maybe people would think she was simply shocked at how quickly he had managed to sweep her off her feet.

He kept hold of Charlotte's hand and gave it a squeeze. She dragged her gaze up from the ring and met his eyes and he tried very hard to give her a silent message.

Trust me. We can get through this without hurting anybody.

And then he turned and pasted a smile onto his face.

'Jendi... What wonderful timing. We wanted *you* to be the first to know.'

CHAPTER FIVE

'I KNEW ALREADY.' Lady Geraldine was coming towards them with surprising sprightliness given her age and state of health. 'Nobody can hide the glow of true love…' Tears were running down her wrinkled cheeks as she got close enough to embrace Charlotte. 'Oh, my dear…I'm *so* happy for you.'

She must feel like she was hugging a tree, Charlotte realised, but she couldn't make her body soften. Or even raise the arms now hanging by her sides like dead branches. One of them was even weighed down with an enormous rock. No… She had to be dreaming. He couldn't *really* have shoved that ring on her finger, could he?

Still dazed, Charlotte lifted her left arm. It looked like she was returning her grandmother's effusive hug but, in reality, she was getting her hand to a position where she could see it.

Yep. There it was. On her third finger. A quite respectably sized solitaire diamond in an antique gold setting. Definitely an engagement ring. What on earth did Nico Moretti think he was playing at, walking around with an engagement ring in his pocket?

Words floated into through the sludge in her head. His grandmother's ring. *A long story*.

No story could be long enough to rescue her from this escalating nightmare. What was that saying Gran used to deliver with a wagging finger? Something about the complicated web you weave when first you practise to deceive. Charlotte shook her head to clear the mist. This had to end. Now.

'This isn't what is seems, Gran. I'm not engaged. This is…ridiculous.'

'Oh, I know, darling.' The grip Lady Geraldine still had on her increased a notch. 'You weren't expecting this, were you?'

'Of course I wasn't.' A snort of something like laughter escaped her throat. 'Nico and I have only just met. We're not even…' Charlotte raised her gaze as she searched for the right word to explain the total lack of a genuine relationship between them. It brought her line of vision directly over her grandmother's shoulder. And it locked with Nico's gaze.

He had one eyebrow raised and a curiously disappointed stillness to the rest of his face . What dismissive word was she going to come up with here?

That they weren't even *friends*?

That they weren't connected in any way, shape or form?

Except they were, weren't they?

They'd become connected totally by chance when they'd formed a united medical team to help the man who'd had the cardiac arrest and fallen from the scaffolding. Having him present when she had been floundering in front of so many distinguished symposium

attendees this morning had been what had given her the strength to give any kind of presentation at all. The thought that he might have been impressed had made her feel like she hadn't failed.

Having him right there when she had been already starting to grieve for Gran had been what had given her the strength to try and make whatever time her beloved grandmother had left as happy as possible.

And the way she'd felt when he'd looked at her like that at the table. As if he was in love with her. As if he'd wanted to kiss her.

Oh, yes…she couldn't deny a physical *and* emotional connection to him even if she didn't want it to be there. Somehow Nico had broken through her safety barriers. Despite the short time they had known each other—less than a day, for heaven's sake—he was already enmeshed in her personal life in a way that no man had ever been.

'I know, darling.' Lady Geraldine's soothing words took her back. Way back to when it had seemed that nobody could ever understand. Or put things right. And yet the words had always been sincere. And Gran had always put things right, no matter how long it had taken. 'People will think it's too soon. *You* think it's too soon.'

'Of course I do. It's…it's…' *Ridiculous.* But Charlotte's gaze was still holding Nico's as she tried to read the silent message he was sending. It was a reassuring message, whatever it was. How was she supposed to interpret that? Or believe that this was somehow okay.

'It's love at first sight, that's what it is,' Lady Geraldine said happily. 'The best sort. Wearing Nico's ring doesn't mean you have to get married next week, dar-

ling. It's just a promise of commitment. You can take all the time you need to make sure that it's perfect.'

All the time they needed to keep Gran happy for as long as she lived?

Time.

That's what Charlotte needed.

'It will take time.' Nico's voice was strong. Amazingly calm, considering. 'And you're right, Jendi. I have…what's that expression? Jumped the gun.'

Something about the way he recited the phrase made Charlotte think his choice of words was deliberate. He was reminding her of the euphemism she'd used about kicking the bucket. Reminding her of what was important here. And maybe it was a warning, too.

If she destroyed this illusion she would be ruining not one but two of the items on Gran's bucket list. There was no way the train trip could provide the slightest pleasure if the number-one item on the list was revealed as a deception.

Geraldine let Charlotte go with a final pat. She turned and looked up at Nico, who smiled at her.

'We will have to be apart a lot in the coming weeks,' he said sadly. 'I have commitments in the United States and Europe. In Australia, even. But I had to do something to make my intentions as clear as possible. To achieve what I know will make us *both* happy.' Make us *all* happy, his glance reminded Charlotte.

'Of course you did.' Lady Geraldine beamed.

Charlotte's mind was clearing rapidly. Nico was presenting an easy way out here. He could be her fiancé but he would be absent. She could keep her grandmother happily believing that a wedding was on the cards with-

out any further awkwardness of them having to keep up the pretence for real. Or, if she couldn't bear to be less than honest, she could say that things had fizzled out in a few weeks and use the excuse that it would never have worked. They would never have enough time together to keep the relationship alive.

'Mmm.' The sound came out in a strangled fashion. 'I'm still not sure—'

'Of course you're not.' Lady Geraldine slipped her arm through Charlotte's and began to lead her back to the restaurant. 'You like to be in control, child, and you've been swept off your feet.' She slipped her other arm through Nico's. 'Come on. We'll all go and have another glass of that lovely champagne and give Charlotte time to get used to this delightfully unexpected state of being an *engaged* woman.'

Dio mio...

What, exactly, had happened there?

It wasn't the unexpected twist of events that had led to Charlotte now wearing his grandmother's ring that was disturbing Nico most as he followed the women back to the restaurant.

No. It went far deeper than a pretence that was now a little more complicated than intended. Something had happened when Charlotte had been caught in that loving embrace and had looked at him over her grandmother's shoulder. When she'd been searching for a way of trying to explain that this was all a lie. That there was nothing of any significance between them.

She hadn't been able to, had she? Because she'd felt the same thing he had when their gazes had touched

and locked. Somehow, over the course of this crazy day, they *had* connected. And on a level that was totally alien to Nico. Inexplicable and deeply disturbing but, at that moment, he would have overturned heaven and earth to protect Charlotte. To extricate her in a dignified fashion from this mess he had created.

He had no idea what had triggered such a strong urge. Guilt from knowing he'd pushed her into this? Or maybe he'd caught another glimpse of that lost and frightened child in her eyes. He'd certainly seen desperation that had been coming from not wanting to hurt somebody she loved so much. Maybe that explained why he was feeling as though the ground was shifting beneath his feet and that the rules he lived by were no longer relevant.

Knowing that Charlotte was capable of that kind of love when, to outward appearances, she was incapable of that much emotion. Knowing that she was such a different woman from the one he'd met years ago. Curiosity was a powerful motivating force and Nico wanted to put as many pieces of this puzzle together as he could before he moved on.

Maybe when he had the full picture he would be able to understand why he was feeling as if he was caught in some invisible web. And then he would be able to avoid it happening again. He liked his life exactly the way it was, thanks very much. He did not like this feeling of long-held beliefs wobbling and his footing being less than secure in his world.

Back at the table, Lady Geraldine waved a bejewelled hand and waiters willingly rushed to refill glasses and serve exquisite-looking desserts. Charlotte was sit-

ting very still, staring at the chocolate creation on the small plate in front of her as though unsure whether it was, in fact, edible.

Or maybe she was unsure whether anything was real. Perhaps she was hoping to wake up and find that this whole evening had simply been a bad dream. Her grandmother was also watching her and then she turned to Nico and smiled. It was an expression of understanding. And reassurance. Charlotte just needed a little more time, the glance suggested. And then she would be able to embrace the joy of this new event in her life.

She certainly needed something. A gentle reminder of why they'd started this charade in the first place?

Nico smiled back at Lady Geraldine. 'Tell me about tomorrow,' he invited. 'I hear you have an adventure planned. On the Orient Express?'

Lady Geraldine beamed at him. 'It's been a long-held dream of mine. One of them, anyway.' She slid another glance at Charlotte and there was a moment's pause as she sighed happily. Then she collected herself and focused on Nico. 'Have you ever travelled on the Orient Express yourself?'

'No. I've heard of it, of course. It has a wonderful history, doesn't it?'

'Right back to 1883.' Lady Geraldine nodded. 'It's the world's most famous train and it's been totally restored to its original glory. You step back in time and travel in the kind of elegant luxury that only the very privileged could afford a hundred years ago. It's an experience everybody should have at least once in their lifetime, don't you think?'

'Absolutely.' Nico was happy to agree. This was what

this evening was about after all. To make Charlotte's grandmother happy. To encourage her to make the most of whatever time she had left in her own lifetime. To tick off those 'bucket-list' items. 'I hear that the food is amazing and isn't there someone that plays a grand piano in the bar?'

'Oh, yes.' Lady Geraldine's smile was misty now. 'Everybody dresses in their best and is on their best behaviour. We'll all be thoroughly spoiled as we glide through Italy, Austria, Switzerland and France and back to London just in time for Christmas.'

She eyed Nico over a spoon containing a tiny portion of chocolate mousse. 'I expect you'll be visiting your mother for Christmas Day, Nico?'

'Ah…no.' Nico shook his head. 'I believe her new husband has whisked her off to New Zealand to have Christmas in the sun.'

'But you have other family?'

Uh-oh… Any moment now he was going to be invited to have Christmas dinner with Charlotte and her grandmother. He needed to head this one off at the pass.

'Sadly, I have work commitments in London I can't break. That's partly why I'm taking a day or two at my leisure in Venice now.' This was true enough, wasn't it? He was always happy to work over family-oriented holidays to give his colleagues time off. He didn't have a family to spend time with. And he didn't want one. Nico shifted in his seat, which brought his knee into contact with Charlotte's. He heard her sudden intake of breath and she finally seemed to become aware of her surroundings again.

Good. He needed some help here to avoid being pres-

sured into joining the Highton clan for Christmas dinner. Who knew how many other distant but formidable relatives Charlotte might have waiting in the wings?

Lady Geraldine had a very benign smile on her face right now as she apparently enjoyed her taste of the dessert but Nico had the distinct feeling that the impression of a sweet old lady was probably deceptive. There was an ironclad will beneath that perfectly groomed exterior and that improbable red hair. What Lady Geraldine wanted, she would no doubt get. Except, maybe, the chance to live to an even riper old age.

He reached for his glass of wine. He increased the pressure on Charlotte's knee a little to encourage her to say something but she was watching her grandmother, who was shaking her head as she put down her spoon.

'Absolutely delicious,' she said sadly. 'But I can't eat it.'

Nico could feel the tension in Charlotte's focus. 'You've hardly eaten anything, Gran.'

'I'm too excited,' Lady Geraldine said.

'About the Orient Express?' This was a good direction to steer the conversation back to. A safe one. 'I'm not surprised. It's probably a good idea to save your appetite for all that wonderful food.'

'Mmm…' Lady Geraldine nodded thoughtfully. 'I *am* excited about the train trip but not nearly as excited as I am about this engagement.' She reached over and took hold of Charlotte's hand, bending the fingers so that the diamond ring took centre stage. 'I don't think I've ever been so happy.' She was locked in eye contact with her granddaughter. 'You will be, too, Charlotte Jane. I just know you will.'

Charlotte's indrawn breath was ragged. 'But...'

'I know, darling.' Nico could see the way Charlotte's fingers were being squeezed. Lady Geraldine's voice was soft. 'And it doesn't matter if I don't live to see the wedding. This is enough. To know that you've met such a wonderful man and the attraction is strong enough to be totally irresistible. It's a promise of a happy future for you...and I intend to enjoy every single moment of it.'

She straightened in her chair and turned her gaze to Nico. 'I have two cabin suites booked on the Orient Express,' she said unexpectedly. 'I wanted both Charlotte and myself to enjoy this trip as much as possible, without being cramped.'

'Good thinking.' Nico nodded. Thank goodness the topic of conversation was getting back onto safe territory. 'I'm sure you'll enjoy every moment.'

'Oh, I will. Especially now.'

There was something in the gaze from those faded blue eyes that made Nico feel like a small child again. A small child confronted by someone in ultimate authority.

'Because of the engagement?' Nico's smile was a little forced. He should be pleased because this represented exactly what he'd set out to achieve but he had a sinking feeling that he wasn't going to get off quite this easily.

'Exactly,' Lady Geraldine purred.

Maybe he was. Nico's smile widened.

'I can't think of a better way to celebrate,' Lady Geraldine continued, 'Can you?'

'No. What could possibly be a better way to celebrate

than the very best of food and wine while you travel in ultimate luxury?'

'I'm so pleased you agree. I'll let the train manager know that you'll be joining us.'

'What?' Both Nico and Charlotte uttered the horrified exclamation simultaneously.

'It's perfect,' Lady Geraldine said calmly. 'You don't have commitments until Christmas Day, Nico, and we'll be back in London by Christmas Eve. As you said yourself, what better way could there be to celebrate? It sounds as though you and Charlotte are going to have a lot of time apart in the near future and I'm sure we all agree that we should all make the most of every moment we can have together. Who knows how many of them there will be?'

Her voice wobbled just a little as she finished speaking. Charlotte's jaw had been dropping but now it snapped shut.

'You can't do this, Gran,' she said slowly. 'You can't use something like your illness to make people do what you want them to do. It's…it's emotional blackmail.'

'Nonsense.' Any hint of frailty vanished from Lady Geraldine's demeanour. 'It's common sense, that's what it is. You're both important, busy people. You'd never make the time for something like this unless someone pushed you into it. And this is a once-in-a-lifetime opportunity. Do you have any idea how hard it was for me to get a booking on this train? And *two* cabins. If it had only been one, I would have given up my place so that you and Nico could have done the trip together.'

'But this is *your* dream, Gran.' Charlotte was shak-

ing her head now, looking bewildered. 'Why would Nico and I want to do it?'

'Because it's the most romantic journey on earth,' Lady Geraldine said. 'You've found each other in the most romantic city and by astonishing good fortune you now have the chance to build on that by travelling together to the destination you were both heading for anyway. I'm not going to take you away from Nico the day after you've just become engaged, Charlotte. This is my engagement gift to you both—some more time together. If he won't come with us on the train, then you can stay here and I'll go by myself.'

'No...you can't do that. I won't let you. You're not well enough.'

It was a stand-off. Nico didn't need the combined effect of both women looking at him to know he was expected to say something to defuse the tension but, for the life of him, he couldn't think of anything to say. For heaven's sake, all he needed was an excuse that would keep him at least somewhere in Europe for the next twenty four hours but his mind was blank. Stunned at the way this...diversion had taken on a life of its own. Moving at a pace that appeared as unstoppable as the train he was now expected to board tomorrow.

Tables were being cleared around them and any moment now the waiters would come and interrupt this awkward silence, but clearly it wouldn't be soon enough for Charlotte. She made an exasperated sound as she pushed back her chair and got to her feet.

'I need some air,' she announced. 'I'll leave *you* to talk to Gran, Nico.'

Her tone suggested that he was unlikely to get any-

where but that it was his problem. He'd got himself into this mess and now he could get himself out of it. Her body language as she headed towards the balcony suggested that she was washing her hands of the whole situation because it was clearly uncontrollable. The slump of her shoulders said that she didn't believe he could do it without causing harm.

And maybe she was right. Maybe now he was going have to confess his part in this deception. Was there a way he could do that and convince Lady Geraldine at the same time that it had been done with the very best of intentions and that Charlotte had only gone along with his stupid idea because she loved her grandmother so much?

Nico took a deep breath and opened his mouth but Lady Geraldine got there first to fill the silence.

'Oh, dear…' she murmured. 'And there I was, hoping that she'd finally got over it all…'

Nico couldn't help himself. 'Over what, Jendi?'

Lady Geraldine looked uncomfortable. 'That's the problem, Nico. I've never been able to find out.' She raised her eyebrows. 'I was hoping you might be able to tell *me*.'

'Scusi?' The Italian word popped out, as they often did in moments of great stress or surprise.

'There's only been one other occasion when I've thought that Charlotte might have found the right man for her. The person she was going to spend the rest of her life with. To raise her own family with. And it was *years* ago. Back when she was just a baby doctor and everybody could see how brilliant she was. *Is*,' Lady Geraldine corrected herself but she was frowning. 'I

don't know what went wrong,' she continued softly, almost as if she was talking aloud to herself, 'but Charlotte…changed.'

Yes. He was getting to the heart of the mystery now.

'That was the time I first met her,' he confided to Jendi. 'When she was the star of the emergency department and nobody could sing her praises highly enough. And she was so happy. There was a sparkle about her that lit up a room. A smile that advertised such confidence…' His voice trailed off as he realised the extent of how radically Charlotte had changed.

The confidence was still there but it was only professional. Cold. That's what had hit him this morning—that lack of sparkle for want of a better word. It was only when he had pushed himself beyond any acceptably professional boundaries that he'd seen a hint of a woman capable of *real* emotion. That buttoned-up outward appearance was like a suit of armour around the old Charlotte.

Whatever had happened had killed her personal confidence. Her hopes for a future outside her work ambitions. Had she been brutally dismissed by a man she'd been deeply in love with?

How could the man have been such an idiot to pass up a woman like Charlotte?

And why did the thought of her being passionately in love with another man stir up a nasty sensation in his gut that he couldn't identify? Was it jealousy? No. That was absurd. He had never felt jealous in his life.

'I saw her out with that man,' he told Jendi. 'At a very exclusive London club. I think we were even introduced. Was he a *prince*?'

Lady Geraldine made a dismissive sound. 'That's what he called himself. He was a long way down the tree of some obscure European royal family. He was certainly a very charming young man. And very sure of himself.'

'So what happened?'

'Charlotte will never talk about it. I didn't see her for a few weeks. She said she had flu and didn't want to pass it on. And then she always had an excuse of being too busy at work to come to see me and when she finally did I was…shocked.'

'Why?' Nico leaned forward, unconsciously holding his breath.

'She looked…ill. So thin. And…' Lady Geraldine shook her head very slowly and when she raised her gaze to Nico's he could see tears in her eyes. 'You hit the nail right on the head, my dear. Her sparkle had gone. It was like it had been when she first arrived in my care as an orphaned child. When she was so lost and unhappy that she wouldn't even speak. For *months*.'

'She wouldn't speak to you?'

'Oh, no. She wasn't a tiny child any more. She would talk but only if we didn't talk about *him*. Siegfried. All she would say was that the relationship was over and it wasn't important. The only thing that mattered was her work.'

Lady Geraldine looked away. 'I thought if I gave her enough space that she would eventually talk to me about it, but it's been nearly six years and after the first attempt or two I had to give up. It's the one thing that's never discussed but is always there. The elephant in the room, you know?'

'The elephant?' How many odd English phrases were going to test him today?

'The huge thing. You can't ignore it because you always have to walk around it to get anywhere. But you're not allowed to mention it because, if you do, the door gets slammed shut and you can't get anywhere at all.'

'Hmm...' Nico was digesting the information. He was silent for a long time and when he spoke, his voice was uncharacteristically grim. 'He hurt her,' he said softly. 'He hurt Charlotte badly, this *Siegfried*.'

'Yes.' Lady Geraldine dabbed at the corner of her eyes with her napkin.

'Physically?'

The gasp was shocked. 'Oh, *no*... If he'd done that, she would have gone to the police, surely?'

'But you said she looked unwell.'

'She'd had flu. There was a very bad flu going around that year. One of those bird varieties, I think.'

Nico wasn't listening. How could anyone have wanted to hurt Charlotte? She had been so beautiful. A girl testing the wings of womanhood. In love and totally trusting. What kind of bastard had he been and what had he *done* to her? Nico didn't believe the 'flu' excuse for a moment. And something was telling him that the pain of the broken relationship had not been simply emotional.

'I need to talk to Charlotte,' he said, his chair scraping on the stone-flagged floor as he pushed it back.

Lady Geraldine caught his arm as he turned to leave. Her age and state of health disappeared from Nico's awareness as he read her expression. It was the look of a mother as well as a grandmother. Ageless. She needed

to protect her child and she wasn't sure if she should
have spoken about her concerns. There was a plea in
her eyes that Nico could read only too well.

'I'm not going to hurt her.' The words came out like a
vow and Nico meant every one of them. 'I never would.
That I can promise you.'

Charlotte was freezing.

An evening dress was entirely inadequate for a win-
ter's night in Venice but she couldn't go back inside.
She could see that the evening was winding up now and
people were leaving.

Good. If she waited a little longer, there would be no
audience for when she had to go back in and face her
grandmother after Nico had explained why he couldn't
accompany them on the Orient Express.

She could see them through the tall, arched window.
Their body language was intense as they leaned towards
each other, oblivious to anyone else in the room. The
fairy lights made the room seem like another world and
Charlotte could see the Christmas images still scroll-
ing against the far wall. Snowmen and sleighs. Christ-
mas trees and prettily wrapped parcels. Happy people.
Families. Parents with excited children.

Parents who had once been lovers. Engaged couples.

Charlotte was twisting the ring on her finger without
realising it. She gave it a tug. Good grief...it was a tight
fit. She was going to need soap to get it off. Maybe she
should go into the bathroom and find some.

But then she saw Nico get to his feet abruptly and
she saw the way her grandmother caught his arm. For
a moment that seemed suspended in time she saw the

way they looked at each other and the light was enough for her to see the expression on Nico's face. Such a *kind* expression. Loving. Intense. The kind of look someone might have if they were making a promise they intended to keep.

Or maybe he'd been apologising. Was he coming out to tell her it was safe to go back in now?

Charlotte's heart picked up as Nico came out onto the balcony. He moved with such grace, this man. A calm assurance that he could command his environment and protect anyone within it. Powerful but not intimidating because there was a softness about him. That slow, easy smile. The glint in those dark eyes that advertised the ability to find joy in life. To play.

That's what they'd been doing tonight and Charlotte couldn't deny that, for a while, it had been…fun. No. Fun wasn't the word. What had drawn her in had been the illusion. The need to taste something that was so seductive it was irresistible. The illusion of being in love.

With Nico.

She had to turn her head and stop staring at him as if the charade was still continuing.

'Did you talk to Gran?'

'I did.' Nico was close to her now.

'Did you tell her the truth? Does she understand why you can't come on the train with us?' Charlotte couldn't repress a shiver. Was it the cold or the disappointment of failure?

'Not exactly.' Nico was shrugging off his jacket. He stepped closer and draped it over Charlotte's shoulders.

Her first instinct was to shrug the garment off with a dismissive shake. She wasn't a child who needed some-

one to take care of her. She could look after herself, thanks very much.

But the gesture had been unexpectedly thoughtful. *Caring.*

And the warmth was astonishingly comforting. Charlotte could feel her fingers creeping to the edges of the jacket to pull it closer around her. The warmth was the warmth of Nico's body. The slide of the silk lining against the bare skin of her arms and shoulders made it feel as though *he* was touching her.

It was disturbingly intimate now. Charlotte could even catch a whiff of a scent that was pure male. Pure Nico? She had to close her eyes for a heartbeat as she tried to stop herself inhaling deeply.

'Your grandmother loves you very much,' Nico said quietly. 'She does not want you to be hurt…again.'

Again? Her eyes snapped open. Oh, my God…what had they been talking about in there? But Gran didn't know the truth so she couldn't have told Nico. She was safe.

So why didn't she *feel* safe?

'W-what did *you* say?'

Nico looked more serious than she'd seen him look all day. Even when he'd been arriving at a potentially fatal incident. The subdued look didn't sit well on a face that was made for laughter. Her heart skipped another beat.

'I told her that I would never hurt you.'

'So she still thinks that we're…we're *engaged*?'

Nico's mouth twitched. 'I'm afraid so. I couldn't bring myself to cause her pain.'

It shouldn't be such a relief. Not when Charlotte couldn't see any way out of this.

'And the train?'

Nico shrugged. 'I have a free day. I have to get back to London. Why not?'

'Because…it's impossible. How could we keep this up for thirty hours?' Charlotte had another try at tugging the ring off her finger, looking away from him as she did so.

She could see past Nico to where the final guests for the evening were leaving. Only her grandmother remained and the maître d' was looking concerned, helping the elderly woman to her feet. Lady Geraldine was pointing towards the balcony. And now she was walking towards the door.

'Nothing is impossible,' Nico was saying.

'She's coming. She'll guess. She's not stupid.'

'She won't guess if you stop trying to remove that ring.' Nico caught her hands. 'If we…'

His hands moved, pulling hers up to his neck before he let them go. His hands kept moving, though, burying themselves in her hair. Cupping the back of her head and tilting it as he leaned in to cover her mouth with his own.

He was *kissing* her.

Just for show. To cover an awkward moment when Gran might have picked up on the tension between them.

Except…it didn't feel like a pretend kiss.

Or maybe it did, for that first, startled moment as their lips made contact, but then Nico's lips moved with a kind of question that Charlotte couldn't help respond-

ing to on some deep, instinctive level that totally overruled any conscious thought. Her lips parted beneath his and when she felt the touch of his tongue against hers all ability to control her thoughts vanished.

A fleeting hope that her grandmother would see them and stay well away to give them a private moment evaporated, along with any awareness of what was around them. Charlotte was completely lost in this kiss. Transported to a place she'd never been. A place where passion and tenderness combined to create an all-consuming fuel that could burn away anything and everything and leave only peace and fulfilment in its wake.

A kiss that promised everything. So much more than this touch of lips and tongues.

More…

And that was when Charlotte stopped being lost. She couldn't do more. If she tried, Nico would find out and he would know what was so wrong with her.

That she could go so far and no further. Because she was not a real woman. Real women liked going further. They weren't…*frigid*.

That did it. Just the tiniest echo of that hateful word was enough. Charlotte wrenched herself back from Nico's touch. His jacket slid from her shoulders and puddled on the stone terrace. She could turn to see what had happened, scoop up the jacket and try to collect herself before acknowledging her grandmother standing in the restaurant doorway.

'Oh…Gran… I'm so sorry. I…lost track of time.'

'So I see.' Lady Geraldine's smile warmed the winter's night.

Nico was rubbing his lips slowly with his forefin-

ger, staring at Charlotte, but now he also turned towards the door.

'You must be tired, Jendi. Let me see you both back to your hotel.'

'That would be lovely, Nico. Thank you. We have an early start tomorrow. I think we have to be at the Santa Lucia station by nine a.m. to catch the train.'

It was Charlotte's turn to stare at Nico but he didn't meet her gaze. Instead, he put an arm around her waist as they began moving.

'No problem,' he told her grandmother. 'I'm an early riser.'

CHAPTER SIX

'WHERE IS HE?'

'I don't know, Gran.' Charlotte allowed a small seed of hope to blossom that Nico might fail to show up in time. Or maybe that odd squeeze in her chest was disappointment?

Yep. There was definitely an internal struggle going on here. The safest thing was to never see Nico Moretti again and that's what she should want. And, yes, she could try and convince herself that she only wanted him around, continuing this pretence of a relationship, because it was such a joy to see her grandmother so happy, but there was no way of hiding the real truth. Part of her—a big, rebellious part of her—simply wanted to be close to him again.

'Maybe something came up.' Like a bout of common sense? 'He doesn't have our phone numbers so he might not have been able to let us know.'

The train was already here at the station, the sleek, dark blue carriages with the gold trim, the coat of arms featuring two rampant lions and the lettering announcing that this was, indeed, the Venice Simplon Orient Express. As if anyone could mistake it! Among the or-

dinary modern European trains in the station, this one
stood out like a beacon. So did the attendants. The gold-
trimmed blue uniforms looked positively military and
the pillbox hats the stewards were wearing made them
look ready for a fancy-dress party.

The check-in desk stood out on the grey concrete of
the platform in equally startling contrast. A red carpet,
of all things, with brass posts holding tasselled ropes to
create an oasis of luxury amidst the mundane. Even the
people milling around looked different. Like that young
woman in a long coat that belonged to another era, its
fur collar turned up around her neck. The people were
generally better dressed, certainly, but that wasn't the
only difference. There was an air of excitement that en-
cased this part of the station and separated it from the
rest. From the real world.

'I knew we should have offered to let him share our
water taxi.'

'It would have been a bit of a squeeze with all your
luggage, Gran.'

It had, in fact, taken an impressive tip to get the
water taxi driver to leave his boat tied up and carry
Gran's bags up the daunting flight of stairs leading into
the train station from the road beside the canal. 'You
did know you're only supposed to have one cabin bag
and one piece of luggage to be checked in, didn't you?'

Her grandmother sniffed. 'If you're going to do the
Orient Express, it must be done in style. Everybody
knows that. Goodness knows how you get away with
nothing more than an oversized handbag.'

Cabin luggage hadn't been all Charlotte had been
carrying on her way to Venice, of course. She'd had

her laptop bag to contend with as well. An accessory that was now lying on the bottom of a Venetian canal. She could remember the expression on Nico's face as he'd realised what had happened. So apologetic, even though it hadn't exactly been his fault. The willingness to do whatever he could to put things right.

He was a kind man. And a generous one. The tailored suit jacket Charlotte was wearing again today suddenly felt tight. Scratchy, almost, as her senses replayed the sensation of the silk lining of Nico's jacket against her bare skin. A sensation that morphed almost seamlessly into remembering that kiss.

How kind was he? Kind enough not to reveal astonishment…*disgust*…when he found out what Charlotte was lacking?

And then there was that very tiny seed of what was definitely hope because that kiss had made her feel things that no other kiss ever had—even Siegfried's. And if just a kiss felt that different, maybe other things would feel different too and maybe…just *maybe*…she'd be able to—

Oh, *help*… Wasn't it enough that her memory of that little scene had kept her awake virtually all night? She couldn't allow it to keep distracting her like this. Charlotte balanced her cabin bag on top of Gran's biggest suitcase and grabbed the handle of the other with her free hand. With a determined shove she began moving the luggage towards a check-in desk that looked suspiciously like an antique mahogany piece. Lady Geraldine pulled the handle of her smaller bag as she followed.

'You're going to have to wear the same dress for dinner tonight that you had on last night, aren't you?'

'What was wrong with my dress?' It had been the first time Charlotte had worn the slinky, silver number but she'd been delighted with how it had looked when she'd put it on. How good it had made her feel.

'It's a lovely dress, dear. You just need more than one of them.'

It was a lovely dress. And if Charlotte was honest, she'd felt way more than simply 'good' in it. The way Nico had run his eyes over it more than once, as though the experience was a pleasure all in itself. Yes…that dress had made her feel *beautiful*. An odd experience for a woman who did virtually nothing to enhance her appearance in order to attract the attention of the opposite sex.

'Nobody's going to know I'm wearing it two nights in a row.' Charlotte smiled at the woman behind the desk and handed over the tickets.

'Apart from your fiancé.'

The woman behind the desk was smiling. 'You must be Lady Geraldine. We got your message. We're delighted to be able to welcome Dr Moretti on board to accompany you and your granddaughter.'

'Um…there could be a small problem…' Charlotte began. But the woman wasn't listening. She wasn't even looking at her and the expression on her face suggested that she was looking at something far more interesting.

A tall and extremely attractive man, perhaps?

'*Cara…*' The endearment was a caress. 'I'm so sorry I'm late.' Nico pulled Charlotte into his arms and then bent to brush her lips in a perfectly acceptable kiss for a public place. Except it lingered for just a heartbeat too long. And his eyes lingered on hers even longer. Char-

lotte dragged in a breath. The part of her that wanted to be close to Nico was winning. Doing a happy dance inside her chest that made her heart thump and send extra blood up to warm her cheeks. The wash of relief was unmistakeable and hot on its heels was something she hadn't felt in years.

Excitement. The kind a small child would have creeping downstairs too early on Christmas morning and seeing the magic of the gifts under the tree. Gifts for *her*.

Did she dare to pick one up and rattle it? Tear off a tiny piece of wrapping paper to see if she could guess what was inside?

But what if it wasn't what she wanted? Maybe the anticipation was better than reality.

'I went to the hospital,' Nico explained. 'I knew you'd want to know how our man from yesterday was getting on.'

To her shame, no doubt due to the emotional rollercoaster the day had presented, Charlotte had barely given the man another thought. So much for her heartfelt presentation yesterday about the medicine they practised being about the people. But Nico was right. She could feel her face light up in her eagerness to know the outcome. This was the kind of excitement she was used to. *This* was what she needed to focus on.

'He's doing well.' Nico's smile was one of pure delight. 'He had an angioplasty and half a dozen stents put in. His broken leg's been sorted and he's sitting up in the coronary care unit and you'd never know he'd been dead for a while. No evidence of any brain damage even.'

'Really? That's…astonishing. Our CPR must have been up to standard, then.'

'A little more than that, I think.' Nico put his arm around Charlotte's shoulders as he turned towards Lady Geraldine. 'We are an amazing team. And here we are, about to have an adventure. I am the happiest man on earth.'

Lady Geraldine was beaming at them. The check-in clerk was smiling mistily but then she collected herself. 'Here are your boarding passes. We'll take care of the suitcases and you can take your cabin baggage with you. I wish you the happiest of journeys.'

Lady Geraldine merely nodded. 'It will be,' she said softly. She winked at Charlotte. 'All that remains to be seen is which of us is the happiest *woman* on earth today.'

Lady Geraldine needed some assistance to climb up the steps and negotiate the narrow corridor of the train carriage. The first impression was the glow of polished wood and brass. And lights. Lamps casting a soft glow. Fairy lights in honour of the season, looped at ceiling height on the internal wall and twinkling merrily. The doors had small wreaths festooned with artificial cherries and tiny golden bells.

Even more overwhelming than the warm glow of the wood and lights was a sense of confinement. The cabins were tiny with no more than a richly upholstered double seat and a tiny table beneath the window. A washstand was cleverly incorporated into a corner.

For most passengers this would have been their total space but with a suite, a door beside the washstand cabinet was open, leading to the adjoining cabin where the

seats had already been turned into comfortable-looking bunk beds with crisp white linen and soft-looking towels folded on the ends.

For one person, it would have been the ultimate in spaciousness aboard the train. For a couple, it still would have been more than enough. To share this amount of space with Nico Moretti was something entirely different. There didn't seem to be enough oxygen in the small spaces.

Their personal steward served champagne as the train pulled out of Santa Lucia station while Charlotte was checking that Lady Geraldine was settling comfortably into her suite. Nico joined them as the steward pointed out features of the cabins, including the bell that would summon him for assistance at any time of the day or night.

'The maître d' will visit your cabin soon to take your lunch and dinner reservations. Our restaurant cars have tables for two or four people.'

'We are a party of three,' Charlotte informed him. And how lucky was that? No chance of an intimate table for two with soft lighting and too much champagne. If she could put up good enough barriers around that part of her that was so drawn to this man she would be safe from making a complete fool of herself.

Was that a significant look that her grandmother was sharing with Nico?

'This is your gift,' Charlotte added, for good measure. 'And we intend to share every possible moment of it with you. Don't we, Nico?'

Nico seemed to be relishing the champagne and he merely lifted his glass in a toast of agreement.

There wasn't room for three people to sit in one cabin. Charlotte sat beside her grandmother as they opened and perused the map of the journey. Nico stood near the door, apparently enjoying the scenery through the corridor windows and chatting to other passengers as they went past.

They chose the first sitting for lunch and it was Nico who insisted on helping Lady Geraldine negotiate the route and cope with the sometimes jerky motion of the train. It took a long time to get through several carriages and through the bar car before they got to one of the restaurant cars, especially when everything had to be explored and admired.

'The bathroom is amazing,' Lady Geraldine declared after their first stop to wait for her, which was right beside her suite at the end of their carriage. 'The toilet seat is made of mahogany and everything else is brass. Even the cover for the paper. And it's all so clean and shiny.'

The resident pianist was not yet playing the baby grand piano in the bar but they had to stop there as well.

'Play something, Charlotte,' Lady Geraldine commanded.

'I can't do that.' Charlotte was horrified. 'I haven't played a piano for years and I'm quite sure it's not allowed, anyway.'

But the handsome young man polishing glasses behind the wooden bar grinned. 'Go ahead,' he invited. 'It's too early to bother anyone.'

'Please, Charlotte.' Lady Geraldine was heading for a nearby seat. 'For me? It's so long since I heard you play.'

And she might never hear her again?

'Yes… Please, Charlotte.' Nico's smile was mischievous. 'I'm curious about your splinter skills.'

Oh, for heaven's sake. Charlotte realised she wasn't going to win and the best way of avoiding stress in getting through this voyage was clearly going to be taking the path of least resistance. She slid herself onto the piano stool and raised the lid on the gleaming keys. She had taken lessons for years as a child and playing for pleasure had been a feature of every visit to her grandmother's house. Until…until her life had changed overnight.

Her hands shook for a moment as she held them over the keys. Maybe the least stressful response would have been to refuse to do this but now it was too late and if she didn't, she might be expected to provide an explanation.

Flicking a glance upwards Charlotte knew that Nico had seen the tell-tale tremor of her hands. She willed them to be still. Willed herself to continue, much as she'd forced herself to start that presentation in Nico's presence yesterday. The only piece she could think of to play by heart was Beethoven's 'Moonlight Sonata'.

The first notes were tentative but the piano was beautiful and within a few bars Charlotte was drawn in to the haunting sound of the music. Her stiff fingers relaxed as she remembered the release that this had once brought her. The pleasure of doing something for herself that had nothing to do with work. Mindless and satisfying and restorative. Just…pleasure…

'Bravo…' Nico's eyes were full of admiration as the last notes died away.

'I knew those piano lessons were worth every penny.'

Lady Geraldine held her hand out for Nico to help her to her feet. 'Now, let's go and have some lunch.'

The lunch was three courses of beautifully prepared and presented food but Lady Geraldine only picked at hers and didn't touch the tarte tatin served for dessert.

'I'm a little tired,' she confessed. 'I think I'll go back to my cabin and rest for a while.'

'I'll come and keep you company,' Charlotte offered immediately.

'No. I might need some help to get back without being knocked off my feet but I need some quiet time. I might have a nap.'

Charlotte felt her level of concern ramp up. Gran hadn't eaten much and now she looked pale. Was she in pain?

It was Nico's arm that Lady Geraldine chose to lean on to keep her balance and they had to stop at frequent intervals to allow other people to pass on their way to the restaurants.

One of those people was another elderly woman whose head turned in surprise as she took another look.

'Lady Geraldine? Jendi?'

'Oh, my goodness. Winsome Black. What on earth are you doing here?'

'I could ask you the same thing. What an astonishing coincidence.'

Lady Geraldine's head shake was incredulous. 'It's a small world, isn't it?' She turned to Charlotte. 'Winsome's an old friend that I haven't seen for years. We worked together once on a huge fundraiser for that children's charity.'

'One Last Wish.' Winsome nodded at Charlotte.

'Such a worthy cause. They made wishes come true for terminally ill children.'

'This is my granddaughter, Charlotte,' Lady Geraldine said.

'And this is my grandson, Connor.' The good-looking young man, who was clearly aware of how much space they were all taking up in the narrow corridor, smiled at Charlotte and offered her his hand.

She shook it with an equally conspiratorial smile. They had something in common, didn't they? Here they both were in the company of grandmothers with…personality.

'Charlotte and her fiancé are keeping me company,' Lady Geraldine was confiding in Winsome. Her smile was poignant. 'This trip is my last wish…'

'Oh, surely not.' Winsome smiled. 'I seem to remember you telling me that age is only an attitude.'

Lady Geraldine opened her mouth but then noticed the human traffic jam they were creating in the corridor. 'We'd better get a move on,' she said. 'But we must get together, Winsome, and have a proper chat.'

'That would be lovely.'

'How about afternoon tea? We could meet in the bar at, say, four o'clock?'

'See you then.' With a smile, Winsome continued on her way.

Charlotte wondered if the arrangement might be too much given that her grandmother had already said she needed a rest, but the sparkle in the elderly woman's eyes chased away the worry that her condition was deteriorating and that this trip would prove too much for her.

'Oh, look…the queue at the gift shop has gone. Let's see what they have.'

Charlotte was quite happy to linger and look at the souvenirs available. The more time they spent doing things like this, the less time she would have to spend with Nico, alone in their cabin while Gran had a rest.

You could buy hand-blown crystal glasses and crockery with the Orient Express insignia. There were salt and pepper shakers, travel accessories in blue velvet, photo frames and even jewellery.

Lady Geraldine chose a specially bound copy of Agatha Christie's *Murder on the Orient Express*. And then she ordered Charlotte and Nico to choose a gift for themselves.

'A selection of wine glasses would be a lovely engagement present,' she suggested.

'You are celebrating an engagement?' The tall man with a heavy accent who ran the gift boutique sighed happily. 'I tell everybody that this is the train of love…'

'This trip is the gift, Gran. Remember? We don't need anything else.'

But the tall man was putting things on the counter in front of Nico. 'For your beautiful lady?' he murmured. 'A special memory, perhaps?'

Blue velvet cases were being opened to display pearl necklaces on silver chains that had clasps engraved with the train's insignia. Silver and gold bangles were similarly engraved. A chain bracelet had tiny silver charms like a train carriage, a conductor's whistle and a pillbox hat but Nico was picking up another bracelet. He held it up to show Charlotte.

'Do you like this, *cara*?'

Tiny silver hearts linked together. A delicate piece of jewellery.

Romantic.

Charlotte opened her mouth to tell him that she didn't wear jewellery but out of the corner of her eye she saw the way her grandmother was pressing a hand to her throat. Holding her breath as she witnessed evidence of the love her granddaughter had finally found?

'It's…lovely.' Let him buy it, she told herself. She could reimburse him later.

Nico not only purchased the bracelet, he insisted on putting it on Charlotte's wrist. His fingers brushed her skin as he fed the rod of the clasp through the silver circle engraved with the name of the train.

He smiled at her then. Just the way he had when he'd sat at their table last night. As though she was the only woman in the world for him. As if he was so deeply in love that nothing else mattered.

She knew he was going to kiss her. The tall man wanted it to happen. Her grandmother wanted it to happen.

And, God help her, *she* wanted it to happen.

It was just a kiss and her lips were ready for it this time, already soft and slightly parted. If she sat down at a piano any time soon again, she would probably find that her fingers were instantly ready for the release of music too. The pleasure to be found. The connections between her fingers and her brain and her heart had unexpectedly been woken up after a very long sleep.

Like her lips had been?

Not that it was a passionate kiss, of course. Just a gentle pressure. But the promise was there. And no mat-

ter how fiercely Charlotte told herself that she didn't want this and couldn't go there, her body was defying her. The shaft of desire was so much more intense after last night. How on earth was she going to cope with the rest of this journey? Where were some new barriers when she needed them?

At least Nico left her alone to do some more exploring after Lady Geraldine was settled back into her cabin behind a closed door. It gave Charlotte time to try and rebuild her defences. To plan how she could get through the next hours. Maybe one of them could sleep in here, on the seat? At the very least she could choose the top bunk so that she wouldn't have Nico climbing past inches away from her face. What did he wear in bed? Oh, God…imagine him climbing up wearing nothing but a pair of silk boxers or skin-hugging cotton knit underwear. And even with the highly unlikely possibility that he had a pair of flannelette pyjamas in his bag, she'd still be aware of him sleeping beneath her, wouldn't she? She would hear his breathing. Feel the warmth of his presence. *All* night.

Heavens, it was warm in here. Charlotte adjusted the central heating radiator beneath the window and even opened the top window a little for some fresh air. She was just beginning to feel calmer when Nico returned to the cabin.

He was carrying a bottle of champagne in a silver ice bucket. Two crystal glasses dangled from his other hand. He leaned against the door with a smile of invitation curling the corners of his mouth.

What woman would be able to resist?

Charlotte, that's who, with her grandmother safely

shut away and all the good work of calming herself down undone in an instant.

It wasn't hard to glare at Nico as though he was committing an unpardonable sin. 'What on earth are you thinking?' she snapped. 'I hope you're not planning to get me drunk so you can take advantage of me again.'

Again?

Nico shoved the cabin door shut with his foot. The champagne had seemed like a good idea. They were supposed to be celebrating their engagement, weren't they? They didn't have to drink the damned stuff. And what was wrong with trying to make this journey as pleasant as possible, anyway?

What *was* Charlotte's problem?

'Take *advantage* of you?' He kept his voice quiet but allowed it to cool noticeably. 'Is that how you see this?'

Her voice was small. 'No.'

At least she had the grace to look embarrassed but it wasn't good enough.

'On balance, I suspect most people would consider you to be taking advantage of *me* right about now.'

'You agreed.' Charlotte had two bright spots of colour on her cheeks and her tone was accusing. 'This was all *your* idea—'

'I have gone out of my way to help you,' Nico interrupted, dumping the ice bucket and glasses on the table by the window, oblivious to the glorious scenery of the Italian Dolomites rushing past in the distance. 'And it is *not* because I have any intention of "taking advantage" of you. You are the complete opposite of the type of woman I find attractive.'

A curious expression changed Charlotte's features. She looked...hurt? Disappointed? Surely not. The expression was gone as quickly as it had appeared but it took the wind out of Nico's sails. His anger evaporating, he sank down onto the seat beside her. 'Do you want to know the real reason?' he asked.

'Mmm?' The sound was somewhat strangled but Charlotte was looking at her hands, which were clasped tightly together in her lap.

'You fascinate me,' Nico said simply. An honest statement, dragged from a deep place, possibly against his better judgement.

There was a long moment of silence but Nico let it ride as he tried to shut down the implications. Why did this interest feel so very different from the attraction a woman usually had for him? Was it a threat?

Very slowly, Charlotte finally raised her head. Her eyes were a dark, stormy grey and they were wide and puzzled. Fearful, almost.

'Why?' The word was a whisper.

Why indeed?

'You're a beautiful woman, Carlotta.' The Italian version of her name came to his lips unbidden. 'You are also very intelligent and successful. I have a great admiration for your professional abilities.' He could feel a corner of his mouth quirk. 'You are also surprisingly talented at playing the piano.'

A snort of mirth escaped Charlotte as she shook her head, encouraging a lock of hair to escape the tight ponytail she was wearing today.

Nico couldn't resist catching that lock and smoothing it back behind her ear. 'I believe that people come into

your life for a reason,' he added quietly. 'I find myself in an extraordinary place, if only for a limited time, and I have to wonder if fate has brought us together because we have something we can learn from each other.'

She was looking at him now as if he'd grown two heads. 'Like what?'

'I don't know.' Nico shrugged. 'Maybe it's your astonishing grandmother I was destined to meet. To learn how one can make the most of life until the very end. Or how to face the prospect of that end with such dignity and courage.'

'Oh…' Charlotte caught her top lip between her teeth but it wasn't enough to stop tears rushing to her eyes.

Dio…he hadn't intended to make her cry. Nico extracted one of her still-clasped hands and held it between his own.

'Or maybe I need to learn about family,' he said. 'The love you have for your *nonna* touches me very much. Right here.' He brought her hand up to press it against his heart. 'I don't have a bond like that. Perhaps I pushed my mother away because of the childhood sadness of losing my father. Maybe that's why I never want to marry or have a family of my own because I can't imagine inflicting that kind of pain on children.

'But half of me is Italian and it doesn't feel right. I've ignored that sense for many years but seeing you with your *nonna* opened my eyes.' His smile was wry. 'I don't know if it will change how I live my life but it feels right to be helping you.'

'But you wouldn't inflict that pain on your own children.' He could feel the pressure as Charlotte started holding *his* hand instead of just letting hers be held.

'Because you'd know what it was like. And even if the marriage didn't work, you'd still keep your bond with your children. You'd fight for it. And win.'

She believed that. She believed in *him*. It gave Nico an odd frisson of…what, pride? Invincibility? Oh, yes… he could conquer the world if a woman like Charlotte truly believed in him. Except…

'It's not going to happen…' The admission was being torn from somewhere that had been so well locked away maybe he hadn't even been aware of it himself. 'The kind of love that leads to marriage…and children…can only happen if you can fall in love. I think…I think that I'm not capable of doing that.'

There it was. His deepest, darkest secret. Something that he'd never said to anyone. From the shocked expression on Charlotte's face she must realise the significance of his confession. But she didn't believe it.

'Why not?'

Nico had to swallow hard. Why was he putting himself through this? Because it seemed like a pathway to get Charlotte to open up about herself? If he stopped now, he'd never reach his goal.

'I love my mother,' he said quietly. 'I can't blame her for wanting to find happiness in her life and the men she falls in love with don't seem to be able to provide that for very long. But I loved my father too and, even as a child, I could see that he was destroyed by losing the woman he loved so much. Falling in love can create so much pain. You either end up being destroyed yourself, like my father, or destroying others, like my mother has—more than once.'

'That doesn't have to happen. Not if you choose the right person who can give you what you need.'

'What if you don't know what it is that you need? How can you possibly make the right choice of a person to be with for the rest of your life?' Nico shook his head. 'No. It's safer to never fall in love. Perhaps I'm lucky that I have that inability.'

Charlotte was still staring at him, a crease of concern between her brows.

'But you don't want to end up like Gran,' she said, with a wobble in her voice. 'Old and sick but with nobody to care about you. No child. No grandchild.' Her voice trailed away as if Nico wasn't supposed to hear her next words. 'That's what terrifies *me*...'

'So why are you alone?' Nico turned so that he could look directly at Charlotte. 'A beautiful, talented woman who should be thinking of having children of her own so that she can have grandchildren one day.'

There was no response other than a withdrawal Nico could both see and feel. As if the white witch from Narnia had waved her wand and turned his companion to stone.

Nico had bared a part of his soul here. A part that had never been shared before and never would be again. Charlotte wasn't going to be allowed not to take her turn.

'Tell me about Siegfried,' he said.

'No.' The refusal was absolute. Charlotte pulled her hand away and turned to stare out of the window.

Nico leaned back against the seat, letting his head rest on the lace-covered cushion. 'I'm a patient man,' he said lightly. 'We have the rest of today. And *all* night.'

He couldn't miss the way Charlotte's chest heaved as she gasped silently. Struggling for control? Interesting. He was getting somewhere, at least.

Nico watched her profile closely. 'We are in this extraordinary place and time and we never have to see each other again after tomorrow. I believe I have something to learn from you, Carlotta. And I think that maybe you have something to learn from me.'

He touched her arm and she flinched. Nico sighed. He should give up. Accept that Charlotte wasn't prepared or ready to learn anything. Except he didn't believe that. She just had to unbutton herself a little more. And if she did that, maybe he would get the answers to the mystery of why she'd changed so much. And then his fascination with her would fade and his life could get back to normal.

'In order to learn something,' he offered carefully, 'maybe you have to be prepared to admit that there's something you don't know. To be open. And honest. Being honest makes you vulnerable, I know that. But I've been honest with you.'

Charlotte nodded. 'You have.'

'More than honest. I've told you something that I've never told anyone else. That I never *will* tell anyone else. Something that I see as…shameful. What kind of man am I if I cannot fall in love or be the kind of husband and father a woman would want?'

She was still struggling. Did she even realise that she was shaking her head very slowly? That her hands were gripping each other tightly enough to have cut off any useful supply of blood?

'You have the power to hurt me, Charlotte, if you

chose to share that information with anyone. I'm trusting you not to do that.'

The slow headshake turned into an equally measured nod. A promise.

Nico lowered his voice to something just above a whisper as he touched her again. And this time she didn't flinch. 'You can trust me.' He cleared his throat and spoke more strongly. 'So...will you do me the honour of being honest with me?'

Dio, that had disturbing echoes of some kind of marriage proposal. Except it wasn't, of course, so he didn't need to feel as if he was getting completely out of his depth.

Even when Charlotte raised her eyes to his and he could see that she wanted to tell him.

Wanted to trust him.

She was just having to gather so much courage that it broke his heart to watch.

'I loved him.' She finally choked the words out. 'I thought he loved me. But he wanted... I couldn't...' There was agony coating the words now. 'We weren't... *compatible*.'

There was another message in her eyes now. One that said Charlotte was unbearably alone in the world but that there was nothing she could do about it.

Nico sighed again, more heavily this time, as though utterly defeated. He held out his arms and gathered Charlotte to his chest.

And held her while she cried.

CHAPTER SEVEN

'THERE'S NOTHING LIKE a *proper* afternoon tea, is there?' Lady Geraldine sighed happily as she stirred sugar into her second cup and listened appreciatively to the sound of silverware tapping against real bone china. 'Did you know you can buy these lovely cups and saucers from the gift shop?'

'I'll have to have a look. I'm planning to go there after this.'

Lady Geraldine couldn't help noticing the glow of Winsome's smile. Her old friend certainly looked very happy these days. She could return the smile easily. She had a lot to be happy about herself at the moment.

Like meeting an old friend unexpectedly. Being on her once-in-a-lifetime dream journey. Actually sitting in this famous bar carriage with the pianist now in residence playing some soft, classical music interspersed with Christmas carols. Remembering Charlotte playing on the beautiful instrument earlier when it had been the first time she'd heard her in so many years. Could it be that it was Nico who was bringing back the part of her granddaughter she'd been missing for so long?

She picked up the elegant white cup with the blue

ribbon pattern around its rim and the VSOE logo under a small crown. 'Maybe a set of these would make a lovely engagement gift for my Charlotte and her Nico.'

'You said they'd only met yesterday? In Venice? When they both saved that man's life?'

'Yes...' Lady Geraldine pushed aside that tiny niggle of doubt. 'But they'd met before. Years ago, at Charlotte's hospital. Fate has just thrown them back together and...' She sighed again. 'It's obviously meant to be. Like your Connor and...what was her name again?'

The conversation paused for a moment as the steward removed the plates that had contained tiny sandwiches and replaced it with a platter of warm scones, adding small silver pots of jam and clotted cream.

'Mmm...' Lady Geraldine eyed the cream. 'Proper Cornish clotted cream, by the look of that.'

'Kelsie,' Winsome said as she followed her friend's example and picked up one of the scones. 'Kelsie Summers. But I don't think she and Connor are about to fall into each other's arms like your Charlotte and Nico. She jilted him, in fact, fifteen years ago and I have the feeling he hasn't forgiven her.'

'Really?' Lady Geraldine had spread the jam and clotted cream onto her scone and was just about to take her first bite but the conversation had just become more enticing than the calorie-laden treat. 'They must have been very young. Oh, *do* tell...'

They both dropped their voices to a more discreet level and Lady Geraldine listened to the story with avid interest. Young love could be such a fragile thing, couldn't it? She had to hope that there wouldn't be

any unforeseen twists in the road ahead for Charlotte and Nico.

She finally turned her attention back to her scone but her expression was thoughtful.

'We might be able to help things along,' she suggested.

'What do you mean?'

'The dinner seating is very strict, I hear.'

'It certainly is. I've tried to change tables at the last minute on some of my previous journeys and it almost never happens.'

'It's not the last minute yet,' Lady Geraldine said firmly. 'And if we both had a little chat to the maître d', I'm sure we could persuade him to juggle things a little.'

'In what way?'

'By making an extra table available. We've still got a lot of catching up to do, haven't we? We haven't even started talking about that terrible business with Deirdre Wilkins defrauding the charity so that she could run off to the Maldives with that "personal" trainer of hers.'

Lady Geraldine knew her smile would reveal how much she enjoyed an occasional bit of juicy gossip. 'If we asked to be seated together, that would mean leaving both your Connor and this Kelsie and my Charlotte and the lovely Nico alone at their tables.'

'Yes... If we could make sure they gave them a table for two or didn't put another couple to join them at one of the bigger tables.'

'It would be so romantic, wouldn't it? Everybody dressed up and the lighting all soft and lots of delicious champagne to add to the atmosphere?'

Winsome was smiling. 'Why don't we ask our nice

steward to go and see if the maître d' might be able to spare us a minute or two?'

Charlotte drifted towards consciousness with reluctance.

She had never felt so comfortable. So relaxed. So *safe*. She was floating, supported by a strength she knew she could trust. Cradled against it and it was warm and...moving?

Yes. A steady, gentle movement like breathing. And there was an equally steady but gentle thumping against her ear.

A sound she normally only heard through a stethoscope.

Awareness of where she was kicked in. Or should that be who she was with?

Asleep on, in fact?

'Ohhh...' Charlotte pushed herself upright with a groan. 'I fell *asleep*?'

'You did.' There was amusement in Nico's tone. And a tenderness that touched something that felt raw inside Charlotte.

The last thing she remembered was bursting into tears and Nico holding her. She'd expected him to want more information about what had gone so wrong with her relationship with Siegfried. For her to define what she'd meant by being incompatible. But he hadn't asked anything. He'd offered her comfort instead, as though he understood. As though everything could somehow be put right.

And it had been too much for Charlotte. Her defences had collapsed completely and she'd sobbed out the tears

that had been bottled up for years and years. And then she must have been overcome by sheer exhaustion and fallen asleep.

And he'd just continued to hold her?

'How long?' Charlotte put a hand to her hair, which felt like a rat's nest. She closed her eyes in disbelief and found that her eyelashes felt all clumpy when she blinked. She probably had mascara all over her face. She opened them again. The short winter's day was ending already and it was dark outside but their cabin was glowing in the soft light from a lamp on the table. 'How long have I been asleep?'

Nico was tilting his head to one side and then the other, stretching his neck. 'I wasn't watching the clock.' He smiled. 'I may have dozed off myself, in fact.'

Charlotte could feel a smile stirring. A joke about them sleeping together forming.

'Only until the steward woke me to tell me about Jendi.'

The smile and joke evaporated. 'What? Oh, my God…and you didn't wake me? What was wrong? Why—?'

Nico put a finger against her lips and the gentle pressure stopped her anxious flow of words.

'He merely came to ask if I could accompany her to the bar for the afternoon tea she had arranged to have with Mrs Black. As soon as he saw that I was…ah… otherwise occupied, he said it was no problem, he would accompany her himself and ensure that she didn't lose her balance.'

Charlotte couldn't believe she could have slept through the whole exchange. 'I'm sorry,' she muttered.

'I must have been more tired than I realised. I…um… didn't sleep much last night.'

'Of course not. You're worried about your *nonna*.'

'Mmm. That, too…'

She saw the flash of understanding in his eyes as he considered what else might have been keeping her awake. Like that kiss…

Distraction was needed. Charlotte looked around. The bottle of champagne was still sitting in the bucket. There were a few small cubes of ice floating on the water inside. Nico must have followed her glance.

'It may still be cold enough,' he said. 'Shall we have a toast?'

'To what?'

'To making this evening as enjoyable as possible? For everyone involved. It will be time to get ready for dinner before long, I expect.' Nico was dealing with the foil on the champagne bottle. 'We need to prepare ourselves to put on a good show.' The cork came out with a satisfying 'pop'. He smiled that slow, easy, irre-sistible grin as he filled the glasses and held one out to Charlotte. 'Dutch courage?'

'Will I need it?' And then Charlotte remembered what her hair and face must look like and she smiled ruefully. 'Don't answer that. I know I look a complete mess.' She took a sip of her drink. 'It's just as well I won't see you again after tomorrow. I would be morti-fied. I can't think of anyone who's ever seen me look this terrible.'

Apart from Siegfried, of course. Charlotte took a longer sip of the wine.

Nico touched his glass to hers. 'You are beautiful, Carlotta.'

He looked as though he believed the words. He was giving her *that* look again. Like the one he'd given her last night. And again, in the gift shop. But why? There was no one around to see. He didn't have to pretend here.

And hadn't he told her that she was safe because she was so completely not *his* type?

She wanted to be his type. Heaven help her but she wanted Nico to kiss her again.

Dammit. Where were her safety barriers when she needed them? At the very least she needed to break their eye contact but it seemed impossible.

Charlotte searched for a barrier she could put up to protect herself but couldn't find a trace of one. All she could find was a memory of how it had felt to know that Nico had shared his shameful secret with her and how cathartic it had been to finally share her own with another living person. How it had felt to wake up in Nico's arms.

How was it possible to feel so vulnerable and yet so safe at exactly the same time?

She still couldn't break the eye contact either. And Nico wasn't looking away. Charlotte could feel the distance between them closing. The kiss that she wanted so badly was only a heartbeat away.

Until a knock sounded on the cabin door.

'Dr Moretti? Dr Highton?' The steward sounded as if the matter was urgent. 'I'm sorry to disturb you, but you are both needed.'

* * *

It was just as well the moment had been broken by the interruption.

Perhaps it had been a mistake to let Charlotte sleep in his arms for so long but what else could he have done?

The depth of pain he'd heard in those words '*not compatible*'. They couldn't have had anything other than a sexual reference and for it to be so hard for Charlotte to have uttered them meant they were the key to the puzzle of what had changed her so much.

A horrible suspicion had formed in Nico's mind. Something unthinkable. So dark it couldn't be given a name. So horrific all he'd been able to do was hold onto this damaged woman as he'd tried to fit in the other pieces of the puzzle and control the rush of pure fury on her behalf.

He had to control it. Nico hadn't known if his assumption was correct. Maybe Charlotte would never tell him and even if she did, what on earth could *he* do about it?

Nothing, that's what. It was none of his business. Not his problem. But it would provide an explanation to the mystery and that was what he'd wanted, wasn't it?

So Nico had done nothing. Said nothing. As the minutes had ticked by he'd continued to do nothing and that was when he'd felt Charlotte's heartbroken sobbing subside. When the exhaustion in her body had taken over. When she'd slipped into a peaceful, bone-deep slumber.

He could have eased himself away at that point, found a pillow and blanket to make her comfortable on the seat. Or carried her to a bunk, maybe, and left her to sleep for an hour or two. What was it about this

bizarre situation he'd been caught up in since early yesterday morning that made it impossible to walk away?

He could have ignored Charlotte when he'd first seen her crying on the terrace below his window. He certainly hadn't needed to come up with the dangerous notion of posing as her lover, let alone shoving a ring on her finger. And he could have found an excuse not to accompany the women on this train journey.

But he hadn't. Every step of the way he had hesitated and then been drawn in deeper by something he couldn't explain. And if the steward hadn't rapped on the door at that particular moment, he would have kissed Charlotte again.

More than kissed her, actually. He could have asked gentle questions with his mouth and his hands that would have confirmed what he suspected was the answer to the puzzle that had intrigued him ever since he'd recognised Charlotte on that cobbled Venetian street.

He would have got answers to those questions, he was sure of that. Just as sure as he was of the fact that Charlotte had *wanted* him to kiss her. He had seen that desire darken her eyes and soften her lips and he'd felt that knowledge kindle his own flame because it was part of what intrigued him so much. The contradictions. The ice queen on the surface and the woman capable of such deep emotion within. Was the single, ultimately professional doctor desperately in need of physical release, possibly without being consciously aware of it?

Whatever. The desire had been wiped from her eyes the moment that sharp rap had sounded on the door and the tone of the steward's voice had told them that they were not only needed but needed urgently.

Charlotte's assumption was, of course, that Jendi had become ill. She moved swiftly to wrench open the cabin door.

'It's my grandmother, isn't it? She needs us?'

The steward nodded. 'Only you, Dr Highton. She's asking for assistance to get dressed for dinner.'

'But you said you needed both of us.'

'Yes. I'm hoping that Dr Moretti could come with me to see another passenger in the carriage who requires a doctor. He thinks he might be having a heart attack.'

Nico could actually feel his professional persona taking over. Smothering anything personal, like his desire to kiss Charlotte. There was still a flicker of something personal there, though. He stepped closer, needing to touch her, and put his hand on her shoulder.

'You go and help your *nonna*,' he told her. 'I'll deal with this.'

'But…' Was it his imagination or did Charlotte lean into his hand a little, as if she was trying to return the touch? Her gaze caught his and he could read the message so easily. She was reminding him of what he'd told her grandmother only hours ago. That, together, they made an amazing team.

'I'll send for you,' Nico said softly. 'If I need you.' He stepped past Charlotte into the corridor, where the steward was waiting anxiously for Nico to follow him. The last personal thoughts evaporated. 'What equipment do you have on board?' he queried. 'Oxygen? A defibrillator?'

'Yes. We have oxygen. And an AED.'

'Good.' Nico picked up his pace as they made their

way to the cabin at the far end of the carriage. 'Show me which cabin and then fetch them for me, please.'

The man in the end cabin was in his sixties. His colour wasn't good and he was clutching a small red and white canister of glyceryl trinitrate spray in his hands. His wife was beside him, looking even paler than her husband and virtually wringing her hands.

'How long is it since the pain came on?' Nico asked.

The anxious woman checked her watch. 'Nearly fifteen minutes.'

'And how many doses of the spray have been taken?'

'Two? Maybe three... I've lost count.' The woman was struggling to hold back tears. 'It's not working and...and they said that if it didn't work it could be a heart attack and we'd have to get Douglas to the hospital as quickly as possible.'

Nico had his fingers on the older man's wrist. His pulse was a bit rapid but quite strong and regular.

'Tell me about the pain.'

'It's like a bus parked on my chest. Right here...' Douglas pressed a fist to his sternum. 'It's hard to breathe.'

'Just in your chest?'

'Yes.'

'Have you ever had a heart attack?'

'Yes. Ten years ago. That's when this whole business started. But it's been stable. Always comes on the same way...and if I sit down and use the spray it... does the trick.'

He was starting to sound breathless. Thankfully the steward had returned now. He was carrying an oxygen cylinder in one hand and the small red case of an

AED in the other. Hopefully the automatic defibrillator wouldn't be needed but it was great to know that such a lifesaver was available if it came to that. Even with the best team in the world performing CPR, it could only buy time. The only way to restart a heart was through defibrillation.

The best team in the world. Unbidden, a memory of Charlotte working with him on the man at the building site flashed into the back of Nico's mind. He shook it off as he uncoiled tubing and fitted nasal prongs to give Douglas some oxygen.

'This may help the pain,' he said. 'Are you on any medications?'

'Yes. Too many.'

'Can you tell me what they are?'

Douglas shook his head, closing his eyes and screwing up his face as though the pain was becoming unbearable. A sheen of perspiration was beginning to show on his bald head. Nico's heart sank.

'I've got them.' The anxious older woman was rummaging in a small suitcase. She pulled out a plastic bag containing numerous packages of medication. They were all things that a cardiac patient could be expected to be on.

'Have you had your aspirin today?'

'Yes.' It was his wife who answered. 'He's taken everything.'

'Let's try another dose of the GTN.' Nico took the canister from the man's hands. It was a bad sign if the spray that normally worked on his angina was failing to be effective but was it possible that it hadn't been used correctly? Nico rolled the canister in his hands, mak-

ing sure the contents were mixed and then sprayed a dose into the air to check that the metered dose mechanism was working. The spray came out but, oddly, Nico couldn't smell anything.

He held the canister up and peered at the base. 'This spray expired two years ago,' he exclaimed.

'Oh, my goodness!' Douglas's wife clapped a hand to her mouth. 'Really?'

'Really.' Nico reached for the portable pharmacy in the plastic bag. Yes. There was a small box in there that contained a replacement canister. And the expiry date was a year away. He ripped open the box, took the lid off the canister and squeezed off a test shot. 'Open your mouth,' he directed Douglas, 'and lift your tongue.'

He gave Douglas two sprays under his tongue and then kept his fingers on his patient's pulse and watched his breathing while they waited. Within a matter of minutes Douglas started breathing more easily and deeply. The lines on his face relaxed and when he opened his eyes he actually smiled.

'It's almost gone,' he said.

'Oh…thank God…' His wife was crying. 'I'm so sorry, Doug. This is my fault. I should have thrown that old spray away as soon as we had the new one.'

'Waste not, want not.' Douglas patted his wife's hand. 'If you weren't so good at being thrifty we'd never have been able to afford this trip, would we?' He turned to Nico. 'Thank you, Doctor. I'm not having a heart attack after all, am I?'

'It certainly looks like nothing more than an episode of angina. Let's keep the oxygen going for a little

while and see how you go. Someone can always come and find me later, too, if you're worried.'

The only person looking worried now was Douglas's wife. 'I'm so sorry to have disturbed your trip,' she told Nico.

'It's not a problem.'

'Is it your first time on the Orient Express?'

'It is.'

'Isn't it wonderful? Are you enjoying it?'

'Of course.' But Nico had to consciously smile instead of allowing a puzzled frown to crease his forehead. Enjoyment wasn't a word that he would have chosen to describe his state of mind so far. He'd started out being intrigued and then he'd been impressed by Charlotte's piano playing. He'd had a spell of being angry when he'd been accused of planning to take advantage of her and then he'd had that cold chill of horror when he thought he'd guessed her secret.

But the overwhelming emotion that he would remember from this trip was going to be the way he'd felt sitting in that cabin and holding Charlotte while she slept. The feeling of protecting her. Of knowing that she trusted him enough to fall asleep in his arms like that. That he could trust *her* enough to not ever share the personal information he had given her.

A good feeling.

An incredibly powerful feeling.

Even more powerful than the desire that had kicked in when he'd realised that Charlotte had wanted him to kiss her as much as *he'd* wanted to kiss her?

Yes. Strangely, it was. He was used to desire and he

knew there were countless women in the world who could make him feel like that.

But that other feeling was completely unfamiliar. And deeply disturbing. Powerful enough to feel like it had a life of its own and could take control. Was this what falling in love was all about?

Nico couldn't answer that because he'd never been in this space before. He wasn't capable of falling in love. He knew that. But maybe he was getting a glimpse of what it might be about.

And it was disturbing enough that he never wanted to experience it again so maybe it was time to take charge and make sure he wasn't ambushed by any other strange emotions. The distraction of being a doctor for a little while was definitely helping. The fact that the train seemed to be coming to a halt was less helpful.

Had something happened? Maybe there was engine trouble or something on the tracks and he'd end up being on this train for a lot longer than expected. Just how long could he keep up the level of control he might need when he was sharing a compartment with Charlotte?

The steward, who'd been hovering outside the cabin while Nico treated Douglas, stooped to peer through the window. 'We're coming into Innsbruck,' he announced. 'I need to attend to other duties.'

Nico nodded. 'Thanks very much for your help.'

'I can put the AED away now?'

'Yes. Thankfully, I don't think we need it.' Nico raised his eyebrows as the train jerked and came to a complete halt. 'Why are we stopping?'

'We have to change engines whenever we come to an international border. This is a thirty-minute stop and

most people like to get off the train and stretch their legs a bit.' The steward hurried off, probably to open doors and then to stand, looking very smart in his blue uniform, to give people another photo opportunity.

Douglas certainly wasn't going to be jumping off the train to stretch his legs right now. Nico adjusted the setting on the oxygen cylinder and settled in to watch the progress of his new patient.

The contents of Lady Geraldine's larger suitcase were spread out over the seat and hanging from the edges of the bunks as she chose her outfit for dinner.

'The long black taffeta skirt,' she decided. 'With the black, silk camisole and the velvet bolero jacket.'

'Very Gothic,' Charlotte smiled. 'Shall I do your hair so that you've got a bit of fringe covering one eye?'

'Don't be naughty, Charlotte Jane. The black is merely a canvas to show off my diamond jewellery. I'm going to need my necklace and the brooch that goes on the jacket. And I've got my bracelet and best rings in my jewellery case. Oh…we mustn't forget that darling little tiara either. The one I wore last night, remember?'

'How could I forget?'

Lady Geraldine eyed her granddaughter suspiciously. 'I don't think you're taking this seriously, Charlotte. This is the dinner of my lifetime and I intend to look the part.'

'Sorry, Gran.' Charlotte kissed her fondly. 'I want you to enjoy tonight as much as possible. Are you sure you're feeling all right? Did you have a good rest?'

'I had a lovely rest. And then I had an even better

time having afternoon tea with my old friend, Winsome. We still have lots to talk about.'

'Maybe you'll see her again after dinner.'

Oddly, Lady Geraldine looked evasive now. 'Help me into my skirt, child. And then you'd better start doing something to get ready yourself. Fancy suggesting I wear my hair over my eye. Have you looked in a mirror recently? What have you and Nico been up to in your cabin?'

'Gran...' But Charlotte couldn't help thinking about the look in Nico's eyes just before the steward had interrupted them. About how much she had wanted that kiss to happen. Even now, the curl of desire the memory could evoke was enough to make her close her eyes for a heartbeat. To make her lips curl in pleasure at the memory.

If that kiss had happened, would it have stopped there? Would she have wanted it to? The bite of fear that kicked in was enough to make her shake her head as if she could banish the hateful sensation.

She needed to try and locate at least a shimmer of her old armour. To pretend to be in control. Normal. Maybe it would help to make a joke of it. 'Have you *seen* the size of those bunks?'

'You're young,' Lady Geraldine said with a smile. 'I'm sure you'll cope.' She reached out and stroked Charlotte's cheek. 'Oh, darling. You're so in love with him, aren't you?'

Charlotte had to turn away. To find something solid to focus on as she felt the ground shifting beneath her feet with a curious spinning sensation. She lifted the hanger holding her grandmother's astonishing skirt with

the ruffled hem down from the top bunk and pretended to notice some lint that needed brushing away.

In love?

Ridiculous. Nobody fell in love that quickly. She felt safe with Nico, that was all. He knew more about her than anyone. More than her grandmother, in fact, in a rather significant area.

She liked him. A lot. Who wouldn't? He was clever and kind. So kind that he'd sat, getting cramp, for hours, holding a woman in his arms because he hadn't wanted to wake her?

She trusted him, too. Who couldn't trust someone who put the kind of trust in you that led to sharing the kind of secret she could so well understand him wanting to keep to himself? Not that it was true, of course. Nico was more than capable of falling in love if he'd only let himself.

And that feeling when she'd woken up in those arms. As if she had been floating in the most blissful place on earth. She'd never felt so safe.

So *protected*.

Superimposed on that memory came that look of desire in Nico's eyes when their lips had been drifting closer together in the moments before that rap on the door.

That mix of safety and desire was a chemical combination that could only mean one thing.

That…yes. She *was* in love with Nico Moretti.

No. Maybe it meant two things.

She was not only in love. She was in trouble.

CHAPTER EIGHT

MAYBE IT WAS her new awareness of how she felt about Nico. Or perhaps it was the incongruity of him appearing in these surroundings looking impossibly gorgeous in his dinner suit. Whatever it was, it completely stole Charlotte's breath away when she opened the door of her grandmother's compartment to his polite knock.

Did her grandmother actually bat her eyelashes?

'It's been a long time since I was escorted to dinner by such a handsome young man,' she said with delight. 'Charlotte Jane? You can have him later but I really do need Nico's arm while we're walking. This train is remarkably jerky at times.'

'No worries, Gran.' Charlotte smiled. 'He's all yours.'

But then her gaze caught Nico's and the smile got stolen away like her breath had been. Oh…Lord…that look in his eyes.

'I love that dress,' was all he said. 'I'm so glad you've worn it again, *cara*.'

Lady Geraldine made a tutting sound. 'I'm trying to train Charlotte to expand her wardrobe, Nico. It won't

help if you tell her you're happy she's worn the same thing two nights running.'

'But it's true, Jendi.' Nico's smile for her grandmother was so warm and genuine that Charlotte's heart squeezed painfully. How could she not love a man who was clearly already so fond of her beloved gran? 'And I am an honest man.'

The comment did something strange inside Charlotte. Echoes of his voice telling her that he'd been honest with her and asking her to give him the honour of being the same with him. It was a bond she knew she could never have with another person. Did he feel the same? No. How could he when she hadn't shared the most shameful part of her secret? When she'd been less than completely honest?

But his gaze flicked past Charlotte's again. 'Most of the time,' he added.

All the time, Charlotte suspected. This pretence they were engaged in was an aberration. Sure, Nico had approached it as an amusing diversion but any control had been lost very quickly, hadn't it? At about the time he'd pushed that ring onto her finger, probably.

No wonder he was feeling uncomfortable but Lady Geraldine didn't seem to pick up on the loaded comment. 'I'm ready to go,' she announced. 'I want as much time to enjoy seeing everybody else dressed up as I can before I start feeling too old and tired.'

Or before she felt too sick and sore? Charlotte followed Nico as he carefully escorted Lady Geraldine through the rocking carriages towards the dining cars. She needed a break, she said, when they reached the bar car. She wanted to sit for a few minutes and enjoy listen-

ing to the piano. And…how nice…her friend Winsome
was sitting at one of the side-facing seats and seemed to
be saving space for her. Perhaps Charlotte could order
a nice cocktail for her?

Charlotte perused the cocktail menu while Nico
made sure her grandmother was seated comfortably.
Heavens, but there were a lot to choose from. She'd
never even heard of a Moscow Mule or a Planters
Punch. Both her grandmother's favourites were there,
though, so all she really needed to choose between was
a Singapore Sling or a Gin Fizz.

Nico came back to the bar as she ordered a Gin Fizz.
When he was only a step or two away the train gave a
sudden and rather dramatic lurch. A cry rippled through
the carriage as people spilt their drinks but the pianist
didn't miss a beat of the Viennese waltz he was play-
ing. And Nico's arm was right there to steady Charlotte
as she lost her balance.

It was the first time he'd touched her since that al-
most kiss when they'd been interrupted earlier and it
seemed to ignite a peculiar magic. How else could Char-
lotte explain the fact that a steadying touch morphed
into an embrace that moved in time to the music?

They were dancing?

Yes. On a minuscule patch of blue carpet, in the
space between the bar and the piano, Nico was very
competently leading her through a confined version
of a Viennese waltz. Charlotte could have laughed out
loud. Except that this was giving her the same kind of
feeling that she'd had when she'd woken from that deep
sleep in Nico's arms, and she wanted to recapture that
bliss for just a few seconds.

So, instead of holding her head in the correct position for a waltz as she'd been trained to do in those lessons Gran had insisted on when she'd been a teenager, Charlotte let herself droop enough to put her head on Nico's shoulder. And he tilted his head so that it rested against hers. It was no waltz now. Just a slow, close dance.

To anyone watching, and no doubt that included Lady Geraldine and her friend, they must look like a couple madly in love. Nobody, meaning Nico, needed to know that it was actually genuine on her part now.

And maybe that was a good thing. Maybe…just a very small maybe…this didn't have to end when they got off the train in London tomorrow.

No. That tiny, unbidden seed of hope died away as Charlotte remembered Nico saying he never wanted marriage or children. That she was safe because she was so completely not his type of woman.

Oh, well…at least if Gran lived long enough for her to have to confess that the relationship wasn't going to work long term, she wouldn't have to pretend to be heartbroken, would she?

Oh, God…she really was in trouble now.

Released from Nico's arms to a round of applause from the crowded carriage, Charlotte headed back to the bar. She was going to order one of those potent-sounding cocktails for herself because she needed something strong if she was going to cope with the rest of this journey. She needed some bottled courage. Or stamina.

Moving towards Lady Geraldine's seat to wait for the bartender to bring the drinks, Charlotte found that introductions were being made. Winsome's grandson Connor was with a young woman called Kelsie, who

was now sitting beside Lady Geraldine. They were discussing seating arrangements.

'Winsome and I have arranged a table for ourselves,' Lady Geraldine said. 'We don't want to bore you young things with our gossip.'

The implications were immediately obvious. Nico and Connor exchanged a glance as if they were measuring each other up and considering the prospect of a foursome for dinner. Kelsie was watching the older women as if she knew there was more coming. And there was.

'So, instead, we have three tables,' Lady Geraldine smiled. 'One for each couple.'

Charlotte almost groaned aloud. 'I don't think you're allowed to change arrangements like that, are you, Gran?'

Lady Geraldine merely tapped the side of her nose. 'Wait and see where the maître d' puts us all,' she murmured. And then she winked at Winsome. 'Being old doesn't entirely deprive us of our ability to charm men into doing what we want, does it, Winnie?'

'Not at all, dear. As you say, age is only an attitude.'

Charlotte caught Connor's gaze and his expression said it all. This was a done deal and there was absolutely no point trying to make changes now. She was now faced with the prospect of being alone with Nico for a dinner that might go on for hours. An intimate, romantic kind of dinner. Her heart sank. One strong cocktail was not going to be enough.

Nico had to admire the persuasive powers of older women. Tables had to be at a premium on the train, even if there was more than one sitting for dinner, but

here they were at a table that could seat four people and it was only set for two.

It was beautifully set with crisp, white linen, sparkling silverware and immaculate crystal that caught the soft light of the Tiffany lamp on the window side of the table. The carriage might be crowded with other diners but it felt like he and Charlotte were enclosed in a bubble of their own. He was glad that she hadn't had a different dress to wear because this silver sheath was gorgeous and so very appropriate for the season. It made her eyes look like a dark shade of silver instead of grey. Or was that because they were catching such a warm glow from the light?

Or perhaps it was the champagne he had ordered. She certainly seemed to be enjoying the Moët, even if she wasn't clearing her plate with each delicious course that arrived. He had polished off the entrée and then demolished the main course of traditional roast turkey with chestnut stuffing.

Conversation had proved easier than he'd expected, having been deprived of Jendi's company. They'd started out with the practical matter of sleeping arrangements for the night.

'I'll stay in the bar for a while,' Nico had told Charlotte. 'And then I'll come back to the cabin and sleep on the seat. You can close the connecting door when you go to bed.'

He'd asked if she knew what would happen tomorrow.

'We get to Paris around dawn,' she'd told him. 'When we get to the end of the French line for the Orient Express, we have to get off and there are special buses that

we stay on for the channel crossing. The English branch of the train takes us into Victoria Station. I think we get in at about five p.m.'

As the plates for the main course were taken away, Charlotte allowed her champagne glass to be refilled. Did her smile look a little forced as she held it up to Nico in a toast?

'What will you do?' she asked brightly. 'When we've arrived back in London? For Christmas Eve, I mean.'

Nico shrugged. 'I expect I'll go to work and catch up on any inpatients. I'm covering a big area for the next few days. I like to give my colleagues as much time as possible to be with their families over Christmas. And you? What will you be doing?'

Charlotte turned her head to look out the window, although there was nothing to see in the darkness.

'I'll go out to Gran's. Her estate is a good hour out of London. I'll stay with her for Christmas Day, of course, and then it'll be time to face up to what needs facing up to.'

Jendi's cancer. Dio…but it was going to be a difficult time ahead for Charlotte. Nico wanted to reach across the table and catch her hands. To offer to be there for her as a friend in the weeks or months ahead.

But this faux relationship wasn't supposed to continue, was it? Charlotte wouldn't want it to. Having her in a committed relationship with a potential family in the future might be at the top of her grandmother's bucket list but Nico could still hear the vehemence in Charlotte's voice when she'd declared that it was never going to happen.

So he said nothing. Instead, he followed Charlotte's

example and stared out of the window. There were sparkles of light swirling outside in a mesmerising kaleidoscope.

'Look at that,' he exclaimed. 'It's snowing. It'll be a white Christmas for some people.'

'I love a white Christmas,' Charlotte said softly. 'It makes you feel like you're living inside a Christmas card. I think the best Christmas I ever had was one where Gran and I got completely snowed in and the electricity went off. We ended up cooking the chipolatas that were supposed to go in with the turkey on sticks on the open fire. I was only about nine but I was so impressed that Gran knew how to do stuff like get the fire going and cook sausages.'

'Sounds special.'

'What's the best Christmas you remember, Nico? Was it white?'

'No. It never snowed in our part of Italy.' Funny that to remember his best Christmas he automatically wiped out any year after he'd been whisked off to Ireland. 'It would get cold, though. I think the best Christmas I can remember was outside. We had a terrace with a long wooden table that was under grapevines. In the summer it was leafy and cool and in the winter there was an open fireplace big enough to roast an ox. For some reason we had Christmas dinner outside that year. Possibly because so many family members had gathered. There were aunts and uncles and cousins I never knew I had.'

'How old were you?'

'About six.'

'Did you have turkey?'

Nico shook his head. 'That wasn't traditional. We

have the feast of the seven fishes on Christmas Eve and then on Christmas Day we have lots of pasta and then roast meat like chicken or beef. And potatoes.' He frowned. The food hadn't been what had made that Christmas memorable.

'There was music,' he continued softly. 'My father was at the head of the table and he was *so* happy. Between courses he would drag my mother away from the kitchen and dance with her in front of the fire. There were so many people. So much laughter. So much love...'

'Family.' The word was a whisper and Charlotte's eyes were as bright as he'd ever seen them when Nico turned from the view of the snow. 'It's what Christmas is all about, isn't it?'

'It was once...' Nico had to clear his throat. The memory of that particular Christmas was disturbing because it evoked a yearning he'd thought he'd put behind him many, many years ago. Part of the heartbreak he would never want to inflict on a child. Or a woman. Or have inflicted on himself ever again.

Dessert of a classic plum duff with crème anglaise and brandy butter came and went with a noticeably more sombre mood at their table. It was a relief when a steward came to tell him that Lady Geraldine was ready to be escorted back to her cabin whenever it was convenient for him.

'Or I can arrange another escort?' The steward tilted his head to include Charlotte. 'If you and your fiancé wish to stay longer?'

'No.' It was Charlotte who spoke up quickly. 'We

can finish now.' She didn't meet Nico's eyes. 'If that's all right with you, Nico?'

'*Sì*. Of course it is.

The last thing Charlotte expected when she returned to her suite after helping her grandmother get undressed and settled into her bunk for the night was to find Nico still there.

She had thought he would be long gone. Having a nightcap in the bar and ready to wait until he thought she was safely asleep before coming back to get what rest he could on the seat in this compartment. Not that she expected to get much sleep herself but it would have been a relief to shut the connecting door and have a space entirely to herself for a good few hours. No chance of losing control and making a fool of herself that way.

Now she was distinctly unsettled. Not only was Nico here but he'd taken off his dinner jacket and rolled up the sleeves of his dress shirt. His bow-tie was undone as well, hanging down beside the undone top buttons of his shirt. His hair was rumpled, as if he'd thrust his fingers through it more than once, and it was long enough since he'd shaved to give his jaw a dark shadow. He looked ever so slightly disreputable lounging on the padded upholstery of the seat.

And ultimately desirable.

Maybe that was why Charlotte's words came out more sharply than she'd intended. 'I thought you were going to the bar.'

Nico raised an eyebrow. 'It occurred to me it might be a good idea to wait until Jendi was asleep. What if

she wanted to go to the bathroom and saw me abandoning my beautiful fiancée?'

Oh, God…this was getting way beyond a joke. Charlotte had had enough.

'It's not funny, Nico.'

'No…it's not.' Nico got to his feet. 'Shall I tell you the real reason I haven't gone to the bar?'

He took a step closer and Charlotte was pinned by the heat in his gaze. She still had a hand on the door to help her keep her balance as the train rocked, and Nico was swaying on his feet but his gaze didn't waver in the slightest.

She couldn't respond to the question but it didn't seem to matter. Nico was going to tell her anyway.

'I didn't want to,' he growled.

Charlotte didn't have to ask why not. She could see the see the answer in his face. Could feel the flicker of heat spiral deep in her belly. The words forced themselves out anyway, though, as she tried to buy enough time to process what was happening. 'W-why not?'

'Because I wanted this instead.' Nico closed the gap between them. He steadied himself with one hand over Charlotte's against the door but he slid the fingers of his other hand behind her neck and then up into her hair as he cradled her head and dipped his own so that their lips could touch.

His mouth felt familiar now. Safe. Charlotte knew that the touch of his tongue against hers would provide a pleasure so intense it was almost pain but her lips parted eagerly and her tongue met his halfway to begin the dance. And this time the give and take of the kiss

changed into more than an exploration and taste of pleasure. This time it had an urgency that demanded more.

And that was enough to make Charlotte pull away. To snatch a gasp of breath and then shake her head.

'I...I don't understand...'

'Yes, you do, *cara*,' Nico said very softly. 'I want you.'

She shook her head again, more insistently. 'But... *why*?'

Nico leaned against the door. He still had a hand cradling her head and she felt his fingers move in a caress. 'Why wouldn't I?'

'Because I'm...not your type. You said so.'

Nico smiled *that* smile. The slow, lazy one. Except that this time it seemed to be gentle. Reassuring? 'I say stupid things sometimes.'

Charlotte had to drop her gaze. Dammit. The train seemed to have picked up speed and the way it was rocking made her more acutely aware of the proximity of Nico's body. Of how it would take nothing for her to fall just a little closer and mould her own body against his.

'This can't go any further,' she said.

'Why not?' The words were a whisper. A question, not an accusation. If she said the word Nico would stop but he genuinely didn't understand, and why would he? He must have seen her own desire for him. He had to be well used to reading those kinds of signals from women.

'Because...' Charlotte couldn't look up. She couldn't stop herself continuing either. Good grief...far from giving her the stamina to maintain control in a difficult situation, the amount of champagne she'd knocked back

this evening was having the opposite effect. Her control
had slipped so far she'd lost the handle for the door be-
hind which she kept her secret so well shut away. She
hadn't been completely honest with Nico earlier, had
she? *He* had been with *her*. Guilt bubbled up inside her
and something snapped.

'I can't do it,' she whispered. 'I…can't have sex.
I'm…' No. There was no way she could utter that horri-
ble word. A shudder went right through her entire body.

Nico's hand slipped out from her hair and he let go
of the door. This was it. He was going to excuse him-
self and go to the bar for a stiff drink, and who could
blame him?

But, instead, he gathered Charlotte into his arms and
held her close to him. His mouth was close to her ear
and he spoke softly.

'You've been hurt, *cara*,' he said. 'I know that.
You've been raped, haven't you?'

Charlotte's gasp was shocked. 'No…it…wasn't rape.
How could it have been? He was my…my boyfriend. I
had chosen to be with him. I'd chosen to go to his apart-
ment. It might have been my first time but I knew what
was going to happen.'

For a long moment Nico simply held her in silence.
Then he spoke gently. 'But it didn't happen the way you
wanted it to, did it?'

'N-no.' Unbelievably, the tears were gathering again.
After not having cried for so many years, she was cer-
tainly making up for it now.

'And when you wanted him to stop, he wouldn't,
would he?'

'H-he said it wasn't his fault if I was frigid. He wasn't

going to have his evening ruined by a—a tease.' There. The word had come out all by itself. 'And—and he was right. I hated it and…and when I tried again, more than a year later, with someone else…I couldn't do it…so he—'

'Was a stupid, arrogant bastard,' Nico whispered vehemently. 'Who had no idea what he was talking about and didn't deserve to be in the company of any woman, let alone someone like you.'

Charlotte felt his lips press against the top of her head. And then she felt Nico's hand under her chin and a pressure that made her raise her face to meet his gaze.

'It's not true,' he told her. 'You are a beautiful, *passionate* woman and all you need to do is believe that.'

Maybe there'd always been a glimmer of hope deep inside that that was true. Maybe when she'd tried again, it had been too soon. Or with the wrong person. Charlotte had always thought that she might have conquered her demons if she could have talked to someone professional about it but the shame of anyone knowing had always stopped her.

And now Nico knew. And he was still here.

And he was gorgeous and kind and he'd said that he wanted her.

They wouldn't be seeing each other again after tomorrow so would it really matter if it didn't work. She might never have an opportunity like this again. To find out…

Charlotte licked suddenly dry lips. 'Did you really mean it?' The words were incredibly hard to utter.

'That I want you?' Nico's eyes were so dark they looked black. His hands on her back slid lower until

they cupped her bottom. He pulled her even closer so that she had no need of any verbal confirmation of his state of arousal.

'Oh...' Charlotte couldn't look away from his eyes.

'Do you trust me, *cara*?'

She didn't have enough breath to say anything. Instead, Charlotte stretched on tiptoe so that she could reach Nico's lips with her own. She slid her arms around his neck at the same time as she felt herself being lifted off her feet and carried into the adjoining cabin and a bunk that would simply have to be big enough.

Well...

He'd been right, hadn't he?

Not just about the reason why Charlotte Highton's personality had changed so much.

He'd been right about the fact that she was a beautiful and passionate woman.

It was well after midnight when Nico eased himself out of the bed that was far too small for two people to sleep together comfortably. He got dressed again and let himself quietly out of the cabin with the intention of going to the bar for that long-postponed nightcap.

Charlotte was deeply asleep again, which wasn't surprising. She'd been on an emotional roller-coaster for the last two days and she'd had rather a lot of champagne tonight.

Had he taken advantage of her lack of inhibitions?

Or would she thank him for proving what she should have been able to believe in all along? That there was nothing wrong with her. Nothing she needed to be afraid of or hide from.

That was a minefield in itself. Charlotte was a passionate woman. The way she'd responded to him had been a joy. No…it had been by far the most tender love-making he'd ever experienced. So overwhelming that he could only hope Charlotte hadn't noticed she hadn't been the only one with tears wetting her cheeks in the aftermath. The way he'd felt when she'd started to touch him back… To offer herself so completely…

Even now Nico had no idea what to do with the sensations that made it hard to breathe. It had made him feel like he was the most special person on earth. As though she was the only woman in the world he ever wanted to be with again because he would never experience anything like this with anyone else.

He knew how ridiculous that was. The world was full of beautiful women who were eager to share his bed. But Charlotte was naïve in such matters. She might believe he was the only man who could make her feel like that. She might mistakenly believe she had fallen in love with him when she was now capable of having a fulfilling relationship with any man she chose.

It didn't have to be him.

He didn't want it to be him.

So why was he feeling so…uneasy? So in need of a stiff drink?

Because there was a voice in his head that was trying to insist that being with Charlotte for just a little longer wouldn't hurt? That he could, at least, have one more night like last night? Just to check whether it had actually been so extraordinary?

He knew perfectly well how wrong that would be. *That* would, without any doubt, be taking advantage of

Charlotte, and Nico had far too much respect for her to even consider it.

The strange sound Nico heard as he made his way through the seemingly deserted carriages in the early hours of the morning only added to his disturbance.

He'd heard that sound before. The cry of a baby who'd only just entered the world.

A newborn on the Orient Express? Impossible.

The echo of that cry of new life stayed with him, though, imagined or not. And Nico didn't like it.

He didn't want a new life.

He wanted his old one back.

CHAPTER NINE

CHARLOTTE KNEW SHE was alone even before she'd surfaced from sleep enough to open her eyes.

Had it been a dream?

Her memories certainly had a dreamlike fuzziness to them. Sensations rather than clear thoughts, and the gentle rocking of the train beneath her seemed to encourage her to close her eyes and explore them. She could feel each one as clearly as if it was happening all over again.

The surprise of finding Nico in the cabin when she'd finally got Gran settled, so closely followed by a breath-robbing fascination generated by seeing him with his shirt buttons undone and his tie hanging loose. As if she'd interrupted him in the process of getting completely undressed...

The explosion of that sensation that had sent shafts of desire into every cell of her body when she'd seen the reflection of her own desire in Nico's eyes. When she'd felt his fingers steadying her head for the kiss that had sent her straight over the edge.

Into that abyss of fear and self-loathing. The feeling of falling without a parachute, knowing that death was

inevitable, as she'd uttered the words that had been her confession of her inadequacies as a woman.

The soft cloud that had gathered and cushioned that fall…first with Nico's words of reassurance and then the physical invitation to see how right they'd been.

And…oh…Charlotte had never known it could be like that. Maybe she'd had fragments of glimpsing it from haunting, erotic dreams but this had been reality.

Or had it?

Shifting a little in her bunk, Charlotte could feel the sweet, inner tenderness that could only be the result of having been passionately loved. With a small sound that was almost a groan, she let herself sink into the last sensation she remembered. Of falling asleep in Nico's arms again but this time feeling as though it was the only place in the world she could ever want to be. Falling asleep with the utter bliss of knowing those arms would still be around her when she woke.

Except they weren't.

How had Nico managed to extricate himself from this tiny space without waking her? He must have been very determined not to, which meant that he'd wanted to be alone.

Why? Did he regret what had happened between them?

Well…why wouldn't he? For heaven's sake, he'd been sucked into her private life because of her meltdowns in front of him. She'd cried all over him. Twice! He'd seen her with her panda eyes and he'd heard all the sordid details of her mortifying past. He must think she was needy and pathetic virtually all the time.

Did he think that she might remain clingy? That she

would try and keep him in her life longer than the period they'd agreed on? Ask him for more than he was prepared to give?

It was odd but the notion of being seen as pathetic and clingy was worse than revealing herself as physically frigid. Nico had shown her that what she'd believed about herself had been so not true.

What she needed to do was show him that any fears about how else she might behave were also untrue. She was in love with him, certainly, but that was *her* problem. It didn't need to be Nico's and he didn't deserve it to be. Not after giving her a gift so far beyond price by restoring her self-esteem.

Creating the magic that had been her night on the Orient Express.

She would have to thank him, of course, but she had to do it in a way that let him know he was not under any further obligation to her. And she needed to make him believe it. To present herself in a way that showed confidence and independence. The way she presented herself at a conference might be a good start.

With a determined shove Charlotte got rid of the bed covers and climbed out of the bunk. Finding herself naked was a reality check that made her blush. She'd never slept naked in her life and the comfort zone of well-fitting clothes had to be her first priority. Washing her face in the tiny corner basin a short time later, she eyed herself in the mirror. The smudged make-up and rat's-nest hair that advertised a night of totally wanton behaviour were the next things she had to take control of. Only then would she be able to face her day.

And Nico.

* * *

He was going to have to face Charlotte at some point. Having caught a few hours' sleep on the seat in the daytime area of the suite and making sure he was not there when Charlotte woke up, Nico had successfully whiled away a good portion of the morning with coffee and newspapers in the bar car.

Brunch was being served already in the dining cars and there was still no sign of Charlotte or Lady Geraldine. It wouldn't be that long before they reached Calais and would have to board the buses for travel to England via the channel tunnel. There would be no private cabins on the train leg to London, during which they would apparently be served afternoon tea, and they would be going in different directions as soon they reached Victoria.

Nico could well imagine how chaotic it was going to be in that huge station on Christmas Eve. It probably wasn't going to be much less private from the time they had to share a bus with dozens of other people. If he wanted a conversation alone with Charlotte, he would have to do something about it now. Clearly, she wasn't planning to come and find *him* this morning.

Their suite was empty and Lady Geraldine's door was closed but Nico tapped on it anyway. It was after ten a.m. Surely Jendi would be up and about by now?

Charlotte opened the door. For a long moment they simply stared at each other. Nico had to process the startling change from when he'd last seen Charlotte, asleep with her glorious hair spread across the crisp, white pillowcase, her lips devoid of any artificial colouring and swollen from so many kisses.

He was facing Dr Highton right now. Dressed in that power suit he'd first seen her in when she'd been on her way to the symposium. She had her hair scraped back into that complicated knot arrangement that gave her the look of an air hostess and her make-up was perfect. No smudged mascara from tears being shed and her perfect lipstick made it look as though her lips had never been licked, let alone kissed.

And, apart from a flash of something that was gone too quickly to analyse, even her gaze looked professional. Impersonal enough to make Nico take a mental step backwards, at any rate.

'Is everything all right? It's…getting quite late.'

Charlotte wasn't meeting his gaze now. 'I can't believe I slept so late,' she said, loudly enough for her grandmother to overhear. 'No wonder you went off to find some breakfast. There's something about the motion of a train, isn't there? It makes you sleep so well.'

Nico raised an eyebrow. Surely Charlotte would realise that *he'd* had virtually no sleep.

'Is that Nico?' Lady Geraldine called. 'Bring him in, Charlotte Jane, for goodness' sake.'

There wasn't room for three people to sit. Charlotte remained standing as well.

'How are you this morning, Jendi?' Nico enquired politely. 'Did you sleep well, too?'

'Not bad.'

Nico could feel the tension emanating from Charlotte. She didn't believe that and she could be right. Lady Geraldine did look rather pale and she was gripping the windowsill with one hand, as though the movement of the train was making her uncomfortable.

'Apparently there was a baby boy born on the train last night, have you heard?'

'No...*really*?' Lady Geraldine turned and was unable to disguise her wince of pain. She ignored it, however, and her expression suggested that everybody else had better follow her example. 'How do you know?'

'The steward in the bar told me when he gave me the newspapers. He said that we'd be reading about the unexpected event on the Orient Express very soon. I actually heard it crying late in the night when I was walking through the carriage. Apparently the young girl had disguised her condition very well, by wearing a large, old-fashioned coat.'

'Oh...I think I saw that girl at the station in Venice,' Charlotte said.

'What on earth were you doing, walking around the train in the middle of the night?' Lady Geraldine asked.

'I needed to stretch my legs,' Nico said, after a moment's awkward silence. 'The bunks are...rather small, aren't they?'

'Depends on what you're doing.' Lady Geraldine managed a smile. 'I'm delighted that Charlotte felt the need to sleep in, I must say. It's probably been years since she hasn't been up at the crack of dawn.'

There was a very noticeable flush of colour on Charlotte's cheeks now and when she flicked a glance towards Nico the shutters were down. She was most definitely thinking about what had kept her awake last night. The relief at seeing what he now knew to be the real Charlotte peeping out was enough to make him try and hold that gaze. And convey the message in his

smile that he agreed it was well worth remembering. Unforgettable might be closer to the mark.

'Oh, for heaven's sake...' Lady Geraldine flapped a hand at them. 'Go and make sheep's eyes at each other in your own cabin and leave an old lady in peace.' The tone was authoritative but she was still smiling as she delivered the order.

Charlotte looked as though she was about to refuse but then shook her head and signalled Nico to go ahead of her. He stepped into their suite and she barrelled in straight after him, closing the door behind her.

'I don't want to leave her too long,' she said. 'I'm pretty sure she's not feeling nearly as well as she's trying to make out.' Biting her lip, Charlotte stared down at her hands. 'I *think* she wants me out of the way so she can take another dose of her painkillers.'

'Is there anything I can do to help?'

'I don't think so.' Charlotte shook her head. 'But... thank you...'

Nico had the distinct impression that the hesitation meant that Charlotte had something else she wanted to say. So he waited. Sure enough, her chin rose as she took a very deep breath.

'I don't mean just for offering to help with Gran...' The movement of Charlotte's facial muscles suggested acute embarrassment. 'Thank you for...you know...'

Nico raised an eyebrow. Was this it? So much for fearing that Charlotte might think she'd fallen in love with him! Was last night going to be a polite 'Thank you' and 'You're most welcome' kind of exchange?

He felt distinctly piqued even though he knew he

should be relieved. But it deserved something more than that, surely?

He stepped closer. Close enough for them to be breathing the same air. He bent his head as if he was about to kiss her but stopped halfway there.

'I can assure you it was very much my pleasure.'

Her eyes widened and he heard her catch her breath but then she stepped back. Only a tiny step, admittedly, but it was enough to send a very clear message. Charlotte didn't want to be kissed again this morning. And there was enough tension in the air to make Nico wonder if she was trying to get back into her old comfort zone. That might explain the way she was dressed and the hairstyle that defied anyone to try and run their fingers through those long tresses.

'Don't....' The word escaped from him as a whisper. A soft groan almost.

'D-don't what?' she stuttered.

Nico had to close his eyes for a heartbeat. He hadn't intended saying this but maybe it needed to be said. 'Don't dismiss last night as a one-off.'

Oh... *Dio*...would she think he was asking to see her again?

Maybe he was...

With a mental shake Nico forced a smile to his lips. 'Don't ever stop believing that you're special. That what you have to offer would be more than enough for any man you chose to be with.' He straightened his spine and tried to keep his smile from faltering. 'There's a whole world of men out there, Charlotte. You'll find someone one day and you'll know he's the person you

want to share your life with. Don't let your past hold you back.'

She was nodding. Blinking hard as though determined not to cry. And when she spoke, her voice was remarkably strong.

'Back at you, Nico Moretti.' Okay, her smile was a bit wobbly. 'Don't be afraid to fall in love in someone or let your past hold *you* back. You need to trust yourself and find someone who can appreciate all you have to offer because…it's a lot.'

Find someone?

Someone else, she meant.

It was Nico's turn to nod. To smile. This extraordinary connection they had was because they'd shared things they'd never shared with others. It was a new experience—much as this train journey was new. Totally unrelated to normal life and it couldn't be expected to continue. They both knew that. At least, this way, they could part with special memories of their brief time together.

Charlotte was twisting the ring on her finger. 'I should give this back,' she said.

'There's no rush.' Nico shrugged. 'Despite your wise words, I'm not about to go hunting for a wife. And even if I found someone, I don't really think she'd want to wear such an old-fashioned ring.'

'It's a beautiful ring,' Charlotte said immediately. 'A family heirloom. A symbol of what's held you back even. *I'd* wear it.'

'You *are* wearing it.' He had to smile. 'Not that I gave you much choice about that.'

Charlotte's breath came out in a huff. 'I mean, you'd

have to make sure that whoever you really give it to un-
derstands its significance. The promise. You'd have to
tell her everything you told me.'

As if he was ever going to find someone to share
soul-deep secrets with again. Once was enough. Like
this train journey.

They were both staring at the ring.

'I'll have to take it off as soon as I get back to work,'
Charlotte said. 'I wouldn't be able to wear a ring like
this even if I *was* engaged.'

'There's no rush,' Nico said again. 'Just see how
things go with your *nonna*. You know where I work.'

Charlotte nodded again. 'At the Hammersmith, yes?'

'Yes. And it doesn't matter if I'm not there for some
reason. You could just leave it with my secretary.'

'But…' There was a lot not being said here. About
how long she might want to keep up the pretence. How
long it would take for her grandmother to die. Her lips
trembled. 'But it's precious…'

'I trust you.'

It wasn't hard to sound sincere. He'd trusted Char-
lotte with far more than a family heirloom, hadn't he?

The only sound for a long moment was the clack of
the train wheels. Rhythmic and steady. Like a heart-
beat. And then Charlotte raised her eyes.

'I trust you, too,' she whispered.

That was a lot bigger than the trust he'd placed in
her, even by confessing what he knew could be seen as
an inadequacy. Being a commitment-phobic male was
far more socially acceptable than the stigma of having
been labelled a frigid woman. Or having been raped.

He was holding a secret that could potentially wreck her carefully ordered world. It was huge.

A gift that no one else could have given him.

Like the one he'd given her by showing her that it wasn't true? Being the man who'd had the privilege of holding her as she'd come apart in someone's arms for the first time?

They were even. Equals.

And, as long as he didn't do something stupid and make a fool of himself, they could keep this respect for each other. Part as friends. They would get back to reality and their own lives soon enough.

It was time to lighten the atmosphere.

'I'm hungry,' Nico announced. 'Would you care for breakfast in the dining car?'

'Gran's ordered cabin service. I need to stay with her and see if she actually eats anything. You go.'

So the separation was to begin already. The countdown was on.

Fine. Nico knew that was sensible. What they both wanted. There would be plenty to distract them for the rest of the day because it was unlikely that they would be alone again together. They would probably never be alone together again. This was it. The last intimate moment he would have with Charlotte Highton.

He had to kiss her. Just a soft farewell.

'I won't forget.' It was a promise. A deliberately ambiguous one. Charlotte could assume he was talking about her wise words regarding his future. She didn't have to know that he meant *her*.

Her quiet words followed him like an echo that

seemed to be picked up by the train wheels as he made his way to the dining car.

'I won't either.'

The rest of the journey seemed interminable.

Lady Geraldine was keeping up a brave face but she ate virtually nothing of her brunch and didn't touch the champagne or afternoon tea on the English leg of the trip. The weather was cold enough to make her look pinched and it was clearly a struggle to join the excited conversations around them that were predicting a genuine white Christmas as fat snowflakes began to fall more and more heavily.

'I'm just tired, love,' she told Charlotte. 'But I wouldn't have changed anything about the last couple of days. Not a thing.'

And Charlotte had been able to smile back and tell her grandmother that she felt exactly the same.

Victoria was heaving with people desperate to get to where they wanted to be for Christmas Day. It was Nico who helped collect their luggage and carve a pathway through the crowd to where Lady Geraldine's chauffeur had arranged to meet them.

They offered Nico a lift but he declined with palpable regret.

'I've made an appointment with a colleague at the Hammersmith,' he told them. 'You need to go in the opposite direction and it'll be bad enough already. I hope you don't get caught in a traffic jam or the snow. If I can't find a cab, I'll take the tube.'

He took Charlotte in his arms to say goodbye. For her grandmother's sake? Was that why he said that he

was going to miss her and that seeing her again couldn't be too soon for him?

It wasn't why Charlotte returned his kiss and agreed that it couldn't be too soon for her either.

She meant every word.

The bleak feeling of watching the crowd swallow Nico only got stronger as they inched their way out of London.

Lady Geraldine took her hand and gave it a squeeze.

'I know it's hard, darling. It's such a shame that Nico's going to be so busy for a while.'

'Mmm...'

'You're lucky, though.'

'Oh?' Thank goodness her grandmother couldn't possibly have any idea of just *how* lucky her granddaughter had been.

'Yes. Much luckier than back in my day. You've got your mobile phones and...and Scope.'

Charlotte smiled despite herself as she sighed. 'Skype, Gran.'

'Whatever.' Her hand got another squeeze. 'It's not quite the same as the real thing, though, is it?'

'No. It's not.' There was an odd pain in Charlotte's chest as she tried to draw in a new breath.

Her heart starting to break perhaps?

CHAPTER TEN

CHARLOTTE'S FAVOURITE CHRISTMAS ever had been the one she'd told Nico about when they'd been snowed in and Gran had cooked sausages on sticks over the open fire in the drawing room.

Maybe, some time in the future, somebody would ask her about her *least* favourite Christmas and she knew that, coincidentally, it would also be one of the rare, truly white ones.

This one.

She stared out of the V-shaped gap in the snow piled on the sill of her latticed window and there was the eerie, early morning light that only a thick blanket of snow could create. There was nothing to disturb the perfection of the Christmas-card scene in the gardens of Highton Hall. The footprints on the lawn below had probably been made by a fox but if her grandmother had seen them in years gone by, she would have told a small Charlotte that they were the tracks left by Santa's reindeer.

The thought should have brought a poignant smile

to her face but instead Charlotte felt the lump in her throat get bigger.

She had never felt this...bleak.

This lonely.

This...*empty*.

As if she'd lost something huge that she would never have back again. Like her heart? Or maybe it was part of her soul. The part that she'd shared with Nico. Yes. That's what it felt like. He had brought light into the darkest part of her being and, by touching it, it had somehow become his, even if he didn't want it.

Was that what love was? Giving away the most important part of yourself?

No... Charlotte found her picture-perfect view becoming blurry. It was finding someone who recognised that part. Accepted it. Made it better than it had been before simply by being there.

And it wasn't one-sided, that had been the clincher. Nico had shared that part of himself with her. The lonely little boy who was still there deep inside. The one who'd been hurt and had seen people he loved get hurt, and was determined to never be the cause of such hurt himself.

Nico thought he didn't know what he needed. That he couldn't possibly make the right choice of a person to be with for the rest of his life. He thought he was incapable of falling in love.

And maybe he had the kind of strength to hold himself back from that kind of surrender but it was blindingly obvious what he needed.

A tiny robin, its bright red breast a decoration in it-

self, fluttered into view and landed on the windowsill, tilting its head and to give Charlotte a cheeky glance.

'He just needs what we all need,' she informed the robin. 'To be loved.'

The robin fluttered off like an echo of laughter.

As if it was that simple…

It was. Charlotte had found that person, hadn't she? She had given him that part of herself she could never give to anyone else.

But it was that impossibly difficult at the same time.

Because finding someone that you connected with at a soul-deep level wasn't enough. They had to feel the same way or it could never begin to work.

And Nico didn't feel the same way. How could he when they'd only known each other for a couple of days?

But he didn't even want to *see* her again. Good grief, he'd told her that she could leave the ring with his secretary, if he wasn't around.

It had meant nothing. A bit of harmless pretence to make an old lady happy before she died. Repayment for the imagined debt of losing her laptop. A bonus of a one-night stand as well?

Charlotte forced herself to move. She couldn't stand here dwelling on how miserable she felt. It was Christmas Day after all. And her toes were freezing. Dressing quickly, she chose clothes for warmth, donning black woollen leggings and an oversized crimson pullover on top of a black bodysuit. No doubt her grandmother would expect her to change for dinner but that was a

few hours away yet and it would be warmer downstairs when the open fires were stoked up.

Maybe Christmas dinner wasn't so far away after all. The rich aroma of roasting meat caught Charlotte's nostrils as she went downstairs. Betty, the cook, must be busy in the kitchen, probably under Gran's strict supervision. Charlotte would probably be given a laden plate of bacon and eggs and an admonishment about the perils of laziness and sleeping in.

The Christmas tree in the huge foyer of this grand old house had coloured lights twinkling merrily and there were gifts beneath, enticingly wrapped in pretty paper and tied with bows of satin ribbon.

It looked like one of the festive pictures that had played against the wall of that Venetian restaurant… good grief, only three days ago? On the evening when she'd given in to the temptation of pretending that Nico was her lover. When she'd accidentally become 'engaged' to him.

The ring was still on her finger. Touching it, Charlotte found she could twist it more easily now. Because she was away from the efficient central heating of the Orient Express and in a huge, chilly ancestral home?

Or was it because she felt so cold inside? So bleak…

Whatever. She couldn't take it off yet, could she? Not on Christmas Day, when it would be the first thing Gran would notice. She would have to find a solution to this situation but not today.

And she couldn't let Gran see how miserable she was either. Pasting what she hoped was a bright smile on

her face, Charlotte walked past the Christmas tree and went down the long hallway to the kitchen.

Betty was basting an enormous turkey. Her husband, John, was polishing silver serviette rings over newspaper spread on one end of the kitchen table. Her daughter was peeling Brussels sprouts and scoring an X into the stalks.

'I was just about to put some breakfast on trays and bring it up,' Betty said after Christmas greetings had been exchanged. 'I was getting worried.'

'Has Gran not been down yet?'

'Not a peep from her. And she's always the first up on Christmas Day.'

'I'll take her up a cup of tea,' Charlotte said. She was worried herself now. 'I expect she's just tired out after her big adventure.'

'You look a bit peaky yourself, pet.' Betty and her family had been a part of Highton Hall for as long as Charlotte could remember. They were more like relatives than staff. Family. Charlotte's smile was genuine this time.

'I'm fine, Betty. I just need a cup of tea, too.'

Betty had been patting her hand. Her jaw dropped.

'Oh…my…. Is that what I *think* it is?'

Charlotte held up her hand and the diamond flashed as it caught the light. Her heart sank. The game had to go on a little longer no matter how much worse it was going to make her feel.

'I guess I had a bit of an adventure myself, Betty. You'll hear all about it as soon as Gran's up, I'm sure.'

'I'd better.' Betty busied herself with a teapot and a

china cup and saucer. She added a couple of tiny gingerbread stars to the saucer. 'Go on...tell Lady G that we're waiting to hear all about it.'

Her grandmother's bedroom was still dark.

'You awake, Gran? I've got a cup of tea for you.' Charlotte balanced the cup in one hand as she drew back the heavy drapes to let the bright, mid-morning light into the room.

And then she turned, and didn't notice how much tea she was spilling on the Persian carpet as she raced to her grandmother's bedside and dropped the cup and saucer on the bedside table. Gingerbread stars floated in a saucer full of tea.

'Gran...'

Lady Geraldine was lying with her knees pulled up and the bedcover gripped between clenched fists. Her face was white with a sheen of perspiration on her forehead. Her pulse was racing. And weak. Her abdomen was swollen and hard to the touch. And it only took the lightest touch to make her cry out in agony.

'Oh...*God*...' Charlotte picked up the phone beside the half-empty cup of tea. She dialled only three numbers.

'I need an ambulance,' she said crisply as soon as her call was answered. 'It's urgent.'

Emergencies like heart attacks and strokes were no respecters of what day it happened to be.

Extreme weather was more of a problem on days when people simply had to be somewhere else for an important occasion and the number of accidents rose.

And there were plenty of people like him who had no family to be with and no desire to celebrate Christmas and carried on with stupid behaviour like getting into fights and getting beaten up or stabbed.

Worst of all, there were the people who found the season too much of a reminder of what they didn't have so the rate of attempted suicides always went up, too.

It was not a good day to be in charge of an emergency department but the staff always did their absolute best to make it as cheerful as possible, and Nico had always managed to join in and encourage them.

Why was it *so* hard this year?

Why did he feel so...bleak?

So...*empty*?

It was *ridicolo*. Ridiculous.

He had his life back the way he wanted it to be. *Needed* it to be.

So why did he feel so off-kilter? So *perduto*, almost?

And why was it always Italian words that came into his head when something stirred him deeply? The past was behind him and best forgotten. Even dredging up happy memories, such as the favourite Christmas he'd shared with Charlotte, was not a good thing to do. No wonder he couldn't settle into doing what he most loved to do and lose himself in the demands of his work.

He would go and do another thorough neurological check on the elderly gentleman in cubicle three who had fallen when he'd gone outside to sweep snow off the steps in preparation for his family arriving. He'd hit his head hard enough to need a period of observation before they could consider letting him go home

to his Christmas dinner. Maybe it hadn't just been the slippery steps and the fall responsible for him losing consciousness either. Perhaps a more thorough cardio-vascular work-up would be justified.

Imagine what would have happened in Venice if Charlotte hadn't been there to see beyond what others had seen?

'Incoming, Dr Moretti,' a nurse told him as she hurried past. 'Eighty-something-year-old female with an abdominal mass and acute bowel obstruction. She's tachycardic, short of breath and vomiting. GCS of thirteen.'

Dio… An elderly woman with a bowel obstruction that could potentially be due to a tumour? Was everything today going to remind him of either Charlotte or her *nonna*? They were probably sitting in front of an open fire right now. Drinking mulled wine or eggnog, perhaps and listening to Christmas carols. Maybe there was a piano and Charlotte would be playing carols. Or maybe they were opening their gifts to each other.

Or…maybe something terrible had happened. Nico could see the ambulance team coming through the doors of his department now. He couldn't see much of the figure on the stretcher because she was bundled up in warm blankets and her face was covered by an oxygen mask. The person holding the bag of IV fluids aloft wasn't part of the paramedic crew, however.

It was Charlotte.

No. Could this be the beginning of the end for Jendi? Surely not today, of all days…

'Resus One,' Nico ordered, before the triage nurse

had a chance to consider priority. 'And get a surgical consult down here stat.'

He ushered the entourage into the resus area reserved for major cases. There was no time for any more than brief eye contact with Charlotte as Nico listened to the handover from the paramedics and prepared to launch an investigative and stabilisation protocol that could deal with this emergency. There was no way he was going to let Lady Geraldine Highton die in his department on Christmas Day.

As awful as it was, this was just the kind of challenge he'd needed. That disturbing, *empty* feeling had completely vanished and Nico had never felt more in control. Or more determined to do his absolute best for his patient. And her family.

The waiting was the worst.

At least all the tension and drama and fear since the moment she'd found Gran in such a dreadful state had been balanced by the swiftness of action and the company of others. The paramedics had been brilliant, using a four-wheel-drive vehicle to get to the estate and then transferring Gran to a faster ambulance to get her into the city. The roads had been appalling with all the snow and traffic jams from a big accident on the M1. They'd had to stick to routes that had been cleared in the city and get to an emergency department that was not only open on Christmas Day but prepared to accept a major case.

It had taken too much time and all the while Lady Geraldine's condition had been deteriorating. It was

becoming hard for her to breathe and her level of con-
sciousness was slipping. By the time they'd arrived
at the totally unexpected destination of the Hammer-
smith—*Nico's* hospital—she was unconscious and the
situation was looking bad enough for Charlotte to be
unaware of anything except the relief of getting to a
place where they might be able to help her grandmother.

And then there'd been the drama of trying to get
Gran stable enough for the surgeon to consider that op-
erating might be an option on an eighty-two-year-old
woman. There'd been fluid resuscitation and ventila-
tion assistance, blood tests and scans and ECGs. Peo-
ple rushing in and out with the kind of controlled chaos
Charlotte was all too familiar with, but this was her
gran being treated and she'd never felt less like a doctor.

Waiting like this in an area set aside for the families
of patients undergoing surgery was a new experience
too. It was nerve-racking and felt interminable. There
were only one or two theatres being used for absolute
emergencies today and just a skeleton staff on duty so
it felt like she was completely alone and she'd been here
for what felt like hours. Surely the surgery was over by
now? Why hadn't someone come to tell her what was
going on?

Had they forgotten she was even here?

No… Charlotte could hear footsteps echoing in the
wide, empty hallway outside. Coming closer. Someone
was coming to see her and what they had to say could
possibly be devastating news.

She couldn't move. Could only stand there, with her

fingers pressed against her mouth to stifle a cry. Afraid to breathe. Unable to blink even.

And then a tall figure filled the doorway. A powerful presence entered the small space of the waiting room and...

And Charlotte wasn't alone any more.

'Carlotta...*cara*...' Nico gathered Charlotte into his arms and held her close. '*Grazie a Dio ho trovato voi.*'

He'd had to come even though he had no real news for her yet. Standing there, in the observation deck of the operating theatre, it had come back with a vengeance.

That empty feeling.

Had it really been the challenge of fighting for Jendi's life that had made it go away? The focus on medicine that was the most important thing in his life? Or had it had been because Charlotte was so close to him again?

He had to find out. His shift in the emergency department was finished and there would be no professional distraction for him now. If he found Charlotte and that empty feeling disappeared then he would know the truth.

And it had. *Dio mio*, but it had evaporated like mist in hot Italian sunshine as soon as he'd gathered her in his arms and held her close to his heart.

The truth was irrefutable. It wasn't work he needed like the oxygen in the air he breathed. It was this woman. *Charlotte*. Without her, he would have that horrible, empty feeling for the rest of his life.

'*Carlotta...*' The word was a breath that got lost in her hair.

'I don't understand,' she said.

Neither did Nico. But it was wonderful. So joyous.

'I can't speak Italian, Nico...' She was wriggling in his arms, pulling back so she could see his face. 'What's happening?' Her breath was a fearful gulp. 'Where's Gran?'

How could he be so selfish? Nico stroked her hair and focused enough to change languages.

'There's a break in surgery. They're doing a biopsy of the tumour. It will be a bigger operation if they decide to try and remove it all and it would be too much of a risk if it's...'

She knew what he was saying. If the tumour was aggressively malignant, they would only attempt a palliative procedure to deal with the bowel obstruction.

But Charlotte's eyes had widened. 'The surgeon thinks there's a chance it's not malignant? That it's... *benign*?'

Was it cruel to give her hope or a gift that he could share with her for at least a little while? The point was moot because she knew the answer. They wouldn't be interrupting surgery for the length of time it took to use a technician on Christmas Day if it wasn't a good possibility.

'Are you going back? Can you find out?'

Nico shook his head. 'They'll come and tell us. I want to wait here with you. I...I *have* to.'

'You *have* to?' Charlotte's tone was as odd as his had been. A note of wonder? '*Why?*'

'Because…' There was no point in being less than honest with her. There never had been and never would be. 'Because being with you…it makes the empty feeling go away.'

'Oh…' Charlotte's gaze was holding his and he could actually see it melting. Getting misty. 'It does… It *so* does, doesn't it?'

'*You* feel it too?' A surge of emotion was threatening to explode inside Nico's chest. Gratitude? Relief? *Hope*? No. It was bigger than any of those. 'I've never felt like this,' he confessed. 'I don't know what this is… but it's…it's…'

'I think it's love,' Charlotte whispered. 'I'm in love with you and that's why I have the empty feeling when you're not here.'

'I'm in love with you…' Nico tested the words out loud. Strange and new but…yes…they felt right. He tried them in Italian to make sure. '*Cara mia, innamorata di te.*'

And that made them real but still unbelievable. 'How?' he whispered. 'How did this happen? So fast?'

'I don't know…' But Charlotte was smiling. Almost laughing, but there were tears in her eyes at the same time. 'But it's Christmas…and it's the most wonderful gift I could ever have been given. I love you so much, Nico. I've never felt like this before. It feels like everything that's ever happened to me, even all the bad things, were worth it because it led me here. To *you*.'

He had to kiss her then. Slowly. Tenderly. The bursting feeling inside him intensified and turned to molten

joy. It was a long time before he could lift his head to look into Charlotte's eyes again.

'When I was in Venice,' Nico told her with a smile, 'a moment or two before I saw you at the accident scene I was having to push my way through the crowd and I heard this old woman and you know what she said?'

'No.' Charlotte was smiling up at him. A tear escaped and Nico let go of one of her hands so that he could brush it away for her. 'What did she say?'

'That it was almost Christmas. A good time for a miracle to happen. I think that's what this is, Carlotta. A miracle.'

Charlotte sniffed and the sound was so unromantic that Nico could feel himself fall even deeper in love with her. Had he really thought he was incapable of doing this? He was good at it. With a bit of practice he would be the best.

When Charlotte scrubbed at her nose, he caught her hand. The one with the ring on it. He seemed to remember it had been quite a struggle to get it onto her finger but it came off quite easily.

Charlotte went very, very still.

'You know what this is.' Nico had to clear the sudden gruffness of his voice away. 'Of all the people in the world, you are the only one who can know the symbolism of this ring. The...' His voice cracked again. 'The promise it carries.'

Her gaze clung to his. Her head dipped and rose again in a slow, solemn nod.

'I didn't give you a choice about wearing it before,' Nico continued. 'I'm giving you that choice now. Will

you wear this ring, *inamorata*? Will you accept my promise?'

'Oh...*yes*, Nico.' Her hand was shaking as she held it out for him to slip the ring back on her finger. 'But...'

He stilled her words with a gentle finger on her lips. 'It's like your *nonna* said,' he murmured. 'It doesn't mean we have to get married next week. It's a promise of commitment. We can take all the time we need to make sure it's perfect.'

The sound of footsteps outside the waiting room sent a sudden chill down Nico's spine. Someone was coming to give them news.

What if it was bad news?

The only way this could be truly perfect would be to have Jendi at their wedding, wouldn't it? To see her, at some point in the future, cradle her first great-grandchild in her arms.

To know that the biggest thing on that bucket list of hers had been well and truly ticked off.

It was the surgeon, who'd come straight from Theatre to find them. He'd stripped off his gown and gloves but he was still in his scrubs and white gumboots. He still had a hat covering his head and neck.

But he was smiling. 'Your gran's a real trouper,' he told Charlotte. 'Tough as old boots, in fact. She's come through this astonishingly well. You'll be able to go and see her in Recovery very soon.'

'Oh...thank God...' Charlotte was clinging to Nico's hand with a vice-like grip. 'And...and the tumour?'

'Benign. We got it all out. Can't see any reason why

she won't keep ticking along for a good few years yet.'
The surgeon's smile widened. 'Merry Christmas.'

Charlotte was sobbing in his arms now. Nico had tears on his own face.

Buon Natale, indeed.

The best ever, without a doubt.

EPILOGUE

CHRISTMAS WAS LONG GONE.

Lady Geraldine Highton didn't remember it at all. She remembered Venice, of course, and the magic of the Orient Express journey. How could she ever forget when it had made her most cherished dream come true? Her beloved Charlotte had found the love of her life.

And here they were, in the gardens of Highton Hall, in the springtime. Surrounded by daffodils and bluebells with the gentle perfume of apple blossom and tiny puffs of cloud in an otherwise blue sky making this day perfect.

Their wedding day.

They'd waited until she was fully recovered, bless them, and these last few months had been a gift in themselves. She hadn't been allowed to rely solely on the wonderful care Betty had co-ordinated. They'd both moved into Highton Hall themselves, despite the hassle of commuting to London for their busy working lives.

And somehow Nico had got out of all those overseas commitments that had threatened to keep him and Charlotte apart for the foreseeable future. They hadn't

had to rely on that new-fangled Scope thing at all. It had been, in fact, as if they couldn't bear to be apart from each other for a heartbeat longer than they had to.

And when they were together, they couldn't keep their hands off each other. Not that anyone minded today, of course. It was only expected that they would link hands when Charlotte had wound her way through the chairs set out in the bluebell woods under the ancient oak trees to join her husband-to-be in front of the celebrant. That Nico had immediately bent his head to place a lingering kiss on her lips might have been a tad premature but…he was Italian. What could one say?

And it wasn't as if Charlotte was wearing a veil to cover her face. She may have chosen a traditional, stunning white dress that made her look beautiful enough to bring a tear to anybody's eye, but she'd left her hair loose and flowing.

It had been a joke when Geraldine had offered her beloved tiara as the 'something borrowed' but there it was, sparkling in her blonde hair as a shaft of sunlight found a way through the unfurling leaves of the oak trees. A glint of silver on her wrist was the only other adornment Charlotte had chosen. That tiny ring of hearts that had the emblem of the Orient Express engraved on its catch.

Geraldine eyed the rings on her own fingers as she smoothed the skirt of her lovely new pink silk dress. Maybe she should tone down her own accessories? No. That would be tantamount to curbing all sorts of things. Acting her age even, and that would never do, would it?

She had to shift a little on her chair in the front seat

as the proceedings started. There were still moments of discomfort as she recovered from the major abdominal surgery that had removed that thankfully benign growth but she would never complain.

This was more than a bonus of time that she hadn't expected to have.

What had occurred during this last Christmas season had been the most amazing gift ever.

Although…

She'd interrupted something last night. A moment between Charlotte and Nico that had looked like more than an intimate goodnight on the eve of their wedding. Nico had had the palm of his hand on Charlotte's belly. She'd had her hand resting on top of his and the look they'd been giving each other was one of those that could speak volumes.

She hadn't let on that she'd seen them.

And she certainly wouldn't advertise the fact that her bucket list now had a new item on the top.

She was already the luckiest woman in the world, even though she knew her granddaughter would dispute that title. It would be her secret that she would be keeping her fingers crossed for another amazing gift next Christmas.

A gift they could all share.

A *baby*…

* * * * *

PREGNANT BY MORNING

KAT CANTRELL

Kat Cantrell read her first Mills & Boon novel at school and has been scribbling in notebooks since she learned to spell. What else would she write but romance? She majored in literature, officially with the intent to teach, but somehow ended up buried in middle management at Corporate America, until she became a stay-at-home-mum and full-time writer.

Kat, her husband and their two boys live in north Texas. When she's not writing about characters on the journey to happily-ever-after, she can be found at a soccer game, watching the TV show *Friends* or listening to 80s music.

One

Matthew Wheeler stepped into the fray of Carnevale not to eat, drink or be merry, but to become someone else.

Venice attracted people from all over the globe for its beauty, history or any number of other reasons, but he doubted any of the revelers thronging Piazza San Marco had come for the same reason he had.

Matthew adjusted the tight mask covering the upper half of his face. It was uncomfortable, but necessary. Everyone wore costumes, some clad in tuxedos and simple masks like Matthew, and many in elaborate Marie Antoinette–style dresses and feathered headpieces. Everyone also wore smiles, but that was the one thing he couldn't summon.

"Come, my friend." Vincenzo Mantovani, his next-door-neighbor, clapped Matthew on the shoulder. "We join the party at Caffe Florian."

"*Va bene*," Matthew replied, earning a grin from the Italian who had appointed himself Matthew's Carnevale guide this evening. Vincenzo appointed himself to a lot of things, as long as they were fun, reckless and ill-advised, which made him the appropriate companion for a man who wanted to find all of the above but had no clue how to accomplish it.

Actually, Matthew would be happy if he could just forget about Amber for a few hours, but the ghost of his wife followed him everywhere, even to Italy, thousands of miles from her grave.

Vincenzo chattered in accented English as he and Matthew pushed through the crowd along the edges of Piazza San Marco and squeezed into Caffe Florian, where it was too loud to converse. Which suited Matthew. He had the right companion, but he wasn't sure Vincenzo did.

Like most Venetians, the man had never met a stranger and had immediately latched onto the American living by himself in the big, lonely palazzo next door. Vincenzo's description, not Matthew's, though he couldn't deny it had some truth. He'd outbid an Arab prince by the skin of his teeth to buy the palazzo overlooking the Grand Canal as a wedding gift to Amber, but they'd never made it to Italy in the eleven months after the wedding. He'd been too busy working.

Then it was too late.

Matthew sipped the cappuccino his new friend had magically produced and summoned up a shred of merriment. If he planned to think about something other than Amber, dwelling on her wasn't going to work. She would hate him like this, would want him to move on, and he was trying. His sole goal this evening was to be someone who wasn't grieving, someone who didn't have the weight of responsibility and his family's expectations on his shoulders. Someone who fit into this fantastical, hedonistic Carnevale atmosphere.

It was hard to be someone else when he'd been a Wheeler since birth.

Matthew, along with his brother, father and grandfather, comprised the foundation of Wheeler Family Partners, a multimillion-dollar commercial real estate firm that had been brokering property deals in North Texas for over a century. Matthew had firmly believed in the power of fam-

ily and tradition, until he lost first his wife, then his grand-father. Grief had so paralyzed him the only solution had been to leave.

He was a runaway from life, pure and simple. He had to find a way to get back to Dallas, back to the man he'd been.

The beaches of Mexico had failed to produce an answer. Machu Picchu had just exhausted him. The names of the other places he'd been had started to blur, and he had to do something different.

A month ago, he'd ended up in Venice. Until real life felt doable again, this was where he'd be.

Near eleven o'clock, Vincenzo herded a hundred of his closest friends—and Matthew—the few blocks to his house for a masked ball. The narrow streets allowed for only a few partygoers to pass simultaneously, so by the time Matthew arrived at the tail end of the group, the palazzo next door to his was already ablaze with lights and people. In marked contrast, Matthew's house was dark.

He turned his back on it and went up the stone steps to Vincenzo's back entrance. The sounds of Carnevale blasted from the palazzo, drowning out the quiet lap of the canal against the water entrance at the front.

Inside, a costumed attendant took his cloak. An ornate antique table in the hall blocked Matthew's path to the main area, an oddity with its large glass bowl in the center full of cell phones.

"It's a phone party."

The gravelly voice came from behind him, and he turned to find the owner.

A woman. Masked, of course, and wearing a delicate embroidered dress in pale blue and white with miles of skirts. The neckline wasn't as low cut as almost every other female's, but in combination with so much dress, her softly mounded breasts drew his eye. Whimsical silver butterfly wings sprouted from her back.

"Was my confusion that obvious?" he asked, his gaze firmly on her face.

She smiled. "You're American."

"Is that the explanation for why I don't know what a phone party is?"

"No, that's because you have more maturity than most of the people here."

So she must know the guests, then. Except for Vincenzo, who had disappeared, Matthew knew no one. This little butterfly was an interesting first encounter.

Most of her face was covered, with the exception of a full mouth painted pink. Caramel-colored hair hung in loose curls around her bare shoulders. Stunning. But her voice...it was sultry and deep, with a strange ragged edge that caught him in the gut.

He'd been looking for a distraction. Perhaps he'd found one.

"Now I'm curious. Care to enlighten me?" he asked.

She shrugged with a tiny lift of her shoulders. "Women drop their phone into the bowl. Men pick one out. Voila. Instant hookup."

His eyebrows rose. Vincenzo partied much differently than Matthew had been expecting. "I honestly have no good response."

"So you won't be fishing one out at the end of the evening?"

A tricky question. The old Matthew would say absolutely not. He'd never had a one-night stand in his life, never even considered it. This kind of thing had his brother, Lucas, written all over it. Lucas might have pulled out two phones and somehow convinced both women they'd been looking for a threesome all along. Well, once upon a time he would have, but in a bizarre turn of events, his brother was happily married now, with a baby on the way.

Matthew did not share his brother's talent when it came to women. He knew how to broker a million-dollar deal for

a downtown Dallas high-rise and knew how to navigate the privilege of his social circle but nothing else, especially not how to be a widower at the age of thirty-two.

When Matthew left Dallas, intent on finding a way to move on after Amber's death, he'd had a vague notion of becoming like Lucas had been before marrying his wife, Cia. Lucas always had fun and never worried about consequences. Matthew, like his father and grandfather before him, had willingly carried the weight of duty and family and tradition on his shoulders, eagerly anticipating the day his wife would give birth to the first of a new generation of Wheelers. Only to have it all collapse.

Becoming more like Lucas was better than being Matthew, and nothing else had worked to pull him out of this dead-inside funk. And he had to pull out of it so he could go home and pick up his life again.

So what would Lucas do?

"Depends." Matthew nodded to the bowl. "Is yours in there?"

With a throaty laugh, she shook her head. "Not my style."

Strangely, he was relieved and disappointed at the same time. "Not mine, either. Though I might have made an exception in this one case."

Her smile widened and she drew closer, rustling her wings. The front of her dress brushed his chest as she leaned in to whisper in her odd, smoky voice, "Me, too."

Then she was gone.

He watched her as she swept into the main room of Vincenzo's palazzo and was swallowed by the crush. It was intriguing to be so instantly fascinated by a woman because of her voice. Should he follow her? How could he not follow her after such a clear indication of interest?

Maybe she'd been flirting and it hadn't meant anything. He cursed under his breath. It had been far too long since he'd dated to remember the rules. Actually, he'd never understood the rules, even then, which was saying something

for a guy who thrived on rules. But this was Venice, not Dallas, and he was someone else.

There were no rules.

Matthew followed Butterfly Woman into the crowd.

Electronic music clashed with old-world costumes, but no one seemed to notice. Dancers dominated the floor space on the lower level of the palazzo. But none of the women had wings.

Along the edges of the dance floor, partygoers tried their luck at roulette and vingt-et-un, but he didn't bother to look for his mystery woman there. Gambling was for those who knew nothing about odds, logic or common sense, and if she fell into that category, he'd rather find a different distraction.

A flash of silver caught his eye, and he glimpsed the very tips of her wings as she disappeared into another room.

"Excuse me." Matthew waded through the dancers as politely as he could and chased after the only thing he could recall being interested in for eighteen very long, very cold months.

When he paused under a grand arch between the two rooms, he saw her. She stood at the edge of a group of people engrossed in something he couldn't see. And he had the distinct impression she felt as alone in the crowd as he did.

Tarot junkies crowded around Madam Wong as if she held the winning lottery numbers. Evangeline La Fleur was neither a junkie nor one to buy lottery tickets, but people were always amusing. Madam Wong turned over another card and the crowd gasped and murmured. Evangeline rolled her eyes.

Her neck prickled and she sensed someone watching her.

The guy from the hall.

They locked gazes across the room, and she gave herself a half second to let the shiver go all the way down. Delicious. There'd been something about the way he talked to

her, as if truly interested in what she had to say. About Vincenzo's stupid phone party, no less.

Lately, no one was interested in what she said, unless it was to answer the question, *"What are you going to do now that you can't sing anymore?"* They might as well ask what she'd do after they nailed the coffin shut.

Hall guy's suit was well-cut, promising what lay underneath it might be worth a peek or two, his lips below the black velvet mask were strong and full and his hands looked…capable. The man trifecta.

The music faded into the background as he strode purposefully toward her without so much as glancing at what he passed. Every bit of his taut focus was on her, and it had a powerful effect, way down low in places usually reserved for men she'd known far longer.

Boldly, she watched him approach, her gaze equally as fixed on him.

Bring it, Tall, Blond and Gorgeous.

The mystery of his masked face somehow made him more attractive. That and the fact he couldn't possibly know who she was behind her mask. This…pull was all about anonymity, and she'd have called anyone a dirty liar who said she'd like it. But she did. When was the last time she'd been within a forty-foot radius of someone who wasn't aware of how her career had crashed and burned? Or the number of Grammys she'd won, for that matter.

For a time, she'd dwelled in the upper echelon of entertainers—so successful she didn't require a last name. The world knew her simply as Eva.

Then she was cast aside, adrift and alone, with no voice.

"There you are," he murmured, as if afraid to be overheard and determined to keep things between them very private. "I'd started to think you'd flown away."

She laughed, surprising herself. Laughter didn't come easily, not lately. "The wings only work after midnight."

"I'd better move fast, then." The eyes on her were beau-

tiful, an almost colorless, crystalline blue that contrasted with the black border of the mask. "My name is—"

"No." She touched a finger to his lips. "No names. Not yet."

As he looked very much like he wanted to suck her fingertip into his mouth, she dropped it before she let him. This stranger was exciting, no doubt, but she had a healthy survival instinct. Vincenzo's friends were a little on the wild side. Even for her.

Yet she'd been following Vincenzo around Europe for a couple of months and couldn't seem to find anything better to do. She wanted to. Oh, how she wanted to. But what?

"Are you seeking your fortune, then?" He nodded to Madam Wong and the crowd parted.

Madam Wong shuffled her cards. "Come. Sit."

Tall, Blond and Gorgeous pulled the brocade chair away from the draped table. Evangeline couldn't see a way to gracefully refuse without drawing unwanted attention, so she sat, extremely aware of the capable hand resting on the back of the chair inches from her neck.

When Madam Wong shoved the deck across the table, Evangeline cut it about a third of the way down and let the fortune-teller restack the cards.

After that quack doctor butchered her vocal cords, Evangeline had spent three months searching for a cure, eventually landing on the doorstep of every Romanian gypsy, every Asian acupuncturist and every Nepalese faith healer she could find.

No one had a way to restore her damaged voice. Or her damaged soul. In short, this wasn't her first tarot reading, and she had little hope it would be any more helpful than all the other mumbo jumbo.

The only positive from the nightmare of the past six months came from winning the lawsuit against the quack doctor, who no longer had a license to practice medicine, thanks to her.

The costumed crowd pressed closer as Madam Wong began laying out the spread. Her brow furrowed. "You have a great conflict, yes?"

Oh, however did you guess? Evangeline waited for the rest of the hokey wisdom.

The withered old woman twirled one of the many rings on her fingers as she contemplated the cards. "You have been cut deeply and lost something precious."

The capable hand of the masked stranger brushed her hair. Evangeline sat up straighter and frowned.

Cut.

She had been, in more ways than one.

"This card…" Madam Wong tapped it. "It confuses me. Are you trying to conceive?"

"A baby?" Evangeline spit out the phrase on a heavy exhale and took another breath to calm her racing pulse. "Not even close."

"Conception comes in many forms and is simply a beginning. It is the step after inspiration. You have been inspired. Now you must go forth and shape something from it."

Inspiration. That was in short supply. Evangeline's throat convulsed unexpectedly. The music in her veins had been abruptly silenced and she hadn't been inspired to write one single note since the surgery from hell.

Madam Wong swept the cards into a pile and began shuffling. "I must do a second spread."

Speechless and frozen, Evangeline tried to shake her head. Her eyes began to burn, a sure sign she'd start bawling uncontrollably very soon. It was the wrong time of the month for this sort of emotional roller coaster.

She needed a code word to get her out of this situation. Her manager had always given her one, so if the press asked a sensitive question, she'd say it and he'd rescue her.

Except she had no manager and no code word. She had nothing. She'd been rejected by everyone—music, the industry, fans. Her father.

"I believe you promised me a dance."

Tall, Blond and Gorgeous clasped her hand and pulled her out of the chair in one graceful move.

"Thank you," he said to Madam Wong, "but we've taken enough of your time. Good evening."

And like that, he whirled her away from the table, away from the prying eyes.

By the time he stopped in an alcove between the main dance floor and the back room, her pulse had slowed. She blinked away the worst of the burn and stared up at her savior. "How did you know?"

He didn't pretend to misunderstand. "You were so tense, the chair was vibrating. I take it you don't care for tarot."

"Not especially. Thanks." After a beat, when it became apparent he wasn't going to ask any questions—which almost made her weep in gratitude—she made a show of scouting around for a nonexistent waiter. "I could go for a glass of champagne. You?"

The thought of alcohol almost made her nauseous, but she needed a minute alone.

"Sure. Unless you'd rather dance?"

"Not right now."

Actually, she was thinking seriously about ditching the party and going to her room. A headache had bloomed behind her eyes. Except her room was right above the dance floor and Vincenzo's other guests had taken the rest of the rooms.

"Be right back. Stay here." Her stranger vanished into the crowd.

Maybe she could quietly gather her things and check into Hotel Danieli, with no one the wiser.... She groaned. As if. She had a better chance of finding solid gold bars on the street than an empty hotel room in Venice during Carnevale.

The stranger returned quickly with two champagne flutes, and she smiled brightly, clinking her rim to his in a false show of bravado. Yes, he was gorgeous and intui-

tive, but she wasn't going to be good company tonight. She nursed the drink and tried to think of an exit strategy when over his shoulder, she caught sight of her worst nightmare.

It was Rory. With Sara Lear.

Of course he was with Sara Lear. Sara's debut album full of bubblegum pop and saccharine love songs had burned up the charts and was still solidly at number one. The little upstart hadn't worn a mask, preferring to bask in the glow of stardom. Rory was also unmasked, no doubt to make doubly sure everyone knew who was with Sara. He was nothing if not savvy about his own career and his band Reaper made few bones about their desire to headline one of the major summer concert series. Hitching his wagon to a star was an old pattern.

Evangeline had flushed his engagement ring down the toilet after he dumped her and gladly told him to go to hell when he asked for it back.

Rory and Sara strolled through the main room as if they owned it, and why wouldn't they? Both of them had functional vocal cords and long, vital careers ahead of them. Six months ago, Evangeline would have been on Rory Cartman's arm, blissfully in love, blissfully at the top of her career and still blind to the cruelty of a world that loved a success but shunned a has-been.

The headache slammed her again.

She knocked back the champagne in one swallow and tried to figure out how to get past Rory and Sara without being recognized. Sara, she wasn't so worried about; they'd never officially met. But her ex-fiancé would out her in a New York minute without a single qualm. A mask only went so far with someone who knew her intimately.

She couldn't take the questions or the pitying looks or the eyes watching her navigate a very public meeting with the guy who'd shattered her heart and the woman who'd replaced her in his bed. And on the charts.

"More champagne?" her companion asked.

Rory and his new Pop Princess girlfriend stopped a few yards from the shadowy alcove where she stood with the masked stranger. She couldn't step out into the light and couldn't risk standing there with no shield.

Desperate times, desperate measures.

Praying she'd read him right, she plucked the half-empty flute from her savior's hand, set both glasses on the ledge behind her and grasped the lapels of his tux. With a yank, she hauled him into a kiss.

The moment their lips connected, the name Rory Cartman ceased to have any meaning whatsoever.

Two

Matthew had only a moment to register her intent. It wasn't long enough. When the winged woman pressed her lips to his, his body lit up and flooded with heat. She was like a conduit to a nuclear reactor, and the shocking sensation of her warm mouth on his threatened to bring on full meltdown.

He knew precisely what Lucas would do in this situation.

Cupping her face with both palms, Matthew tilted her head to slant his mouth against hers at a deeper angle. Her lips parted on a sigh, and the hands holding his lapels tightened, drawing him closer.

Nearly groaning, he kissed this nameless butterfly until he couldn't think, couldn't stop, almost couldn't stand. The shock of awareness and incendiary carnal lust picked up where his brain failed.

Shocking. And yet familiar. As if they'd done this before, exactly this way, pressed against each other in the shadows. Their lips fit, their bodies slid together with ease. He was kissing a stranger—a nameless stranger—and it should feel wrong, or at least odd.

It was so very right.

This woman was not at all his type—too glittery, too sensual, too beautiful. He couldn't imagine introducing her to his mother or taking her to a museum opening where they'd rub shoulders with the elite of Dallas.

But he didn't care.

For the first time since Amber died, he felt alive. His heart beat in his chest and blood flowed through his veins and a woman was kissing him. He reveled in these small clues that he hadn't been buried alongside his wife.

After an eternity passed in a blink, she broke away and stared up at him, her breath coming in short gasps. "I'm sorry."

"For what?"

He hadn't kissed a woman other than Amber in five years and as a reintroduction to the art, it was off the map. Surely she'd felt some of the same heat.

"I shouldn't have done that," she said.

"Yes, you absolutely should have."

He might be out of practice, but she was still firmly in his arms, and a woman who hadn't just had her world shaken to the foundation would have stepped away by now.

She inhaled sharply, her chest pushing against his and stroking the flame higher. "Not under false pretenses. I have to come clean. My ex is here, and that was a poor attempt to hide from him."

"I beg to differ. As attempts go, I thought it was pretty good."

A quavery laugh slipped out from her kiss-reddened lips and then she did step away, out of his embrace. But not too far.

"Just so you know, I don't go around kissing random men."

"There's an easy way to fix that. I'd be happy to introduce myself and thus eliminate the randomness."

"That would be awesome because I'm pretty sure I'm going to kiss you again."

She *had* felt it.

The thrill swept all the way to the soles of his feet. To-night, he was someone else, and as it seemed to be working out well so far, why screw around with it?

"Matt. My name is Matt."

It flowed from his mouth effortlessly, though he'd never been Matt in his life. But right here, right now, he liked Matt a hell of lot. Matt wasn't bogged down in inertia and terrified he'd never find his way out. Matt hadn't walked away from all his responsibilities at home or lain awake at night, eaten with guilt over it. Matt hadn't drifted around the world in search of something he suspected didn't exist, only to land in Venice holed up in a cold, lonely palazzo.

Matt had fun and kissed costumed women at parties and maybe got to second base before the end of the night.

She smiled. "Nice to meet you, Matt. You can call me Angie."

Angie. It was too harsh, too common for such a delicate and ethereal woman. The careful phrasing tipped him off that it wasn't her real name, but since he'd similarly hedged, he couldn't exactly complain.

"Which one is your ex? So we can steer clear."

Since she'd been trying to hide, he assumed the breakup had been nasty and not Angie's choice.

Surreptitiously, she glanced behind her, then faced him again. Her soft brown eyes bored into his, luminous with appreciation. "He's over there, on the couch with the little blonde."

Matthew located what had to be the couple she meant. They were locked in a torrid embrace, and the guy's hands were down the blonde's dress. Ouch. Not only was her ex at the same party but also not much for public decency.

"They didn't get the memo? This is a masked ball."

"I like you," she said with a decisive nod.

He grinned. "I like you, too."

"That's good, because I intend to thoroughly use you. I hope you won't be offended."

Matthew's eyebrow shot up. "That depends, I suppose, on what you plan to use me for. And I really hope it's in the same vein as kissing me to hide from lover boy over there."

Apparently Matt knew how to flirt, too. There was no other explanation for such blatant come-ons.

Her tongue wet her lips, and the way she did it—while eyeing his lips at the same time—clamped down hard on his lower half. "You just became my new boyfriend."

"Excellent. I didn't realize I'd applied, but I'm gratified to have survived the rigorous selection process."

She laughed, and that gravelly timbre sliced through his gut anew. "Just for tonight. I can't stand the thought of anyone feeling sorry for me because I'm here alone. Pretend we're together, and I'll buy you breakfast."

Breakfast? He might be in for an evening with a little more action than he'd envisioned.

Was that what he wanted?

"I'm not the slightest bit offended. Unless I'm the backup choice. Is your real boyfriend otherwise engaged?"

"Very nicely done. But unnecessary. You don't have to be all casual-like if you want to know whether I'm available. Just ask."

Dang, he *was* out of practice. But dating had felt like such a betrayal. For so long, he couldn't, and when he finally deemed himself ready, no one appealed to him. Even if he'd dated every one of the sophisticated, demure women in Dallas angling for an invitation to dinner, none of them had wings.

He swallowed and dived in. "Angie, are you seeing anyone?"

"Yeah, this guy named Matt." She stood on tiptoe to whisper in his ear, like she'd done in the hall when they first met. It was becoming something he enjoyed thoroughly. "And he's really hot, too."

"Really?" No one had ever referred to him as hot. At least not to his face. The notion buzzed through his heightened senses and settled in nicely. "I must know more about this guy."

"I'd like to, as well. Vincenzo's got a great balcony on the second floor. Grab a couple of glasses of champagne and meet me there."

She turned and threw a saucy glance over her shoulder as she swayed in the direction of the stone staircase beyond the roulette tables.

He couldn't comply fast enough. Lucas would definitely see what this sexy little butterfly had in mind, and Matt was pretty curious, too. This was one night where anything might happen, and for once, he was looking forward to the possibilities.

The balcony overlooked a closed-off side courtyard that had fallen into disrepair. The small space above was poorly lit and cold, but had the bonus of being Rory and Sara free.

Evangeline was confident Matt wouldn't recognize Rory, as her new friend didn't seem the type to listen to punk rock, but her ex-fiancé's picture did end up next to hers with alarming frequency, even six months later. She couldn't be too careful.

Vincenzo's entertainment system vibrated the stone below her feet. In the distance, the revelry at San Marco drifted along the streets, wrapping the city in festive noise. Singing, instruments, the pop of what might be fireworks, all of it blended into the mystique that was Carnevale. And, for a moment, she was by herself at the world's largest party.

She didn't have to wait long for Matt. Her masked companion came through the unlocked French door with two champagne flutes balanced expertly in one capable hand. It was February in Venice, but the shiver that twisted her back had nothing to do with the temperature.

Thank God she hadn't ditched him. If she had, she'd have

run smack into Rory and missed the single most perfect kiss in the history of time. As stand-in boyfriends went, Matt had it going on. And he'd kissed her headache away, too.

She could find worse company to stave off the perpetual loneliness. Especially among Vincenzo's friends.

Matt handed her a glass and clinked the rims in an echo of their first toast. "This balcony is very difficult to find. How did you know it was here?"

Without the muddle of loud music, his voice was nice—clear, with a hint of the South running through it.

"I'm staying with Vincenzo. My room is down the hall."

"Oh? How do you know Vincenzo, Angie?"

Only her mother called her Angie, so it had seemed safe enough to use the name, though she regretted the necessity. Matt was a genuinely nice human being, someone she'd probably never have connected with under normal circumstances.

"Friend of a friend. You?"

As he was well-spoken and had far more class than Vincenzo's typical wealthy, spoiled buddies, she'd pegged him as a casual acquaintance.

"I'm staying next door."

Well, that made sense. Here on business and renting for the duration, most likely.

"Will you be in Venice long?"

Below the mask, his mouth turned down. "I'm not sure."

As she knew exactly the tone one used to say *back off*, she didn't press him, though now she was curious what his business in Venice might be. Shipping, maybe. She'd never dated a businessman and rarely interacted with people in that realm unless it involved contracts.

Whatever his livelihood, it was to remain a secret for the time being, and since she had secrets of her own, that was fine. She tossed back some champagne, let the bubbles fizz across her tongue and contemplated this very intriguing stand-in boyfriend.

Of course, if they stayed on this balcony, she didn't really need a companion, coerced or otherwise, as a shield from questions and ex-fiancés. So maybe she needed him for something else entirely.

She was alone in the most romantic city in the world, and Matt represented a golden opportunity to change that for one magical evening, then leave before he realized who she was. Loneliness went hand in hand with the fresh scars of rejection that kept reminding her not to let anyone get too close.

But an anonymous encounter—that was a horse of a different color. If he didn't know who she was, he couldn't reject *her*.

The direction of her thoughts heated her up fast despite the chill in the air. But who could blame her for going there when the man's mouth made her blood boil?

There was this strange awareness between them, which she'd felt the moment he'd turned to face her in the foyer. It was almost a recognition, as if she'd seen him many times, but had never quite caught up with him to start a conversation.

Yet he'd never removed his mask. She knew he had a chiseled jaw to match his well-defined mouth and a solid chest under his lapels, but that was it. The rest of his face remained hidden, like his body, his hopes, his disappointments...the mystery of it whet her appetite for more.

"Ever been on a speed date?" she asked him.

He took a sip of champagne and shook his head. "Can't say that I have."

She doubted he'd ever have a need to resort to such a thing. Dating as a whole never worked for her. Men usually fell into three categories: starstruck, unavailable or opportunist.

Rory was firmly in the last category. His rejection had been crushing, especially after losing her voice. She'd thought of all people, he'd understand and would sympathize. That he'd be there for her during the worst crisis of

her life. Instead, he couldn't dump her fast enough. On the bright side, he'd cured her of any desire to have a man in her life permanently.

Which made her masked friend exactly what the doctor ordered.

"I haven't either, but I always wanted to. It seems like fun."

"I'm always up for fun. What does it entail?"

She loved the way he talked, like it never occurred to him that normal people's vocabulary didn't usually include words like *entail*. And like it never occurred to him that she hadn't gone to college. He treated her as if she possessed intelligence. That was potent.

"Well, to the best of my knowledge, there's a time limit. We have to get to know each other as quickly as possible before the bell rings. It's designed so you can figure out if you're compatible in a short period of time."

He cocked his head, lips pursed. "I already know I like you. Why do we need to have a speed date to figure that out?"

She shook her head, gaze glued to his. A part of her wanted to take this instant attraction to its natural conclusion as fast as possible. But no smart girl jumped into the pool without at least some clue how deep it was.

"Consider it part of the application process. There's a spark here, and I'm curious to see what happens if we fan it."

His irises flared. "Just so I'm clear, how does the time limit factor in?"

"Ask as many questions as you want, as fast as you can, and when the timer on my phone goes off, you're going to kiss me."

His palm cupped her face, tilting it up to almost meet his. "What if we skip the timer and I kiss you right now?"

"That's no fun." She firmly removed his hand from her chin, only to lose it to her hair as he threaded his fingers

through the loose curls not caught up in her feather head-piece.

His warm thumb rested in the hollow behind her ear, brushing it lightly. "Clearly you need a refresher on how good my lips feel on yours."

The shiver went deeper this time, and a nice little hum zipped along her skin, tightening all her erogenous zones into an ache she'd not experienced in a long time. Apparently the speed date was unnecessary to fan the spark.

"Where's your sense of adventure? Five minutes."

She pulled her phone from the clutch tied to a string at her waist and tapped up the timer. She set it on the stone ledge behind Matt, then locked onto the ice-blue of his eyes. Anticipation was one of her favorite parts, and she'd happily drag it out as long as she could.

"I'll go first," he said. "How many times have you seduced a man on a balcony?"

She couldn't help but laugh. Was that what she was doing? "Never. I'm making all sorts of exceptions for you."

"How many times have you seduced a man period?"

"Once or twice. I'm not one to apologize for having a healthy sex drive. Should I?"

"Not to me. Maybe to all the other men down there who are missing out. Your turn."

"I'm naked. What do you do first?"

"Fall down on my knees and weep with joy. Did you really mean to ask what I'd do second?"

Oh, yeah, she really did like Matt. There was something to be said for a guy who could make her laugh with such regularity. "That is what I meant, and before you get all smart-alecky with me, go ahead and hit me with third, fourth and fifth."

"Did I buy you dinner first?"

"Who cares? I'm naked or did you forget?"

"Oh, no, my gorgeous little butterfly, I did not forget. I

asked because I'm trying to get a solid picture in my head of the scene."

His hand pressed on her nape, oh-so-slightly, and her head fell back. His lips grazed the corner of her mouth, not quite touching, but close enough to send a frisson of sparkling heat all the way down to her core.

Well, she hadn't intended for this speed date to descend into foreplay, but okay. It was *sizzling*. And personal information, like their secret professions, or lack thereof in her case, wasn't likely to come up.

"Are you naked on a bed after I've undressed you?" he murmured against her jaw, breath fanning the uncovered part her of face and making her ache to turn into those lips to complete the connection. "Or naked in the shower and have no idea I'm about to join you? Naked, but asleep and I'm going to awaken you slowly?"

Her lungs hitched. "Cheater. You've played this game before."

She felt his mouth turn up against her cheek. "Let's assume I'm a quick study. Your answer? I believe that was three questions."

"It was?"

Who was seducing whom here? And how far did she want this to go? Never had she contemplated such a dangerous liaison with a mysterious man she'd only just met but who touched her on so many levels.

"Bed, shower or asleep? I must know in order to tell you what I plan to do. Or perhaps you'd prefer I show you?"

Yes, yes she would. Except she couldn't speak, as he slid an arm around her waist, drawing her taut against his warm body. She clutched his shoulders and they were amazing and strong underneath his jacket. "There's no shower on this balcony."

"So true," he murmured. "The alarm's going off."

It wasn't. She didn't care.

He covered her mouth with his and turned her into liquid

mercury for the second time. The man was a master, hot and forceful, and her lips fell open under the divine pressure. He plunged in, tongue skimming against hers, deliciously rough and tasting of champagne.

She moaned and changed the angle, inviting him deeper, urging him forward with small tugs of her hands against his shoulders. *More*, she needed more, needed to quench the thirst raging in her veins with this extremely arousing man.

Judging by the full-fledged blaze between them, he felt the same. About *her*, not Eva. How great was that, to be with a man who hadn't already made a bunch of snap judgments?

"Touch me," she commanded hoarsely, her damaged voice even more raw with desire.

Almost hesitantly, he palmed her breast through the thick bodice of the dress, and she nearly growled in frustration. Forget that. She reached down and gathered up the hem of the ridiculously full skirt and tucked it under the sash at her waist. She guided his hand through the opening, straight to her bottom.

It was his turn to groan as he flattened his palm against her bare cheek. "A thong? That is unbelievably sexy."

"Not nearly as sexy as your hand on it while I'm still fully dressed." He explored the uncovered flesh and traced the strings into her crevice and back out again. Her knees almost buckled. "Don't stop. Keep going."

He took her mouth again, ravenous and greedy, as his fingers nudged underneath the silk. Just far enough to steal her breath for a long second. Blatantly, she circled her pelvis, silently begging him to go deeper.

Whether she'd planned to go this far or not, her body wasn't holding back. She was about to come apart under his capable hands.

Instead, he withdrew entirely and blew out a heavy breath, smoothing her skirts down with a confusing finality. "Angie, I have to confess something."

"You're married." Disappointment swamped her so quick

and so fast she nearly convulsed. The ache, which had moments ago been a vortex of desire, cooled. She should have known.

"No." He shook his head in vehement denial. "I'm completely unattached. It's just…I don't…"

"You're not attracted to me." But his impressive length had ground hard against her, evident even through the monstrosity of fabric at her waist.

He swallowed hard. "How could you possibly think that? I've never been so turned on in my life. There's this one small problem. I've never seduced a woman on a balcony, so I'm ah…unprepared."

Oh. "You don't have a condom."

The giggle slipped out before she could stop it. He was just so flustered and so cute, running a hand over his dark blond hair with evident frustration. It caught her quite unexpectedly in a soft, warm place inside. Talk about being unprepared.

Was he ever going to stop being so unexpected and amazing? God, she hoped not.

Three

"I'm glad you find my lack of preparation amusing." Matthew certainly didn't. He'd never been so mad at himself and so happy she wasn't angry, all at the same time.

And he had never been in quite so much physical pain. Yes, the women in his social circle were sophisticated and demure, rightly so, but lukewarm in their approach to everything.

He never realized how truly hot it could be with someone so uninhibited.

"It's not funny. Trust me, it's not." She pulled him down by the lapels and kissed him sweetly. "That's for not having a condom."

"What?"

She shrugged with a delicate one-shoulder move. "I've been around my share of dogs. It's nice to find someone who isn't always thinking with what's in his pants. Besides, this isn't the dark ages. You can easily be mad at me for not having one."

"I take it that means you don't."

She shook her head. "And I can't do birth control. Everything gives me headaches. But we're in luck because it's

Carnevale. I bet we can score a boxful of very festive condoms from Vincenzo's room."

So now Matt had been reduced to stealing condoms. Brilliant. Condoms were not first and foremost on his mind, yet he'd gladly jumped into her wicked game without hesitation.

What was he doing on this balcony?

"Maybe it's a sign."

"A sign? Like what, we're not supposed to hook up tonight?"

Hook up. Matthew Wheeler did not *hook up*. He'd been happily married to the perfect woman and would still be if an aneurism hadn't killed her. Commitment made him tick.

Angie might discount the idea of signs, but he couldn't. This wasn't meant to happen and probably for a very good reason. Did he really want a one-night stand with some woman he'd met at a party? It just wasn't his style.

The empty palazzo next door called his name, offering a place to retreat and lick his wounds. Where he would go to bed alone, dream about Amber and wake in a cold sweat. If he slept. Sometimes he lay awake, racked with remorse over leaving his family in the lurch.

That was his real life. This interlude with a winged woman at a masked ball was nothing but a fantasy born of desperation and loneliness. It wasn't fair to use Angie to appease either.

But God Almighty, it was difficult to walk away from her. When she'd been in his arms, pliant and sizzling, he heard the distinct sound of his soul waking up.

Angie's kiss-stung lips and luminous brown eyes nearly did him in. She'd asked him to be her fake boyfriend at this party, a role he'd stepped into with ease and enthusiasm, but without really considering what enormous pain must have driven her to ask.

He couldn't abandon her.

Matthew might not hook up, but neither did he have to listen to Matt, who despite Angie's belief, was very much

thinking with the bulge in his pants. He needed to cool down and evaluate his goal here before he got carried away by the fantasy.

So he'd split the difference.

"Let's dance."

Wary surprise wrinkled her mouth. "At the party?"

"Sure. Why not? You haven't had a chance to throw your new boyfriend in lover boy's face yet." Neither of them had done much spelling-it-out and some clarity might be in order. "And I'd like to take a step back. Make sure we're both headed in the same direction."

"I hear you. The balcony *is* cold and I do like to dance," she mused. "How about this? I'll dart into Vincenzo's room and stuff my clutch with as many condoms as it'll hold. We'll dance. If you move to music like you do on a speed date, we'll be headed in the same direction all right—back upstairs and into my bed."

His pants grew tighter. Exactly how many times did she envision having sex? He shook his head to clear the erotic images she'd sprung loose in his brain. It didn't work.

"I'll consider myself warned."

She smiled and it was a whole lot wicked.

Matthew took her hand and led her toward what promised to be a provocative round of dancing. At least in a room full of people, the temptation to dive under Angie's skirt would be lessened.

If he did that again, he'd like to be much more clear-headed about it.

Unbelievably, more people had gathered in the rooms downstairs, filling the dance floor to overflowing. Couples swayed and dipped to the slow song. Matthew drew Angie into the sea of dancers, carefully navigating to protect her wings. He hadn't danced in a long time but the ballroom classes he'd let Amber drag him to came back in a rush.

He positioned his arms and prepared to try some semblance of a modified waltz, or at least do the best he could

in such a crowd. Angie melted against him, undulating her hips against his in a hypnotic, sensual rhythm. A hot lick of need coursed through his gut. She hadn't attended the same classes. Obviously.

He held her close, mimicking her moves. All he could think about was the scrap of silk underneath her skirt. And the foil packets rounding the sides of her clutch. He wasn't doing a very good job of splitting the difference.

Angie's ear was right by his mouth, and he had the most insane urge to nibble on it. Instead, he cleared his throat to ease the knot of sexual tension that had stiffened everything in his body.

"What if we continue our speed date but take it down a notch?"

She repositioned her head so it was lying in the hollow of his shoulder. The feathers anchored in her hair brushed across his neck. "I'm listening."

"What's your favorite color?"

"That's more like forty-seven notches. I don't have a favorite color. I like the rainbow." Someone bumped into her, shoving them closer together, not that he minded. "What's yours?"

The smell of her hair weakened his knees. Outside, it hadn't been so noticeable, but in the close, heated confines of the room, the exotic scent curled through his nose. Even her shampoo was unearthly, as if he needed another reminder they came from different worlds.

"Black. It goes with everything."

"How practical. I like that in a man. Where were you born?"

"Dallas. And please don't ask me if I've met J. R. Ewing. I've never been to Southfork, and I don't watch the TV show." That was one constant about Europe. Everyone knew Dallas from either reruns of the old drama or the reboot version on cable. "What about you?"

"Toronto. My mom moved to Detroit when I was a baby and became a U.S. citizen. That's where I grew up."

So maybe their worlds weren't as far apart as he'd assumed. "You're American?"

The silence stretched long enough for Matthew to wonder if he'd said something to offend her. But she had to know her ragged voice didn't carry a discernible accent and was unusual enough to warrant such a question.

"I'm nothing and everything," she said with a laugh that wasn't a laugh. "Usually I tell people I'm French Canadian. But I haven't been to Toronto in years. Or Detroit for that matter."

"Is your mom still in Detroit?"

"She lives in Minneapolis, for now, working on her fourth marriage. I have fam—other people in Detroit."

Other people? He didn't ask. The undercurrent of pain in her voice had been strong, and if she'd wanted him to know, she'd have said.

"Your home is in Europe then?"

"Or wherever the wind takes me." She injected a note of levity, but he wasn't fooled. Nowhere felt like home and it bothered her. "Do you still live in Dallas?"

"No." Lack of a home was something they shared. He'd sold his house, his car, everything. The only possessions he had to his name were the clothes in the closet at the palazzo and a few childhood mementos stored in his parents' extra bedroom. "I'm going where the wind takes me, too."

At least until he found the way home.

She stopped dancing and collided with the next couple, earning a dirty look from them. Impatiently, she pushed Matthew off the dance floor toward the side wall and peered up through her mask, eyes liquid with sympathy. "I'm sorry."

"For?"

"For whatever happened."

She didn't question him,, though she could obviously read between the lines as well as he could.

A wave of understanding rippled between them. Both of them were searching. Both of them carried secrets full of pain and misery and loneliness.

They weren't different at all.

She whispered, "I'm glad the wind blew us to the same place."

All pretense of speed dating evaporated. Something much more significant was happening.

"Me, too."

Amber's death had broken his heart, nearly broken him entirely, and he couldn't fathom feeling that strongly about anyone else. For months and months, he'd despaired of ever feeling *anything* again, and like a foghorn echoing through the mist of his grief, this gravelly-voiced fantasy had appeared.

She was a gift, one he wasn't ready to give back.

No, he didn't want a one-night stand with some random woman, but he couldn't resist exploring what two damaged souls might become to each other.

With his brain firmly in command, he drew her hand into his and smiled.

"Instead of directions upstairs, I have a better idea. Come home with me."

Home. Evangeline liked the sound of it. She'd never had a home.

She'd had new stepfathers every few years. A half sister, Lisa, whom their father had obviously preferred since he'd married Lisa's mother. Plenty of hotel rooms and airplanes—all of that, she'd had.

She wished she could indulge in something so simple, so achingly honest as *home*. But imagine if she took off her mask and Matt turned out to be a reporter. Or worse.

At Vincenzo's, masks were part of the ambience, the ano-

nymity. Masks kept things surface level. Masks kept a man at arm's length and promised nothing more than one night, a brief, sizzling interruption of loneliness. Masks prevented rejection. And scars. She'd had enough of both, thanks.

And there was no doubt Matt had a couple of his own scars.

With a light laugh, she blinked at him coquettishly. "What are you proposing?"

"A continuation. No exes. No crowds. No rules. Just me and you and whatever feels right."

Oh. That might be okay. "What if I wanted to keep our masks on? What would you say?"

"No rules. For anything."

Her insides shuddered deliciously. "That's a little open-ended. How do I know you aren't into some very naughty things?"

"You don't. We're both taking a leap of faith."

The wicked gleam in his eye didn't reassure her, but it certainly piqued her interest. "I might be into naughty things."

"I'm counting on it." He tugged her hand as the music switched to another electronic number. The crowd went crazy, pressing in on them from all sides. "Come on."

To her left, she glimpsed Sara Lear posing for a picture with two men in drag. Rory was nowhere in sight, but he might pop up again at any moment. That decided it. The last thing she wanted was to be at this party alone, constantly reminded of how she wasn't Sara.

Matt was clearly lonely, too. She'd head in his direction and see where it led.

"Let's go. Right now."

He kept her hand in his and led her out of Vincenzo's palazzo via a side entrance. They crossed a moonlit court-yard and climbed an ornate outer staircase to the second floor. Matt held the door for her to enter ahead of him. Lights flashed.

"Welcome to Palazzo D'Inverno," he said.

Evangeline's breath stalled in her throat. Relief frescos lined the walls and extended to the ceiling, where the colors exploded into Renaissance-style art of unparalleled beauty. Modern terrazzo floors studded with chips of marble and granite spread underneath her feet and met three sets of glassed French-doors leading to what appeared to be a marble balcony overlooking the Grand Canal.

Three long leather sofas in sea-foam green formed a U in the center of the living room, and all three afforded an amazing view of Venice, lit for Carnevale with breathtaking splendor.

"This is unbelievable." There were no other words. Vincenzo's palazzo had been in his family since the time of the Medici but it couldn't hold a candle to this one. "I had no idea anything like this still existed in Venice."

Matt's mouth twisted into a semblance of a smile. "Keeps the rain out."

"Whoever owns this place hit the jackpot. You're lucky they agreed to rent it out. It's amazing."

He shot her a quizzical look. "I'll be sure to pass on the compliment."

"Do you have all three floors, or just the *piano nobile*?"

"Top two. The bottom floor isn't restored. The bedrooms are upstairs. Would you like to see them?"

"Was that a line?" She grinned at his chagrined expression. He was endearing in a way that shouldn't be possible in conjunction with his forceful, compelling personality. "If so, I must say it worked extraordinarily well. I not only want to see the rest of the house, purely for aesthetic reasons of course, but I want to get out of this dress in the worst way."

She took a step toward the twisting staircase, but he tugged her back and pierced her with his beautiful crystalline eyes, capturing her gaze with his and refusing to let her go.

"Angie, I didn't invite you here solely to get you naked.

When I said no rules, I meant no expectations. If nothing happens, that's all right. I don't mind if we talk until dawn. Whatever feels right. Remember that."

"Matt—" The rest froze in her throat.

He was nothing like the people in her world. He carried a hint of vulnerability, a depth that pulled at her. And his restraint—that she couldn't fathom. All the men she knew took what they wanted, when they wanted it.

Not this one. He was very clearly telling her she still had choices, regardless of how brazenly she'd thrown herself at him all night. He didn't just see her as an outlet to slake his thirst but as a valued companion. That was powerful. And seductive.

She whispered his name again. "I don't mind if we talk, either."

She never talked. Talking sucked, especially when the sound of her own voice made her cringe. But they both deserved to have choices.

"Is that what you want?"

She craved the attention of this man, who seemed to understand exactly what she needed, when she needed it. To understand the weight of loss and the pain of being adrift, desperate for an anchor.

Something momentous swelled in her chest. "I just want to be with you."

"You've got me. For however long you'd like. I'm not going anywhere." As if to prove it, he lowered the lights, creating a romantic ambience instantly. He sat on the couch and spread his hands. "Think of me as a smorgasbord."

She laughed, and it blew away all the thick implications of the moment.

"Now that's something I've never had before. By the way, I wasn't kidding about getting out of this dress. I can hardly breathe, and it's heavy."

"Would you like a T-shirt?"

"Um, not really. What I'd really like is your help." She

stepped out of her heels, crossed the room and sat on the couch facing away from him. "The laces in the back are too hard to reach."

"What would you have done if we hadn't connected? Slept in it?"

Connected. That hit her in all the soft, warm places again. This was a connection, a greater one than she'd been looking for, or had expected, and far more precious—thanks to the custom of wearing masks for Carnevale. She'd never have let her guard down otherwise.

"I would have figured out something," she murmured as he gently lifted her curls and swept them up over her shoulder. Her skin prickled as she felt his gaze on the bare expanse from her hairline to the strapless bodice.

His hands skimmed down her back on either side of the wings, stoking the fire he'd built on the balcony, which hadn't extinguished at all. Those strong fingers pulled on the threads, unknotting them and drawing them through the grommets with deliberate, aching leisure.

She kept expecting to feel his lips on her shoulder, on the column of her neck, or at the place where fabric met her skin. But the longer he held back, and the longer her skin burned for his touch, the crazier it drove her.

Yes, he was a master at this anticipation game. Among other things. When she finally got him naked and under her, she'd show him a thing or two.

Except she still wasn't sure they were headed for the bedroom. It was disorienting to have her temporary, surface-level liaison morph into something undefinable. Something so much more than a quick fix for loneliness.

So what was it?

Finally, after an eternity, the laces pulled free from the bodice, loosening the corset and spilling her breasts partially over the neckline of the dress, and he still hadn't made a move.

"It, uh, has to come over my head," she said without turning around. She raised her arms. "Can you...?"

He grasped the bodice but she was sitting on the skirt, so she wiggled and he pulled, until the yards and yards of lace tulle eased past her waist. The mask popped up onto her forehead, but she repositioned it before the skirt fully came off.

Then she was naked except for her thong. And the mask. What would he do first? The way he'd answered that question back on the balcony had been maddeningly vague.

He draped her dress over the back of the couch. She faced the canal, away from Matt, and he had yet to say a word. Screaming sexual tension whipped through all her nerves until she thought she'd pass out.

"So. What did you want to talk about?"

His soft laugh settled inside her. "I'm wondering about this."

He traced the trail of eight notes tattooed in a string at the small of her back. The smooth touch unleashed a tremor she couldn't control. "It's a tattoo."

"The notes are all the colors of the rainbow. I like it."

No one had ever noticed that before. "Music is important to me."

It was more than she'd meant to say and communicated none of the shock of pure grief the words had unearthed. She shoved the grief back, like she always did, shoved back the longing for a voice to express the pain. If she had a voice, she'd have no pain to express. It was a cruel, vicious circle she couldn't escape.

Except this was one night she didn't have to face the darkness alone. "Matt."

"Angie."

The smile in his voice warmed her. "Just making sure you're still there. Are we going to talk some more or is there something you'd like to do instead?"

"Was that a line?"

"Yes. It was." The ache at her core spread, and only the man behind her could ease it. She'd never wanted to be with someone more. What did she have to do to get him to make a move? "Obviously not a good one since you're still sitting there like yo—"

"Stand up and turn around, Angie."

She did slowly.

His hooded gaze swept her from head to toe, lingering along the way and unleashing a delicious tingle in all the places his eyes touched.

"You are the most beautiful woman alive. Come here."

He grasped both her hands and stood to meet her. In one breath, he drew her into his arms and kissed her.

Flames exploded at their joined mouths, between their bodies, crackling down the length of her bare skin where the soft fabric of his suit brushed it. Oh, how wrong she'd been. He *was* a man who took what he wanted. And he wanted to consume her whole.

She wanted to let him.

They *connected.* On every level.

When he tilted her head back to access her throat with his firm, gorgeous mouth, their masks caught at the corners. Patiently, he disentangled them and glanced down into her eyes, suddenly still. "No expectations. Does this feel right?"

Without warning, he skated a hand down her spine and fanned it at the small of her back, cradling the tattooed music notes in his capable hand as if he knew he held her very center.

Her eyelids fell closed and she moaned. "More right than anything I've ever felt. Please don't say you're really in the mood to talk."

He laughed against her throat, and she felt the caress of his lips clear to her toes. "I'm not. But I would be happy to talk, if that's what you wanted."

She shook her head almost imperceptibly, terrified she'd dislodge his mouth from her skin. "I want you."

"Good. Because I'm about to make love to you."

Yes, she wanted that, too. To be filled by this very different man, to the brim. To connect, bodies and minds. Souls.

He threaded a hand through the hair at her neck, his fingers solid and firm against it. "Angie," he murmured, almost reverently.

"Stop." Tears stung the corners of her eyes. Baffling, irrepressible tears because she wanted something else from him, something she'd resisted all evening. "Just stop."

"Okay." His hands withdrew and the sudden lack of support buckled her knees.

"No! Don't stop touching me. Stop calling me Angie." Before her subconscious could come up with one of the hundreds of reasons it was a dangerous idea, she reached up and yanked off her mask. "My name is Evangeline. Make love to *me*, not the mask."

Four

"Evangeline."

It flowed from Matthew's mouth like a prayer. Yes. *That* fit this angelic, winged woman who had bared herself to him in more ways than one.

He drank in her face, and it jolted something inside, as if his soul had done a double take and said, *There you are*.

"Angie is a nickname. Evangeline is who I am."

A nameless emotion tightened his throat. "I'm honored you trusted me with it."

She'd done far more than simply remove her mask. The significance of it sent a flood of guilt through him. Guilt because he could shed his physical mask—but not his internal one.

And still he drew off his mask and dropped it to the floor. "Allow me to reciprocate."

For a long while, she fixated on his face. His neck heated. Who would have thought taking off a mask could provoke such intensity?

"God, you're gorgeous."

"Most people call me by my given name, but if you want to address me as God, I won't argue."

She laughed, pushing her firm breasts into his chest. "Way to defuse the moment. That's a rare talent."

He'd intended to diffuse his own embarrassment at her frank admiration, which even Amber had expressed infrequently. But if Evangeline chose to believe he had superpowers, so much the better.

"Are we finished with the revelations?" he asked.

"Not even close. Now that I've seen what's under that mask, I'm dying to peel away this suit—" she flicked his bow tie "—and get a look at the rest of the goods."

"I hope it meets with your expectations." His voice dropped. Nerves. Of all things.

Before fully internalizing the implications, he swept Evangeline into his arms and carried her up the stairs to the bedroom.

"Any man who can do that without having to catch his breath most definitely has a body that'll meet my expectations," she said as he laid her on the bed. "Oh, wow. That's quite a fresco."

Matthew glanced up at the ceiling, where stucco divided sixteen individual paintings last touched by a brush during the Renaissance. "It's my favorite."

"I like it, too. I'll lie here and look at it while you fetch the condoms out of my clutch. Which is downstairs." She flipped him a cheeky grin as he cursed.

He cursed some more as he tromped back down the narrow stairs in search of the errant bag. It was still attached to her dress, but instead of pulling out a couple of condoms— because who was he to question how many they'd need—he untied it and brought the whole thing.

The bulging sides of Evangeline's clutch induced a healthy dose of reality. He was about to have sex with a virtual stranger, one whose face he'd seen for the first time less than ten minutes ago. Halfway up the stairs, he paused.

Was he really going to go through with this?

It was one night. One night in which he had an oppor-

tunity to turn the tide of his grief and rejoin the living by spending time with a beautiful woman who made him feel ten feet tall—feel being the operative word. One night when he could act recklessly with no one the wiser. He was in the most romantic city in the world, perhaps on purpose, and he wanted all that Venice had to offer.

Evangeline was draped across the cream-colored comforter when he strode through the bedroom door. She studied the ceiling with pursed lips, hair spread out underneath her and breasts freely on display. That lack of inhibition—it staggered him. Excited him.

His body hardened in anticipation, and his fingers tingled as he recalled the smoothness of her bare skin. This one night was a rare offer from the universe, and he was incredibly lucky to get it.

She glanced over with a sultry smile. "You. Come here."

Only a fool would pass up what was clearly fate.

With one hand, he got rid of his shoes and socks as he crossed the room. He tossed her clutch on a pillow and stared at her gorgeous form, flawless in the lamplight. "Hold on a minute."

He pulled a book of matches from his bedside drawer and lit the candles lining ornate sconces on each side of the bed, then clicked off the light.

"Nice. You could have gotten me here a lot faster if you'd said that was the first thing you'd do once I'm naked." She sat up and grasped his lapels, drawing off his jacket with a quick yank. "And you have on too many clothes. I'm feeling self-conscious here."

He let the jacket fall to the floor. "I can't imagine why. You're beautiful."

Flames flickered over her skin and threw honey highlights into her curls.

Her hands, which had been busy with his tie, rested flat on his chest, and she rose up on her knees to meet his gaze.

A hundred emotions poured from her expression, passing between them in silent communication.

"You know why," she said.

He did. In her eyes, he saw the same things she no doubt saw in his. They had an understanding, nonverbal and mystifying, but very real. He'd felt it from the first moment in the hall. He felt it now.

She was self-conscious not because of her nakedness, but because she'd removed her mask and feared learning she'd made a mistake in trusting him.

This night was about two damaged people seeking a port in the storm. He was going through with it because he wanted to live up to her trust. Wanted to fall into a woman so different from any he'd ever met, one so wrong for a real estate broker from Dallas, but perfect for a man who didn't know who he was or how to live his life anymore.

He wanted to see what happened if he let go of all the rules. It couldn't be worse than the purgatory of the past eighteen months.

If he did it right, it would be spectacular. Meaningful. And Matthew did *everything* right.

"I'm not going to disappoint you," he said hoarsely.

"I know. I wouldn't be here otherwise." Her voice had grown impossibly huskier as well, skating across his skin, burrowing its gravelly hooks into his center. "I've just never done anything like this before. Never wanted to."

Well, that made two of them. Hopefully they could figure it out together. "No expectations. No rules."

"I remember. Except I have this one rule." She made short work of removing his bow tie and began slipping his shirt's buttons free with deliberate care as she peeked up from under her lashes. "I get to explore first. You have to wait your turn."

He went so hard, his spine curved. Had a woman ever undressed him so provocatively?

"That's a pretty unfair rule. Why can't we do it at the same time?"

"Because I said."

The last button popped from its mooring, and she slid blazing fingertips across his bare chest on her way to his shoulders. His shirt came off in her hands and she yanked it halfway down his arms, trapping them against his side.

"Actually," she added, "the rule states I get to explore twice, once with my eyes and another time with my mouth."

Said eyes roamed over his exposed skin as she pulled him closer with the grip she had on his shirt. Without warning, she spun him and tied his hands behind his back with the fabric.

"Oh, now that's *really* not fair."

"All's fair in love and war." Still on her knees, she turned him back around to graze a fingertip down his chest and into the waistband of his pants. "I'll let you go when I'm done exploring."

She drew him closer and dropped his pants and briefs to the floor, ravishing his erection with her eyes, as promised.

He kicked his pants away. "I can easily break out of this you know."

"You won't." Her light tone fooled him not in the least.

This was love *and* war. And holy cow, did that get his juices flowing in a way he'd never have guessed. He'd play along, but she better believe he'd be dishing it out when he got the chance.

With a soft sigh, she twirled her finger. "Turn around. I want to see it all."

He faced the wall opposite the bed, slightly uncomfortable and enormously turned on by the notion of her eyes traveling up and down his naked body.

"When does the mouth exploration start?" he called over his shoulder.

Her answer came with a soft touch at the base of his

spine. Hair brushed his skin as she nibbled upward and his long-neglected body erupted with heat.

By the time she reached his neck, her tongue had joined the party. He groaned at the wicked swipe of wet heat against his earlobe, and allowed her to spin him slowly as she followed the line of his jaw with her lips.

Then there was no more talking as she kissed him.

He wanted to drag her into his arms and respond in kind. But he couldn't. His honor forced him to stay constrained as she did her best to drive him mad. He spiraled closer to the edge as she tilted his head in her palms to take the kiss deeper, teasing her nipples across his chest in a tantalizing back-and-forth dance.

Evangeline broke the kiss, arching her back sensuously. The silk of her thong brushed his length, and he nearly came apart right then and there.

No. He breathed heavily through his nose and clamped down on his reaction.

"Matt," she breathed into his ear, and the low croak was the sexiest thing he'd ever heard. "When I first saw you, I noticed those capable hands. I want them on my body. Now."

She reached around to pull the knot of his sleeves apart, but he'd already yanked his wrists free.

His mouth was on hers instantly as he slid both palms down the heat of her back to cup her bottom. Smooth. Arousing. He crushed her against his erection and plunged into sensation, freely allowing his body to revel in the impressions, the awareness. Finally, he felt something other than frozen and disoriented.

As he dipped underneath the triangle of silk at her thighs, she moaned and strained forward, seeking his fingers, throwing her head back in pleasure.

That was as arousing as the feel of her skin.

She was nothing like Amber.

He willed away the comparison—ghosts had no place here. But the thought circled and grew. Amber had been so-

phisticated, elegant. Beautiful in the way of a glass swan with special handling requirements.

He'd always held her in slight reverence as the future mother of his children, and they'd shared a strong relationship anchored by common interests and goals. Their love life had blossomed into something wonderful and good. But conducted in the dark, under the sheets, which Matthew never minded.

This was something else, something erotic and animalistic and wicked. Evangeline wasn't Amber. And there were no rules tonight.

He wanted to bury himself in this woman and be resurrected a new man.

Evangeline enfolded Matt with her arms and willed him to hurry. But there was no rushing the man she'd been goading with tied hands for the past few minutes.

His fingers wrapped her in a veil of pleasure as they slowly traveled across her skin, spinning magic through her center as he touched her everywhere—inside and out.

Yes. Exactly what she needed—to be filled, valued, appreciated. Accepted.

With incredible restraint, he lowered her to the mattress and drew off her underwear, then crawled up the length of her body, laving every inch of skin as he went. He reached her throat and tilted her head back to taste with hard suction. Simultaneously, his thigh separated hers, relentless against her sensitized flesh and setting off pyrotechnics behind her eyes.

She'd never dropped into such heavy desire so quickly, never been so hot and ready to explode. Usually it took a while. But then, they'd been engaged in foreplay in one form or another since their first meeting in the hall.

Was it any wonder Matt was about to take her under with only his thigh?

His tongue circled her breasts, then treated her to the

same intense suction he'd used on her throat. Her back came off the bed, arching, as her feminine parts contracted. She gasped.

"Now, Matt."

It was supposed to be a demand, not a plea. But the words left her lips on a broken sob, and she no longer cared that a man had reduced her to begging.

He extracted a condom and fingered it on. It took an eternity but then he was back between her thighs, sliding into her. Watching her as they became one and their gazes locked. Something powerful, divine even, swelled between them and her heart thumped in time with the throb in the air.

No, she'd never done this before because she had no idea what *this* was.

It certainly wasn't a random hookup. But neither was it safe. The deeper the connection, the deeper the eventual pain.

She'd taken off the mask in a calculated gamble, and Matt hadn't recognized her. It should have allowed her to simply revel in this one night where a man couldn't hurt her because he didn't really know her. It should have been freeing. Not confusing.

Desperately, she cast about for a way to eliminate the swirling mass of vulnerability this man evoked by simply looking at her. Through her.

"Not this way." She wiggled and he rolled to his side, confusion evident.

"Too soon?"

"Too missionary." Waggling her brows, she knelt on the bed and glanced back at him. "Try this on for size."

He grinned and instantly heated her back with his torso, mouth to her neck as he filled her again from behind. Much better. Now she couldn't see all that depth of emotion. And vice versa. They'd pleasure each other and stave off the loneliness for a night and go on.

His fingers teased her flesh. Clearly this was not his first

rodeo. She let her senses flood with Matt and moaned as he lit her up expertly. His name fell from her lips and too late she realized it didn't matter if she could see his face. His touch conveyed more depth than she'd dreamed possible.

Tears pricked her eyelids. She wanted that touch to mean everything she sensed it did. But was terrified to admit it. How could she convince herself this was nothing but a brief divergence if he kept touching her that way?

The orgasm, quick, powerful and amazing, swallowed her whole long about his second thrust, and he exploded with his third.

She collapsed, chest to the bed, and he spooned her into his arms, both of them still shuddering. He held her tightly and she curled into him, shocked at how natural it felt, how right, when normally she preferred not to be touched as her body cooled.

"I have never come so fast in my life," she gasped. "I think that's my new favorite position."

Though somehow, it hadn't been quite the cure for her confusion that she'd envisioned. And lying here in his arms with his thumb tenderly stroking the curve of her waist wasn't helping. The powerful flames of desire he fanned weren't sexual. She wanted Matt to be different. Special.

She should get dressed and leave. Right now, before she found out he wasn't.

But if she left, what then? Spend the rest of the night alone, huddled in the dark, listening to Vincenzo's guests party till dawn?

"It's definitely my new favorite position." He cleared his throat. "Though I'm willing to try a couple of others to verify. In a few minutes. I know we have all these condoms, but you're not an easy woman to recover from."

She had to smile at that. Nice to know it had been staggering on both sides.

A part of her had prepared to be kicked out. Maybe hoped she would be—it was safer that way. Not all men liked a

woman hanging around afterward. Finding out Matt didn't fall in that category thrilled her. Dangerously.

"What if we just talk?"

Where had that come from? She never stayed.

She nearly took it back, but her soul ached, and Matt inexplicably salved it. Morning was soon enough to escape. For now, she wanted one whole night of fantasy, where nothing mattered but being with a man who liked her and wanted her around.

His lips curved up against her temple. "A continuation of our speed date?"

The chilly palazzo air raised goose bumps on her arms. "Well, I'm not sure how we could find any more levels of compatibility. But okay."

He laughed. "Yeah, we gel. At least in bed, which is fantastic. It's been a while."

"Really? How long?"

Rolling her gently to the side, he pulled the covers free and nestled her back in his arms underneath them, like he'd read her mind. "A year and a half. Or so."

Oh, God. "Are you like, religious or something? Did I make you break vows?"

"No." He was quiet for a long time. "That's when my wife died."

Something hot exploded in her chest. His pain—she'd seen it, knew it was there, but never would have guessed its roots went so deep.

"Oh, Matt. I'm so sorry."

She rolled and took his lips with hers in a long kiss of sympathy. Why, she didn't know. It wasn't like she could fix anything or erase his agony, not with a million kisses.

"Thanks," he whispered against her lips. "It was a long time ago."

Her heart hurt for him and furiously demanded she find a way to salve his soul in return. "There's no statute of limitations on being sorry that someone you loved is gone."

"I guess not." His smile flipped her stomach. "When you said *talk,* that's probably not what you meant. But I thought you should know."

Because there was something more here than either of them had expected. He felt it, too.

"That's why you're drifting. To find some sort of closure." His nod confirmed what she'd guessed. "You're not in Venice on business, are you?"

"I wish it was that simple. If only there was a way to close the deal on grief, I'd be all set."

Matt was a widower. It felt weird. "People our age shouldn't die."

People their age shouldn't lose a career over botched surgery either, but crappy things happened with no rhyme or reason.

He smoothed a curl away from her face, his expression unreadable, and she waited for a demand that she slice open a vein in kind, share her personal pain with him. She wouldn't. Couldn't. And it wasn't fair to Matt that he'd hooked up with someone nowhere near as willing to be vulnerable.

But he didn't hand her a scalpel.

"Are we the same age? Wait, am I allowed to ask that? Isn't there a rule about asking women their age?"

A laugh slipped out. "No rules, remember? I'm twenty-seven."

"Thirty-two." He grinned. "Not nearly old enough to need *that* long to recover."

She let him change the subject by kissing her breathless and rolling on top of her, bracing himself on his strong forearms. He met her gaze, his eyes full of her, not pain. They'd connected over their mutual search for a way to combat the darkness, and it was working.

For one magical night, they had each other.

Five

When Evangeline awoke, Matt was watching her, cheek to his pillow. The drapes were flung apart, and sunlight spilled into the room, across the bed. With strong features and those amazing blue eyes, he was more gorgeous by morning light than he was by candlelight.

"Hey there." He smiled and laced their fingers, bringing hers to his lips.

She smiled back. "If you're always this cheerful in the morning, you might want to keep sharp objects under lock and key."

With a laugh, he tucked a curl of her hair behind her shoulder. "I'm not this cheerful ever. You have the unique effect of being a good influence."

Or the unique effect of breaking his dry spell with women. The sunlight had returned her cynicism, apparently.

"Are you watching me for a reason or auditioning to be my stalker once the boyfriend job is over?"

"For a reason. But you'll think it's weird."

Her eyes narrowed. "Weirder than watching me while I sleep?"

"I like your face." He shrugged. "It was covered most of the night, and I haven't seen it nearly enough yet."

"There's nothing special about my face." Other than how famous it was. She sat up and threw off the covers, intending to flee before the discussion went in a direction she didn't like.

Besides, it was morning. She'd stayed long enough.

His hand shot out from under the sheet to grab her wrist and tug her back. "I could look at you for hours."

"I'm naked. Of course you could." *Men.* But his eyes weren't on her uncovered body.

She was trying so hard to assign typical male qualities to Matt, and he wasn't letting her.

"You still have feathers in your hair."

"I do?" Her hand flew to her hair and sure enough, a mess of pins still held part of her headpiece in place. Wonderful. Her hair must resemble a bird's nest after a monsoon.

"Let me."

He rose up from the cocoon of sheets, which fell from his body in a slow waterfall, and her belly contracted. There was very little typical about Matt, and his prime physique was no exception.

He scooted up behind her, but not close enough to touch. It didn't matter. His heat radiated outward, stroking her skin with delicious fingers of warmth. With aching gentleness, he plucked a pin from her hair, then another, his breath fanning her scalp as he worked.

Awareness prickled her skin and ignited a slow burn in her center.

"That was the last pin."

But his fingers stayed in her hair, combing it lightly, patiently untangling the snarls. Then his fingers drifted to her shoulders in a caress. He lifted her curls and touched the back of her neck with his warm, talented lips, unleashing an unexpected shiver.

She shouldn't stay. Her one magical night was over, and

morning light put a damper of reality over everything. In fact, she should have left before he woke up. Why hadn't she?

"Matt."

The lips paused in their trek across her nape. "Are you about to tell me you have somewhere to be? Nice knowing you, but party's over?"

Was she that easy to read? "I don't have anywhere to be."

Well, that was a stupid thing to admit. Now she had no exit strategy if she decided she needed one.

"Then don't go."

His hands gripped her arms, drawing her backward into him, supporting her with his chest as he ravished whatever he could reach with his mouth. Her insides erupted.

She wasn't going anywhere, not yet. But she also wasn't doing this backward. Not this time.

She spun in his arms and wrapped her legs around his waist. The delight playing with the corners of his mouth sent a shaft of heat through her. "Just try and get rid of me, cowboy."

His laugh rumbled against her flesh. "Not everyone from Texas rides horses."

"Who's talking about riding horses?" She shoved his chest and knocked him back against the comforter, moving onto her knees over him. "Giddyap."

Now there was a sight. Gorgeous, masculine magnificence spread underneath her thighs. Matt was hard all over, had a nicely defined torso and a wicked smile. She'd won the man sweepstakes and had been daft enough to miss out on watching him last night.

Eyes stormy with dark desire, he lifted his chin. "Your turn to fetch the condoms."

She stretched to pull one off the bedside table and ripped it open with her teeth. "Done."

"Then saddle up, sweetheart." He shoved his hands under

his head with a mischievous wink. "You don't have to tie me up this time."

Which she'd only done to ratchet down the emotion of the moment. It had failed miserably.

"Liked that, did you?"

The flippant response almost caught in her throat. Because she didn't want to be flippant. Didn't want fun and games. She wanted the tender, profound Matt of last night who made her feel cherished.

When had she turned into such a *girl*? Five minutes ago, she was halfway out the door—mentally, at least—and here she was wishing for the opposite. Matt had her completely messed up.

"I have yet to discover something about you I don't like," he said.

"I've got you good and fooled then."

He pierced her with the force of all that depth behind his eyes. "I don't think so."

She looked away, letting the condom fall to the bed. "You don't know me. Not really."

No one did—by design. How much worse would rejection hurt if someone dug through all the protective layers and exposed her core? Well, she already knew. It would feel an awful lot like when her dad hadn't wanted her.

"That's not true." He sat up, resettled her against his thighs and cupped her chin. "I recognized you as soon as you took off your mask."

Her heart plunged to the floor and tried to keep going. "You did?"

Why hadn't he said anything? Duh. He hadn't because he'd wanted to score with Eva. Of course. Disappointment nearly wrenched a sob from her frozen chest. He wasn't special. Big surprise.

"Something inside me did, as if I'd always known you." He shook his head with a half laugh. "Sorry. I'm no good

at this, and to top it off I sound like a starry-eyed teenager. They must put romance in the water here."

"What are you saying?"

He huffed out a frustrated breath. "I don't know. I mean, it wasn't like, hey didn't we go to the same high school? It was an elemental recognition. Inside. Nothing like that has ever happened to me before." Matt's fathomless eyes begged her to understand, but she couldn't sort through the panic in her abdomen to put definition around his words. "I thought you felt it, too."

He meant that indefinable swirl between them. The *connection*.

Cautiously, slowly, her heart started beating again.

"The first time I kissed you. It didn't feel like the first time. Is that what you mean?"

He lit up, zinging her in the stomach. "Yes. That's it exactly. Everything between us...it's just right. We're sitting here naked having a conversation, and it's not strange."

The smile cracked before she registered that he'd pulled it from her. "Feels pretty good to me."

"Me, too. I know as much about you as I need to. You're my butterfly."

His lips claimed hers in a kiss full of promise. And like that, he turned the tables on her again, making her yearn for things she shouldn't, such as another night of absolving her loneliness in the arms of a man who wasn't eager to get rid of her. A man who made her feel valued.

If she stayed, how long could that possibly last?

The sooner she left, the sooner that yearning could dry up and blow away. But the second she walked out the door, she'd be back in the real world, lost and alone, with only the thin layer of Eva for protection—and that didn't go very far anymore.

Rock. Hard place.

With Matt, she was simply an anonymous woman enjoying the uncomplicated company of a man, and it gave her

room to breathe she hadn't known she needed. One night hadn't been enough. But if she stayed, it was like giving Matt permission to get closer. That couldn't go well.

She stared into the depths of those almost-colorless-blue eyes.

A small voice in the back of her mind insisted she was selling this completely atypical man short.

Matthew palmed Evangeline's chin and kissed her until his brain sizzled. She was naked in his lap, legs around his waist, and the position was so sensually erotic, he was one rub of her flesh away from going off like a bottle rocket.

Last night had been a fantasy. This morning—still pretty unreal. He'd awoken with a start, afraid Evangeline had evaporated like so much mist in the sunlight. But there she was, hair draped over the pillow, breathing deeply in sleep, beautiful against his sheets. The way she filled his bed was so very nice.

Their one night was over. It wasn't enough, and he wasn't ready to say *ciao*.

Her hands cupped his butt, urging him closer and he was already almost inside her. One quick thrust and he would be. His thighs strained. He groaned against her mouth, blindly seeking the condom wrapper with clumsy fingers before it was too late.

His fingers closed around it, and he eased back a bit to roll it on, still kissing her because he couldn't stop.

Finally, it was in place. He lifted her bottom and slid in, all the way, and she breathed his name as he situated her flush against him.

His eyelids slammed closed as Evangeline washed through him, blasting away all the cobwebs until that incredible light of hers flooded the darkness inside. They moved together, heightening the pleasure, heightening the sense of completion until they both exploded simultaneously.

He wrapped his arms around her and held her tight

against his torso as the ripples went on and on. As they faded away, they left the warmest glow in their wake. His lips rested on her temple, and he couldn't have moved if his life depended on it.

"I like that position pretty well, too," she murmured, and he grinned.

"It has its merits." Her cheek rubbed his, bristling his morning stubble. As decadent as it was to still be in bed, they had to get up sometime. "Are you hungry? I'll make you breakfast."

It probably sounded as much like a stall tactic to her as it did to him. He didn't care. Too many things in his life had ended prematurely, and if she left, he'd probably never see her again. That would be a true shame.

"Do you mind if I take a shower first?" She made a noise. "I forgot, I don't have any of my stuff. Does the offer of a T-shirt still stand?"

"Sure. Give me a minute in the bathroom and then it's all yours." He eased her off his thighs and took shameless delight in watching his uninhibited butterfly roll onto her back, still breathing heavily.

Matthew pulled a T-shirt from the dresser and tossed it next to her on the bed. He bent down to kiss her thoroughly because he could, then whistled as he dressed and went downstairs to scare up some breakfast.

Whistled.

He'd be shocked, except his ability to be shocked had disappeared right around the time Evangeline had presented her naked backside and told him to hop on board. She was the most exciting woman he'd ever met, and under normal circumstances, real-estate mogul Matthew Wheeler would bore her instantly.

But this was Venice, and he was a guy who could keep up with Evangeline and talk about spiritual connections without flinching because there were no rules. Being Matt was liberating.

The updated plumbing in Palazzo D'Inverno only went so far, and when Evangeline turned on the shower upstairs, pipes rattled inside the kitchen walls. It was like music. His cold, lonely house was filled with Evangeline, and he liked it. A lot.

When she came downstairs clad in only his T-shirt, bare legs on display and wet hair dark against her shoulders, every drop of saliva in his mouth dried up.

"How do you make cotton look so good?"

He handed her a glass of orange juice.

"One of my natural talents."

She stood on her tiptoes to kiss him as if they were a couple comfortable in the kitchen dance from having performed it so many times. Sipping the juice, she perched on one of two stools at the center island and watched him at the stove.

"I hope eggs and toast are okay." He glanced over his shoulder and nearly dropped the spatula at the sight of such a tousled, stunning woman in his kitchen. "I guess I should have asked."

"It's fine. I don't do whacked-out diets or lament about animal rights. I just eat."

"I like that in a woman."

"I like a man who cooks."

They traded scorching hot glances until the scent of toast filled the air. He pulled it from the toaster and plated everything, then sat next to her at the island.

This was the first time he'd eaten a meal with a woman in...too long to recall. He'd missed the simple pleasure of awaking to warm female, of sharing a bathroom. Laughing and making love whenever the mood struck.

He missed being married, more than he'd realized. No amount of wishing, cursing, grieving or wandering could bring Amber back, though he'd irrationally tried it all. He could only embrace what *was* possible.

"So," he said after swallowing a bite of toast. "Do you have plans for the weekend?"

"It's Wednesday. The weekend is a long way off."

At home, his calendar filled months in advance and he lived by his schedule. In Venice, he'd learned calendars were a dirty word, which he still hadn't adjusted to. "I'd like to see you again. Maybe go on a date."

He definitely wasn't done with what Evangeline made him feel.

She put her fork down with all the fanfare of a royal announcement. "I'm not so big on dating."

"Oh." The brush-off. Apparently he was rustier at this than he'd realized, because he'd have sworn they had something going on here. "What are you big on?"

Her gravelly laugh surprised him. "You."

"Uh, okay." To stall, he shoveled food into his mouth and chewed slowly. His wits did not gather. "Can I assume you *are* that into me then?"

"Matt." She sighed, and it didn't reassure him. "You're the best thing that's happened to me in a long, long time. But—"

"Why does there have to be a *but*? I'm the best thing. Roll with that." He encouraged her with a finger twirl, unable to keep the grin off his face.

Negotiation time—his best skill. She was in for a surprise if she thought there was a chance in hell he was letting her get away.

Shoulders slumped, she stared at her plate for a long time. "What if I said I'd like to see you again too, but here? At your house?"

Her body language told him volumes about the importance of his answer.

He shrugged. "The last time I dated, dinosaurs roamed the earth. I'm not so big on it, either. I just want to see you. When? Pick a day that works for your life."

A firm commitment would settle the uneasiness prickling his spine quite well.

When she looked up from her plate, tears had gathered

and one slid down her face. A giant fist clenched his gut as she wiped away the tear.

"I don't have a life," she whispered.

"Evangeline…" What was he supposed to do? Say? Feel?

Instinctively, he slid from the stool, gathered her into his arms and held her, mystified, but happy to be doing *something*. She melted into him, her hands clutching his shoulders as if she couldn't get close enough, and he ached over her unidentified agony.

"I'm sorry. I don't usually fall apart in the middle of being asked out on a date." Her watery chuckle gave him hope things hadn't gone entirely to hell.

"I'm not asking you out on a date. No, ma'am. I have it on good authority you aren't big on dates. I'm asking you to my house for…dinner?" he offered, praying that would get a thumbs-up. "I'll cook."

"Dinner would be nice," she said into his shoulder. "Tonight. Tomorrow night. Any night."

"Tonight. In fact, just stay," he said, voicing the invitation he should have issued from the outset. This place needed her light. *He* needed it. "Unless you're sick of me or need to go hang out with Vincenzo since you're his guest."

"Vincenzo is probably sleeping off his hangover and won't notice if I'm there or not."

The forlorn note clinched it. Unless he'd completely lost his marbles, she wasn't ready to say *ciao,* either.

"I'll definitely notice if you're here or not. Italian TV leaves a lot to be desired, and I'd rather be with you. Spend another night, or better yet, through the weekend." The words rushed out before he'd hardly formed the thought, but the relevance of it, the weight of what he asked, was already there, inside him. He'd finally woken up from an eighteen-month stupor, and there was no way he'd let it end. "Will you stay?"

She hesitated, lids closed in apparent indecision. When

she opened her eyes, the flicker in their depths warned him something he might not like was about to happen.

"Why haven't you asked me about my voice?"

He blinked. "Was I supposed to?"

"It's damaged. Aren't you curious? You can't tell me you haven't noticed."

Damaged? It hadn't always been that way? "You noticed my hands and I noticed your voice. I love your voice. It's one of the sexiest things about you."

"It's not sexy. It's horrific, like a sixty-year old with a four-pack-a-day habit."

He laughed, but it didn't sound like he was amused. Because he wasn't. "That's ridiculous. Your voice is unusual. That's what makes it special. When you say my name, it latches onto me, right here." He grasped her hand and slapped it to his stomach. "I love that. I love that you can affect me by speaking."

She pulled her hand free. "You're being deliberately obtuse."

Frustrated, he shoved fingers through his hair. He'd invited her to draw out their one night, not solve world hunger—couldn't it be a simple yes or no?

"Fine. Evangeline, what happened to your voice?"

"When you sing a lot, polyps grow on your vocal cords. Sometimes they rupture. It requires a special expertise to perform the surgery to fix it. Adele had a good doctor. I didn't."

His brain nearly curdled at the lightning-fast subject change. "What's a lot? Like you sang professionally, you mean?"

"Yeah. Professionally. A lot." Her eyes searched his, hesitating, evaluating, and he got the impression she was feeling him out. They were still very much in the throes of negotiation, and he couldn't stumble now.

"No false pretenses," she said. "If I stay, I need you to know. When I sang, it was by another name. Eva."

"Eva."

The name flashed an image in his mind of the woman before him, but transformed into a lush, heavily made-up singer on stage in a tiny gold dress, with a hundred dancers weaving around behind her.

"Eva-who-performed-at-the-Super Bowl-Eva?"

She nodded, expression graveyard still as she waited for his reaction.

"Is that supposed to scare me?"

"I don't know what it's supposed to do. I just couldn't stand it being between us."

Matthew went cold. "Are you disappointed I didn't recognize you?"

When she'd removed her mask, he'd thought the jolt of recognition was uncanny. Had his subconscious simply remembered her from a halftime show?

The disappointment sharpened and stuck in his gut. Then faded abruptly. He'd felt something between them long before he saw her face.

"No, relieved." She clutched his hand. "My fame doesn't bother you? I have a lot of money. Does it change anything?"

"Not in the slightest."

She wasn't just wrong for Matthew Wheeler; she was in a whole other stratosphere of incompatibility, with a life full of limos, designer drugs and glittery celebrities. Hell, she *was* a glittery celebrity and glittery didn't gel with the blue bloods in his circles. But he'd realized they were wrong for each other five minutes after meeting, and though he desperately wanted to find a way to get back home, that wasn't happening today.

This was a finite Venetian affair, and Matt didn't care who she was. She made him feel alive for the first time in eighteen months, and that made her perfect for right this minute.

"Since we're going full bore on disclosures, I have money, too. I bought this palazzo as a wedding gift to Amber, my

wife. In Dallas, I was a partner in a multimillion dollar real estate firm and drove an Escalade. Then I dumped all my responsibilities and jumped on a plane. I have little to offer anyone right now. Should I have told you that before we got involved? Does it change things for you?"

If it did, he wouldn't blame her. He was a bad bet emotionally.

"Is that what we are? Involved?" Some snap crept back into her eyes.

"Yeah. Wasn't looking for it, wasn't planning on it. I left Dallas to regain my sanity after my wife died, and I finally feel like that's possible, thanks to you." He slid a thumb down her jaw. "Stay."

"Matt," she whispered, and her palms came up to frame his face. "This is crazy. We just met."

"Tell me you're ready to walk away and I'll show you to the door."

She shook her head. Hard. "But you don't want to be seen in public with me. Someone always recognizes me. Then the harassment starts, rehashing how my career is over." Her eyes filled again. "It's not a lot of fun."

There was the source of all that anguish he'd sensed. This amazing, beautiful butterfly had been damaged beyond repair, and the public refused to let her forget. A fierce, protective instinct tightened his arms around her, filling him with a heavy impulse to do something to fix it for her, to help her.

They'd both lost something, and perhaps she needed him as much as he needed her, though she seemed much less willing to admit it.

In order to get her to stay—to give them *both* the peace they desperately sought—the terms might have to be less structured than he would like.

"Good. I don't want to go out. I don't want to share you." He gestured toward the room at large. "Inside these walls, we can block out the rest of the world and just be together. I need that. If you do too, then go to Vincenzo's, get your

stuff and stay here for as long as that's true. When it's not, leave. No rules. No expectations."

It *was* crazy. And rash. So unlike a guy who missed his wife and valued commitment. That was the reason it worked, why he and Evangeline gelled, because he wasn't that guy right now.

Crazy was what made it great.

Six

Evangeline sneaked into Vincenzo's without stumbling over any passed-out revelers.

Once in her room, she threw on a sweater over Matt's T-shirt and stabbed her legs into jeans. Then she packed her suitcases in preparation for either the biggest mistake of her life or the smartest thing she'd ever done.

Jury was still out on which one Matt was. But she was willing to see what unfolded as they blocked out the world for a few days, especially with the caveat of his consent to leave whenever things got too stifling.

Roots weren't possible for someone like her, who fed from new experiences and new destinations. Who knew the dangers of staying in one place too long and allowing someone to matter. Being with a man who got that was huge.

So was the fact that he wasn't in a hurry to get rid of her.

When he'd asked her to stay, he still had no idea who she was—she could tell. And somehow, that had been the clincher. Eva ceased to have any relevance. Actually, it hadn't been a factor between them all along and she'd never had that. What started as a short-term anonymous encounter had accidentally turned into something else.

It was scary to be just Evangeline, scary to be so exposed, but deep inside, she yearned for someone to see beneath the layers and value *her*.

As soon as she found out Matt wasn't that someone, she'd be out the door.

In record time, she shut the lid on her second suitcase and zipped it. She had packing down to a science.

As she carried the suitcases down the marble staircase to Vincenzo's first floor, one of his buddies who'd passed out on the couch stirred. Franco. Or maybe it was Fabricio. He sat up and blearily evaluated her as he scrubbed his jaw.

"Eva. Didn't know you were here." A night of hard drinking slurred his accented English almost unintelligibly. He zeroed in on the suitcases. "Leaving already?"

"Yeah. Tell Vincenzo I said later."

"Wait. Do my show this week." He lifted his chin. "*Milano Sera* will treat you well."

She took in his too-handsome face and two-hundred-dollar haircut that not even a night of couch surfing could ruin. Now she remembered him. Franco Buonotti. He was the host of a late-night talk show on an Italian network. He'd bugged her a couple of times before to do an exclusive with him.

"I don't think so."

"Aww. Not even for me?" He batted his eyelashes, and she almost snorted.

Italian playboys were so not her type—she was more into blue-eyed blonds Regardless, she hadn't broken her silence on the botched surgery in six months and didn't see a reason to change that now.

"Not even."

She escaped to the haven her blue-eyed blond had offered.

Upstairs in Matt's bedroom, she unpacked her clothes and arranged them in the empty spots he'd cleared for her in the closet and dresser. Unable to resist, she opened a drawer to finger his shirts. Very few of his items lay folded inside

or hanging in the closet. He traveled as light as she did. But then, neither of them had a permanent home.

Oddly, seeing their clothes mixed felt very permanent. It shouldn't have put a smile on her face.

Matt ordered lunch to be delivered, and the soup grew cold because they were too busy talking to eat. He was transparent and genuine, and his willingness to share covered her tendency not to. He never ran out of stories, and she forgot to be wary by the middle of the afternoon.

That's when *Milano Sera's* host intruded on her haven. Matt answered a knock at the door, and she glimpsed the too-handsome face of Vincenzo's friend through the crack.

"I'll take care of it," she told Matt and shooed him away from the door. "I already said no."

"*Cara*, no one says no to me."

He'd cleaned up and squeezed his impressive build into tight Dolce & Gabbana jeans and a distressed T-shirt. That kind of sexy might work on tittering schoolgirls, but Evangeline couldn't titter to save her life.

"Yet I did. This is a private home. Please respect that."

She shut the door in his face and turned to see Matt watching her.

"Sales guy?" he asked with raised eyebrows. "What was he selling? Ice to Eskimos?"

And somehow he pulled a smile from her. Matt's talents were amazing. "He hosts a talk show on an Italian network and wants me to do an interview."

"Badly, I guess, to chase you here."

"I'm sorry he bothered us." She sighed. "It was a nice idea, to block out the world. Unfortunately, the world tends to camp out on my doorstep."

With it came the intrusion of Eva…and a reminder of all the reasons she'd latched onto the suggestion of a place to hide. If she knew the answers to the questions, interviews might not be so hard.

Her phone beeped, as if to underscore the point. Like an

idiot, she checked it to see an apology text from Vincenzo. Well, that was something, at least.

Matt took the phone from her fingers and tossed it on the credenza to his left without checking his aim.

"Hey, the world may come to you, but you don't have to answer to it." He swept her hand into his, holding it tight. "No rules at Palazzo D'Inverno. You don't have to do anything you don't want to."

"Thanks." It was therapeutic to have someone validate her choices.

He pulled her to the couch and settled them both into it comfortably. The sun was low enough in the sky to cast a glow over the whitewashed building opposite the palazzo.

His fingers tangled in her hair, and she experienced the deepest sense of harmony she'd experienced in a long while. Maybe the deepest ever.

"You drove an Escalade?" she asked in a blatant attempt to change the subject. "Really?"

It seemed too domestic for a guy who liked to throw rules out the window.

Matt chuckled. "Yeah. But I sold it, along with everything else. Seemed easier, since I had no idea where I was going or when I was coming back. Sometimes it feels like that part of my life was a dream, and I have a hard time remembering who that guy was."

So he hadn't really fit into that suburban existence. Venice was more his speed, and he'd obviously taken to the laid-back lifestyle. She wondered if she would have given him a second glance if they'd met at a party in the States.

"Did you end up in Venice because it reminds you of your wife? You said you bought this palazzo for her."

The fingers in her hair stilled. "Amber. Yeah, I did buy it for her. But she died not too long after we got married. She never got the chance to visit."

"That's a shame."

His wife had never seen this beautiful place Matt had

given her. But Evangeline couldn't quite squelch the thrill of knowing she was the only woman who had slept in Matt's bed, who had lain with him on this couch and eaten at his table.

"The lack of ghosts is the most attractive thing about Palazzo D'Inverno. You know what that means in English? Winter Palace. Seemed appropriate to come here. My soul felt pretty frozen."

Her heart ached for him. He wandered in search of a cure for his grief. Maybe he'd found one—her.

Silly. Probably a recipe for disaster to imagine herself a healer. But the notion was still there, pinging around inside her.

"The Italian who built this palazzo called it that because he came here during the winter from someplace colder. So did you."

"True." The expression on his face caught her right in her aching heart. "But it's only warmer because you're in it. I wouldn't have come to Venice if Amber had stayed here. I sold the house in Dallas we'd bought together. I can't be around things with memories. I get too attached."

Of course he did. Anyone with Matt's depth would be shattered by the loss of someone he'd obviously loved. He and his wife had shared a house and a life and a level of commitment she couldn't comprehend.

He was staring out the window blindly when she glanced at him. "Is it hard to talk about her?"

"Yeah." He didn't elaborate, and the hard set of his mouth said he wasn't going to.

For a guy who had easily told stories at lunch about his college days, closing off must mean it was a very taboo subject. She had an extra store of mercy for that kind of pain, especially for someone who'd been so very nice about Franco's invasion.

Maybe she'd stayed in the worst sort of foolish gamble—

betting that Matt wouldn't hurt her because he empathized with her pain.

Through the glass, she watched a bird pecking at the marble balcony. "When I was in an interview and the reporter asked a question I didn't want to answer, I'd use a code word. My manager would smoothly and quickly rescue me. We'll have one, too. Whenever one of us touches on a sensitive subject, the code word is sacred. It means 'get me out of this. No more questions.'"

That melted the stone from his expression. "What kind of code word?"

"You pick. Make it silly. That way, we can lighten the mood at the same time."

"Armadillo," he suggested immediately. "They walk funny."

The way he said it, all serious about the assignment, made her giggle. "See? It works. So do you want to call *armadillo* about Amber?"

His mouth twitched. "Maybe. And maybe I'm starting to get through it. I can say her name out loud without flinching. Progress."

Because of her? Maybe she hadn't given herself enough credit in the healing department.

Then he tipped up her chin and pierced her with those pale blue eyes. "I'll be your manager. In the interview."

Her lungs seized. "What are you talking about? I'm not doing the interview."

He didn't get it at all. Had she lost her gamble already?

"But if you wanted to, I'd stay right there with you. Say the word and I'll rescue you." He smiled and it was so gentle, she almost smiled back. "Nothing wrong with both of us making progress."

So, he'd obviously drawn a few of his own conclusions about her reasons for saying no.

She shook her head. "I don't want to do the interview."

"Okay."

And like that, he dropped the subject in favor of launching into a discussion about what she might like for dinner. She responded, but most of her attention was back on Matt's offer to be with her during the interview.

If he'd pushed, her heels would have dug in. But he never forced her to explain herself—backing her into an emotional corner was the fastest way to irritate her. It was almost like he knew.

"Matt?" He didn't even comment about how she'd interrupted him. "You'd do that for me? Rescue me if I say *armadillo?*"

"Sure." His brows wrinkled in confusion as he squeezed her hand. "I said I would. Does that mean you're going to do the interview?"

Patiently, he waited her out, his silence nothing more than encouragement to go on if she chose. Or not, if she chose, which was usually the path she took. "I don't know. I've had a strict no-interviews policy since the surgery."

"Do you get stage fright in front of all those cameras or something? Just picture them in their underwear."

The mental image of cameras wearing a pink, lacy bra-and-panty set made her giggle. "That's not the problem. I just don't like the questions."

"Well, no offense, but that guy doesn't strike me as a hard-hitting news journalist. If he asks you about anything more strenuous than where you shop, I'll fall over in a dead shock." He brushed a thumb across her cheek. "If I was going to jump back in the water, I'd get my feet wet with a small-time Italian talk show first."

"I'll think about it."

She'd think of nothing but. Because his point was valid.

He gave her plenty of space by bounding up immediately to cook dinner. She trailed him to the kitchen to watch him beat the raw ingredients into submission, which she thoroughly enjoyed.

"While you're sitting there," Matt said as he pulled cov-

ered platters from the refrigerator. "You should start thinking of the proper way to thank me for this fantastic dinner."

She returned his wicked grin. "Exactly how good of a cook are you?"

"My mama taught me well. Though I believe she intended for me to feed myself. Not use my culinary skills to seduce women."

"But you're so good at both. She should be proud."

They laughed and traded banter, and dinner was everything she'd anticipated when he'd asked her to stay—a low-key, enjoyable evening with a man who liked her.

Matt wasn't the only one who needed to heal. She got that. But he had a prayer of getting there one day, especially if she truly helped him along. Unfortunately, there wasn't anything he could do in return to fix her vocal cords. She was permanently scarred, and at best, this Venice interlude was a distraction from the rest of her life and what she would do with it.

For ten years, she'd worked hard, so hard, to climb the charts. Nothing had been handed to her. Only by tapping into her emotions and feeding her muse with the next greatest adventure had she found success. Being aimless and idle grated on her almost as much as having no voice. She wanted—needed—meaning again, but what if she invested in something and it kicked her to the curb like music had?

The public's hostile clamoring for a piece of her just increased the difficulty in answering the questions. But how long could she go on ignoring the fact that the person who really needed that answer was Evangeline?

Milano Sera was a benign compromise, and the addition of Matt's strength made it somehow seem a lot safer. She should do it, if for no other reason than to gain some progress toward the answers. If Franco put her back against the wall and demanded an explanation of who she was going to be from now on, all she had to do was say *armadillo*.

* * *

Evangeline's former publicist agreed to work with *Milano Sera*'s team to arrange an interview, with two important stipulations—Matt must be given free rein on the set, and Franco had to tape the show remotely from Vincenzo's house.

No one argued. Two days after Evangeline tucked her belongings into Matt's dresser, the taping was a go.

She checked her makeup one last time in the framed mirror above the marble double-sink vanity. A remote taping meant limited resources, so she'd handled her own clothes and hair in the ensuite bathroom she'd been sharing with Matt. No change from regular life; the days of stylists and three dedicated makeup artists were long over. She didn't mind. The activity gave her a chance to calm her nerves.

Eva stared back at her from the mirror. Whatever happened today was happening to Eva. She had to remember that.

When she and Matt entered Vincenzo's palazzo, the buzz of activity stopped as if a plug had been pulled. A statuesque, authoritative woman in her forties barreled over to pump Evangeline's hand and escort her to the makeshift set, introducing herself as the show's producer.

Gingerly, Evangeline perched in the tall, canvas chair the producer had indicated and smoothed her fuchsia skirt as the camera director lined up the shot, fiddled with the lighting and barked orders at the stressed assistants. Matt watched it all without comment from the edge of the camera zone, one hand shoved in his back pocket. It was a deceptively casual stance, but his keen blue eyes missed nothing.

So far, so good. The anchor of Matt's presence went a long way.

Franco strolled over to take the other chair, appropriately slick in his Armani suit and practiced smile.

"Eva, I'm happy you changed your mind."

Sure he was. The ratings boost would likely make his year.

An assistant clipped the small microphone inside Evangeline's strappy top, which she'd specifically chosen because its design allowed for the microphone to be completely hidden.

"I enjoy watching *Milano Sera* so I'm happy to be here, as well."

Franco nodded, though he surely didn't believe either falsehood. Another assistant dashed over and frowned over Evangeline's microphone as Franco murmured to the statuesque director.

"There's a small difficulty, *signorina*." The assistant unclipped the microphone and dashed away to return with another one. "Speak to Franco now."

"Thank you for having me, Mr. Buonotti," she said obediently.

Franco shook his head and tapped his earpiece. "It's no good."

The producer and another man whispered to each other furiously as assistants milled around.

"What's the problem?" she asked Franco. Foreboding settled in her chest at his blank expression.

"Your voice, *cara*. It's not working well with this remote equipment," he explained, not the least bit apologetic, as if the equipment wasn't to blame, but *she* was. "Too low. They can't get it to register."

Her cheeks heated. Rejected by the taping equipment.

"Try again. Speak directly into the microphone." Franco cleared his throat. "Tell me, Eva. What is your life like now that your voice has been so tragically altered?"

A cold, clammy sweat broke out across her neck. Slicked her palms. Eva. He was talking about Eva's voice. Not hers.

"Um." She shook her head as her brain shut down.

Matt was wrong. The interview hadn't even started yet, and already Franco was probing her wounds with inflammatory phrasing. Fashion tips, she could handle. Why had

she naively believed Matt that shopping would be Franco's focus?

Armadillo.

Her throat clamped closed and she couldn't get the word out. Couldn't make any sound at all.

This wasn't happening to Eva, it was happening to *her.*

But then Matt was there, leading her from the chair and tersely informing the producer that Eva did not deign to give interviews to second-rate talk shows without proper equipment.

"Nice," she said when she could speak again, which happened right around the time she crossed the threshold of Matt's house. "You're the best manager I've ever had."

"I'm sorry I suggested that."

He was still bristling, his expression hard and unyielding. And maybe a little frightening.

"It's not your fault."

"It is. I had no idea he'd be so insensitive."

He muttered a particularly inventive slur on Franco's paternity and heritage simultaneously.

Amazing how Matt could still make her smile in the midst of emotional uproar.

"If it makes you feel better, you made up for it, like by quadruple."

It hadn't been merely a rescue, but an expert extraction completed without letting on to her distress *and* giving *Milano Sera*'s team the impression they'd upset her diva personality. A miraculous feat in her opinion.

"It does not make me feel better." He flipped on the lights to dispel the February gloom. Instantly, she cheered. This *was* still a haven. "You told me exactly what would happen. But I was so sure I knew what would help."

Clearly frustrated, he heaved a sigh.

She tucked herself into his embrace and laid her head on his shoulder, right at the hollow she'd first discovered

while they were dancing. "You've given me exactly what I needed. A place to block all that out."

His arms tightened, drawing her into his body deliciously. "I'm glad, sweetheart. Palazzo D'Inverno is available to you as long as you want it."

Not the house. You.

He helped, in so many intangible ways. In his arms, nothing seemed as bad.

She didn't say it.

If nothing else, Franco had shown her the protection Eva had provided in the past had all but vanished. She had nothing left to be rejected but the deepest part of herself, and that was something she refused to risk.

No matter how much she wished Matt held some sort of magic key to her future, he couldn't be anything more than a brief distraction. There was no question their Venice affair was going to be hot, fantastic…and short-lived.

She refused to become dependent on a man—not just a man, but one with his own demons—to fill the gap music had left behind, and she could see it happening as if Matt's beautiful eyes had turned into a crystal ball. Worse, it would be all take and no give, because her store of trust was in short supply. That was totally unfair.

How much longer did it really make sense for her to stay?

Seven

Matthew blinked and it was somehow Saturday already.

Evangeline filled his house, exactly as he'd envisioned, and blinded him to everything else. They didn't go out, more through his insistence than hers. He'd set up an account at both the local pharmacy and the grocery store so Evangeline could order whatever she needed to be delivered. The creative thank-you she'd given him for his thoughtfulness still ranked as one of the highlights of the week.

And there had been a lot of highlights, especially the gradual lightening of the shadows in her eyes, which he'd only made worse with his meddling. He was gratified she'd stayed long enough to let him undo the hurt he'd caused.

He'd never had a relationship with no promises past breakfast. Certainly never thought he'd have suggested it. Every morning, he expected—braced—to find she'd left in the middle of the night.

It was getting old. But the terms were too necessary to change.

The wanderlust in her eyes was unmistakable. When she talked about performing in Budapest or Moscow, her expression reminded him of when he was inside her. Rapturous.

She couldn't sing, but she still liked roaming. Eventually, she'd move on and leave him behind.

Which was good. This thing between them was amazing, but he couldn't keep it up, not long term.

He glanced at his phone. With the time difference, Mama should be at one of her Saturday-morning fundraisers right about now. The perfect time to call. He dialed and waited for voice mail to pick up.

"You've reached Fran Wheeler. I'm busy saving the world with style and grace. Leave a message."

His mother's voice poured alcohol on the exposed wound of guilt in his gut, which was approximately half the size of Texas. "It's me, Mama. Just checking in to let you know I'm still alive. Talk to you later."

He wouldn't, because he never called when she might actually answer.

What would he say? *Sorry about taking off. No, still not coming home. Still not capable of being the Wheeler you raised me to be.*

He had to go home and pick up his responsibilities with Wheeler Family Partners.

But he'd left because he couldn't do it any longer, couldn't see his grandfather's empty desk every day. Couldn't attend fundraisers and ribbon cuttings without Amber. Couldn't watch Lucas and Cia sneak off during the boring parts of events and return with all that love and affection dripping from their faces.

It was too hard.

So he'd live in the present and wring every bit of pleasure out of it.

He sat at the kitchen island and watched Evangeline wash lunch dishes in the sink. He cooked and she washed dishes. Worked for him—the view was very enjoyable from his stool.

"What do you want to do now?" he asked. She flashed

a naughty smile over her shoulder. "Twice this morning wasn't enough for you?"

"Never enough. I like you too much."

Yeah. He liked her, too. Everything was fun. Showers. Dishes. Long talks in the afternoon. "The weather is supposed to be unseasonably warm today. What if we have dinner on the roof?"

"There's a rooftop patio?" Her gravelly voice was hopeful as she dried the last dish and put it away.

That voice. It still dug in, sharp and hot inside no matter how many times he heard it. It was the first thing he wanted to hear in the morning and the last thing he wanted to hear before he went to sleep.

"Did I forget to mention that?"

"Never mind dinner. Show it to me right now."

"Sure." He took her hand and led her outside.

The breeze from the canal was chilly, but bearable, as they climbed the outside stairs to the roof. Venice unfolded as they walked out onto the patio.

Evangeline gasped. "Oh, Matt. I could live here. Right here in this spot. The view is amazing."

"I know. It's one of the reasons I bought this palazzo."

Several of the plants lined up in clay planters against the railing had withered and died, but a few remained green, fresh against the backdrop of browns, terra-cotta and white from the surrounding buildings.

Millions of dollars of real estate stretched on either side of the canal. Once, he'd have taken in the structures with a critical eye, evaluated the resale value, calculated the square footage. Mapped the location and noted the neighborhood features automatically.

None of that could compare to the gorgeous vision standing next to him. The look on her face—he'd move a mountain with a teaspoon if it put that expression of awe and appreciation there.

"You can see the spires of San Marco. And Santa Maria

della Salute. Isn't it beautiful?" She pointed, but he was busy looking at her. Her loose curls blew against her cheek and her eyes were luminous and his gut tightened. His reaction to her was so physical, so elemental. Would he ever get tired of that?

"Yeah. Beautiful." His fingers ached to sink into her hair. Among other things.

That was the beauty of their arrangement. They did whatever they wanted, when they wanted to do it. And he wanted her, wanted to make her feel as good as she made him feel. Right now.

"Let's go back inside."

"What? Why?" She flicked him a puzzled glance and turned her attention back to Venice.

"Because," he said hoarsely, and the unexpected catch in his throat swallowed the rest of the words.

With obvious concern, she eyed him. "Are you okay?"

No. Not hardly. He tugged on her hand. "Come back downstairs. Please. I want to be with you."

"You *are* with me." Her gaze traveled over him. Finally, she caught on to his urgency and grinned. Wickedly. "Oh. Well, I've got news for you. My girl parts work the same whether I'm inside or outside."

Attention firmly on him, she leaned in and teased him with a butterfly kiss while her hands wandered underneath his shirt. He was already half-aroused, and her fiery touch drained heat south instantly.

"Evangeline." He groaned as her fingers dipped into the waistband of his jeans to cup his bare butt. "We're on the roof."

"Uh-huh," she murmured against his mouth. "If you want me, take me, cowboy."

The kiss turned carnal as her tongue crashed with his and they drank from each other. She stole his reason, transformed his desire into crushing need, drew him out of time and place.

He was totally hooked on it.

Tilting her head, he changed the angle, went deeper, fed his senses with the feast of Evangeline.

Their hips aligned, seeking the heat, the promise of completion just beneath their clothes.

He nearly lost his balance as his shirt came over his head, gripped tight in her fists. She threw it to the concrete. Before he could protest, she had his zipper down and her warm hands stroked his flesh, coaxing him out from behind the fabric of his underwear.

They were on the roof. And he was on display.

Then she knelt. Her mouth closed over his length, and conscious thought escaped him as his knees weakened. Running on pure carnal instinct, he pushed deeper until the licks of fire spread through his blood like an inferno, tightening into a knot at his center. He couldn't keep from coming another second.

"Hold up, sweetheart."

He eased from her mouth and in a flash, dropped to the ground and pulled her into his lap. The breeze cooled his fevered skin. Street sounds wafted from below. And he didn't care. She encouraged him to do new things, things he'd never do under normal circumstances, and somehow it made sense.

In moments, her clothes landed in a heap and her mouth landed on his, legs wrapped around his waist, exactly the way he liked.

Yes. He fed the flames as he slid into her. Eyes closed, he froze, sustaining the perfect pleasure of being inside her sweet body, reveling in the physical, carnal hunger that drove him to join with her.

He'd left Dallas desperate to feel again. She'd burrowed underneath the ice-covered inertia and sensitized him. To the limit.

She moaned his name and rolled her hips, drawing him deeper than should have been possible. The roof, the air,

Evangeline—*something*—heightened the sensations, spiraling him toward oblivion faster, stronger, fiercer than ever before.

Her gaze captured his, and the morning sunlight refracted inside her eyes, brightening them. The ache of near release bled upward, into his chest, his throat.

Lids fluttering, she surrendered to an exceptionally strong climax. It rippled down his length and detonated his own release. The blast echoed in his head, blacking out his vision.

He held her slumped form, dragging oxygen into his lungs. That had been…different. And in a relationship full of different, how could there be so many shades yet undiscovered?

How could he crave still more when they'd delved so deeply already?

When she shifted, resettling in his lap, clarity blew away the awe of the moment.

"Evangeline. We forgot to use a condom."

"It's okay," she mumbled against his shoulder. "It's the wrong time of the month."

Women and their bodies—that was a mystery he'd yet to solve even after being with Amber for years. He heaved out a shudder of a breath.

"Sure?"

"Well, either way, too late now." She smiled up at him. "And it was worth it. I don't know how you do that to me. It was unbelievable. Even for us."

"Yeah. It was."

She'd noticed the difference too, but attributed it to the lack of a barrier. Which he didn't believe for a second. Sure the sensation was mind-altering. He'd do it again in a heartbeat if given a safe opportunity. But there was more to it than forgetting a condom, and he feared it had everything to do with Evangeline. With who he was around her. Because of her.

"We'll be extra careful from now on." She wagged her finger at him. "You have to stop being so adorable and sexy."

"Me?" That he could never get used to. It was disturbing when she told him how much he turned her on, which she did frequently. Disturbing because he liked it, and didn't understand what about her was so compelling, when she and Amber were such polar opposites. "You're the one who was all gorgeous with the hair in your face."

"You've got it bad and you might as well admit it."

His pulse stuttered. "Got what bad?"

A crush? Feelings? Was she staring down the barrel of their relationship and seeing things that weren't there?

Or was he making excuses for things he didn't want to examine too closely?

"An addiction to inventive positions," she explained with a wicked laugh. "And locations, apparently."

His muscles relaxed, and he eased her up to help her get dressed, then stepped into his own clothes. "That's all you, honey. I'm just here for the food."

Her laugh uncurled across his skin with gravelly teeth and stayed there. She affected him in so many ways. And not all of them were good.

A dose of guilt wormed into his consciousness. He'd found a temporary cure for his ills, but how fair was it to keep using Evangeline?

"Hey." He caught her hand and brought it to his lips. "You know I don't have much to offer. Emotionally. Right?"

She nodded, gaze searching his quizzically. "I'm not confused about what's going on between us. We're keeping the demons at bay until it doesn't work any longer. Were *you* confused?"

"No. Just checking."

Keeping the demons at bay. Yeah, that was exactly what they were doing. She knew he wasn't capable of anything more right now.

They meandered downstairs to do absolutely nothing except be together.

It shouldn't have been so easy. They should get on each other's nerves. Or complain about socks on the floor, dishes in the sink. Argue about something.

They didn't.

The longer he spent in Evangeline's company, the less he recognized himself. He hadn't put on a suit since the masked ball; he hadn't ironed a shirt or balanced his checkbook. T-shirts and spending money recklessly felt far too comfortable. As comfortable as Evangeline.

He hadn't dwelled on Amber in days. Wasn't that the point of all this? Why did it feel so strange?

Venice provided a much-needed break from real life as he searched for a way to get back to Dallas, to the responsible, centered, married man he'd been. When he'd understood his place in the world and woke up happy every morning.

He didn't know what would work to turn back time, or if what he sought existed. But he was starting to wonder—if he'd known what to look for, what would he have found instead of glittery, wrong-for-Matthew-Wheeler Evangeline?

And would he recognize it, now that Evangeline had so filled him he couldn't see around her?

Late one afternoon, Evangeline's phone buzzed. She retrieved it and flopped on the couch next to Matt, then glanced up from the text message to catch his gaze.

"Vincenzo's cousin, Nicola, is throwing a small dinner party," she said. "Tonight. Do you want to go? It's casual. He assures me the guest list is well vetted."

They hadn't left the house in a week. Self-preservation warred with the gypsy part of her soul that liked parties and people and experiences. All of her parts liked Matt, so it wasn't a hardship to wake up in his bed every morning.

"Sounds fun. As long as you're okay with it."

And that was why. He was amazing and intuitive and

never crowded her. Gradually, she'd stopped practicing her exit strategy and just enjoyed hanging out with him. Plus, she'd grown rather fond of starring in Matt's rodeo. The man shattered her with those eyes alone.

Was she okay with going out? It was dinner at Nicola's house, not a public flogging. She hesitated.

"Nicola lives on the other end of the Grand Canal. How should we get there?"

With silent, reassuring strength, he covered Evangeline's hand with his. "Private water taxi. Put on a big hat and a scarf. It'll be dark. No one will know it's you."

"Done." She accepted the invitation and deleted the other text message she'd received from her half sister, Lisa, without reading it, then spent an hour getting ready. Which gave her plenty of time to get worked up about her sister.

Lisa was seventeen. And her parents had been married. The anger, the sheer resentment was embedded deep. Their father had chosen a life with one daughter over the other— Evangeline would never forgive that. She sent Lisa extravagant Christmas gifts in a petty attempt to show her father there were no hard feelings. And maybe to quietly announce that hey, no dad needed for her to be a huge success.

Evangeline hadn't spoken to her sister since the botched surgery. How many texts did she have to ignore for Lisa to give up? It wasn't like they were real family.

Putting it out of her mind, she vowed not to let unpleasant history ruin the fun evening she and Matt had planned.

When Evangeline returned downstairs, Matt was waiting for her, dressed in dark jeans and a sweater. His eyebrows rose.

A floppy hat covered her pinned-up hair, a scarf hid the lower half of her face and giant sunglasses completed the disguise.

"Perfect." Matt shot her a playful grin. "Except maybe lose the glasses. It is nighttime."

She slipped them off and returned his smile. "Happy?"

"Always."

That thrilled her to no end, to be responsible for Matt's happiness. That was part of the reason she stayed. It was powerful to watch him slowly heal.

The taxi picked them up at Palazzo D'Inverno's water entrance and motored away from the dock. The driver steered under the Ponte dell'Accademia and up the canal to Vincenzo's cousin's house. Twinkling stars competed with the twinkle of Venice, both lit for the night with stunning brilliance.

They arrived a few minutes later. Once inside, Evangeline started to introduce Matt and realized with no small amount of mortification that she didn't know his last name. It hadn't seemed important, until now.

With a quick grin that said he'd read Evangeline's mind, he stuck out his hand to Nicola Mantovani, their hostess. "Matt Wheeler."

He repeated it to Nicola's boyfriend, Angelo. Vincenzo shook Matt's hand and introduced his lady friend for the evening, whose name Evangeline promptly forgot. He never called his dates again anyway.

Nicola lifted an unobtrusive finger toward a uniformed servant, who sprang forward to pass out wineglasses full of deep red Chianti. The tiny, dark-haired Italian raised her glass. "A toast. To new friends."

Expertly, Nicola finessed everyone to the lushly appointed salon where they took seats and chatted politely.

When Vincenzo launched into an impassioned review of the performance he'd seen at Teatro alla Scala the prior weekend, Evangeline leaned in to whisper in Matt's ear. "Wheeler. That's a nice last name."

Matt grinned. "We haven't formally introduced ourselves, have we?"

"Evangeline La Fleur." She stuck her hand out in mock solemnity. "Nice to meet you, Matt Wheeler."

Vincenzo paused long enough to drain his glass and mo-
tioned for a refill.

In the silence, Angelo asked Matt, "What do you do?"

"I'm a partner at a commercial real estate firm in Dal-
las, Texas."

No hesitation. No dodging the question. It was clearly
how he defined himself or the answer wouldn't have come
so quickly. It put an odd barb in her stomach because she
wouldn't have been so quick with her own answer.

"Oh, do you know J. R. Ewing?" Angelo snickered at his
own joke. Evangeline rolled her eyes, but Matt just laughed.

He was such a good guy to spend time with her friends
and not call them out for being lame. But here she could
relax and just be herself, without the pressure of Eva.

"Real estate." Nicola wrinkled her nose. "Houses?"

"No, we haven't delved into residential. We sell office
buildings. Downtown high-rises." When he warmed to the
subject, the pang in her stomach poked a little harder. He
loved his job. It was all over his expression. "Land for de-
velopment. That sort of thing."

We. Not *I.* An interesting choice of phrasing. Who was
the *we?*

"High-rises. That sounds impressive." Nicola's nose un-
wrinkled and she leaned forward, suddenly a bit more in-
terested in Evangeline's companion now that she scented
money.

"Matt's very successful," Evangeline threw in, though
she didn't know much about the ins and outs of the life he'd
left behind. Neither last names nor pre-Venice activities had
ranked very high on the priority list of their discussions.
She'd always assumed it was by design, since Matt's wife
was a taboo piece of that past.

But really, of course he was successful. Look at him.

He squeezed her hand. "Evangeline's being kind. I've
been on an extended vacation. Wheeler Family Partners

was the top-selling firm in Texas last year, but its current success is due to my brother. Not me."

"You work for a family business?" Nicola asked, and Matt nodded, explaining how the other partners were his dad and brother and the firm had been in his family for over a hundred years.

No one else seemed to notice the catch in his voice, but it sliced at her.

Family meant nothing to her, was almost a foreign word. But to Matt, it seemed as if it had been the cornerstone of his existence before Venice. He'd communicated far more than the simple logistics of a job—he'd belonged to a unit.

He wandered in search of answers now, but did he eventually want to return to his roots? She didn't want to ask. Didn't want it to matter. But the barb in her stomach was also due to realizing they were less alike than she'd assumed.

She waited until after dinner, when they'd settled into the water taxi to return to Matt's house, to bring it up again. "Tell me more about your life in Dallas."

With a laugh, he kissed her sweetly. "Why? Do you need to take a nap? That would be so boring you'd nod off in a second."

Her lips curved. "Boring? You? There's no way the guy who put his hand under my dress on a balcony could ever be boring."

"I drove a sports utility vehicle, Evangeline."

"But you left it all behind." His wife's death had turned him into a drifter. Like her. They'd both been honed by tragedy but had yet to recognize their new shape. She desperately wanted to feel that kinship with him again after learning they'd come from such different places. "So it doesn't matter now, right?"

"It matters. I walked away from a legacy. The name of the firm is Wheeler Family Partners. That pretty much en-

capsulates it. Family is everything. And I abandoned them." His voice never wavered as he listed his sins.

Strength. He had it in spades and it pulled at her. The men in her life were weak. Spineless. Matt regretted his actions but took full responsibility for what he'd done.

"I didn't mean to poke at scars. Armadillo?" she offered.

"Yeah. It's not a great subject." He curled her palm against his. "What was your life like when you were singing?"

"Busy. Lonely." The hand holding hers tightened. Encouraging her to go on. He was so easy to be with—maybe she could open up, just a little. "The guy from Vincenzo's party, Rory, he was supposed to be the cure for that. We were so similar, both with careers in the industry. Both happy being nomads. He had some bad habits, but I stepped over the empty Jack Daniel's bottles because I was in love with him. Turns out he wasn't content to be saddled with a has-been."

"I'm sorry."

"I'm not. Longevity isn't one of my gifts." She'd have tried, for Rory. And probably would have bungled it all up. "That's what made being an in-demand vocalist so great. I sang all over the world, was constantly on the move."

She'd loved it, loved having a new destination, new experiences.

And that was the gist of it, wasn't it? She and Matt had a kinship born of shared pain, but it was tenuous at best. A successful, solid real estate broker who valued family had nothing in common with a music business has-been who sported a giant albatross called Lack of a Career around her neck.

Besides, his heart still belonged to his wife, would always belong to his family. Hers had been cut from her chest by the same blade that destroyed her career. Maybe even before that.

She'd shared this time with Matt because they were both slaying their demons.

How much longer would it take for this refuge to crumble around her?

Eight

Evangeline rolled over and pulled the sheets up around her neck. Cold. And still dark. Though her brain languished in the fog of semiconsciousness, she could tell Matt wasn't asleep. His breathing was too even.

Two weeks and four days into it and she could already gauge his state of consciousness. She also knew his favorite foods, the exact rhythm to move her hips to make him explode, how to get that blinding, sincere smile out of him that shivered her insides.

And if he was awake, she knew she'd never go back to sleep.

They were becoming dangerously entangled for two ships who were supposed to be passing in the night.

Supposed to be. But she was still here.

She kept looking for a reason to leave. Kept waiting for claustrophobia to set in or for Matt's true colors to shine through. The longer she spent with him, the more convinced she became that he was the real deal and she could trust him. He was a genuine guy who wasn't looking for the quickest way to get rid of her. Who treated her like he'd stumbled upon a rare treasure.

Instead of scouting for the exit, she stayed. The longer she stayed, the more obstacles she saw to keeping this Venice bubble afloat.

Why couldn't she have met Matt in six months? A year? At any point in the future when she'd figured out who she was going to be and could give Matt what he deserved—someone a lot more together, at a different place in her life.

She scooted across the cool sheets and nestled into his arms. "You need a glass of warm milk?"

He kissed her temple. "Did I wake you up? Sorry."

"You didn't."

But maybe on some level, he had.

That instantaneous spiritual bond hadn't dimmed in the slightest. Sometimes, he finished her sentences, and sometimes, she didn't have to speak at all. It was more than gelling and she puzzled over the indescribable, powerful nature of their relationship.

It should feel weird. Suffocating. It didn't.

"I'll go downstairs so you can sleep."

Something was bothering him. Matt's ghosts continually haunted him and lots of great sex hadn't produced quite the exorcism she'd have wished.

She snaked an arm over his chest to hold him in place. "Don't you dare. Talk to me."

"It's not a middle-of-the-night subject. But thanks." His hand wandered over to stroke her breast and as lovely as that was, his touch carried a hint of preoccupation.

"Anything is a middle-of-the-night subject. It's dark. Sleepy. What better environment is there to lay it all out?" Unless he was about to call it off. That froze her pulse. She didn't want it to be over.

She'd thought they were both happy to live in the here and now. Both happy to see what unfolded. The lack of boundaries made it easier for her to stay but also made it easier—for either of them—to walk away.

Should she have checked in with him before now?

The hand on her breast stilled, but didn't move away. "You wouldn't rather go back to sleep?"

"I'd rather you weren't upset. Tell me, and let me make it all better. That's what I'm here for, right? To beat back the demons." Which was a two-way street, and he did his part well. "But unlike other forms of self-medication, I don't come with a hangover."

"You don't pull any punches, do you?" A deep breath lifted his chest. "I was thinking I should be over Amber by now."

"What? Why would you think *that*?"

Oh, that was such a better subject than calling it off. He hardly ever mentioned his wife, and she respected his privacy. But curiosity pricked at her, naturally. What had Amber been like? What was so special about her to have shattered Matt into so many pieces?

"It's been a year and a half. How can I still be so messed up?"

"You can't put a time frame to grief. Life doesn't have checklists."

"We weren't married a whole year. She's been dead longer than the length of our marriage."

"So? You loved her." Obviously a lot, more than Evangeline had ever loved anyone, or could even imagine. She could, however, *easily* imagine how it would feel to be the object of such unending devotion.

Especially Matt's.

That put a hitch in her lungs. She suddenly, unreasonably wished for something impossible—the hope that she might one day take Amber's place in his heart. Impossible, because she'd have to open herself up in return and trust Matt with her deepest layer. Impossible, because he was still hung up on his wife. That was the biggest obstacle of all.

Apparently dark-and-sleepy was a good environment for her conscience to spill confessions, as well. As long as she didn't start doing it out loud...

Matt shifted restlessly. "Am I doomed to suffer for the rest of my life because I fell in love with someone? It's not fair."

He was destroyed. No one should have to bear that much of a burden without relief.

"I don't have all the answers." She rested her palm on his heart, which beat strongly despite her suspicion it was badly broken. "The only thing I know for sure is life sucks and then it gets better until it gets worse again. Sometimes I think God likes to see what happens when the carpet is pulled out from under you."

After a long minute of silence, he said, "It doesn't bother you that I'm moping around over another woman?"

Well, now that you mention it...

"I didn't say that." Boy, he'd taken her no-subject-off-limits-in-the-middle-of-the-night seriously, hadn't he? Despite asking, she didn't think he'd actually appreciate knowing about the burning-in-the-gut jealousy of Amber she'd just discovered. "But we're cool. I understand. Of all people, trust me. I understand."

Probably too much. Other women wouldn't put up with being a form of self-medication. But Matt wasn't presenting her with a buffet of choices. What would she pick if he did?

The question bounced around inside her with no answer.

"The pastor at Amber's funeral said something that's stuck with me. The valleys of life are impartial and temporary. If that's true, I should get over it already, right?"

"Is *that* why you're beating yourself up? That's total crap!" Evangeline's vision grayed for a furious moment. Pastors should soothe people in their time of grief—not spew lies. "The valleys of life are anything but impartial. Or temporary. Both of us had the center of our existence ripped from our fingers. No warning. That's as personal as it gets, and I refuse to accept that we don't have the right to be pissed off about it because it's gone forever."

His arms tightened around her, holding her close, calm-

ing her. *He* was calming *her*. "Is that what happened? You had the center of your existence ripped away?"

"Yeah. I did." Her chin trembled.

"You don't talk about it."

Just like he didn't talk about Amber. "No voice. It kind of puts a crimp in the talking thing."

"That's a cop-out. Especially with me. Should I tell you again how sexy I think your voice is?"

She sighed. Transparency was one of the many things she couldn't avoid with Matt. It went hand in hand with the vibe between them. And it went both ways. He'd veered away from Amber on purpose, maybe to avoid talking about her. Or maybe to find some straw he could grasp from her own experiences. They were *both* fighting their way out of the valley.

He was so compassionate and decent and didn't want anything from her but her company. She should honor that.

"I lost everything." She shut her eyes. "Not just my career. I sang my whole life, from as early as I can remember. Back then, my voice was the one thing that belonged to me and no one else. Singing was a coping mechanism."

"What were you coping with?" he asked gently.

"You know, stuff. My home life." She hadn't thought about it in years. But that had been the genesis of using her voice to express all the things going on inside.

"My dad, he was a hockey player for Detroit. A seagull who swooped in, got my mom pregnant and never called her again. She tracked him down, got child support. She moved to the U.S. so he could know his daughter. Guess how many times I heard from him?"

"Evangeline…" Matt nearly pulled her on top of him in a fierce hug, lips buried in her hair.

"It's fine. I'm over it."

"I don't think so," he murmured and softened the contradiction with a light kiss. "You started to say you had family in Detroit. When we were dancing."

God, she had. How did he remember that? "He's not my family. He lost that chance. But, I...have a...sister."

"Are you and your sister close?"

Evangeline laughed but it came out broken. "She worships me. Not like in a million-screaming-fans way. Because she wants to sing."

Lisa texted her all the time asking for career advice. Evangeline still didn't know why she'd ever answered. No one had helped her. But before the surgery, she hadn't been able to stop herself from pathetically responding each and every time. Once, she flew Lisa and three friends to London for a concert for Lisa's fifteenth birthday. It was the last time she'd seen her sister.

After the surgery, Evangeline went into a hole and stopped responding to the texts. One of these days, Lisa's name on her caller-ID wasn't going to cause such deep-seated anguish. She hoped. It wasn't Lisa's fault their father was a bastard.

"Is she any good?" Matt asked.

She shrugged. "I've never heard her sing. Too busy, I guess."

"You've got time now," he pointed out quietly, but his words reverberated in her head like the boom of a cannon.

"Yeah. I should call her." She wouldn't. What would she say? They had no relationship, had only ever connected over their mutual interest in singing. Now they had nothing in common other than a few strands of DNA. "Armadillo."

She was done with midnight confessions. Lisa was a corner she couldn't stand being backed into.

"I should call my brother. I haven't talked to him in a month." Matt rolled away and she missed his warmth. Had she hurt his feelings?

A sick niggle in her stomach unearthed the realization that she'd set up the code word as a way for him get out of difficult subjects, but only she used it.

"Is a month a long time?" she asked.

"We saw each other every day. His office was next to mine. We went to the same college, played basketball with some guys once a week. And you know. He's my brother. It's my job to make sure he stays out of trouble."

"You miss him."

It wasn't a question. She could hear it in his voice and didn't have to ask if they were close. Could Evangeline have a similar relationship with Lisa if she tried harder?

No. Evangeline wasn't cut out for family relationships. Didn't want to be. It hurt too much.

"That was before. When Amber was alive. After, I drifted through everything, disengaging until everyone stopped trying. I kept thinking something would happen to snap me out of it. Then my grandfather died and I realized. *I* had to snap me out of it. So I dumped my entire life in Lucas's lap and left." He chuckled derisively. "I even sold him my house. He's in *my* house with a wife he's gaga over, making new memories, about to deliver my parents their first grandchild. I should be there, living that life."

There. Not here. Venice was a temporary fix. She knew that. So why did it make her so sad?

"Are you jealous that your brother is happy?"

At least they had that in common.

"No. Not really. Maybe a little." He sounded defeated all at once. "Mostly I'm glad. I never thought he'd get married. He was kind of a screwup. But he met this woman who transformed him into a guy I didn't recognize. He's responsible. Committed. Expecting a baby who will be the first of the next generation of Wheelers. That was my role. A role I couldn't do any longer. And I need to figure out how to do it again."

He had more demons than she'd realized. "You're not just trying to get over Amber. You're trying to fit back into the life you had with her."

A life that included lineages. Babies. Roots and new

branches on the family tree. Concepts so alien she barely knew how to label them.

He huffed out a breath. "I can't. I know that. But for as long as I can remember, I've done the right thing. I ran Wheeler Family Partners, and I was good at selling real estate. Successful. Amber was a part of that. She had connections, came from a distinguished family. There were five hundred guests at our wedding. CEOs of Fortune 500 companies. A former U.S. president. The governor. We were happy being a power couple. People could depend on me. I want that back."

Her stomach dropped. No wonder he hadn't cared about her celebrity status or her money. He had his own social clout, in a world far removed from hers.

A cleft, one she hadn't realized was there, widened.

He hadn't embraced the wanderlust—he'd been desperate to find the magic formula for curing his grief so he could pick up the broken pieces of a life he'd abandoned, but yearned to return to.

Unlike her, he *could* go back. And would. Not only did neither of them have a whole heart to give to anyone else, they came from different places and were going different places.

She kissed his cheek. "I depend on you. Right now, you're my entire world."

How pathetic did that sound? He had a career waiting for him. A family. Both would welcome him back with open arms, she had no doubt. No mother who took the time to teach her son to cook would turn her back on him.

"Right now, I'm pretty happy being your entire world."

Shock flashed behind her rib cage. "Really? I thought you were heading toward the big breakup."

He *should* be heading toward the breakup. She should, too.

"What, you mean of us?" He laughed and shifted suddenly, rolling her against him, tight. "You're the best thing

hat's happened to me in a long time. Why would I give hat up?"

"Isn't that what we've been talking about? You want to go home." Home to a place she couldn't follow. Her gypsy soul would wither and die in the suburbs. "This is…our Venice bubble. It's not going to last."

Quiet settled over them, and she waited for him to agree.

But he said, "I don't know if I *can* go home. My family— he obligations. It feels so oppressive. Like it's too much for me to handle. I want to be me again, but at the same time I want to keep hiding." He chuckled darkly. "God Almighty, I sound like the biggest pansy."

No, he sounded like a man in incredible turmoil. For once, she'd stayed. She'd done it as an attempt to block out the future, but instead, quite by accident, she'd discovered this sensitive, wonderful person. What a juxtaposition. She ached to salve his wounds, knowing the moment she did, he'd leave her.

Rock. Hard place.

"I want to sing. I can't. We're both stuck in a rut we can't get out of."

Matthew listened to the sound of Evangeline's heart against his and threaded fingers through her hair.

"Rut. Valley. Same difference."

There was nothing quantifiable about the grieving process. It had stages, or so he'd read. But they weren't easily identifiable so he had no idea if he'd gone through them all, remained immobilized in one, or had stumbled his way back to the beginning to run through them a second time.

He'd been stuck in the valley for far too long. And he was sick of it.

Her lips grazed his throat and stayed there. They'd both lost so much. Did she find it as comforting as he did to be in the arms of someone who understood? She not only understood, she'd given him permission to be mad.

That was powerful.

Because he *was* mad. And felt guilty about being mad Evangeline somehow made it okay to let all that out, let it flow, and the anger cleansed as it burned through his blood

"I was part of something," he said. "In Dallas. Some sons rebel against the family business, but I couldn't wait to be on the team. My parents were proud of me, and I thrived on that. Thrived on being married and looked forward to starting a family. Then it was gone and I couldn't function. I don't know how to get that back."

The sheer pressure of life without Amber had nearly suffocated him. But it was more than missing her. They'd been like cogs in a complex machine, complementing each other. He didn't know how to be successful without her.

"I admire you," she said quietly.

He snorted. "For what, disappointing everyone?"

That was at least half his onus—how did he face everyone again, knowing he'd abandoned them? Knowing they were eyeing him with apprehension, waiting for him to freak out again?

"For recognizing that you needed time away to get your head on straight. It was brave."

"Cowardly, you mean," he corrected. "People deal with pressure gracefully all the time. I cracked. It wasn't pretty."

"But you changed things. You left your comfort zone and struck out to fix it, without any idea how or where that would occur. That's sheer courage in my book."

He started to tell her she should reread that book but closed his mouth. She saw him differently. But that didn' mean she needed glasses. Perhaps he did.

"Thanks. That's nice to hear."

"You had a choice and made it." The unspoken *I didn* wrenched his heart.

"Have you ever noticed the stuff people say when you'r grieving makes no sense?" That was another gripe he'd been carrying around since the funeral.

"What like, 'Sorry for your loss'?"

"Yeah. My favorite is, 'But think of all you do have.'"
He struggled to voice the anxiety whipping through him.
Struggled to phrase it in a way that didn't sound self-
centered. And gave up. This was Evangeline. He didn't have
to pull punches. "It's meaningless. Thanks for pointing out
I still have a mom and a dad. That makes it *all* better. And
oh, yeah, I have my health. The fact that I'm still breathing
is supposed to get me through the valley?"

"I got an, 'At least you still have all the money'. Don't get
me wrong. I'm grateful I can afford to eat. A lot of people
can't after losing their job. But money doesn't make up for
losing who you were."

"Exactly." It was like she peered down his throat and read
the words in his heart, expressing for him what he couldn't
formulate. "Singing was your purpose. So what do you do
now that it's gone, right?"

She laughed without humor. "Isn't that the million-
dollar question?"

He'd meant it rhetorically, but something in her tone
tugged at him. "Is it?"

She didn't answer, and he lightly bumped her head with
his chest. "Middle-of-the-night. Nothing is sacred."

Don't call armadillo. His senses tingled. This was criti-
cally important, he could tell.

Her soft sigh drifted across his skin. "I don't know what
to do now. That's my demon."

"The one I'm here to beat back for you?" The phantoms
in her eyes weren't just from losing her voice. How could
he have missed that? Because he'd been wallowing around
in his own problems instead of tending to hers.

"Singing is all I'm good at. My only talent."

"Not hardly."

"Being good in bed isn't a talent." The eye-roll came
through loud and clear.

He bit back a chuckle and the accompanying comment—
it is the way you do it.

"You're good at making me cheerful. That's something
no one else could accomplish, so don't knock it. But I was
going to say the music industry can't be easy to crack or
everyone would do it. Persistence is a talent. You worked
hard to achieve success."

"Yeah. Hard work." Her voice fractured. "There was a
lot of that."

There was more, something else she wasn't saying, and
she was hurting. The inability to fix it crawled around in
his chest. But this middle-of-the-night was exactly what
he'd asked for—the exploration of what two damaged souls
could become to each other.

Dang it if he'd fail at being what she needed.

"Hey." He brought her hand to his cheek and held it there,
reminding them both he wasn't going anywhere. "This
demon of yours, what does he look like? Big and scary?
Small and quick with a sharp stick? I'll do a much better job
of keeping him away if I have an idea what I'm looking for."

She laughed, low and easy, drawing a smile from him.
"Big. With claws. And he doesn't shut up. Ever."

"What does he sound like? James Earl Jones or more
Al Pacino?"

"Dan Rather."

Ah. "So your demon moonlights as a reporter who asks
you questions you don't like." And he'd bet the demon an-
swered to the name *armadillo*.

"Yeah."

The single syllable quaked through her damaged vocal
cords and snapped something behind his rib cage.

"Like what?" he whispered, his voice nearly as raw as
hers.

"It's not the questions." She shifted and wet pooled into
the hollow of his shoulder right about where her eye had
been. Tears. "It's the lack of answers. Bad stuff happens

They were just vocal cords. Why don't I know what to do next?"

"Because," he countered fiercely. "You're not out of the valley yet. Once you clear it, then you'll see where to go."

He had to believe that was true, had to believe it was possible. He wanted out of that valley—for himself, but also to show her the way.

"Music was a part of my soul." More tears dripped onto his chest, but he didn't wipe them away. Didn't move at all for fear of stemming the tide of her grief. "And I thought it always would be or I wouldn't have inked eighth notes on my body permanently. How do you find a new direction when something so ingrained is gone?"

Silently, he held her, suddenly furious that he didn't have the answers. Her anguish vibrated through him and wedged into a place he'd thought was dead and buried.

"I could have the tattoo removed," she continued brokenly. "Turned into something else. But what? Who am I going to be for the rest of my life?"

Yes. *That* was the million-dollar question. Evangeline voiced things he could hardly define, let alone articulate. They gelled because she struggled in exactly the same ways he did.

And perhaps they'd solve it together.

"Is there no way to keep a hand in music? Do you play an instrument?"

"Piano." She sniffed. "I wrote all my songs."

An odd sense of pride filled him with the admission. She'd produced something from nothing, using a creative energy he couldn't fathom.

"That's amazing. I thought other people wrote songs for recording artists."

A tune filled his head instantly. Hers. She'd written the notes, sang them. He wished he could have heard her live. Wished he could ask her to sing for him, here in the dark.

His gut split in two over the loss of something he'd never dreamed he'd want.

"Other people do write songs, when the artist is just a voice. Like Sara Lear." She growled. "I hate how catty that sounds. But geez, I could trip and fall into a piano and accidentally write a better song than the ones she sings."

Was her ability to connect dots broken or was she too close to see the obvious? "Then do it. Write one for her."

She shook her head against his shoulder. "I can't."

"Can't, or don't want to?" he countered softly.

"The words...they've all dried up."

"They'll come. You're an artist who isn't just a voice." He stroked her hair. "You'll figure it out. We'll both figure it out, and in the meantime, we'll hold each other in the dark and lay it all out there."

"Matt?" More snuffling. "I'm glad I stayed. I don't stay as a rule. No rules is nice for once."

Finally, he breathed a little easier. The conversation could have veered into something ugly. But he'd navigated it pretty well—he hoped—despite a distinct lack of experience with damaged souls, his or anyone else's. His relationship with Amber had been straightforward and undemanding. Safe.

He'd certainly never experienced quite so many highs and lows when she'd been alive.

"It can't last. This thing between us," he clarified. Evangeline was merely passing time with him until she figured out her next steps. She'd said as much. It shouldn't hollow him out—wasn't that what they were *both* doing here?

"I know that," he added, "but I can't stand to be in the valley alone. Please don't think less of me for selfishly dragging it out."

"I don't think you're selfish."

She wouldn't. Evangeline was the single most nonjudgmental person he'd come across. He could tell her anything. Had told her things he'd never said out loud. He didn't worry about disappointing her with his failures. Ironically, be-

cause he'd set out to be someone else with her, his internal censor-switch had shut off. He had the freedom to pour out the angst and fear he'd carried for months.

He wished he had more to give her in return and was suddenly sorry they'd met while they were both still stuck in the valley.

Nine

"Let's go out," Evangeline announced late one afternoon as they watched a movie, snuggled together on the couch.

Convinced he'd misheard, Matthew hit the volume, almost dropping the remote. "Out? As in out in public?"

Other than an occasional rooftop visit, they hadn't crossed the threshold of Palazzo D'Inverno since the dinner party a couple of weeks ago. He was on a first name basis with the grocery store delivery guy, who delighted in correcting Matthew's poor Italian.

"Yeah." She shrugged. "Take me on a date tonight."

"You hate dating."

"But I like you." She fluttered her lashes, coquettishly. "So I'm willing to make sacrifices. I might even let you talk my clothes off after."

"What's going on? Cabin fever?"

It was certainly starting to get to him. As much fun as Evangeline was—and really, was there such a thing as too much sex?—a slight sense of restlessness wouldn't go away, no matter what he did.

"I don't know. Maybe. I haven't worn makeup in for-

ever. I'd like you to see me in something other than one of your T-shirts."

"I like you in my T-shirts. I like you best in nothing at all," he threw in. "But I could go for some dinner with a beautiful woman."

"Dinner and maybe a show." She leaped off the couch, suddenly animated. "Ooh, I have the perfect dress. I haven't worn it yet. I'm going to hog the bathroom. Do you need anything out of it?"

"Nah." He grinned at her enthusiasm and flipped the channel to a cable news station since the movie clearly wasn't of interest any longer. "I'll be here. Waiting. For a long time, I suspect."

An hour later, he'd donned a button-up shirt and ironed some pants, the most effort he'd expended to get dressed in ages. Evangeline still hadn't emerged from the bathroom so he flopped on the couch to amuse himself by flipping through the channels.

She called his name from the stairs.

He glanced at her and his heart locked up.

Evangeline La Fleur had put on yet another mask. She'd transformed into a fantastical vision in a clingy blue dress, honey-brown curls loose around her shoulders, sultry eyes full of mystery and promise, legs shaped by spiked heels that made his mouth water. And he'd kissed every inch of that gorgeous body.

How could she still punch him so hard without a word when they had few secrets between them any longer?

A button-up and kakis were far too casual to have *that* on his arm. Actually, the man in the clothes left a lot to be desired, as well. The glittery superstar walking down his stairs had nothing in common with Matthew Wheeler.

"Ready?" she asked, her gravelly voice raw and thrilling. Like always. It jump-started his lungs again as he stood to meet her. She was still the same person underneath the mask.

"I'm not sure. I think you've stolen my ability to walk. You're…I don't know what to call you. *Beautiful* is too simple a word. You're exquisite." Flustered, he straightened his belt and smoothed his hair. "Sure you want to be seen with me?"

She laughed, throatily, with her head thrown back. It was genuine and elemental, and he hardened in an instant.

"I'll ask you that same question in a little while, when we've drawn a lot of unwanted attention. I thought about playing it down, trying to blend. But it would be pointless. Anyway, I wanted to look nice. For you."

"For me?" That pleased him, enormously, and he yanked her into his arms, careful not to muss this gorgeous creature. "Thanks. It is a pretty good hit for my ego. And I will thoroughly enjoy looking at you all evening as I imagine what I'll say to talk your clothes off."

Her fingers walked down his chest and dipped into his pants to lightly graze his swollen flesh. "It'll have to be good. Maybe with some begging."

He groaned. "We're not going to make it out the door if you keep that up."

Withdrawing her hand, she smiled with a mischievous curve to her lips. "I'll save it for later then."

Eyes still crossed, he helped her into a coat and slipped on his own. Lacing their fingers, he led her outside into the night. Carnevale was long over and the cool March air held a hint of the Italian spring to come.

"Walk or water taxi?" he asked. "I thought we'd go to this little out-of-the-way place I found, instead of somewhere trendy. I hope that's okay. It's only a few blocks."

"Walk. I haven't seen nearly enough of Venice. There's a different feel when you're on the street, in the middle of it all. The view from your living room, or the roof even, is amazing. But removed. You know?"

Yes, he did. He'd been removed from everything for so long. Tonight, he was fully in the land of the living, with

Evangeline, and it did feel different. As if he'd emerged from a dark tunnel and the world had burst open around him.

As they strolled, other couples nodded or called "*Ciao*" upon passing. Streetside shops blazed with light behind glass, wares on display in the window. The pace of life in Venice ebbed and flowed with the canal waters, tranquil and slowed. Peaceful. History—the heartbreak, the triumphs— radiated from the very cobblestones and dripped from the stucco veneer of the ancient buildings.

People had lived and died in this city for centuries before Matthew's Northern European ancestors had jumped the pond to America. Life would continue on after Matthew was long gone. It was the here and now that counted.

He squeezed Evangeline's hand, and she glanced over at him through those soft brown eyes that he liked waking up to every morning. Not for the first time, he wondered if there was a way to stop dragging this thing out and do something crazy, like put a stake in the ground and hash out a plan to make it work long term.

Except he'd been searching for a way to move on after Amber's death, never realizing a step in that process might include falling in love with someone new.

It felt disloyal to Amber to think something like that.

This thing couldn't last. Not because he and Evangeline wouldn't work in real life. That was true, but surface level. Deep down, he wasn't sure he could do it again, give his whole being to someone else. Love someone else. Have a household, a baby, a life with someone else.

He'd created the temporary nature of his relationship with Evangeline to make her more comfortable with staying, but it was really an excuse. He'd latched onto it to avoid the truth—he wasn't ready to move on.

They found the restaurant easily. The maître d' showed them to their table, and Matthew ordered a bottle of Chianti, which the efficient staff brought immediately.

"Well. Here we are." Evangeline raised her glass and they clinked rims. "Our first date."

In a manner of speaking. Seemed strange to be on a first date with a woman he'd made squirm under his tongue as he knelt before her in the shower that morning. "Guess we did things out of order."

"That's okay. I'm not big on tradition."

"Like marriage?" Why in the world had he picked that rock to kick? He already knew her stance on commitment.

She wrinkled her nose. "Well, doesn't seem like it works out for many people, does it?"

It had for his parents and grandparents. Seemed to work tremendously well for Lucas and Cia, what little of their relationship he'd been around to witness.

His own marriage had been perfect. With Amber, he'd done things in the exact right order. They'd gone to the opera for their first date. Amber had worn gloves and left them in his car. On purpose, he knew, so she'd have an excuse to call him. Which she had done, two days later.

After three dates, he kissed her and three months to the day, he surprised her with a suite at the Fairmont, where they'd made love for the first time, in a nice evening full of potential. That's when he'd known he would propose, but he held off until they'd been together over a year, then, for Christmas, he'd given Amber a white-gold Tiffany engagement ring that had belonged to his grandmother. Everything safely unfolded according to plan.

For all the good it had done him.

Voices from the front of the restaurant interrupted his musing. Evangeline's face froze as a couple of sharply dressed teenage boys argued with the maître d', pointing at her.

"Sorry, they followed us in here," she said. "They noticed me on the street, but I figured they'd move on."

"What are you apologizing for?"

"Because it's invasive. Or it will be." She pasted on a

smile as the waiter came up behind her to whisper in her ear. She nodded, and the teenagers rushed over to babble incoherently in a mixture of Italian and English, shoving pieces of paper at Evangeline for her to sign. One of the boys handed her a Sharpie and brazenly lifted his shirt. She scrawled "EVA" in flowery script across his pectoral muscle.

Really? Matthew looked away as something black and sharp flared deep inside. These kids had no sense of decorum whatsoever.

And he absolutely did not want to admit the pain in his stomach had to do with Evangeline's palm on the guy's chest. Jealousy. As if she belonged to Matthew and he had a right to expect he'd be the only man she touched.

Evangeline was a good sport through it all. She posed with the boys for at least a dozen pictures, hastily snapped on their phones by the beleaguered waiter. When she was "on," her otherworldliness intensified, sharpening her beauty but making her seem almost untouchable.

She hadn't put on a mask—but taken one off. Eva was an extension of her essence.

Finally, the teenagers drifted out the door, leaving a tense silence draped over them both.

"My fans mean a lot to me." She flicked her nail across the tines of her fork without looking at him. "The ones I still have anyway. But it can be a bit much for someone not used to it. I knew better. I shouldn't have asked you to take me out."

"It's okay." Her biggest concern had been inconveniencing him or upsetting him, but he got that her celebrity went part and parcel with the rest. He reached out to cover her hand. "It's a small price to pay. You're worth it."

Her eyes grew shiny. "Thanks. We're lucky they weren't reporters."

They ate dinner without any more interruptions. When they left the restaurant, bright flashes halted them in their

tracks, and he got a glimpse of the reason for her earlier concerns.

Two media-hounds lounged a few feet away, easily identifiable by their professional cameras and lack of interest in capturing the Venetian splendor all around them. Their sharp gazes were on Evangeline as she stepped into Matthew's side, snugging up against his ribs closely. Too closely. Seeking what? Protection?

A prickle of warning went down his spine.

The men blocked their path, crowding them with their solid builds and flat eyes. Not guys who looked eager to be reasonable.

"Eva," the shorter one on the left—American—called out. "Mind if we ask you a few questions?"

Matthew was about to calmly suggest it would be in their best interests to let them pass. But Evangeline's sharp intake of breath tripped something in his blood.

"I mind," Matthew said, and stepped in front of Evangeline, shielding her from the men.

"Who are you?" The one on the right zeroed in on Matthew. "*You* got time for a few questions? I'll be sure to spell your name right."

"No comment," Evangeline said and earned both men's pointed attention.

"Is that what your voice sounds like now?" The short one whistled. Nastily. "Like a cement mixer with boulders inside. Can I tape it?"

She was trembling against Matthew's back as she pulled on his arm. "We'll go the long way home."

Home. Not to a show, which she'd chattered about endlessly during dinner. If the reporter had latched onto anything else except her voice, Matthew would have let it slide.

These two idiots weren't ruining their night out. "Back off. We're of no interest to you."

"You're with Eva, you're news, buddy." The taller one

snapped off a few photographs, blinding Matthew with the flash.

"You want to get that camera out of our faces before I do it for you?" Matthew blinked hard in an attempt to clear the white starburst from his retinas.

"Are you threatening me, pretty boy?"

"Obviously not well enough if you have to ask. So I'll be clearer." Matthew nodded to both men curtly, tamping down his fury. "Stop harassing us or you'll be examining the ceiling of an Italian jail cell shortly. Or the ceiling of a hospital room. Your choice."

The men glanced at each other, smiling cruelly. "You gonna take on both of us? Over *her*?"

Her. As if she was worthless because she'd lost her voice. The fury welled up again, traveling through his veins, curling his hands into fists.

Walk away. Now. Before you do something you'll regret.

He pivoted and grabbed Evangeline's hand to escape in the opposite direction. They'd only taken a couple of steps when the men skirted them, blocking their path again.

"Hey, what's your hurry?" the short one asked and leered at Evangeline, his gaze on her legs. "We're just doing our job."

If the smarmy little rat didn't get his dirty mind out of the gutter, Matthew would remove it from his skull. Through his nose. "Insulting people who are trying to walk down the street is not your job."

"No, satisfying the public's curiosity is. And we're all curious. What's Eva up to now? Who's the mysterious man escorting her around Venice?" The taller one shoved a small recorder at Matthew, nearly chipping a tooth. "You tell us. We leave. Easy."

"We already said—" Matthew backhanded the recorder away "—no comment."

He shrugged. "Then we'll write our own story. Eva does Venice with an American schoolteacher on holiday. Eva's

new beau—disinherited playboy after her money? Eva sleeps her way into a modeling contra—"

Matthew's fist connected with the reporter's smug mouth. He reeled backward, smashing into the other reporter.

God, that had felt good. He shook out his throbbing knuckles.

The man regained his balance, touched his bleeding lip and glanced at his fingers. "I'm pressing charges."

"See you in court. Until then, stay away from us."

He spun and herded Evangeline through the throng of wide-eyed onlookers and down a side street free of people. They didn't talk, but she grasped his tingling hand tightly.

His heart rate still in the upper stratosphere, he paused in a dark alcove. "You okay?"

"Are *you*?" She touched his face, tentatively. "I've never seen you like that."

"Never been like that." He'd never punched anyone in his life. Not even Lucas, though his brother had surely asked for it on many an occasion. Matthew handled conflict with his brain. Usually. Nothing with Evangeline worked like usual. "The things they were saying were hurtful. No one has the right to treat you that way."

She melted into his arms. "Thank you," she murmured against his shoulder. "I can't tell you what that meant to me."

It had been pure reaction. No thought to consequences. No reason involved. Just a ferocious drive to protect Evangeline from being hurt.

He held her close and his pulse shuddered anew. Amber would have been horrified. Not grateful. Amber didn't let much affect her and would have blown off reporters with some practiced sound bite. He'd never had a reason to protect her. A reason to be jealous. A reason to feel like he was dancing across a high wire with no net and not only craved the danger but kept asking for more.

Amber was gone.

And if he didn't disentangle himself from Evange-

line soon, the man Amber had married would be gone, too. Then who would he be?

The next afternoon, Evangeline stretched out on the couch with Matt's iPad and downloaded a fluffy beach-read novel to entertain her while he took a shower. She needed a distraction from the slimy swirl those reporters had put in her stomach. The media had been a part of her life for a long time, and they'd never bothered her until after the surgery.

Now they just made her sick—physically, deep inside.

When Matt came downstairs, hair still a little damp and darkly golden, she forgot about the story on the page and watched him cross the room. Delicious. He still made her shiver despite the fact that she knew exactly what was underneath that waffle-print shirt and jeans. Maybe because she knew.

But it wasn't the body that got her going.

Matt had jarred something loose the moment he smashed that reporter in the face. It was far more than what he'd done with *Milano Sera*'s people. That had been simply an extraction. The incident with the reporters—something else entirely. She'd never felt anything like it, the rush of release, the empowerment of knowing he valued her enough to stand up to the evils of the world.

He had her back. No one ever had before.

"Busy?" he asked.

"Nope." She laid the tablet on the coffee table.

What could possibly compete with his attention? She loved being his focal point, morning, noon and night. Sure these were extraordinary circumstances, but no doubt he operated the same in real life, with his full commitment on whatever was in front of him. Matt did everything wholeheartedly.

"Do you know if Vincenzo is home today?"

She shrugged. "I think so. I saw him come home early

this morning when I was washing the breakfast dishes. I
doubt he's even awake yet. Why?"

"I'm having something delivered. A surprise. Call him
and ask if you can hang out over there for an hour. No peek-
ing, either." With a mischievous smile, he snagged her hand
and crossed her heart for her.

The area under her fingertip lurched sweetly. "A sur-
prise? For me? What is it?"

He shook his head and mimed zipping his lips. "You'll
see soon enough. Call."

Mystified and with no small amount of curiosity, she
woke Vincenzo from his postdebauchery sleep and an-
nounced she was coming over.

Vincenzo answered the door with a bad case of bedhead
and a worse attitude. She flounced past him into the living
room and perched on the sofa. "You don't have to entertain
me. Go back to bed."

Their friendship went back a couple of years, hinging on
a mutual love of parties and a glittering social scene, but it
had never been deep and meaningful. Like most of her re-
lationships. Except one.

He eyed her. "Trouble in paradise, *cara*?"

"What, you mean between me and Matt?" She flicked off
his concern with a wave. "He's surprising me with some-
thing."

She'd told Vincenzo very little about her relationship with
Matt. On purpose. It didn't have the same transcendence
when explained to an outsider.

Vincenzo jiggled his dark brows. "An engagement ring?"

Automatically, she started to deny it. But what if it was?
No. Surely not. Venice was a temporary arrangement.

"He'd stick that in his pocket. Wouldn't he?"

She glanced at her hand, bare of jewelry since she'd
ripped off Rory's ring and flushed it. Matt wasn't propos-
ing. No way. He was looking for a way home, not a new

wife. There were too many ghosts flitting through his heart for that.

"I am not an expert in matters of marriage." Vincenzo lifted one shoulder and shuffled in the direction of the marble staircase to the second floor, calling out, "Lock the door when you leave."

Alone, she contemplated what she'd say if Matt did get down on one knee and claimed he'd gotten over Amber....

He couldn't. If he did, she'd have to say no, and their affair would be over. Marriage—she couldn't imagine anything she'd be more ill-suited for.

She fretted about it until he texted her to come home.

When she burst in the door of Palazzo D'Inverno, the surprise nearly knocked her off her feet.

"Oh, my God."

A shiny, ebony grand piano stood in the corner of the living room, overlooking the Grand Canal. Matt sat on the bench, quietly watching her, and the two together put a glitch in her lungs she couldn't breathe through.

"Presumptuous of me, I realize," he said. "But I thought you might enjoy having it to play since going out isn't so fun."

Her fingers curled spontaneously. She hadn't touched piano keys since the surgery. Hadn't wanted to. Didn't want to now.

"Thanks. It's…nice."

His eyebrows rose. "You're welcome, and you seem a little underwhelmed. Did I screw up?"

Vehemently, she shook her head. "It's the most thoughtful gift anyone's ever given me."

"Okay. I'll take that." He slid off the bench and engulfed her in his warm, safe arms. "But there's more. Do you want to tell me, or is the piano now the armadillo in the room?"

The laugh slipped out. "How did you know I was going to call armadillo?"

"You get this closed-in face whenever you're about to say it."

"I don't want to play." It fell out of her mouth. Maybe on accident, or maybe because she couldn't bear for him to be so understanding and not get anything for it.

"You don't have to. I can send it back." He hugged her tighter and then released her. "I'll call the delivery company right now."

"No." That had definitely been said on purpose. She was safe with Matt. She knew that. "*Want* is the wrong word. I can't play."

"Like you've forgotten how?"

"Like the music is a razor blade." *Cut*, Madam Wong had said. The music had been cut from her throat and it cut when she heard it and it cut when she played.

"*Screw up* would be too kind a phrase, then," he said. "I'm sorry. I didn't know it was hard for you to play. I envisioned you gaining something…I don't know, peaceful from it."

Her eyelids shut in sudden memory. The piano had been her refuge in a lonely house growing up, the one thing her mother had given her. Because it was the path to fame and fortune, foremost, but Evangeline turned it into something else. A means of expression she'd channeled in conjunction with her voice. Always together.

The piano still had the music inside. She didn't. But in Palazzo D'Inverno, there were no rules, and the two didn't have to coexist. They could have value individually.

"I'd like to find some peace," she admitted. "I don't know why it's so hard."

"Peace is elusive."

She'd meant playing the piano was hard. He'd cut through the outer layer and exposed the raw truth. But not the whole truth. "Not when I'm with you."

With a smile, he captured her hand and pulled her toward the piano. "Then let's do it together."

"What? You don't play."

But he situated himself on the bench and drew her between his spread legs, placing her fingers on the keys under his own. "Teach me. I've been listening to music my whole life. How hard can it be?"

She snorted out a giggle and leaned back against the solid chest supporting her, his breath teasing her ear and his heart thumping her spine.

Safe. Matt was her anchor in a sea of anxiety.

"Move your hands. That's not how you learn. Here, listen."

Slowly, she picked out the notes to "Twinkle, Twinkle Little Star." The keys sank under her fingers with measured float, producing rich tones from under the raised lid. This was easily a hundred-thousand-dollar piano. And Matt had given it to her because he wanted her to experience peace by gently prodding her toward something she could still do.

She didn't mind that kind of push so much.

"A little elementary of a song choice, don't you think?" he said into her ear, and she elbowed him.

"Try it, smart guy. Go ahead." She nodded to the keys.

He plunked out a few scraggly notes that sounded more like he was dragging a screaming flamingo down the street than playing a song. But he got about half of them right—a hundred percent more than she was expecting.

"Not bad. Practice makes perfect."

"Show me another one." He nudged her with his chin, peering over her shoulder intently at the spread of white and black keys. "Something that takes both hands."

Without prompting, her fingers spread, arranging themselves around middle C and the melody trickled out. Then gained strength as her muscles remembered how to stretch and fly.

Matt's hand crept across her stomach and he held her tight as she played, never once flinching if her elbow caught

him. He'd held her through a lot of difficult stuff. Had since the very first moments in the alcove at Vincenzo's party.

When the last notes faded, she slumped, drained.

"One of yours?" he asked softly.

"The first one I ever recorded." But on a synthesizer and with a faster tempo, when she'd had the energy of a burgeoning career to fuel her performance. "My fingers are tired."

His lips rested against her temple. "You don't have to play anymore. Though I enjoyed every second of it."

"It's a good kind of tired. Thanks for playing with me. It helped." The armadillos were having a throw-down in her stomach, but after last night, the exposure of being Eva again and sitting here at the piano, it was too much to keep from bubbling over. "It more than helped. I'm reminded again of what music means to me."

Reminded again of the peace of simple expression, which had been impossible, until lately.

"What does it mean?"

Escape, she thought. Music had been an escape. It could be again, in a far different way. She could separate music from Eva, peel back that layer and see what was underneath. Eva was gone. Evangeline could be herself.

"It means I have choices."

"You did a brave thing by playing the piano again." It was a gentle echo of what she'd said to him during the middle-of-the-night, nothing-is-sacred conversation. "It was hard, but you did it. Choose to do something else difficult. Write a song for Sara Lear."

"I'll think about it."

"Good." It was all he'd say. Somehow, that encouraged her to fill the silence.

"The music industry..." She cleared her raspy throat—a wasted effort. "It'll rob you of everything you'd hoped to gain. The fame, the money...I readily admit I loved that part. But there's a price. You lose a sense of yourself and who you are without all the costume changes. People don't see

you anymore. Not the fans. Not the execs. Both put you on a pedestal but watch to see if you teeter just a tiny bit. Then the new song doesn't climb the charts as fast as the last one. The fans are fickle, and the producers mutter about profits."

It was a no-win catch-22. Everyone wanted a piece of her until they were done with her. Rory. The industry. And everyone eventually rejected her, even people who should love her no matter what.

"I see you," he murmured.

She nodded. "That's why I'm still here."

Matt made it safe to ditch the mask and be herself. He was the one man on earth she could trust with the deepest part of herself and not be braced for a rejection because she wasn't good enough.

He was the only one who could get her to stay because for the first time in her life, staying was better than leaving.

Ten

Moonlight poured through the panes of glass in the bedroom. Evangeline eased out from under Matt's arm and pulled the covers over his gorgeously muscled torso. He shifted but didn't wake up.

She watched him breathe, unable to tear her eyes away. Sooty lashes brushed his cheeks, and underneath those lids lay the most amazing depths. No matter how many mornings she woke wound up in his long limbs, it wouldn't be enough. She could stand here forever and bask in his presence.

But the words were flowing, calling her with their siren song, begging her to commit the emotion to paper. She couldn't ignore the first stirring of inspiration.

The piano had unwound something inside her, and Matt patiently drew it out, helping her examine it in his clearheaded, logical way.

Downstairs, she plopped onto the couch with the back of a take-out menu and a pen. Fifteen minutes later, lyrics covered every blank space on the menu. Good lyrics. For the first time in *months*, she'd tapped into her center and captured the music.

She rummaged around for more paper and came up empty-handed. Matt's iPad sat on the coffee table and though under normal circumstances she'd never use a digital page, she couldn't lose momentum.

When she hit the power button, one of the squares with the logo WFP caught her attention. It hadn't been there before.

She touched it and the website popped up. Wheeler Family Partners. The header contained the profiles of four men and she recognized Matt's instantly. The chiseled good-looking face next to Matt must be his brother, Lucas. A total player. She could see the look in his eye a mile away and hoped his wife kept that one on a short leash.

The other men must be their dad and grandfather. Andrew and Robert, according to the About page. Matt favored his grandfather. They both had the same piercing gaze and straightforwardness. She could tell neither of them would ever lie, cheat or steal.

Her eye wandered down the paragraph. Geez. Wheeler Family Partners had done eighty million dollars of business in the last quarter of the previous year alone, largely owing to the sale of a communications complex in North Dallas.

And Matt had been the spearhead of his firm. Like she'd assumed, he'd been successful at everything he'd tried. Business. Marriage. Getting her to stay.

He was far more special than she'd imagined.

She tapped the website closed and brought up a free-text application, more than a little concerned she'd stemmed the fountain of words with her side foray into Matt's domain.

A blank page materialized. It didn't scare her.

But the words she typed did. She couldn't stop, didn't even pause as the song fell from her fingers, fully formed. Whereas the first round had taken shape in bits and pieces, this one had structure. Order. And it would be a guaranteed hit. She knew it. All four of her Grammys had been for songwriting, not singing.

The piano hovered in the corner of her peripheral vision, and she glanced up at it, then up the stairs to where Matt lay sleeping. No piano this time. She didn't want to wake him.

The fortune teller had predicted she'd conceive. And this felt like birth, like the beginning of something wonderful and amazing. A metamorphosis.

As the last word appeared, she finally removed her fingers from the screen and read over the song again, hearing the tune in her head as she internalized the words. With the right voice, like Sara Lear's, it would climb the charts instantly.

She saved the file to her cloud account and powered off the tablet, staring out the window at the quiet canal.

The right voice. It wouldn't be hers. She wasn't ready to let the song go to another home, but for the first time, it didn't sting so badly to envision it. Thanks to Matt.

Here in the dark, it didn't seem so frightening to admit she was falling for him. He was so genuine and real, and her stupid heart hungrily latched onto those qualities. She knew better. Knew that nothing could crumble the monument to Amber in his chest. But her heart had its fingers in its ears, refusing to hear the message from her brain.

Matt was a heartbreak waiting to happen.

She should go before it was too late. Nicola had a place in Monte Carlo. Vincenzo had been making noises about shoving off in that direction in a few days and had texted her the address with an open invitation to join the group. Her stomach rolled. It had been off since the reporter incident.

Matt still needed her. His turmoil churned below the surface, popping up in his faraway gaze at odd moments. She'd give anything to ease that note of sheer anguish in his voice when he talked about his family and the life he'd lost.

She didn't want to leave.

Her head fell back against the couch cushion. The riot of colors splashed across the ceiling was dim with only the outside canal lights to illuminate it. The paintings depicted

domestic vignettes; men and women sleeping, eating, playing with children. This had been someone's refuge, built to escape a harsh climate.

She and Matt had both done the same. And despite what she told herself about the reasons she stayed, she needed him as much as he needed her. How much longer could they hide away here before Venice became a stumbling block to healing instead of a sanctuary?

Matt's gentle hands in her hair woke her. Daylight streamed through the panes leading to the balcony and beyond the glass, Venice was awash with the morning.

"You okay?" Matt asked from behind her. "Why didn't you come back to bed?"

"Meant to. But I fell asleep." She yawned. The mist of sleep would not clear her mind, like she'd dunked her head in a vat of Jell-O.

"I'll make you some breakfast."

Food did not sound appealing in the least. "You go ahead. I'm going to take a shower. I'll grab something later."

He leaned to plant an upside-down kiss on her lips. "Want me to scrub your back?"

Which was code for Very-Little-Bathing-To-Occur. "Normally I'd be all over that. But I'm just wiped out. The shower is to wake me up." She smiled to soften the blow.

"If you're sure." He brushed a thumb tenderly across her temple and disappeared into the kitchen. Thumps of cabinets opening and dishes clinking drifted out. Comforting sounds. Sounds of home.

How would she know? She'd never had the kind of home the noises had evoked. Never wanted one.

Until now.

Oh, God, where had that come from? This wasn't her home. It wasn't even Matt's home. Home was for people who wanted to stay together, who implicitly trusted each other and never spent all their energy looking for the exit.

She didn't do the domestic thing for a reason. And her subconscious argued that the reason was because she hadn't done it with the right person yet.

Heavy with fatigue, she wandered upstairs to take a long hot shower and get dressed. Somewhere along the way, she began to feel human again. By the time she returned to the lower level, Matt was watching cable news with the crinkle in his forehead that meant he was bored.

When he caught sight of her, he lit up, his expression radiant, and he was absolutely the most gorgeous man on earth. Her heart squished. Out of nowhere, lines of a new song popped into her head. A sappy, sugary love song.

She wasn't just falling for him, she'd splatted flat on the ground and then a giant cupid had stepped on her.

"Feeling better?" he asked.

"Define *better,*" she mumbled, eyes closed in case her stupid, inadvisable feelings were beaming from her insides. "I'm awake, if that's what you mean."

He leaped off the couch and hustled her into the kitchen so he could ply her with food, though the thought of putting anything in her mouth made her slightly nauseous.

Idiot reporters. Those creeps were still upsetting her. She didn't say anything. There was no point in Matt being upset, too.

Gulping orange juice, she took a seat at the island and watched Matt move around the kitchen. Poetry in motion. He was never content to shove a couple of pieces of bread in the toaster and call it breakfast. His idea of cooking involved creativity usually reserved for master chefs.

Today, he was making an egg-white omelet with prosciutto and sun-dried tomatoes, and a half-moon of cantaloupe on the side. He placed the plate in front of her with a flourish and refilled her empty orange juice glass.

She forked a bite into her mouth and swallowed. It stayed down. "Delicious. As always. You should open a restaurant."

"Nah. I just throw some stuff together and pray it turns out." He waved it off with a pleased smile. "Cooking is fun."

"I'm glad one of us thinks so." Her idea of fun was paying someone else to cook. And clean up the kitchen. Matt had never met a pan unworthy of his olive oil or chicken stock. But he made such fantastic dishes, she really didn't mind cleaning up.

"Well, I never used to." He shrugged. "But I like cooking for you."

"Why, because I'm so inventive with how I show my appreciation?" She waggled her brows.

He laughed. "That is one of the perks. But mostly because you let me. Amber...she was kind of a Gordon Ramsay about her kitchen. I stayed out of it."

The omelet took on a whole new significance. "You never cooked for Amber?"

"Sure, when we were dating. But then, I don't know. She loved to cook and prided herself on it, so I just didn't anymore." He stared out the window at the joint courtyard Palazzo D'Inverno shared with Vincenzo's house, his gaze faraway and dejected. "I paid through the nose to upgrade the kitchen in this place. For her. I didn't expect to be the one who would actually use it. Honestly, I probably never would have started cooking again if you hadn't stayed."

That put a lump the size of a grapefruit in her throat. She couldn't swallow. "Thanks for resurrecting your spatula for me."

He shot her a grin. Lately, it didn't take long at all for him to snap out of his Amber mood, which, if she had her way, he'd get out of permanently.

"You eat too much takeout. Or you used to. You were practically wasted away to nothing when I got ahold of you. At least this way, I know you're putting something healthy into your body."

"Oh, I see. You cook for me because you're concerned about my health," she joked back.

And then it sank in. It wasn't a joke. He'd been taking care of her. All along. Maybe subconsciously she'd known that and hence had begun to equate kitchen sounds with a sense of home.

Matt communicated in subtle, baffling ways she'd never experienced—probably because she never stayed long enough to allow it. What was he trying to tell her with food? That he might have deeper and more lasting feelings for her then she'd thought?

Wishful thinking at its worst.

Her eyes burned with the sudden prick of tears.

The omelet turned to mush in her mouth, and she shoved the plate away. "I didn't get much sleep last night. Think I'll go back to bed."

"Are you coming down with something?" He skirted the island and cupped her chin with both palms to peer into her eyes, concern practically dripping from his touch.

"I'm fine. Just tired."

Narrowed blue eyes locked onto hers. The deflection didn't fool him, but he chose not to call her on it.

Upstairs, she threw herself onto the bed, but it smelled like Matt and that wasn't conducive to sleep, unless she wanted to have red-hot dreams about the way that man's mouth felt on her body. She'd rather be experiencing the real thing, but with something far stronger than desire in his gaze.

She wanted Amber's place in his heart. It was a really inadvisable thing to long for. But that didn't make the longing magically disappear.

Matt had cooked for her. He'd been taking care of her in a way he never had with Amber.

Maybe he just needed more time to get over her. Maybe being here, in the house he'd bought his wife, prevented Matt from fully healing. Was Evangeline falling down on her job by dragging out their Venice bubble?

She rolled over and buried her face in the pillow, ex-

hausted but unable to shut off the hamsters turning the wheel in her brain. She'd never been so tired in her life, probably because she'd rendered herself completely inactive. This was the longest she'd stayed in one place.

Monte Carlo beckoned. The words—the music—flowed again after a long, painful hiatus. If she stayed, all that lovely inspiration might dry up again. The wind had always guided her well enough before.

But if she moved on, Matt might lose all the progress he'd made. Worse, they'd never find out what might be possible between them. He couldn't go home yet; that much he'd made clear in more than one conversation.

What if they moved on together?

A daring question. But what if it worked?

If she said the idea of being loved by Matt didn't thrill her, she'd be lying. A solid, committed man like Matt would never fail her, and in turn, she'd never fail him. They had an unparalleled measure of trust in each other, an understanding. That was the way love was supposed to work. She wanted that, for once in her life.

But what if she asked and he said no? He'd been drifting in search of a way to get his old life back. Just because he wasn't ready to go home this minute didn't mean that goal had changed. Could she really risk Matt's rejection?

After mulling it over for a long time, sleep finally claimed her.

Matthew's slight restless feeling graduated into a full-blown itch to do something productive. He settled for getting out of the house.

He took his laptop to the rooftop patio and sat in the sun. The Venetian spring was unbelievable, still cool in the mornings, but a warm breeze wafted from the Adriatic Sea, laden with the pungent scent of marine life.

He wished Evangeline had come up to enjoy it with him,

but she was taking an afternoon nap for the third time in a week.

Something was up, and he suspected she slept to avoid him. Because she was leaving. He could feel her winding down, becoming less talkative.

Honestly, he was avoiding "the talk," too. It didn't feel finished, this thing between them, but only because he didn't want it to be. For once, the idea of no commitment seemed like a blessing. There would be no broken heart in his future when she took off.

The organ in question gave a quick, painful tug at the thought of Evangeline leaving, and he shut his eyes until it started beating normally again. *No more of that, now.*

Since he had an afternoon to himself, Matthew poked around in his stock accounts, balanced his checkbook and generally killed time with stuff that had no promise of holding his interest.

He logged onto WFP, curious to see if anything new was going on. Lucas had posted a few sales, but nothing major and certainly not at the same clip as his brother had performed last quarter. First quarter historically saw the best sales as companies began the year with clean budgets.

The numbers should be better.

Strategies, marketing, building specs—all of it scrolled into his head and he latched on greedily, gratified both the knowledge and the drive was still there.

They could easily gain visibility by—

Stay out of it.

Lucas was handling it, as he had been. What good could Matthew possibly do from halfway around the world?

Renewed guilt gnawed on his insides.

Real estate was in his blood, and he'd missed the negotiations, the deals, the art of reading a potential seller. But the restlessness was more than lack of a job; it was a lack of setting goals and working to achieve them. Feeling successful and knowing his effort would be rewarded tangibly.

He wanted to be dependable, responsible Matthew Wheeler again, not a grieving, guilt-ridden widower.

Maybe he could check in, casually, without throwing his weight around. That might work. He was still a partner, regardless of whether he'd been acting like one, and there was no time like the present to start making amends.

Evangeline had played the piano. Maybe he could take a step out of the valley, too.

A baby step. The top of the mountain would grow closer with each one.

Before he thought better of it, he fished out his phone and sent Lucas a text message.

The response came instantly. You're alive?

Matthew flinched. Yeah, he deserved that. He shot back: Still have a pulse last time I checked. What's going on with WFP? 1st Q looks like a train wreck.

What do you care?

I care. I'll send flowers to soothe your bruised feelings later. 1st Q?

Lucas's answer took almost five minutes, during which Matthew sweated through some very unpleasant possibilities, like Lucas had fallen off the responsibility wagon or something had happened to their father.

Richards Group opened shop in Dallas.

Matthew swore. That had never crossed his mind.

Saul Richards owned the Houston real-estate market and the Wheelers owned North Texas. It was understood that Richards stayed on his turf and the Wheelers stayed on theirs. The shift wasn't a mystery—Richards had scented Wheeler blood with Matthew out of the picture.

Matthew shouldn't be out of the picture. Lucas had been

handling it. Now he needed help. Wheeler Family Partners had been in business for over a century, and Matthew refused to be the one who let it fail.

It was time to go home.

The thought didn't fill him with dread like he'd expected. His life in Dallas had been inescapably intertwined with Amber, with the expectations of creating a family and upholding traditions. But she was gone and as he'd flippantly, but accurately, told Lucas, he still had a pulse. Lucas had married a wife who helped him succeed, and they were happily working on the continuation of the Wheeler line.

There was no pressure for Matthew to fill his old role until he was ready.

The healing had happened so gradually, he hadn't realized it.

Evangeline called his name, and he glanced up to see her waltzing across the patio from the stairs. Sunlight beamed across her face, and she smiled. It slid down his throat with a jagged edge and sliced something in his gut.

God Almighty, she was almost ethereal. But sexy. Strong. Luminous.

Fingers numb, he dropped his phone to the concrete and pulled her into his lap to kiss her thoroughly. She smelled like sleep and Evangeline and everything good in the world. She'd helped him heal. Brightened up his house. His soul.

As the familiar lightning-fast rush of heat filled him, it suddenly occurred to him that if he went home, he'd have to end things with Evangeline.

Then he had the most dangerous thought—what if she came home with him?

No. He couldn't fathom issuing such an invitation. An invitation for what? To hide away in some lover's nest while he stormed the gates of Saul Richards's blockade on the Dallas real-estate market? She would grow bored with Dallas in about five minutes. She'd grow bored with Matthew Wheeler in four.

He could imagine going home for the first time in a long time. But he could not imagine Evangeline there, fitting into Amber's role as the woman behind the Wheeler. Mostly because bright, glittery Evangeline could never blend into the background the way Amber had, quietly providing support and encouragement, organizing get-togethers and charity events with his mother. The women in his world were beige.

Evangeline shifted in his lap, straddling him, her tongue finding creative ways to tease him. Yeah, she was as far from beige as Venice was from Dallas, and he forgot about everything but the warm breeze on his face and the hot woman in his arms.

She drew back, breathing heavily, with a businesslike glint in her eye. "I came to talk. Stop distracting me."

Talk. That sounded bad.

He scooted her back an inch, off his blazing erection, in deference to the directive. "Hey, I'm not the one looking all sexy and disheveled and climbing all over you."

"Can't help myself," she murmured and sighed, thrusting her chest into his. "You're so tempting."

She wasn't wearing a bra and talking was pretty much the last thing he wanted to do.

"What did you want to talk about?" he asked, and snaked a hand under her T-shirt, which was actually his, and hell if that wasn't the most arousing thing ever. He fanned a palm across her bare back, gradually working it around to the front where her breast fell into his eager fingers.

She moaned and arched against him. "Monte Carlo."

He paused, thumb and forefinger wrapped firmly around her nipple. "What about it?"

The end of things now had definition. She was going to Monte Carlo, and he did not want to think about all the implications.

"There's a party." She gasped. "Don't stop. Whatever you're doing, it feels amazing."

"You mean this?" Tweaking her nipple again, he shoved

her up against his erection because maybe they were going
to talk *and* have sex. It would be the first time in several
days they'd connected outside of bed.

"Yes. That." She writhed against him, igniting his flesh.
His eyes crossed. "I didn't bring a condom. Fair warning."

"Well, now. That sounds like a challenge. Hmm. What
can I do that doesn't require a condom?" He yanked the
T-shirt up and closed a nipple between his lips, sucking for
all he was worth. Her warm skin felt like velvet in his mouth
and she moaned his name, bucking against him.

He loved her responses, loved that *he* could do that to her.

He slipped a thumb down her shorts and inside her pant-
ies to circle her trigger-point, and relentlessly pleasured her
until she came apart. Beautiful. He could watch that over
and over.

Boneless, she slumped against him, and he breathed
through his nose until his erection subsided to merely pain-
ful instead of excruciating.

"You were telling me about a party?" he prompted when
her breathing slowed.

This was it. She was taking off. Maybe later today. This
might be their last time together.

He did not want to give her up.

"I was?" She rolled her head to nuzzle his neck, nearly
sending him off the edge of the chair.

"In Monte Carlo. Talk fast because we're finishing this
in about four seconds downstairs." He stood with her in his
arms, sad it was over.

No, not sad. Devastated.

"Um…" She met his gaze and smiled, but it never reached
her eyes. "Never mind. We can talk about it later. Take me
downstairs."

Swallowing, he nodded. She didn't want to ruin their last
time together with unpleasant reminders of what was about
to happen. Neither did he.

Evangeline was the best thing that had ever happened to

him, enlivening him, encouraging him—but also encouraging him to keep hiding. To keep being a runaway.

It was best to go their separate ways, like they'd always planned. Lucas needed him, and the sting of reentering his old life without Amber had mellowed. When he went home, Matt would disappear forever, and there'd be no more wild and crazy, totally-un-Matthew-like Venetian affairs. He'd have his identity back. A plan. Security.

Evangeline would be free to fly off wherever she chose to go next, chasing the wind to the ends of the Earth.

The thought should have made him happier.

Venice was a transitory interlude, and now it was done. He only wished that truth eased the tightness in his lungs. And in his heart.

If only….well, life didn't give anyone the luxury of "if only."

When he picked up his phone to follow Evangeline back to the lower level, he saw another text from Lucas.

I'm handling Richards. Don't worry your pretty little head about it.

Eleven

Evangeline stared at the half-packed suitcase blindly and gnawed on a fingernail. Not one of her previously mani-cured-within-an-inch-of-their-lives fingernails remained.

Matt had gone for a walk. By himself. She didn't blame him for dealing with reality in his own way. Venice, the temporary fix, was over. It just didn't feel like it should be, and if things went the way she hoped, it wouldn't have to be.

She'd almost asked him to go to Monte Carlo. It had been right there on the tip of her tongue, but at the last moment, she couldn't chance a "no," not after he so cleverly steered her away from talking about it. He didn't *want* to talk about it.

But she had a hunch they'd be doing nothing but talking by the time he came back from his walk, because something huge and frightening and momentous might have happened and it sat right in the middle of her consciousness, scream-ing its presence. All she had to do was verify it.

The doorbell chimed.

Evangeline bolted downstairs and grabbed the package from the delivery guy, slammed the door in his face and

only remembered she'd forgotten to tip him after she locked herself in the bathroom.

Hands shaking, she pulled the pregnancy test from the brown wrapper. It was pretty much a formality. Icing on a cake that had already been baking for over a month, since the no-condom roof incident. The fatigue, the slight nausea, the way she sometimes couldn't get enough of Matt's hands on her overly sensitized body and other times, couldn't stand for him to touch her at all—it meant something much more weighty than a need to move on.

This morning, she'd done the math, then called the pharmacy the second Matt went for his walk. Bless him for his foresight in setting up a delivery account, though she doubted either of them could have envisioned it would prevent unwanted photographs of Eva buying a pregnancy test.

Two minutes passed in a blur, and her life changed forever when the little plus sign appeared as expected.

A sob bubbled from her throat, but it was half shaky excitement and half disbelief. Madam Wong's prediction that she'd conceive had encompassed more than songs.

A baby. She was going to have a baby. Matt's baby.

It would be a girl, with Matt's beautiful blue eyes and her voice. Her heart fluttered. Of course. This baby could be the answer to her future. She couldn't sing, but she could learn to be a mom.

And Matt would be a dad, father to their baby. She'd be giving him the one thing Amber never could—the family he wanted. He'd forget about his wife in a heartbeat, like she never existed, and come with Evangeline to Monte Carlo.

Before, she and Matt didn't make sense long term. Now they did. The baby would clinch it. He'd never reject his own flesh and blood. She and Matt would be happy, deliriously in love, with the proof of Matt's devotion strapped into a baby-carrier on his back.

They'd *both* have a family. Together.

Okay, she was getting ahead of herself. She had to tell

him first. But there was no doubt this would be the cata-lyst to keep them together. No doubt he'd be thrilled. He'd drifted into her life for a reason—to heal, surely, but also to move on with the next phase of life.

Evangeline was his next phase.

When his key rattled in the lock, she jumped up from the couch to greet the father of her child. A powerful twist of emotion welled up, like she'd never felt before. She tried to emblazon it in her memory so she could get it into a song as soon as possible.

"Hey," he said. "I'm glad you're still here. I got you some-thing."

"Funny. I have something for you, too." Did she sound giddy?

His grin arrowed straight to her heart. "You do? What is it?"

She shook her head. "You first."

Pulling a wrapped box from a bag, he dropped it into her cupped hands. "To remember me by."

Wait until she told him he'd already given her the great-est memento possible.

The wrapping paper hit the floor. Jewelry. She flipped the hinged velvet lid and gasped.

"Wow. That was not what I was expecting. I love it."

It was a white enameled Carnevale mask, painted with delicate brush strokes in a rainbow of colors. Teardrop di-amonds spilled from the eyes. She pinned it to her shirt, over her heart.

He grazed the mask with a fingertip and glanced up. "I'm glad. I wanted you to have something unusual but easily carried. Since you move around a lot."

That nearly knocked her to the floor. "Thanks. It means a lot that you understand me."

"I'm trying to." He cocked his head. "What did you get me?"

"My gift is unusual but easily carried, too. I hope you'll like it as much."

She hadn't wrapped hers. Fishing it from her pocket, she handed over the pregnancy test.

"What is it?" He took it with a puzzled expression.

Then his whole body stiffened. His expression, his eyes, everything went absolutely still.

"You're pregnant?" he asked hoarsely, gaze flitting back and forth between her and the plus sign. "The naps. Drinking orange juice like it's going out of style. You're pregnant."

"And you're going to be a father." She couldn't keep the smile off her face. "Congratulations."

Matt sank onto the couch as if he hadn't heard her, still staring at the piece of plastic in his hands. "So I assume this means you're keeping it."

Horrified, she glared at him. "As if there was a possibility I might not? Of course I'm keeping it."

"Okay." He blew out a breath and rubbed his forehead absently, not looking at her. "Okay. I just wanted to make sure I understood. That's the right decision. But I'll support you no matter what."

"I never had a doubt."

Matt wasn't like her father. He was solid, capable. Not weak. Matt was a forever kind of guy and somehow, she'd been lucky enough to find him. A baby changed everything. It gave him more than enough reason to move on. With her.

"It was that time on the roof. Wasn't it? When we forgot the condoms." He looked a little green around the edges. "You said it was the wrong time of the month."

"I thought it was. I miscalculated. But it was already too late, and honestly, I'm glad. We're having a baby and I'm looking forward to being a mom. How do you feel about being a dad?"

Matt shut his eyes. "You've had a little more time to process than me. Give me a minute. Can I get you a drink? Crackers?" He shoved both hands behind his neck, like he

was trying to hold his head in place. "I don't even know what to do for a pregnant woman. Be right back."

She watched him flee, breath rattling in her throat, cutting off all her oxygen as she reevaluated his reaction. It never occurred to her that he wouldn't welcome the news. He'd always wanted a family, hadn't he?

Well, he'd said he needed a minute. She had no choice but to give it to him. When he came back, he'd be ready to talk about the future, and then they could make plans to go to Monte Carlo.

Everything was going to be great.

Matthew escaped to the kitchen, formerly his haven. The place where he went to create, feel productive.

Hands spread wide, he leaned on the counter, head down. There still didn't seem to be any blood circulating in his brain. The walls were too close together and the gap between them narrowed.

Pregnant.

Evangeline was *pregnant*.

He wasn't ready to think about being with Evangeline forever, wasn't prepared to examine why they still gelled when they shouldn't. Couldn't get past the fear that suddenly not one, but two people could easily become the center of his existence. Only to be ripped away.

This was his reward for flagrantly disregarding the rules and living in the moment with no thought to consequences. This was what running away from life had gotten him.

Automatically, he filled a glass full of water and downed it without coming up for air once.

From here on out, he'd have to do the right thing. Ironically, if he'd been doing the right thing all along, this never would have happened. But he was a Wheeler, first and foremost, and it was far past time to start acting like one.

What was he going to do? Evangeline would never fit

into his life in Dallas. But she had to. Because he had to. Neither of them had a choice any longer.

Something rushed through his heart. *Relief.* They didn't have a choice but to make it work, whether he was ready to think about forever or not. Forever had started the moment she spoke to him in Vincenzo's hall. Venice was over, but they could still be together.

He returned to the living room, calm and in control. He hoped.

He sat on the couch next to Evangeline. "I'm sorry. I'm one hundred percent here now."

But minus a drink for her. Maybe he was more like ninety percent here.

"I'm glad." Her eyes were enormous and shiny. Red. She'd been crying and it wrenched his heart. No matter what he was going through, it hardly compared to an emotional *and* physical wallop, like what had happened to her.

Stop thinking about yourself, Wheeler.

"Hey," he said softly and took her hand. "It's going to be okay. Did I make you cry? I didn't mean to."

She shook her head. "I'm all emotional. From hormones, I guess. I've never been pregnant before."

"It'll be fine. I'll be here for you. Take you to the doctor and—" he swallowed against the sudden burn in his throat "—be in the delivery room to cut the umbilical cord."

All things he'd looked forward to doing with Amber. Seeing his wife rounded with their child. Lacing fingers as they watched the image in the sonogram. Never had he imagined it happening with someone else, and *never* would he have anticipated the spike of unadulterated elation at the thought of doing it with Evangeline.

Ruthlessly, he shut off the emotions careening through his chest. Becoming emotional would not help this situation.

"So we're going to be together?" she asked tentatively, and her grip on his hand tightened. "You want to be a part of the baby's life?"

The baby's life. He shook his head, to clear it, to whack something loose that made sense. How would anything make sense ever again?

There was so much more to consider than the pregnancy. The next eight months were only the beginning. He and Evangeline were going to be parents, of a kid who would eventually walk and talk and learn to ride a bike.

A baby. He was going to be a dad. Panic nearly blinded him—but the clearest sense of awe fought its way to the forefront.

"We'll raise it together. Of course we will."

The baby would be a Wheeler, entitled to everything Matthew could and would provide. The circumstances weren't ideal, and this curveball certainly jerked him back to reality.

Venice was *definitely* over. They needed to make plans, decisions. Find a place to live. Insurance. A car with a baby seat. His head spun. He didn't own a car anymore.

Evangeline gave him a watery smile. She was so thrilled, and he hated to squelch her enthusiasm, but they both needed to get real, really fast. Their relationship was now permanent. Two people who had almost nothing in common other than enormously painful events in their pasts were going to be parents.

"Together," she repeated. "I like the sound of that. There was something about you, from the very first, that called to me. The fortune-teller even predicted it. That we'd conceive. Remember?"

What he remembered was chasing down a beautiful butterfly for the sole purpose of feeling something again, and tripping headlong into an affair he'd believed would help him get back home. All he'd wished for was a sign that he'd make it back to his old self. That he might heal.

Instead, one passionate round of rooftop sex had bound him to this woman permanently. A woman who was so dif-

ferent from every woman he'd ever met and with whom *he* had to be different to even keep up.

As stakes in the ground went, she'd presented him with a doozy. A baby. The panic rose again, thick in his throat. He pushed it down.

They'd be together. They'd have a family. It was a blessing, no matter what.

"We can get married quietly." If they didn't have any guests, the date of their wedding didn't have to be publicized. They might be able to hide the fact that the baby was conceived out of wedlock. Anything to avoid causing his parents public embarrassment.

His back teeth clacked together. But he wouldn't lie to his parents—they'd have to know the truth. The vision he had in his head of sitting with Amber on his parent's sofa and gleefully telling them about the coming grandchild shattered. Of course, it had shattered long ago.

"Married? What are you talking about?"

"You're pregnant. We're getting married." Out of order. Once again.

She laughed. "Matt, we don't have to be married to be together. Love isn't dependent on a piece of paper."

Love? Did she think he was in love with her? Was she in love with *him*?

Evangeline made him crazy. She provoked sensual—okay, downright erotic—impulses from him. Pulled his soul from the deep freeze and made it okay to say whatever he wanted. Feel whatever he wanted. He couldn't do that forever. His life—his real life—had order and structure. No surprises. He had to get that back.

And he didn't want to be in love.

Never again. If he was doomed to suffer forever for falling in love with Amber, he certainly didn't want to repeat that mistake. Especially not with Evangeline, who made him feel so much. Especially not now.

How much harder would it be to love his child's mother and lose her?

The thought of losing either the mother or the child squeezed his chest so hard, he couldn't breathe. He cursed—was it already too late?

"A baby isn't dependent on love, either," he said. Harsh. But true. Neither of them could afford to keep up the fantasy they'd been living, and he needed to internalize that fact as much as she did. Real life wasn't about mystical connections and Venetian love affairs between incompatible people.

"We're getting married," he repeated.

Her eyebrows came together. "Who said I wanted to get married? You didn't even ask me."

He dismissed her words with a wave. "That's just a formality. Marriage will be good for you."

Her career was over—but she could be a wife and a mother. He had to make her see that. There was so much more to consider than whether he'd *asked* or not.

She recoiled as if he'd slapped her. "A formality? I deserve to be asked. With a ring. And you know, something along the lines of 'I love you and want to be with you the rest of my life.' Try it and then I'll give you my answer."

She was right. He'd gone about proposing the wrong way, but God Almighty, who could blame him? This humdinger of a development had flipped him inside out.

"I don't have a ring. As far as I knew, we were kissing each other goodbye today. I'm sorry." He took a deep breath and slid her palm to his mouth, kissing it in silent apology before he released it. "Let's figure out the next steps together."

She smiled. "The first step is to remember we're going to be happy."

Happy. Happiness had been a sheer impossibility when he left Dallas. But Evangeline had changed that.

They could be happy outside of Venice. Evangeline was amazing, strong, resilient. Look at how she'd walked into

the lion's den of that horrific interview. Faced down the reporters. Played the piano. She could adapt to the role of Mrs. Wheeler and enjoy a life with roots. After all, they'd have a baby and a household to keep her busy and content.

She'd been searching for the next steps, and he'd give them to her. Being his wife would keep her demons away permanently, and she'd definitely become less...glittery. Then they'd gel in Dallas as well as they did here in Venice.

He returned her smile, and somehow it relaxed him. "Well, at least we already know we can live together without killing each other."

He didn't have to give her up. It was easier to picture her in Dallas if he forgot about all the reasons he and Evangeline wouldn't work and instead focused on what would be great.

"I'll let you cook. All the time. I have no problem with a man in my kitchen. It turns me on."

Her thumb smoothed over his and for the first time since he'd walked into the hornets' nest, he actually felt in control again.

Evangeline tucked her feet up under her and leaned into Matt's warm chest. Finally, things had clicked into place, and he'd lost that panicked edge, poor guy. She got that it was a little rough to have something so life-changing dropped on you out of the blue. The adjustment was still messing with her, too.

Marriage—of course he'd want that, and she was still contemplating it. If he came up with a really good proposal, she might actually say yes.

There was a shock. She'd thought Rory had crushed the desire for marriage out of her forever. But Matt wasn't like other men, and to him she was so much more than a broken voice.

"There's a lot to discuss," he said, and she nodded against his shoulder.

"First off, I'd like to talk about Monte Carlo." Thank-

fully, she hadn't brought it up yet. This way, it was practically a foregone conclusion. "The party is already in full swing but if we leave by Thurs—"

"What?" Matt tilted her head up to pierce her with a puzzled gaze. "We can't go to Monte Carlo. Especially not to a party."

"That's where all my friends are. We can tell everyone the news, and of course I can't drink any champagne, but you can have a glass for me."

It would be a fantastic way to celebrate. Not exactly the kind of party Vincenzo and his crowd were used to, but fun all the same. Maybe someone would volunteer to throw her a baby shower.

"We don't have to stay long," she added. "A week, tops. Then I suppose we can come back to Venice until the tourist season star—"

"There's no more Venice." His lips curved up in a half smile, maybe in apology for cutting her off *again*, but the rest of his face was pure confusion. "Surely you've realized that. We'll be flying to the States. We can leave as soon as you're ready. Somewhere along the way, I'll buy a ring and we'll get married at my parents' house."

A little discombobulated, she frowned. "I thought we already talked about the marriage proposal. And there still hasn't been one. Plus, I don't want to go to America. I hate it there. You think the press is bad in Italy, wait until you've dealt with the gossip websites."

"I don't want to deal with the press at all. Unfortunately we don't have that choice because America is where Dallas is and that's where we're going."

"Dallas? You want to go back to Dallas?" The harsh consonants rang in her ears. She'd always known that was his goal, but things had changed. *He* had changed. And he'd said more than once he didn't think he could go back yet. Monte Carlo was an opportunity to continue healing. "What's in Dallas for you?"

"Dallas is where my family is, my job," he explained, and his tone implied she should have already figured this out. "And that's where I have to live in order to do it. Also, my mother is there. She'll help you with the baby."

"I have a mother."

In a manner of speaking—she'd rather eat Brussels sprouts than ask her mom for parenting advice, and honestly, she might not mention the baby to her mother at all. Evangeline hadn't darkened the door of her mother's in a year or two. It wouldn't be out of the realm of possibility to keep the pregnancy from her.

"Your mother is welcome to come and stay for as long as you want her to," Matt offered, and she tried not to gag at the thought. "But my mother will be involved. I want her to have a relationship with her grandchild."

"There's an app for that. It's called Skype."

"That's ridiculous." He flicked off her suggestion as if she hadn't spoken. "I'll probably buy a house close to my parents. There's a good private school in their neighborhood. How early is too early to get on the waiting list, do you think?"

"Matt." He was babbling about something called Hockaday. It was like they were speaking two totally different languages. She tugged on his shirt. "Matt. I'm not moving to Dallas."

Dallas would be the *worst* place for Matt. He seemed to think he was ready, but it was too soon. He needed more time to heal, more time with her.

"Sure you are. There's a really great arts district, and my mom knows a lot of people. She can introduce you to other moms your age. You'll like it."

The first tendrils of alarm unfolded in her stomach. "*You* don't even like Dallas. You said it was oppressive. Do you really think you can go back to real estate, like you're still the same person you used to be?"

The look on his face when he'd been telling Nicola and

Angelo about his family firm—well, he might love his job, but it wasn't going to be the same. He'd walked away because he needed something else.

He needed her.

"I have to be that person. That's the real me. This?" He pointed at the frescoed ceiling. "This is not me. This is some other guy who'd lost his way. Dallas is where I was always trying to get back to. I have you to thank for getting me on the right track."

"Dallas isn't the right track. You're talking about shoe-horning both of us, and a *baby*, into something that doesn't exist anymore. Monte Carlo is the best option for us. We're moving on together. Don't you see?" Desperation laced her words, because it was clear he *didn't* see.

"Monte Carlo is not a place for the mother of my child." His lips firmed into a no-nonsense line she'd never seen before.

"It is when I'm the mother."

Their gazes locked, and the frozen blue of his irises nearly took her breath. All of Matt's incredible depth—the quality she'd always treasured the most—had vanished.

"I don't want you around those kind of people," he said.

"*Those* kind of people?" Her spine stiffened in shock. "And what kind of people would those be, Matt?"

He had the gall to glare at her. "Alcoholics. Like your ex. People who stumble home after a night of who knows what, like Vincenzo, and throw phone parties."

Eyes wide, she snickered to cover her rising distress. "Would you like a stepladder to see over that double standard you just threw up? May I remind you where we met?"

"That's irrelevant. You're not going to Monte Carlo."

Who was this man talking to her out of Matt's mouth and watching her from his eyes, but who clearly was *not* Matt. It was like he'd put on another mask, but this one scared her.

"Are we really on such opposite sides of this? How can that be?" She looked for some glimmer of the empathy

they'd always had. It wasn't there, as if the link between them had been severed. The tendril of panic exploded. "I don't understand what's going on."

"We're having a baby. A baby that will be raised in Dallas, where it will have the best care and the best opportunities." The corner he was pushing her into grew sharp against her back. He *never* pushed. Why now? "Where we can have a good life and be happy. Like you said."

Dallas was his idea of a good life? "What, exactly, do you envision me doing in Dallas? Tea parties with your mother?"

He shrugged. "Sure. If you want to. Or volunteer. My sister-in-law runs a women's shelter. Maybe that would appeal to you. It'll take a while to get back in the swing of things, even for me, but I usually get invitations to at least one or two social events a week. Charity balls and the like. When the baby comes, you can take it easy and focus on being a mother."

"Charity balls?" Her voice squeaked. Which would be unremarkable except it was the highest tone she'd accomplished in a very long time. "Have we actually met? Hi, I'm Evangeline La Fleur, and I live in Europe. I'd like for the father of my child to live in Europe with me."

"Or?"

The challenge snaked through her.

"Or don't. But you're talking about a life in Dallas that I can't do." If she put down roots in Dallas, what would happen to her if it didn't work out? If he decided he didn't want her to stay after all?

"Can't? Or won't?" His tone sliced through her, and tears burned at the corners of her eyes.

"Can't." She took a deep, calming breath, but it shuddered in her chest. "Matt, have you listened to me at all? I'd die in that environment. Die, as in wither up into a dried bit of nothing and blow away."

They *both* would. Why was he being so stubborn?

"You'll be with me. I'll keep you entertained." His wolf-
ish smile unleashed a nauseous wave in her abdomen.

"Is that all I am to you?"

"No. Of course not." He shook his head, sobering, and
every fiber of her being wished for him to follow that with,
I love you. "I want you to be my wife."

That's when it all snapped into place. The sick churning
in her stomach sped up.

"You haven't been trying to get over Amber. That's why
it's taking so long. What you've been searching for isn't a
cure—you've been looking for a *replacement*. The whole
time. And you found one."

"No one can replace Amber." A lethal edge to his ex-
pression whipped out and knifed her in a tender place deep
inside. "I would never attempt to try."

"Of course. My mistake." One of many. But she couldn't
let it go, couldn't stop from ensuring they both heard the
brutal truth. "I've been falling in love with you. All along.
Tell me that's one-sided."

The harsh lines of his face softened. "I'm sorry. I'm not
trying to hurt you."

"But you're going to anyway."

Her heart froze in disbelief. She'd put it out there, only
to have it slapped down. It had never occurred to her that
she wouldn't be successful at healing him. That the baby
wouldn't be the answer. That her feelings wouldn't be re-
turned.

But Matt was honest to a fault, and he'd never lie to her.
He didn't love her.

He couldn't, because she wasn't Amber. She'd never be
able to fill the empty place in his heart, and she'd been a
fool to think that demon could ever be slayed.

Her whole life had been shaped by rejection at the hands
of people who didn't love her because she wasn't some-
one else. She wasn't Lisa. She wasn't Sara Lear. And she
wasn't Amber.

"Evangeline..." He sighed, and deep lines appeared around his eyes, aging him. "I've never made you any promises. I don't make promises I don't intend to keep. And I'm not ready to be in love again. Might never be."

Brutal. She'd had no idea how severe the truth could really be. "So you're proposing we get married and raise a kid. But as roommates?"

"We've been living together without being in love. Why does being married have to be any different? It'll be like Venice, but permanent. If you don't want to volunteer, then do something else, maybe related to music. Give private singing lessons."

"I can't sing," she choked out, and the final stitch holding her heart together snapped. The organ fell into two pieces somewhere in the vicinity of her womb, where the child she thought they'd love as a couple grew.

"Piano lessons then." He took her hand, squeezing, as if nothing was wrong. As if everything was going to work out fine. "If you taught me, you can teach anyone. It doesn't matter to me as long as the baby is taken care of."

It doesn't matter to me.

She was nothing more than a warm oven for his offspring. Not someone to love and cherish. It was the ultimate rejection of everything she'd imagined their relationship to be.

She yanked her hand out of his grasp.

She'd invented a connection—one that didn't actually exist—out of her own loneliness and fear of an empty future. In the end, Matt wanted something from her far more damaging, and far more heartbreaking, than she could have ever predicted. He wanted her to sacrifice everything that made her who she was, and in return, he vowed to *never* love her the way he loved Amber.

Maybe he wasn't capable of loving anyone other than Amber.

Why hadn't she realized that sooner?

"Oh, the baby will be taken care of. *My* baby," she corrected fiercely. This was one time when she'd be doing the rejecting. "I don't actually need your help, in case that wasn't clear. I'm not a wide-eyed sixteen-year-old, terrified and penniless. I've got a net worth in the eight figures. The baby will have every opportunity available under the sun. You go back to Dallas and attend some stuck-up snobby rich people's charity event. I'll be in Monte Carlo living the life that makes sense for me. *You* can have a relationship with your child through the internet."

She fled up the stairs, tears streaming, and locked herself in the bedroom to finish packing.

Twelve

"Evangeline." Matthew banged on the door again, barely resisting the urge to kick it in. "Open the door. We're not finished, not by a long shot."

What in the name of all that was holy had just happened? Somehow, Evangeline had broken up with him, like they were a real couple.

But weren't they? He was going to marry her. He *wanted* to marry her.

He'd invested considerable energy into figuring out the next steps—marriage, a house, a stake in the ground—and Evangeline was *throwing it back in his face*.

This was killing him. His insides tossed and turned faster than a shoreline in a hurricane.

"Oh, we're finished," she called, and slammed something—a drawer. "A good lawyer will help us work out the visitation rights."

Visitation rights. Lawyers. If this was a nightmare, it was not ending fast enough.

"Lawyers are not the answer."

"Why, don't you have one?"

He rolled his eyes at her scathing tone. "I *am* one.

Granted, not well-versed in the ins and outs of international custody law. But I'm pretty sure I could hold my own given time to acclimate."

Some shuffling. The door flung open to reveal Evangeline's ravaged face. He hated it when she cried. Hated being the reason.

"You're a *lawyer*?" She spit it out like he'd admitted to being a member of the Black Panthers.

But at least she was talking to him again. He had to get this situation back under control before she took off to Monte Carlo and he never heard from her again.

"I passed the bar. Is that really important in light of the other really important thing we should be discussing? The baby?" he prompted.

She crossed her arms. "Well, we're full of disclosures today, aren't we? No wonder you're so sanctimonious. Anything else you forgot to tell me?"

"It's not like I hid it on purpose to make you mad. It just never came up."

"But it perfectly illustrates the point. I *trusted* you." She was so worked up, she bristled. "I've never been anything but honest about who I am yet I don't know you at all."

Direct hit. He had worn his mask far longer than she had.

Punching photographers. Sex on the roof. Midnight confessionals. None of that was really him, and she was calling him on it. This was all his fault.

A doozy of a headache landed right behind his eyeballs.

"I didn't set out to deceive you."

All at once, she deflated. "I thought…well, it doesn't matter now."

"It does matter. Evangeline—" He pressed a fingertip to both eyelids, willing the headache to disappear. It didn't. "I don't want to deal with custody and visitation through lawyers. The baby belongs with both parents."

Evangeline and the baby belonged with him, in Dallas.

Their choices about the future had been taken from them, and he'd think about why that made him so happy later.

"Then come to Monte Carlo with me." Her soft brown eyes beseeched him, pulling at him. Unearthing the confusing, unnatural reaction he had to her. "Prove that you're the man I think you are. More hinges on it than what's going to happen with the baby. You came to me broken. I want you to be whole again. Let me heal you."

"But you've already done that." He couldn't help it. He pulled her into his arms, and the feel of her, the warmth, the familiar scent of her hair, knocked his equilibrium loose, nearly putting him on the ground. "That's why I can go back to Dallas and pick up the reins of who I was. Because you made me feel alive again."

Alive. Yes. And without her, what would he be?

"No." She buried her face in his neck. "You're not healed. If you were, you would be able to love me."

That was the kicker. They had different definitions of *healed.*

"I didn't lie to you. I told you I didn't have anything to give. I'm sorry, but a baby doesn't change that."

She nodded. "I understand. And it doesn't change the fact that I can't marry you. If we were in love, I...well, it doesn't matter, does it?"

She'd sliced through everything, right to the heart of it. She wanted him to love her. And he couldn't.

The purgatory of loss was too painful. He wasn't willing to risk backsliding into a hole of depression again. Not even for her.

Especially for her. She made him feel too much.

This was not the opportune time to figure out all this. He'd been searching for a way to get back on track, not searching for someone like Evangeline.

"No compromise?" He had a sick feeling in his gut that he already knew the answer.

"Oh, Matt." She kissed him, lightly, and her lips lifted

too quickly. "Sure I'd compromise. London. Madrid. Pick a place. Monte Carlo isn't nearly as important as what it represents. You won't fully heal until you accept that your old life is gone. You can't go back. Neither of us can. All we can do is move forward. If that's what you want, Monte Carlo is the answer."

He couldn't chase her around the globe like a teenager with a trust fund and no responsibilities.

"Not for me."

It wasn't the right answer for her, either. She'd never find the next steps in Monte Carlo, and the anguish would swallow her whole if he wasn't around. How in the world did she think she'd survive without him?

The baby belonged with him. *She* belonged with him. He wanted to howl with the injustice of it, that he couldn't make her see the logic.

She stepped out of his embrace, dry-eyed. "Then, this is goodbye."

Matthew called a cab instead of Lucas, though he knew his brother would pick him up from the airport. Family would always be there for him, regardless of the grief he'd put them through for the past eighteen months. But he couldn't face anyone.

Not yet. Not when he still couldn't process that he'd left Evangeline in Venice.

The mother of his child. And he'd had to let her go.

After several more arguments, a bucket of tears—not all hers—and a bunch of slammed doors, he'd finally given up trying to reason with her. Stubborn woman. She refused to see what was best and actually threatened to disappear if he didn't accept her decision.

Ultimately, their connection was nothing but the magic of Venice, blowing smoke and illusion to cover the truth. They weren't meant to be together.

The cab pulled up at his parents' house. The driver hefted

the suitcases from the trunk, accepted the folded bill with a nod and drove off, leaving Matthew on the sidewalk in the middle of the suburban neighborhood he'd grown up in. The neighborhood he didn't recognize at all.

His mother had planted something flowery and purple in the side yard that he'd never seen before, and the house's wood trim had been painted. Maybe the brick had been power-washed. A car rushed by on the street behind him, likely only driving thirty miles an hour, but it felt more like a hundred. All of it lent to the sense of being somewhere unfamiliar.

There weren't any cars in Venice. Boats slipped by quietly in the canal or sometimes the cheerful call of a gondolier announced its presence. People strolled the streets and enjoyed a slower pace. He'd grown used to it. Preferred it.

The front door creaked, and his mother poked her blond head out. "Now there's a sight for sore eyes. Get in here, honey. You should have told me you were coming."

Matthew grinned at the break in her voice. "Hey, Mama. It was a surprise."

"It certainly is. Surprise me less or you'll give me a heart attack." She flew over the doorstep and into a fierce hug.

This, at least, felt very familiar. Very welcoming. He'd missed her.

Mama hustled him into the house and fluttered around, doing a bang-up job of ignoring Matthew's protests about staying in a hotel. To stem the tide, he carried his stuff to the extra bedroom upstairs. Arguing with Mama did not ever end well.

"Sit. Let me look at you." Mama sank onto the couch and he followed. She smoothed a lock of hair from his forehead. "Staying long?"

"Yeah." He knew what she was really asking. "I'm home for good."

That put weight on his shoulders. He'd thought he was

ready. He *was* ready. But it was so permanent. And so Evangeline-free.

Her sharp gaze swept him, twice, with a combination of disbelief and hope. "Did you find what you were looking for?"

The harsh laugh scraped at his throat. "Not really. But I figured out it's because I didn't actually know what I was looking for. I don't do well without a plan."

"You never have. So what's your plan now?"

"I'm going back to WFP. Lucas has managed to get himself into a hole, and I'm going to get him out." First time in a long time he had a sense of purpose. A goal. It felt good. Right.

Mama shot him a puzzled glance. "A hole? Did he tell you that?"

"I know about Richards Group. It's partly the reason I came home." The other part had everything to do with a singular desire to be dependable, straight-arrow Matthew Wheeler again. To do something he excelled at and had ultimate control over.

"I think you should talk to him. We'll have a big family dinner to celebrate you being home. Call your brother. Tell him to come early so you can get on the same page." She smiled. "Far be it from me to get in the middle of my boys, but honey, you left. Lucas has been handling things. I doubt he's going to take kindly to you sticking your nose into WFP and bossing him around. A word to the wise."

Matthew checked the eye-roll out of sheer respect for the woman who had birthed him. But it was hard.

"I'm not going to boss him around, Mama. I'm here to help."

She nodded. "Just you remember that. You're helping. Not in charge."

The transatlantic flight caught up to him then, and he cracked his jaw with a yawn. "I'm going to take a shower and maybe watch TV for a couple of mindless hours." De

compress. Be alone without his mother's shrewd gaze on him. He pulled her into a long hug. "Thanks. For letting me come home."

"Silly." She thumped his shoulder, her eyes shiny and full. "You're still my kid, no matter how big you get. I love you. You're always welcome here."

He almost spilled everything then, all the heartache of the past eighteen months, the depression, the disorientation. How he'd experienced it again tenfold on the flight home at the hands of a different woman. But the wounds of Evangeline were far too fresh and the wounds of Amber far too...faded.

He frowned. When had that happened?

"See you at dinner."

Dropping a kiss on his mother's cheek, he went upstairs to clear his mind with a hot shower, which didn't work.

When he'd last been in Dallas, the burden of grief had turned the sunniest of days dark. Amber was constantly on his mind, how he couldn't go on without her. How everything they'd planned was dashed. He'd expected coming home to bring all that back. It hadn't.

When he thought about Amber now, it was with a hazy sort of warm rush. The prongs of grief had lifted.

The skin he washed was the same. But the man inside wasn't. That's why the neighborhood and his mother's house had been unrecognizable. Despite all his yearning to slip back in time, to a place where he knew everything was safe and right, he couldn't. The only thing he could do was accept that he had changed.

Like Evangeline had said.

But if he accepted that his life was something different now, who would he be?

He called Lucas and then flipped on the TV to lose himself in the oblivion of sleep.

The door crashed against the wall, waking him. Grog-

gily, he sat up and swung his legs off the edge of the bed. The empty bed.

He wasn't in Venice with Evangeline. He was in Dallas. Alone.

A fuzzy Lucas lounged against the door frame, hand in his pants' pocket and a smirk on his face.

"God Almighty, you look like roadkill in August." Lucas tsked.

"Thanks. That's exactly what I needed to hear. I was sleeping, by the way," Matthew groused and rubbed a hand across his eyes. His brother's form snapped into focus. "Though I appreciate that you were so eager to see me you couldn't wait."

Lucas snorted out a laugh. "I just didn't believe you were actually here. Had to see it for myself. You back?"

"Looks that way."

"All the way back?"

"Why does everyone keep asking me that? I'm here aren't I?"

Lucas sat on the edge of the bed a couple feet away, dipping the mattress. "You were in bad shape. I'm concerned. Sue me."

Well, I am a sanctimonious lawyer.

Matthew's head dropped into his hands. It wasn't just jet lag crushing him. Evangeline—knowing he'd hurt her, being without her—weighed more than he could bear.

"Honestly, I don't know if 'all the way back' is possible."

"Amber's death nearly destroyed you. Don't let it finish the job," Lucas advised quietly. "You took some time away. Now rejoin life. I'm working on trouncing Richards Group. Another Wheeler on the job can't hurt."

Matthew nearly laughed. "If only Amber were the problem, I'd be all set. Unfortunately, I traded one impossible-to-solve issue for another."

Lucas nodded sagely. "This has to do with the very sexy lady you met. What happened?"

Matthew met his brother's sharp gaze. "How do you know about that?"

"Everyone knows about that. You photograph well, as it happens. So she figured out she's too good for you, huh? Am I going to be nursing you through a broken heart?"

Matthew growled. "Shut up. You don't know what you're talking about."

"Oh, poor baby. Did she make you cry?" Lucas thumped him on the arm, and Matthew shot him a glare.

"Back off. She's pregnant."

He hadn't meant to say anything. But it came out none-theless, too huge to stay under wraps.

"Then what are you doing here without her?" His broth-er's eyes narrowed. "Oh. It's not yours."

Matthew's fist curled, and he almost let it fly, but curbed the impulse at the last second. Where had that anger come from? He wasn't in Venice, free to do whatever he wanted, when he wanted to.

"Of course it's mine. And God, it's a mess."

Lucas started laughing and didn't stop even when Mat-thew shoved him. Finally, Lucas wiped his eyes. "Oh, how the mighty have fallen."

"What's that supposed to mean?" His brother's face might actually be improved with a good slug to the jaw.

Still sniggering, Lucas crossed his arms. "May I remind you of what you said to me about Cia? I believe you ac-cused me of getting a one-night stand pregnant and self-righteously informed me that accidents happen."

His stomach twisted as he vaguely recalled saying some-thing asinine to that effect. "Is it too late to apologize?"

"Nah." Lucas grinned. "No apology needed. It's nice to know you're human like the rest of us. Where is she now? Did you have a fight or something?"

"Worse. She threw my marriage proposal back in my face and took off with her friends."

"That sucks." Lucas whistled in disbelief. "Women. Can't live with 'em, can't shoot 'em."

Matthew had made it sound like Evangeline was a flighty, irresponsible girl who didn't understand what she'd given up, which was completely unfair and not representative of how badly the whole thing had gone down.

"I guess I didn't actually propose."

Lucas's eyebrows rose. "What did you do then?"

"Told her we were getting married." Out loud, it sounded even worse than it did in his head. "It made sense, you know? You marry a woman you get pregnant. Instead, she's talking about lawyers and custody arrangements."

"Geez, are you that clueless?" Lucas huffed out a disgusted breath. "No wonder she dumped you. You don't have a romantic bone in your body, obviously. How in the world did *you* score with Eva?"

That bristled the hair on the back of Matthew's neck. "I didn't *score* with her. It wasn't like that. We had something—" *Special. Meaningful. Unexplainable.* "I don't know. Different."

"Different than what? Amber?"

Matthew's throat burned, and he almost used it as an excuse to clam up. But once, he and Lucas had been close. That their bond had deteriorated was totally his fault. He wanted it back. And the first step was being honest.

"Different than anything I've ever experienced. Amber fit me, fit my plans. Evangeline…doesn't."

But she fit Matt comfortably, like a second skin. Evangeline *was* different—sexy, arousing, provoking and flat-out frightening.

"So? Life is what happens when you're making other plans."

If only it was that easy.

"Since you're so smart, you tell me. If everything you thought you knew about yourself got flipped upside down,

hat would you do?" Yeah, asking *what would Lucas do* ad gotten him into this mess. Why break tradition?

A perceptive light crept into his brother's eyes. "Well, ow. That very thing happened, as a matter of fact. When did, I looked to my older brother and said, *that's who I ant to be.*"

Matthew flinched. "Me? Which part of dumping all my esponsibilities in your lap did you aim to replicate?"

"Nobody blames you for that. You needed a break. But I uess you forgot the rest of that conversation the afternoon rrandpa died. You said I could be you, and you were going o go be me. I took that seriously. I stepped up because I vanted to be as successful as you."

"I took it seriously, too." Matthew had to chuckle at the ony. "You want to know how I got Evangeline's attention? pretended I was you. It worked."

Lucas grinned. "I've never seduced a pop star."

"Neither have I. I didn't know that's who she was at the me. All I wanted was to feel something again." And he'd one a stellar job. He felt stupid, frustrated and out of his lement. "Then bam! There she was, like an answer to a rayer, only I hadn't prayed for *that*. I didn't have any idea vhat to do with her."

"Well, you must have had *some* idea since she's, you now, pregnant." Lucas ducked, but Matthew hadn't been lanning to smack him. Not right this minute, anyway.

"Yeah, I'm not going to kiss and tell. Hope you get over our disappointment real soon." He flopped back against ue pillow, exhausted. "Now she doesn't want anything to do 'ith me, and my kid is going to be living in Europe while m here. Mama is going to be so disappointed."

"Mama? What about you? Aren't you disappointed in ourself?"

"I didn't need you to point that out."

Of course he was disappointed. He'd dreamed of a family or a long time. Instantly, the image of Evangeline holding

his child, her beautiful face luminous as she smiled at the bundle, popped into his mind, and the sharp stab to the gut nearly doubled him over.

"I don't know what to do."

"You're going to figure it out." Lucas put a brotherly hand on Matthew's shoulder. "I've never seen you fail at something you put your heart into."

He eyed his little brother with new respect. Lucas had stepped into the role Matthew formerly occupied, and with more success than probably anyone had expected, thanks in no small part to Cia. Never underestimate the power of the right woman.

Lucas excused himself so Matthew could get ready for dinner.

When he arrived downstairs, everyone was already at the table. Conversation ground to a sudden halt—obviously because they'd been discussing him—when he came into view.

"Hey, son." His dad, who looked tan and fit, jumped up to give him a brief manly hug.

"Playing a lot of golf lately?"

His dad nodded. "Lucas is running the show at WFH and I'm enjoying life. Care for a round?"

Matthew agreed without really intending to, but he was home. Home meant doing all the things he used to. Might as well reestablish the routine right away.

Cia glanced up at him and flicked her long, dark hair from her shoulder. "You'll forgive me if I don't get up." She pointed to her huge stomach, and he quickly averted his eyes. Pregnancy was a sore subject.

"Cia."

He kissed his sister-in-law's cheek and smiled at Mama, then proceeded to suffer through a long discussion about the strategies Lucas was working to drive Richards Group back to Houston where their competitor belonged. It was staggering to hear Lucas spit out such cogent, well-thought-out plans.

More than once, his attention wandered back to Venice, only to snap back to the present when someone said his name. *Matthew.* He'd been called that more times today alone than in all of the past few months.

It felt weird to answer to it.

Afterward, he flopped into one of the wicker chairs on Mama's porch, across from Lucas and Cia. They giggled and nuzzled each other until he thought he'd throw up.

"Get a room."

"Hey, just because you screwed things up with your woman doesn't mean I can't enjoy mine." Lucas ducked as Cia smacked him.

"Leave him alone," she said with a conciliatory kiss to her husband's jaw.

Matthew did a double take. His sister-in-law had never liked him. "Defending me? What is the world coming to?"

But she shot him a mellow smile instead of flaying him alive like she'd have done in the past. "You tell me. What has your world come to, Matthew?"

"Disaster," he muttered. Louder, he said, "Lucas spill all my beans?"

"No, the internet did. It was quite the discussion at the shelter for a week. Did you at least come home with an autograph or two?"

Yeah. Evangeline had taken a Sharpie to his insides all right.

Matthew grimaced. "I came home with nothing."

"I see your attitude hasn't improved. Shame." Cia clucked. "Now I owe Lucas something that's going to be very hard for me to do in my current state."

The smoldering glance she skewered his brother with said she'd figure out a way to pay up or die trying. They seemed blissfully happy, even almost a year into their marriage. Who would have thought?

"Did you lose a bet?"

"Yeah." Lucas answered for her. "The second she saw

the pictures of you and Eva, she swore you'd never come home. So I won."

Matthew shook his head. "I don't know how you could make such a bet over a picture."

Coolly, Cia evaluated him. "You haven't seen them. Have you?" Without waiting for his answer, she held out a hand to Lucas. "Phone, please."

When she got it, she tapped a few times and handed it to Matthew. Pulse hammering, he glanced at the photo taken in front of the restaurant in Venice, and zeroed in on Evangeline's beautiful, radiant face. The small resolution didn't diminish her light in the slightest. She burst from the screen, burst into his gut. The reporter he'd punched took a great picture.

"That picture is the first evidence I've seen that you have teeth. You have a nice smile," Cia said quietly.

He tore his gaze off the woman in the photo to look at the guy she was with. Him. But a version of Matthew Wheeler he'd never seen before.

"Before you left," Cia continued, "you had a permanent scowl. Kind of like now."

He certainly didn't have a scowl on his face in the picture. He looked happy. Blissful even, with his arm around Evangeline. They were close, so close, as if they couldn't bear to be apart for the few moments it took to reach the street. Her face turned up toward his, ignoring the iconic scenery around her. They looked like a couple. A real couple.

A couple so in love they only saw each other.

Whether he wanted it or not, it had happened. He'd been falling in love with Evangeline all along.

Lucas jumped in with a spectacular double-team. "That's the smile of a man who's a goner. If you're so miserable without her, why aren't you wherever she is, making it right?"

His brother—the relationship expert. Matthew almost rolled his eyes. "We're too different to make it work."

A lie. He was too afraid to make it work. He'd come home because running away was what he did. His eyelids slammed shut. Was that really who he'd become? A quitter?

"That's pure BS. You're not trying to make it work. You're here, and she's there. Trust me when I say pride won't keep you warm at night. Swallow yours. And watch a You Tube video on how to propose properly to a woman."

Maybe his brother *had* learned a thing or two about what it took. As he reevaluated Lucas with his arm around his pregnant wife, Matthew had a nasty epiphany. Lucas wasn't a screwup, or even much of a womanizer. In trying to be Lucas, he'd been chasing a shadow that didn't exist.

He hadn't been acting like his brother—he'd been Matthew Wheeler all along, but a better, braver, bolder version, who went by the name of Matt. Evangeline had tapped into his secret longings, ripped off his "Matthew" mask and enabled him to discover who he really was underneath the name.

The man Amber married had vanished and become someone else—a man in love with the mother of his child. An ocean separated them because he'd been blindly, selfishly hanging on to slim threads of the past, too afraid of descending into depression again to realize he'd lost everything important.

He wanted to be that guy who kept up with Evangeline La Fleur and had sex on the roof and believed in the whims of fate that had seen fit to blow her into his path. He wanted to be with her and their child, regardless of whether it happened according to his plan.

The Screwup hat was firmly on Matthew's head. But the mistake hadn't been the accidental pregnancy—it had been letting Evangeline go.

How in the world could he make that right?

Thirteen

Evangeline lay on the bed and wiped her eyes for the forti eth time. Morning sickness was worse than a slow death a the hands of sadistic monkeys. Crackers didn't help. Ginge ale didn't help. Cursing Matt didn't help and usually mad her cry. Like now.

She craved his egg-white omelets with every pregnancy hormone in her body. All the other hormones craved him.

How could she still be so torn apart over a man who' stripped her down to her base layer and then *rejected* her She'd taken a huge leap of faith and trusted him enough t fall in love, only to be crushed. Again.

Really, she couldn't be angry with him. He hadn't lied t her. She'd been lying to herself about what he needed. He' rather suffer than get over Amber.

But she *was* angry. And devastated. So much so, sh couldn't stand to be around him any longer. The look on hi face when she'd threatened to disappear had nearly kille her, but what else could she do?

Vincenzo's cousin, Nicola, knocked on the open door "You need something, *cara*?"

"Thanks. I'm okay." She wasn't but Nicola didn't hav

any magic capable of fixing her broken heart. Thank God she'd come to Monte Carlo, where people understood her.

"We go to a club soon. VIP lounge. No paparazzi. You join us?" The elfin woman raised a brow. "Maybe you meet someone new who helps you forget."

Ha. If only. "I better pass. I doubt someone new would care too much for me running to the bathroom every five minutes."

The effort required to simply get dressed was enough of a deterrent to a night out. Then there were the smoke machines, which probably pumped out fumes toxic to a baby. Flashing lights were guaranteed to give her a headache. Cocktails would flow—watered down most likely, but with enough alcohol to render them off-limits.

Of course all of that was just noise. She missed Matt, missed Venice, and nothing else held much appeal.

Nicola nodded and left her alone.

Evangeline bit back an urge to call after her, to beg her to come back and sit awhile. But Evangeline didn't want to be a burden on her nonpregnant friends. Which was all of them.

Still, Monte Carlo was beautiful. Outside the window of her room in Nicola's high-rise condo, the city unfolded in a myriad of lights, energy and people, generating an exciting vibe that spilled out into the Mediterranean via the hundreds of yachts lining the shore.

Alone time was good. She'd come here to feed her newly awakened muse. Now she had plenty of time to see what new brilliance flowed from her fingers.

But instead of reaching for the paper and pen on her bedside table—which had sat untouched for two days—she retrieved the printed page from under her pillow and unfolded the song she'd written in Venice the night she'd fallen asleep on the couch.

She'd probably read these words a hundred times now. The theme of connection ran through every line. Of course,

because she craved it. Losing her voice had been devastating because it was the link between her and the listener.

But the song spoke to a different kind of connection. One between people, but deeper than the superficial link between a singer and a fan. It was about bonds, family. Things she'd never had at any point in her life, but somehow the right expression had come from her soul.

Because Matt's soul spilled over into hers with his strong sense of unity, goodness…and now she was crying again. How could she have gleaned so much from his depths when he'd closed himself off? It shouldn't be possible. But the evidence was on the page.

It was definitely a good thing she couldn't sing this. She'd never get through the whole thing without breaking down. Sara Lear would do the song justice, and it would be a nice hit for her already-stellar career.

Why couldn't she imagine Sara singing it? Professional jealousy? Probably.

She read the words again. She had to let go. This was part of moving on, something she must find the strength to do. Her voice was gone, but she had a baby on the way. One day, she'd like to look her child in the face and be able to say *I overcame a huge struggle. You can, too.*

One day, she'd like to tell Matt how he'd helped her realize she was more than just a voice, more than Eva. She still had something of value to give.

The song was proof.

All at once, she knew why she couldn't imagine Sara Lear singing this song. Sara didn't need a hit song writer—she had plenty of those barking at her door. Evangeline hadn't written this song for Sara, but for someone else entirely.

And now was the right time to give it away.

Before she could change her mind, she picked up her phone and dialed. "It's Evangeline. Your sister."

Family.

What had started as a simple phone call was actually much more profound. Her heart hadn't just been opened to Matt, but to a whole new world of connection. Even though he'd devastated her, he'd also introduced the wonders of permanence, longevity—all only possible if she allowed roots to grow.

"Hi." Lisa's surprise came through the line clearly in the one short word.

"Sorry to call you with no warning." How did you build a relationship from scratch? Start slowly or jump in with both feet? "I've been going through a tough time and I wanted to apologize for losing touch. Can we start over?"

Maybe somewhere in the middle, then.

"I'd like that. How are you? Your voice is different."

Evangeline chuckled. "The surgery messed it up. Listen, I wanted to ask you. Are you still singing?"

"Yeah. At school, we have a vocal group. I do that and karaoke on the weekends. Nothing that's going to get me noticed, but Dad said I can record some demos after graduation."

Dad. Her stomach twisted at the label Lisa so easily gave the man who'd done nothing more for Evangeline than donate sperm. But this was part of letting go too, and nurturing those fledgling roots instead of chopping them off at the source.

"I have a better idea. I wrote a song for you. I'd like to hear you sing it, and then if we both agree it's everything I hope, I'll book you a recording session with my former producer. He'll lay it down right."

"Omigod. Are you serious?" Half of Lisa's sentence came out a squeal. "You wrote a song for me? Why?"

A million different throwaway responses rose up, but this was about forging a new direction and exposing the deepest parts of herself. About living up to the bravery Matt had seen in her.

"I'm branching into a new career. As a songwriter. I ex-

pect I'll write quite a few songs. Who better to write for than family? If we work really hard and are fully committed, the partnership can launch both of our careers."

Committed. It had a nice ring to it. She'd had precious little commitment to anything and expected it to drop a weight on her chest. But instead, the idea of collaborating with her sister, long term, carried the most intense sense of peace.

Best of all, if someone asked her, *What are you going to do now that you can't sing anymore?*, she had an answer.

A new direction as a songwriter and a new direction with family. Timely, since she was going to have a family of her own when the baby was born.

A wave of guilt clogged her throat. She'd deliberately ensured that family would only consist of two—her and the baby.

That wasn't fair to Matt, Matt's family or the baby.

Evangeline surprised herself by saying, "I'm planning to be in the States soon. Would you mind if I dropped by Detroit so we can work this song face-to-face?"

"That would be killer. When?"

"I'm not sure exactly. I'll call you. I have a stop to make first. In Dallas."

Matt didn't love her—and she'd almost accepted that—but she didn't want her child to grow up without knowing its family. Her baby deserved to know his or her father. Grandparents. Uncle and aunts. Her child wouldn't have to suffer crushing loneliness its whole life. Like she had.

But none of that was going to happen if she hid in Europe forever.

Pregnancy hormones, or maybe just sheer disappointment in herself and in Matt for not being what she wanted had driven her to make a rash decision she now regretted. What else had she categorically rejected before it could reject her?

She had to figure out a way to be a coparent with Matt no matter how much he'd hurt her. Her baby needed her to

be brave. She had to go to Dallas and forge a relationship with her child's family. She and Matt *were* getting a family together; it just wasn't going to happen the way she'd have liked. Somehow, she'd make it work, no matter where she ended up living.

The flight to Dallas was miserable. Two layovers, one delayed flight and a near-morning-sickness-mishap in the aisle of first class later, Evangeline plunked down in a cab and handed the driver Francis and Andrew Wheeler's address. When Matt had shoved it at her with instructions to mail any legal documents to his attention there, she'd never expected to use it personally.

When the cab stopped, her breath caught. The Wheelers' house was exactly what she'd envisioned. Welcoming. Homey. Located in a quiet, stately neighborhood she'd have no problem allowing the baby to run free through.

A pretty middle-aged woman answered her knock. Matt had inherited his mother's blue eyes and blond hair. The older woman's shocked gaze reminded her an awful lot of Matt's face when she'd handed him the pregnancy test.

"Hello," Evangeline said. "We haven't met but—"

"Matthew's not here."

"Oh. You recognize me." That had not been the greeting she'd expected. Actually, she hadn't known what to expect.

"Of course. You're the mother of my grandchild."

Not Eva. Not Evangeline. But something else entirely— part of a family. She took it as a sign that she'd made the right decision in coming here.

"I am."

Obviously Matt had told everyone about the baby.

Matt's mother blinked and her smile warmed. "And I'm terribly rude. I'm Fran. Please come in. You must be exhausted from your flight. May I call you Evangeline? I'm very happy to meet you."

Fran ushered her inside, chattering as if they'd met years

ago instead of minutes. The Wheeler household engulfed her the moment she stepped into the foyer. Warm, rich creams and teals tastefully accented the formal living room, but it didn't feel stuffy. Framed photographs lined the mantel of a large fireplace. All the pictures contained smiling people, clustered together as if they couldn't get close enough.

A family lived here.

"Your home is beautiful. I see where Matt gets his taste."

The older woman shot her a puzzled glance. "Thank you. You call him Matt? And he lets you?"

"Is that unusual?" Evangeline perched on the edge of the sofa and Fran joined her.

"He hates that nickname. Always has. Says it sounds too much like a frat boy with a skateboard under his arm." Fran patted her arm. "I like you already. Anyone who can unstarch my son is a friend of mine."

Matt starched? Evangeline laughed involuntarily. If only Fran knew how unstarched her son could truly be.

"I hope we can be friends. I'm actually glad Matt's not here. I came to see you."

"You did?"

She had no idea how much Matt had told his parents, but the relationship between her and Fran could and should last a very long time.

"I did a selfish thing by taking off to Monte Carlo. Matt hurt me, and I used that as an excuse to keep everyone away from my baby. But I want you, and all of Matt's family, to be a part of the baby's life. It's very important to me."

Fran's eyes lit up, just like Matt's did when he was happy. "I'd like that, too. I'd like it better if my grandchild's parents were married. But I promise that's all I'll say to interfere with what my son has clearly informed me is not my business."

So maybe he had told her everything. Having that kind of bond with a mother—she couldn't fathom it. This woman had shaped Matt, instilling in him many wonderful quali

ties. And most of them were outside of the kitchen. His depth, his sense of commitment, his patience and kindness. All products of his relationship with his family.

Having roots allowed for magnificent things to grow. She wanted that for her baby, but recognized that *she* had to make it happen by sticking around and creating the connections. Maybe she'd open herself to being hurt. And maybe this family would welcome her.

"Marriage was one of the many areas where we disagreed," Evangeline admitted readily. "But I'm here because I realized I was wrong about a few of them. For example, I'm willing to reevaluate my stance on living in Europe."

"Well, that's a relief. It's a shame Matthew's not here so you can tell him personally. I think he'd be very interested in where else you might compromise. Ironically, you just missed him."

She should talk to Matt. No matter how hard it might be. They were going to be parents, whether she wished they could be more or not.

"Do you mind if I wait?"

Fran smiled. "You might be waiting a long time. He flew to Monte Carlo this morning."

Apparently Matthew *was* going to chase Evangeline around the globe.

He'd done everything short of walking up and down Rue Grimaldi yelling Evangeline's name in order to find her. Vincenzo hadn't realized she'd left Monte Carlo, and his cousin shook her head and said, "Sorry, *cara*. She said *ciao* and nothing else."

Frustrated and quite sick of airports, Matthew slumped against the seat of the final vehicle in a long series of shuttles from place to place to place—a water taxi. He needed to regroup, and what better place to figure out what the hell he was doing than Venice?

Palazzo D'Inverno provided the only bit of sanity he'd experienced in forever.

Matthew tipped the driver and clambered up the dock to the water entrance of his house. The palazzo was the only permanent thing in his life, the only thing he actually owned. Coming here had been a gamble. Evangeline had infiltrated this house, and the memories were likely to be vicious.

When he swung open the door, the quiet hush of peace washed over him. Everything was exactly as he'd left it. The piano stood silently in the corner, draped for protection against lack of use. The U of couches faced the balcony overlooking the Grand Canal. Frescos kept watch from the ceiling, the scenes frozen in time for eternity.

The sense of freedom, as if he could do or be anything he wanted was exactly the same, too.

But that probably had to do with the woman standing by the glass, framed by the grandeur of Venice.

"I was starting to think you'd never get here," Evangeline said, and smiled, punching him straight in the gut. Like always.

Evangeline was in Venice. Inside Palazzo D'Inverno, filling his house with her light. What did that smile mean? Was she buttering him up before she handed over the papers detailing the custody arrangement she hoped to talk him into?

"What are you doing here?"

It was far less than he'd like to say. But far more than his suddenly tight throat should have been able to voice.

"Vincenzo caught me at Heathrow. I changed my connecting flight and voila. Here I am."

Which told him not one blessed thing about her intentions. He hated not knowing exactly where she'd been, where she wanted to go, what she was planning, what she was feeling. Once, he would have known instinctively, would have gleaned a hundred nuances from the vibe between them without a word exchanged.

He missed it. He wanted it back.

"How did you know this was where I would end up?"

His voice broke. She was beautiful—radiant like the Madonna with child. Like Evangeline with his child. There was nothing in Dallas, nothing anywhere in the world worth more. Exactly how stupid was he for not realizing that before screwing up everything?

Was she still in love with him? Or had he ruined that, too?

His stomach pitched. Well, he'd just have to convince her to forgive him for being such a shortsighted moron. Negotiation was his best skill.

She shrugged and crossed the room, stopping short of invading his space, likely because he'd given no indication of whether he'd welcome her. "Lucky guess."

Or maybe something else had whispered his destination to her, something unexplainable and incomprehensible. But still real.

"I was coming to you. In Monte Carlo," he said.

"I know. Your mother told me."

Matthew shook his head. Evangeline scrambled his wits. "My mother?"

"I went to Dallas." Her eyes filled. "Matt, I don't want to cut our baby off from you. Or from your family. I was selfish and stupid. Apologies were in order, all the way around, starting with your mother. Ending with you. I'm sorry. I want you to have a relationship with our baby that's more than holidays and birthday cards once a year."

"Oh." Disappointment wrenched his battered heart. What had he expected, that she'd miraculously decided to give him another chance when he'd plainly told her he had nothing to give? "I'm the one who should apologize. I'm sorry, too. So how do you envision a relationship between me and the baby if you're living in Europe?"

"I'm not going to live in Europe. I called my sister. We talked, and she's going to record some songs that I wrote. I never liked the idea of giving my words to Sara Lear. But

Lisa, that's a different story. It'll be a great partnership. I'm going to stay in the States so we can work together."

Pride filled him. She'd found her way after all. "That's fantastic. Why did you fly all the way to Dallas to apologize in person?"

"Well, I was planning to go from Dallas to Detroit. It made sense in the mixed-up files of my pregnant brain."

He contemplated her slight form. "But you're here. Not Detroit."

"A funny thing happened when I got to Dallas. You weren't there. You went to Monte Carlo. I have to know why."

"Evangeline…" He hesitated, unsure how to undo all the damage he'd done the first time by trying to follow rules that made no sense for the man he'd become. But there were no rules in Palazzo D'Inverno. So he said what was in his heart.

"When I got to Dallas, it took about five minutes to know I was still in the valley. And when I looked up, I realized I couldn't get to the top of the mountain unless I had someone with wings to fly me there."

"Me?" she whispered.

He nodded. "Please, please forgive me for all the stupid things I said before. I can't be me without you. I love you."

Tears streamed down her face. "Really?"

"Really." He bridged the gap, drawing her into his arms and she fell against him, clutching at his shoulders. Warm, light-filled Evangeline was in his arms. "I was the selfish one. Clinging to the past when I had the future right here the whole time."

"I don't understand. You said you weren't ready for that."

"I'm not." Who could ever be ready for someone uninhibited, wild and perfect like Evangeline? "To compensate, I refused to put myself in the position of letting my emotions get the better of me again. The problem with that, of course, is that it was too late. I was already in love with you."

The denial burst from her and he closed her lips with his fingertip.

"Shh. It's true. Amber was an integral part of my life for a long time, and when she died, it was like a car losing an engine. One can't function without the other. But I was never a car to you, and because of that, we fit differently. I couldn't see that until I went home and tried to be a car again."

"Are you saying you don't want to be a car anymore? Or are you trying to talk me into buying one?"

He laughed, shocked at the quaver in it. "I'm saying you were right. I can't pick up the reins of my old life and I don't want to. I want to find a new direction with you and our baby. Wherever the wind blows us. I went to Monte Carlo to tell you that."

Hope spread across her face.

"I want to believe you," she said cautiously. "But I trusted you, and you smashed my heart all to pieces. I can't be a replacement for your wife. How do I know you're really over her?"

"I don't want a replacement. Amber was only one color, and that was right for me before. You're all the colors of the rainbow. It's tattooed on you permanently because that's who you'll always be to me."

Her eyelids dropped for a beat, and when she opened them again, the soft brown sucked him under. "How do you always know the right thing to say?"

Because he'd learned that the right thing had context. The right thing wasn't always the same from day to day, and sometimes you had to do what was right for the person you were at that moment.

He grinned. "Several transatlantic flights in a row give you lots of time to think."

"What do you want? Did you come loaded down with a ring and a fancy marriage proposal?"

The pain in her voice tried and convicted him. He'd hurt

her, and saying the right thing wasn't nearly enough to make
up for it.

"No." He'd gone against the very fiber of his being and
come here empty-handed. "This time we're doing things
according to your schedule. I'll follow you wherever you
go, whether we've got a piece of paper calling us husband
and wife or not. I will never again utter the word *marriage*
until you flat out say that's what you want."

"Your mother will be upset."

Obviously Mama had treated Evangeline to an earful of
the Fran Wheeler Sermon on the Merits of Marriage. Hope
fully it hadn't stacked up Evangeline's disfavor against him
any higher.

"She'll get over it. This is about us and what we want."

"And you don't want to marry me."

"On the contrary. Nothing would make me happier than
to claim you as my wife before God and everybody. But it's
your choice. Our relationship will be how you define it."

Amber had been his wife; that role fit her and what they'd
shared. Evangeline was something else and fit the man he
was now. The harder he tried to pin her down, the harder
she'd flap her wings to escape. And he wanted her to be free
to fly, as long as she waited for him to catch up.

A shrewd glint in her eye set off a frisson of nerves.
"What if I wanted to live in Dallas? What would you say?"

"I'd say who are you, and what have you done with the
woman I love?"

Her gravelly laugh clawed through his stomach with how
he'd missed. "My name is Evangeline La Fleur. And your
name is?"

The best question of all and the easiest to answer. "Matt.
My name is Matt."

"Nice to meet you, Matt." She shook his hand solemnly.
"That's a nice name. I like it. You know the funny thing
about names? They change. You think you're this person

he one the name refers to, and then all of a sudden, you have to redefine yourself."

"And with it comes a new name," he said.

That ripple of understanding passed between them, as strong as it had from the first. Finally, finally, the knot of tension at the base of his skull unwound, and he started to believe he'd leave the valley and crest the mountain with her by his side after all.

"So," he continued. "I'm getting a picture in my head of you living in Dallas. What else should I add to this picture? Will you be living by yourself? Or might I convince you to stay with me?"

A deep smile spread across her face. "You're pretty good at convincing me to stay. I'll give you that. If I stay with you, do I get my own room?"

"Nope. The baby gets his or her own room, but you have to share with me, whether we have a marriage license or not. See, I don't need a replacement wife, but I do need a lover. I seem to have an addiction to inventive positions. And locations, apparently, because I'm envisioning a very sturdy table in the kitchen. And maybe a screened-in porch. A large shower is a must, as well. Sound like something you might consider?"

Say yes. He'd be happy to throw in some begging if it turned the tide.

She shook her head. "You're crazy. I like that."

Crazy. Yes, he was. But only because he'd fallen in love with a woman who allowed him to be and feel and do whatever he wanted.

"Please tell me I haven't totally screwed up things between us. I'm open to discussion on how we'll raise the baby, and I don't care where we live. We can stay here in Venice if you want. I love you and want to be with you the rest of my life, wherever you are, whether we have a marriage license or not."

Her eyes grew misty. "That was the most romantic non-proposal I've ever heard."

"Is that a yes?"

"Not yet. I wasn't done with my apology. I'm sorry I was so stubborn. Before. I never should have tried to force you to heal my way or discounted the idea of living where you wanted to. I've been pretty selfish for a long time, excusing it because I'd lost something important. Important, but not crucial. I can't sing but I haven't lost my voice."

"Of course you haven't. You're *my* voice. You articulate the things in my soul far better than I could."

"Geez." Her lids flew closed and she swallowed heavily. When she met his gaze once more, the powerful connection swept through him again. "I was already going to say yes. But if you want to say some more romantic things, I'm all ears."

His heart took flight. "You were? What swayed you, the sturdy kitchen table or me finally gathering enough wits to tell you I love you?"

"The fact that you flew to Monte Carlo. The rest was nice to hear, though. I came to Venice to tell you I wasn't letting you go again, by the way."

He couldn't help but laugh. They'd chased each other around the globe. "I told you, I'll follow you anywhere."

"Then start walking." She turned and flounced up the stairs, hips swinging saucily. Halfway up, she called over her shoulder, "I'll be naked on the bed, thinking about how much I love you. I'm dying to see what you're going to do first."

Matt was pretty curious too and raced up the stairs to find out what two healed souls could become to each other

Epilogue

Evangeline shoved the Murano glass bowl directly into the center of the art niche outside the baby's room. Much better. Decorating the home she and Matt had bought—together—down the street from his parents' turned out to be the most fun she'd ever had. Who knew?

Fran came out of the nursery. "Carlos tacked up the border. Do you want to check out the placement before I have him glue it down?"

Matt's mother had taken on the role of Contractor Supervisor and ruled the workers with an iron fist covered in ice. The two women became friends instantly, and Evangeline fell into the habit of consulting the older woman on just about everything. Fran knew color and style and had fantastic taste.

Since Evangeline had never created a home from scratch, the partnership worked beautifully—as long as neither of them mentioned the word *marriage*. She and Fran had politely agreed to disagree about the status of Evangeline's relationship with Matt.

"I'm sure the border is fine, but I do want to see it." Evangeline stepped into the explosion of red, white and blue, the

color scheme she'd chosen for her son's room. The borde
looked perfect. Once the walls were finished, they coul
start arranging the room to welcome the highly anticipate
arrival of Matthew Wheeler Jr., which frankly, couldn'
occur fast enough.

She couldn't wait to see Matt's gorgeous eyes peekin
out from her child's face. But she'd have to, because sh
wasn't due for twenty-two very long weeks. The ultrasoun
the doctor performed yesterday had confirmed both gende
and delivery date. The little blob on the monitor was th
most beautiful thing she'd ever seen.

"Andy's still out of town," Fran remarked after Evan
geline had given Carlos the okay. "Would you like to hav
dinner with me and Cia? The boys can fend for themselve
for once."

"Thanks, that would be lovely, but I have plans wit
Matt. Special plans."

"Next time then." Fran smiled and turned her Souther
charm on Carlos to get his help with dragging the rocke
into a corner.

The ladies spent a few hours in decorating heaven unt
Matt strolled through the door from work, his smile fc
Evangeline alone.

"I'll make myself scarce." Fran winked, clearly havin
interpreted the definition of "special plans" in her own wa
and let herself out the door.

Evangeline forgot to be embarrassed as Matt folded he
into his arms.

"Hey."

"Hey, yourself." God, he smelled good, like hom
Home—simple and achingly honest, and she'd never love
something so much. Roots with Matt had grown strong an
solid. "Sell anything?"

"Lucas closed the deal on the Watson property. Esp
cially sweet since I yanked it out from under Richards Gro
without them realizing it." His grin fluttered her stomac

He was so happy to be working with his brother again. And she was happy she'd agreed to live in Dallas so he could. Palazzo D'Inverno waited patiently for them to return, which they planned to do after the baby was born.

"I confirmed with Lisa," Evangeline said. "She'll be here next week to start learning the new songs I wrote."

"Great. I'm looking forward to seeing her again."

Evangeline had gone to Detroit twice already, Matt firmly by her side as she worked through reconciling with her dad. Family dynamics were still new and often frustrating, but she was trying. Matt assured her that was the important thing.

"You know what today is, right?" she asked.

A guarded expression leaped onto his face. "That sounds dangerous. Is this one of those rhetorical questions that I'm already supposed to know the answer to?"

She laughed. "I'll assume that means you don't. Four months ago today, I walked into Vincenzo's palazzo, praying that no one would recognize me. I even wore a mask to ensure it, but there was this guy in the hall blocking my way. If I'd arrived one minute later, he'd have already been gone."

Matt's arms tightened, smushing her softly rounded belly into his solid body. "Sounds like fate to me."

"Absolutely. How else would I have found the one person who recognized me with a mask on?"

She tilted her head up to kiss him lightly, and lost her train of thought as he cupped her jaw to deepen the kiss.

Fate. If she still had functioning vocal cords, they'd never have met. The center of her existence had been ripped from her fingers, but its loss had made room for this man and their family. Thank goodness the fire of tragedy had refined her into someone worthy of Matt's unending devotion.

With a squeak, she broke the kiss. Reluctantly. "Let's get back to that in a sec. I got you something to commemorate our anniversary."

"You did?" He lit up. "I like your presents. The last one will be hard to top, though."

His warm hand spread over their baby, safely tucked inside her womb. "Maybe. I gave it a shot. You'll have to tell me how I did. It's in the kitchen."

She clasped his hand and led him into the kitchen he'd designed from the ground up, with dark cabinets and top-of-the-line appliances. He never minded when she invaded his domain but threatened her daily that if she hung around while he was cooking, she'd better learn something. So far, nothing had sunk in because she was too busy watching the chef's butt as he moved between the stove and the prep area.

A small bag sat on the island. Snagging it, she handed it to him. "It's an armadillo."

"A what?" One eye narrowed. "You put an armadillo in this bag?"

"Yeah. There's this thing that I need to be rescued from. So I'm calling armadillo."

With a puzzled glance at her, Matt tipped the bag up and slid the contents into his hand. She plucked the box from his palm and cracked the hinged lid to reveal a platinum band inside.

"Rescue me from being single. Will you marry me?"

His eyes went so dark with pleasure, her heart fluttered. "Nothing would make me happier. What prompted this?"

"I find myself in need of another name change." Evangeline Wheeler—another role she had no idea how to perform but couldn't wait to figure out. "This time, I'd like to be permanent. I can't risk letting that guy from the harbor get away."

And he'd promised to never again push her into a corner and demand she do something she wasn't ready for. No rules. No expectations. The decision had to be hers. She loved that about him.

"Are you sure this is what you want?" His beautiful

rystalline-blue eyes sought hers and held, hope and love
hining from their depths.

She nodded. "I thought I wandered in search of fulfill-
ent, but I was really looking for you. I love you so much.
e my armadillo."

He grinned and pulled her into his firm, safe arms. "As
unny as you've been walking lately, you should be the ar-
adillo."

"Nice. You're the one who put me in this condition. I
as busy trying to soak up the Venice view, but no. You
ad to go and look at me like you wanted to swallow me
hole." Wicked heat sizzled through his expression and
rrowed straight to her girl parts. She sighed, but it came
ut sounding happy and content. "Yeah. Like that. I love it
hen you get that look."

"And I love it that we do everything out of order. I'll buy
ou an engagement ring tomorrow," he promised.

And then he kissed her.

* * * * *

The perfect gift for Mother's Day...

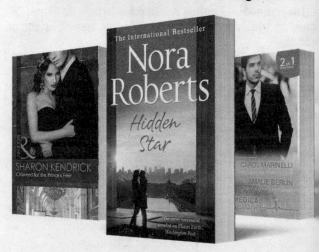

a Mills & Boon subscripti

Call Customer Services on
0844 844 1358*

or visit
millsandboon.co.uk/subscripti

* This call will cost you 7 pence per minute plus your
phone company's price per minute access charge.

MD16